AFFLICTION

BOOK ONE OF THE ALPHA SERIES

JENNIFER JARNIGAN

DORRANCE
PUBLISHING CO
EST. 1920
PITTSBURGH, PENNSYLVANIA 15238

Dorrance Publishing Co
585 Alpha Drive
Pittsburgh, PA 15238
Visit our website at *www.dorrancebookstore.com*

ISBN: 978-1-6853-7133-3
eISBN: 978-1-6853-7977-3

AFFLICTION

BOOK ONE OF THE ALPHA SERIES

CHAPTER

One-

I'm alone now. They've thrown me in my room, and the stone walls block out the screams of my family as the door slams. My family—I can only imagine that they will all meet a similar fate. I know my father is gone, though his loss was not a huge surprise, nor is it particularly painful. Watching my mother's life slip away was what drove me to reveal myself, to rush forward towards the creatures that saw my use and decided I was better alive.

I clutch my knees to my chest as I allow the tears to come forward; hearing a strangled sound only to realize that it is me.

I'm alone. They're all dead.

We shouldn't be surprised; my father was not a merciful person. He was dubbed the Lord of Magic, Darrius Matesscu, and he wore the title like a true dictator. In his mind, he was the god of all magical beings, and his word was law as far as our civilization was concerned. He was an immortal warlock who had ruled for over two centuries, and he, alone, was responsible for a considerable amount of suffering in the current world.

As magic users became more powerful, their bodies weakened, diverting all energy to their abilities, and that meant there was a distinct lack of workers and laborers to do the manual work that living in a city required. This left a vacancy, there became a need for slaves, and the Magic Lord devised a plan.

He captured children of the moon, werewolves, a nearly extinct species that lived among the humans. They remained hidden from the public eye and were only responsible for a small percentage of the murders that chalked up to life in the city. Nobody would miss them, their packs were small, and their societies lacked the structure to warn their species, so one by one they rounded up and then laid a curse upon them, a curse that would force them into a purely mortal form.

The strength of their wolfen half was concentrated into a human body, making them the ideal slave. They were resilient beings that could last through the brutality that came from spoiled elite sorcerers who saw them as nothing more than attractive equipment.

In other words, they were hard to kill and easy to covet.

In their defense, my people were not kind to them. They were in high demand, and the Magic Lord saw money to be made. He auctioned them off to the highest bidder; we did not care where they went or what kind of life they would have. Families were separated, lives broken apart, and children ripped away from their mothers.

To ensure demand, the curse caused the tortured beings to become sterile. With no way to reproduce and create more, their worth skyrocketed, and only the insanely wealthy could afford the designer slaves. Our most frequent buyers came from the Elven kingdom. Our particular stock fit right in with their high expectations, and they bought large quantities of our captives.

I remember the screams all too well.

Their wolf counterparts were forced into hiding, and their bodies were bending, breaking, and stretching to accommodate the new muscle tone. I remember watching the workers whip the tired backs to demand submission, feeling disturbed by their anguish. Still, it had never stopped me from accepting them into my home, from demanding labor from them or expecting their obedience. It was how we were all accustomed.

When you observe them from when they're first caught, when you witness the look of desperation in their eyes once they know what is about to happen to them, you can't help but feel maybe something wasn't right. A looming murmur that this would not end well for anyone.

Of course, we underestimated them.

A species does not want to be held captive; we knew there would be retaliation but not of this magnitude. The curse had not been as clear as we had hoped; in his old age, my father had gotten lazy and felt as though his magic was unbreakable. Not a soul could have predicted that one of them would figure out how to 'change.'

Magically enhanced, there was no way to fight them off. They no longer relied on the moon; instead, they could summon this new being. The wolf that we had thought was erased entirely had only been lying dormant in their bodies, and in this state, they were no longer human, but something separate altogether.

Now that it was estranged from the human form, it was faster, more durable, and superior.

He figured they would kill themselves off or disappear altogether, how could they possibly control this form? It had never been seen before, never been heard of even. A man transforming into a wolf. There were shapeshifters in our realm, obviously, but nothing on this scale. The size of the wolf, it was only something that magic could produce, and blame lay squarely on my father's shoulders.

Nobody could have predicted they would form a culture, an army, an ability to come for us and use our learned weaknesses to their advantage. They knew us, they served us, and they would end us.

So, when it happened, nobody stood in their way. As if we could.

They formed an army, destroying our city with frightening ease. We had no defenses to speak of anyway, my father was the only thing standing between them and the throne, and he seemed as though he was too bewildered to stop them.

He stood, cackling like a mad man as their leader approached. Their voices were inhuman, gravelly, and broken. As if English was not their native language and as if speaking was challenging for them. The leader did not want to bargain; he only wanted to assure my father that his death would be slow and painful and that he hoped he would be challenging to kill.

They had not anticipated the older man's frail state, these past twenty years had taken a massive toll on him, and as the beast's teeth sank into his throat, he laughed until the life left his eyes, and the stone floor stained in his blood.

My mother had rushed over to heal him; it was the only gift she had possessed. She was not an actual magical being, her powers were minimal, but her tender heart and love for my father were all she needed. She pleaded with the creature, her knees smearing the warlock's blood as she tried to stop the bleeding. Her power would never have been enough to revive him.

The beast's teeth clutched her throat, and her shrill scream cut off as his jaws crushed the life out of her. I was blind with fury; I don't know what I would have done, my abilities were fresh, and my capability to use them in a situation like this was quite minimal.

My gift is unique, different from those in most of the magical realm. But not honed nearly to the precision it would have taken to prevent their deaths.

So here I sit, awaiting whatever it is they are going to do with me.

Maybe they will kill me after all. Perhaps they will torture me since my father died so quickly. I sigh, pain is something I've become accustomed to. It is not something I fear any longer though the thought of being chewed on by wolves makes my skin crawl and my blood run cold.

I didn't like being alone with these thoughts, but that is all you have to do when you're being held captive. I realize that it is becoming morning, and I wonder how long I've been in this room, my father's bedchamber.

Reluctantly, I climb to my feet. My legs threaten to fail me, but I gulp in a breath of air and convince myself to take tentative steps towards the vast wardrobe. As I pull open the door, my fingers run over the oak wood, and I try and find any hints of hidden bookcases or trap doors. There is nothing for me here, a depressing metaphor for my entire childhood. I find myself wishing I had paid more attention to the revealing spell classes.

I make my way around the room and check all the cracks. Nothing. This, too, is not surprising. My mother frequented this room, and my father would not have put her life in danger with magical items. Most of his spellbooks were probably encrypted anyway; it would have been unlikely that I would have been able to open them and read from them.

I am left feeling utterly helpless as I search his drawers only to feel like a grave robber, which brings on a whole new wave of emotion that brings me back to my knees and makes me realize just how exhausted and hungry I am.

I feel selfish; how can I feel tired with my family murdered before my eyes? Angry at myself, I numbly bump the back of my head against the stone wall and soak in the ache it brings. Pain means that I am still alive, it means I can do something.

The pang of hunger makes me wonder what time it is, and I walk to one of the windows and see that the sun is in the middle of the sky. Where are my captors? Maybe they're just going to let me starve to death. That would be a punishment; it would save having to torture me. It isn't like I know anything; I've only read about my father's deeds.

It wasn't like I helped him plan any of this. That would have been my brother's job. My brother, who I remind myself, is now dead. The pain wards off any hunger I might have been feeling, and I return to my father's bed to climb into it only to quickly succumb to my exhaustion.

When I wake up I see that the sun is just peeking over the horizon, did I really sleep for that long? Reality hits me all over again as I realize my situation, and with a newfound determination, I get up and go to the windows.

Pressing my fingers into the glass, I look out into the courtyard. I see them out there, men walking among the woods that surround our castle and through the yard in formation. Is that all of them? Or are they like vermin, and there are so many more that you can't see? I force myself to look at them though I feel my heart pounding in my chest.

They don't look so scary; they are just men. At least for now. I don't see any of the wolves that slaughtered my family from last night. I'm not waiting long; my door opens and closes, and I freeze in my place.

I smell him before I see him, the scent of the woods hits my nose, and if I hadn't known it was coming from a murderous creature, it would almost be welcoming. He says nothing; he must be wondering if I'm deaf, considering I haven't acknowledged his presence or even moved since he entered. Slowly, I glance over my shoulder and catch sight of the man who is watching me with a look of frustration.

The look immediately offends me, so I turn to face him, crossing my arms over my chest defiantly. "Well?" I challenge. My boldness surprises me, but I'm infuriated, and it urges me to hold my ground; to not break eye contact.

He is tall, taller than me by at least six inches. I take in his clothes, his leather vest over his thin shirt that stretches over his broad chest. His worn leggings and rugged leather boots suggest clothes aren't something he invests much time into.

He must think I look ridiculous in my white robes. His light eyes take me in, we regard each other, he's as cautious of me as I am of him.

"I suppose I expected more." He speaks. His voice is smooth and low, with a hint of an accent. Where is he from? I'm taken aback. More? What more does he want from me?! He's taken everything I have! I laugh only to shrug half-heartedly.

"Sorry to disappoint." My response is tight. *What did he want me to say?*

His expression morphs into a slightly more amused look. I find myself frustrated as I don't see what he could possibly find amusement in.

"Your family is dead." He confirms and gives me what I'm assuming is a moment to process. I don't allow my face to break; I knew this already, but hearing it confirmed makes me crack. I know that if I allow myself to feel it, I will lose it right here. I stand a little taller and wait for him to continue. "I have spared you because you are the heir to the throne, and I want your help to destroy your father's spellbook."

At this, I scoff and roll my eyes only to hear a low sound, a rumble, a growl. It causes my eyes to widen, I watch this man and realize—*he is the one who is growling.*

"Why on earth would I do that? And, once again, I'm sorry to disappoint you, but I am not the heir. I'm the one my father sent away; you killed the heir." My father had always favored my brother. He stayed and learned battle tactics while I was sent off to be slaughtered; or trained.

I don't think he minded which one.

Restraint crosses the man's face; he's angry, which quietly pleases me.

"You are the only one who's capable of magic, you will assist me, or there will be consequences. Punishment." Here it comes. Torture. He is going to torture me. I swallow as I do my best to appear un-afraid.

"I'm sure there is little you can do to me that hasn't already been done." I'm impressed at how strong I sound, though the smirk that crosses this evil man's face causes me to question if this was someone I should challenge.

He is beside me quicker than I can blink, staggering me with his presence. His scent is strong, mixed with the woods, sweat, and leather. His sun-kissed skin contrasts starkly against my pale olive flesh, but I refuse to give up my position. I meet his gaze, his body is vibrating, and I feel the heat radiating off him. He feels as if he is a thousand degrees, almost unbearable in such close quarters.

His steady hand grips my arm, causing me to flinch at the iron-like fingers that threaten to crush my forearm. Dragging me to the window, he shoves me against the glass to command that I look out it.

Rubbing my arm, I scowl out the window only to see my staff, the people who raised me when my family was too busy to bother. They are on their knees, terrified, in between two massive wolves. I inhale sharply through my teeth as my fingers close on the grasp, cap-turing my resolve.

He has my attention; my physical pain is nothing compared to those I love dying because of me. I have lost enough family by his hand.

Smug, he's pleased with the effect his words have on me. "You will do as I say. Or every hour, on the hour, I will bring one of these people out here in front of this window. I will have my men gut them while you sit here, just like this, and watch them bleed out. We will repeat this process until you decide you want to be more helpful. Do you understand?"

My heart is pounding in my chest; I can't allow this; I am a prince. I spin on my heel and hurl my balled fist towards his face only to have it deflected as he grips my wrist with his heavy hand. Once more, his body begins to vibrate, the heat makes me want to pull away from him, but I'm trapped between the window and his body.

His jaw sets as those light eyes bore into me, wondering if I'm worth the trouble but that amusement flickers, and I know my life is not in danger while in that same breath, I'm bound to obey. I can't allow him to kill anyone else, my love for my people is not limited to the horrors inflicted on me by my family.

"I will help you." I spit.

"I don't think I like your tone." He presses, and when I'm about to retaliate, he continues. "You will refer to me as Alpha. You will do what I say when I say it without question. You will be *my* personal slave. Any falter in my instructions, and there will be consequences. Try a move like that again, and I will have you bound. I am your Alpha now."

I can't believe what I am hearing, twisting in his grasp there is little hope in escaping. Even if I did, I knew what would become of my staff and of my city. I would have to devise a way to free my people. The only way to do that would be to play along. I glare up at him with my own dark eyes.

"I understand." I breathe.

He tightens his grip on my wrist and pulls me against his body. "You understand, 'what'?" He demands as I cringe away from the overwhelming heat.

"I understand, Alpha." I managed through clenched teeth. It makes a hint of a smile curl at the corner of his full lips, true to his word, he releases me to take a step back. I gulp in the fresh air, relieved to be away from the suffocating inferno.

"Well, you can prove your loyalty to me by drawing me a bath, a test of your capabilities as a servant." His words stun me, and I stare at him, bewildered, though I see he is completely serious.

My society had not yet stepped into modernized plumbing. "We don't have running water here, and you know that." I snap at him; he has that amused but aggravated look again. I'm starting to believe that's just his natural face.

"Then I suppose you better start carrying buckets. You have an hour before I return. If you try and run, you know what will happen. I have your scent; it wouldn't be hard to track you. One hour." He leaves the door open, but I don't run.

CHAPTER

Two-

I just stare after the open door and press my back against the glass. I think about what it would feel like to crash my elbow through the window and fall from this height. Would it hurt? What would it feel like to fly through the air, and would I know when I hit the ground, or would I just die?

My toes tingle as I envision it, thinking about lying on the ground as I die and knowing there would be nobody to protect my people. No. I'm not done yet. I must do this. The easy way out could no longer be an option for me.

Self-sacrifice had been something I'd grown accustomed to; in my young life it had been the only reason I'd been tolerated by my father. My red hair had set me apart from my siblings who were all darker complexion and darker in their various hair lengths. The black, voluminous tangles looked quite strange when compared to my own near blood-red locks. More than my birth order had descended me from the opportunity of wearing the crown, my complexion discounted it entirely.

I had known I was different from my siblings before anyone had pointed out to me the complete lack of resemblance. The bred in bravado of my brothers and the cat-like, mysterious nature of my sisters

11

never touched my animated, stubborn personality. As my father liked to remind me, I was not fit to wear the crown, though my mother often recanted with I was made for much more important matters.

I had no way of knowing they were grooming me, preparing me for the day when I would be sent to do the task that very few returned from when I would be stripped of my title as Royal Prince and turned into, for better words, a monk. If I was to return, it would be as a beacon of all that was light and good, reborn in a vision of prosperity and I would be assisting my bustling hometown with creating a new era of abundance. As a farming nation, I was to be much more important than a future king.

I had never dreamed of becoming King, I never wanted such a title. With my two older brothers so adamant in the war room, coveting my father's every word, and his complete disinterest in my person, I had nestled myself with my mother and the servants and yet, even there I didn't seem to quite fit in.

Never having seen the point in gossip and idle chat around wine glasses, I had thrown myself into the academics that our vast libraries had to offer. Befriending the staff suited for the perfect cover story to my continuous tardiness in mundane tasks such as Court and fine art schooling. I didn't wish to paint, I had wished to read, to escape the ever-dismissive pass over of my father.

Now, I'd give anything to attend another boring history lecture. I would walk through hot coals to entertain at dinner or sit in on Court.

I tread to the kitchen before fetching the first pale of water, snagging some bread to soothe the ache in my stomach. There was little fear of the overlord Alpha finding me, I doubted the mongrel even knew how to find the kitchen, and if he did there were a plethora of hiding places. I'd spent plenty of time here in my youth, baking or more so, stealing baked goods.

The rounded male chief offers me a plated sandwich, a simple slab of meat between two slices of bread. While it wasn't my norm, I wouldn't turn it down. I thank him quietly, not wishing to draw any more attention in case a wandering ear were to pass.

My aversion to meat had suited me fine as we were a heavily farmed community, rich with various vegetables, nuts, bread, and even sweets when my parents imported the chiefs for our special events when dignitaries would visit. Seeing the halls now left an ache in the pit of my stomach, nothing had changed on the walls and yet everything was different. As if the very life had been sucked from the depths with the death of the matriarch, my mother.

"Would you like some help, M'lord?" A small voice echoes as I carry the first bucket. Her frail hands circle the other side of the handle and I sigh in relief, though I want to refuse her help, I can't say that I'm not grateful. Physical labor wasn't exactly something I was good for. I hadn't done much for labor in my short twenty-some-odd years.

"If he catches you, he'll have you killed," I warn her, not quite turning her away. The fair skin and brown eyes watch me gently from under the heavy cover of crudely cut bangs. Her thick black hair pulled back into a tangled bun, stuffed under a bonnet.

"It's a risk I'm willing to take, M'lord. I hate to see you suffer so. It's not right, forcing one of your blood to do such a task. Is it true? Are the royal family…" her voice trails off. Was she saddened that only I remained? Would she had much preferred one of my brothers?

"Dead," I conclude. "I'm the last one." It does go by quicker with help, without her, I don't know how I would have managed. My body protests already, despite my schooling, I had been home for nearing on a month, and I had, admittedly, been partaking in the comforts that the crown had to offer. Mutilated, I had no desire to lift a finger for the foreseeable future. It would seem that dream had been cut horribly short.

Her lips purse as she considers this, pulling her eyebrows down in a way that I might even admire if I could find it in my heart to look at a woman in such a way. The crease causing the most quizzical look to form in those chocolate eyes. Her lower lip curling to capture between her admirably straight teeth. Her freckled cheeks rounding with the grimace of deep thought, she was acceptable for a servant.

Gena, a personal servant, more so a maid than something so grand as a lady to one of my sisters. She had desired me for longer than I care to think, I remember in my boyhood her presence as often as I have fond memories and yet, I don't recall anything particularly remarkable about her person.

She'd been a ward of my family most of her life, a constant admirer from afar as I was the only of my siblings to never have been courted. Perhaps it was her wishful thinking that I had other things in mind, that I'd not yet met the right woman. Wouldn't she shudder to find out my lack of suitable mates had been my mother's doing, for she knew well as I did where my tastes lie? "Have you not learned much from school? I thought..."

She had thought about what all the others had. That I would return some great sorcerer, not a downtrodden prince who hid away in his room to hide his shame.

I had been sent away, by my father, to a particular school to hone my skills. While some might see it as a gift, the reality was it was an almost guaranteed death sentence due to the trials a 'Solomonari' must go through to unlock their full potential.

From the ability to control water, more importantly, the weather, I had been deemed one of the rare few worthy of the approval of the dragons. I would be capable of crafting ice, summoning small dragons, and even a bit of healing, a Solomonari was as powerful as his surroundings called him to be. The once peaceful beings who oversaw delivering the weather to poor villagers were now dispatched to areas of famine as miracle workers.

There had been nothing left to do but accept my fate, my ill-prepared fate. I hadn't even known of my 'calling' until moments before I was sent away. I had played with magic, many of the other boys I'd grown up with had some sort of magical ability, but I had always felt stunted in away. It'd never come easily for me as it had for them and then to be accepted into such a school, well, I had not believed I would return either.

A shudder rolls through me at her question. "Not enough to fight them off on my own." I lie. I had learned plenty; I just hadn't learned in an honorable way. Where my companions had left as masters of our craft, I was dwindling at the back of the class. I had only passed due to unsavory measures, defaulting to my only survival method, the one thing I had had to give was myself.

At the school, our teachers were brutal, and our testing was strenuous. Many did not survive the trials, with most eaten by the dragons that they summoned. Every day we prayed to survive; in a twisted sense of humor, they encouraged us as hope allowed us to last longer. We prayed to our gods that they would see us through, and every day fewer and fewer of those pleas were answered.

I watched as my classmates were killed off one by one until only a few of us remained. We were congratulated, told that we had passed. Only, it did not feel like a victory. We felt guilty, why had we survived when so many of our friends had perished? Some horribly so.

Using now felt foreign to me, the disconnect of the higher element of my magic wrought with the agony of the trials and shame of the beds I shared to find worth in my meager existence. I wasn't meant to live, this was revenge for cheating death, this was my personal hell on earth.

It was my job to end this, perhaps that would allow me to atone for giving myself to them willingly in exchange for my survival. "M'lord, the tub is almost full. Is there anything else I could bring you? Perhaps something more to eat...? If I could be so bold... I'm... I'm so sorry that this has occurred."

Was she? Was she sorry? The lone prince, the only heir to this bloody throne, who had used her as a servant her whole life? Much as I like to feel the hero now, I was not much more to my people than a prince frolicking through their town whenever my parents grew bored of me. My sense of duty was all that I had left, a default, not a call to action as my training might have prepared me for.

These people were unlucky to be stuck with me for a savior, I couldn't even save myself. "Were any of your Lycan friends a part of the resistance?" I ask, curious. She blinks at me, clearing her throat. The royal family had kept a few of their own slaves, it wouldn't surprise me if this was crucial to the entrance into this domain.

"No, M'lord. Well, obviously they have joined now, but they surrendered with the rest of us."

Her words play on a loop in my head. Surrendered, that's exactly what my people had done. Given themselves over because my mother strode into Lord Darrius's life, there was little to be done for the people of Dezna. We were estranged, a commodity, they weren't any more our people than we were their hosts. We had abandoned them, handing them me in exchange for decades of neglect had been a failed exchange.

Perhaps it was this that spurred me to do something right, to do whatever I could to change this.

It was an opportunity to be more than the lesser Prince.

I'm most likely not strong enough to choke or drown this man, though I could probably knock him out. As I dump the last bucket, I catch a glimpse of my reflection in the water.

My dark eyes have shadowy circles beneath them from exhaustion and lack of sleep, I can't say this comes solely from my current situation. As I run my fingers over my cheekbones, haunted by the faint echo of my mother's voice, she scolds me that I've allowed myself to get too thin. It makes me smile and I feel tears threaten to spill over.

My hands travel up to tangle in my thick, blood-red hair and I sink to my knees and rest my elbows on the basin as I find myself feeling overwhelmed by the loss, once more. I would do it for my mother so that she had not died in vain. "You may leave me now, Gena," I command her.

Shuddering, I take a few deep and ragged breaths as I compose myself upon hearing him approaching. I cannot allow him to see me like this, I cannot show weakness. I am still a prince; I am still far above his status. Her eyes widen with panic, she curtsies as she rushes out of the room, and I pray that she made it before he caught sight of her in here with me. It is not for my own life that I fear but for hers, the one who was still willing to help me.

His boots echo off the stone floor and I fight to compose myself. There was no time for me to wallow in my own self-pity. I adjust my robes firmly, trying to rid my breath of the tremble. "You're a prince, get a grip." I hiss at myself, glowering at the man staring back at me in the clear water.

He enters the room and I place my hand on the basin, mumbling a few quick words as the water begins to steam. "There. It's warmed up for you."

Three-

My cold tone piques his interest, and he watches me, his nose wrinkles in what might be disgust. He is displeased by something, and he tips his gaze to the bath suspiciously. I roll my eyes at the hesitance, "It's water. I know you slaves rarely bathe but there it is. Just get in."

I opt to leave, startled as he grasps my wrist and I flinch away, trying to wrench free from the iron grip. "You could use your words! What gives you the right to grab me?" I snap, watching this animalistic man in bewilderment.

"I don't trust you. I want you to wash me, as it is a sign of loyalty. You must be accustomed, I'm sure your servants have bathed your spoiled self." I see no sign of jest in his eyes. He wants me to perform an act as if I were a common maid.

Staring at him, I wait for the humor. "I think you are up to the task; it is quite simple, I trust you'll figure it out," I respond and his expression clouds with that same look, annoyed with me but somehow finding me amusing.

As I move to leave, his voice catches me in my tracks. "Didn't we talk about this earlier?" His response has me scowling, so he was fully intent on turning me into his servant?

This vile creature, wishing to reduce me to the lowest form. "Undress then!" I command, gesturing to his clothes and he waves a finger at me, condescending in his mannerisms.

"Is that any way to speak to your Alpha?" His tone is patient and yet restrained, he looks at me as if I am dense. An uneducated youth of a great Lord. "I feel as though you are more qualified for the task of undressing me."

Alpha stands patiently and I allow my eyes to travel down his form. He is a mess, his clothes and skin covered in dried blood and grit, the smell of masculinity, and the woods emanating from him.

"As you wish, Alpha." I try not to sound sarcastic as I throw in a half-hearted bow. My long fingers look ghostly against his dark colors, the stiff material of the garments is rough to the touch. I unbutton his vest, pulling it off him.

The leather is worn and aged; a handmade garment with crude stitching and offering little protection for the large form it conceals. I fold it and set it aside, ignoring the patience in which he regards me. As I approach, I gesture for him to put his arms up and pull his stained shirt over his head, only to gasp at the sight of him.

Jagged scars stretch over his left shoulders, into his pectoral muscle. They're deep, ragged claw marks. His neck bears the scars of a bite wound, deep, light-colored mars on the sun-kissed skin. I realize my hands have frozen and I'm staring, but I'm unapologetic at the discomfort my gawking seems to cause him.

"A gift. From my father." Alpha answers my question before I can ask, and his cryptic expression suggests it's a sensitive subject. My eyes travel over the light peppering of chest hair on his broad chest. I notice the hair is gray and I steal a glance back up at the tangled locks on his head and notice that, too, is gray—not silver. He can't be that old, not with this physique.

My hands find his pants, as I unbutton them the shame begins to wash over me, here I am undressing the man who has killed my family. I jerk them off his sculpted hips and allow them to fall to the ground only to turn away quickly, not allowing myself a glance and quickly travel over to the shelf to grab a few clothes, towels, and soap.

The heavy belt and multiple knife sheaths land on the floor with my dignity, a dull thump. When I turn, he is no longer watching me, as he stands before me completely naked, his body taut and rigid. It brings back memories of my time at the school for Solomonari, and the atrocities that occurred there.

My instructor had favored me, I was his pet for lack of a better word. I shudder at the thought and my eyes are unseeing as I dip the cloth in the water and press it to his chest. He stiffens under my touch, I pause in disgust, but it's not a pleasurable thing for him.

I scrub his chest and reveal more and more tanned skin as I rub away the dirt and blood only to wonder how much of this is his own as I reveal healing cuts. We are silent as I wash one of his arms. Even so, my instructor knew my status, I was never forced to bathe him as a servant.

Running my fingers over the coils of muscle in his arms; his hands are rough against my own. As I finish with his chest, I reluctantly start on his legs. Surprised at his lack of commentary, I steal a glance up but he's not looking at me and it almost sparks a sense of anger that he has so little interest.

He's focused on anything but me, staring off into the distance. He denied me even the dignity of acknowledgment. I move to his back, once more, I'm floored by the tapestry of what a body can endure. The scars run over his shoulder blade and slash across his back in jagged lines that stretch towards his lower back.

Alpha visibly shudders and the muscles in his neck tighten at my touch. I note this for later; this has to weaken him somehow. There is no way someone with this much damage doesn't see impairment from it. It was a shame, really, it must have made his master very disappointed to see it considering he is a fine example of what my father was trying to accomplish.

The thought embarrasses me, I shouldn't consider this man a piece of equipment, but I immediately forgive myself when I think of all the suffering he has caused me in the past few days.

As I return to his front, I work my way over his toned abdominal muscles and feel the heat radiating off of him on my chilled fingers. We are opposites, he and I. When I meet his eyes, I see a spark that is known to me as the same gaze has fallen on my form many times in my short existence, desire is my curse.

I take a deep breath before filling one of the fluffier cloths with water to ring it out on his head. The action brings a startled inhale from Alpha, his height causes the water to splash down my sleeves in an icy blast as I come to realize that my healer's robes are not in the best condition after this activity.

"Well, if you wanted a proper bath, you should have brought a chair. You're too tall to bathe standing, really you should be in the tub." The complaint is half-hearted as I strip off my vest and robe. I have a silk undershirt that is tucked into my pants, guarding my chest against his eyes. I do not allow anyone to see my chest, not anymore.

"You don't get out much, do you?" Alpha's voice is disapproving, trailing his fingers casually over my ivory skin. Hints of the damage under my shirt peek out beneath the sleeves.

"No. I have responsibilities. Besides, I just got back from my train-ing." *Don't allow yourself to go there,* I remind myself as I reach up to soap his hair. His expression darkens with my tone, with the insinuation that I work harder than him. *I do, I'm not a criminal.*

"I don't think you can compare your responsibility to mine." His voice is low. I've offended him. I almost want to laugh.

"No. I suppose you really can't. Considering that I'm mastering a craft and you're trying to destroy my Kingdom and everyone in it." My voice is tight; I feel myself teetering on the edge.

"Your people enslaved mine, treated us worse than dogs, I feel this judgment is just." The heat that is radiating off of him is starting to climb, getting hotter with each moment that passes. I take another fluffy cloth and wring it out on his head to rinse away the soap, an act of defiance.

A low growl curls from his throat; I toss a towel at him. I'm done playing this game, I cross my arms as I walk away from him.

I can't do this. I can't talk politics with him, speak of fairness to a monster. "My mother did not deserve to die. You took vengeance on the innocent." My voice trails: I feel it coming so I wrap my arms around myself and try to hold it back. I can't cry in front of him. "She did not deserve to die," I repeat.

"People die every day, your mother was no exception. Any being who owned a Lycan slave was just as guilty as your father who cursed us. All magic users, the elves in Ziduri, as are the men who sit in the capital of the human cities, and they will all see the same fate as your father."

I wheel around to face him, feeling the tears building. "Then kill me! Don't draw this out. Take your vengeance and leave to slaughter another society." His body vibrates as he struggles to control himself. The heat is unbearable, and I realize the weight of my words. I can't help but think of my servants, the ones who truly raised me. The people of my city would be without hope should I perish here.

"I need you to find your father's book and destroy it so that this cannot happen to another species. We cannot leave until you do so."

He is exhausting!

I stare at him, exasperated. My eyes search his face, how can he not understand? "It doesn't work that way! You can't just destroy the book! It, itself, is probably cursed! I'm useless to you, I can't control the spells from that book and even if I could—I wouldn't use it to help you! You deserve what has happened to you, you can hardly even control what you are. An animal!"

I'm yelling now; I take my hands and slam them into the tub. It forms an ice layer beneath my fingertips, the water cracks, and groans as it freezes. He takes a step back and for the first time, I feel like he actually feels I'm a threat.

I smash the ice with my fists and inky black snake-like creatures curl from the basin, tiny dragons. The blood from my freshly cut hands drives them mad and they flicked their forked tongues at the scent.

I hear the snarl curl from Alpha's throat. All I have to do is command these little dragons and they will burn him to a crisp, yet young dragon magic is hard to control. There stands a good chance I will not live through this attack. But that would be okay, I'm alone here. I can't rule a kingdom or lead a destroyed people back into thriving. *I'm not my father.*

Alpha's smooth voice pulls me out of my musings.

"This is not going to bring them back. None of this is going to bring them back. I'm not sorry about killing your father, he was a vile person and he had to be stopped. But it is unfortunate your mother had to suffer for his deeds and for that, I am sorry. I know what it's like to lose a mother."

I can't tell if he's sincere or just trying to tell me what I want to hear, probably the latter. I blink slowly, my eyes filming over with tears, I just miss her so much. "I'm sorry about your mother." He repeats again.

Breaking, I wave my hand over the basin and the hissing creatures slither back into the water. I feel like I'm going to drop to my knees, only, he steps forward to catch me. I allow him to support my weight as I lose myself in grief for my mother.

My bloody hands smear his clean chest and I want to be anywhere but here but at the same time, his arms are so warm, and I allow myself this little bit of comfort.

I can always kill him later, for now, even the slightest bit of remorse is welcomed.

Looking up, his light blue eyes are wide and unsure of me, I must appear as though I've lost all sense. Perhaps I have.

I feel his hand close around mind as he lifts it to examine it. "You really did just get out of school, not the best magic trick."

"You're lucky I don't have my ax. You would be dead." The threat is very real, but I can't bring myself to look threatening. I'm too exhausted, so, it comes out as more of a joke. Regardless, he allows for a hint of a smile.

Then, to my surprise, he runs his tongue over the palm of my hand on a particularly deep cut. I retract my hand quickly; he has found a way to make me flush which is not easy to do. "Gross." I snap and examine my hand only to see that the cut is already fading, nearly healed.

"You could explain it better than I can."

"Well don't do it again." Though I am intrigued. I can see the command annoys him and he frowns, pulling his eyebrows together.

"Don't speak to me that way." His voice is low as his eyes meet mine and I give him a look of defiance, a challenge.

"Or what?" My retort is stifled as his lips meet mine and I consider pulling away, but the warmth draws me in. He commands from me a response; I snake my arms around his neck to deepen the kiss as it feels so good to *feel* anything at this point. His tongue invades my mouth and I taste my blood which causes me to break the kiss, shoving away from him roughly.

His eyes are blazing as he gauges my expression.

"Do not touch me, dog." Yet as he seizes my arm, his chest heaving with restraint, I can't help but yield to the intensity. I kiss him and my hands tangle in his hair as I pull his face roughly to mine. My body clings to his hard form, the damned clinging to the pyre.

His hands travel to my hips, and he pulls me against him, sending my body blazing. It is my way to preserve my own life, to use my body as a means of trade for my mortal form.

"Spoiled brat." He breaks the kiss and moves to attack my neck. I inhale sharply as I envision him tearing my throat out, pulling firmly on the tangled damp hair. My eyes search the ceiling, hoping to find what little remained of my self-worth.

He slides his hands up my thighs and his fingers slip under my shirt; I grasp his wrists as a form of defense. Alpha stops, retracting from me, yet I don't want him to pull away. I retreat inside myself, if it meant surviving for my people, I would do what I must.

"No." I breathe, warning him with my eyes. "I... I want to leave my shirt on." I manage and he regards me curiously as I press my lips to his again. Having to stand on my tiptoes is hardly getting the job done so I fist my hand in his hair and pull him closer to me.

I'm rewarded with a groan as he catches my lower lip in his teeth and before I know I'm pressed against the cold stone wall. It chills me and I cling to his warmth.

Endure. I could endure if it meant survival.

"What do you want?" I gaze up at him, surprised by the question. Consent? What does he care about my consent?

"What do you think I want?" I go to kiss him, but he avoids me, going low to kiss under my jaw. The sentiment is wasted on me, I block his mouth with my hand to protect my neck.

I don't need someone to love me, I don't need him to care. I need treatment for my disease, that I can only find relief from through the use of my body. Isn't it obvious what I want? I grind my body against him in frustration. "Do you want permission? It's a bit late for formalities?"

"Tell me what you want." He extracts every ounce of my focus. I press against him, digging my fingers into his shoulders, and yet I cannot produce the words as I shut my eyes and will him to do his bidding. His hand captures my jaw, between his thumb and forefinger as I feel the weight of his gaze bearing down on me.

This isn't what I want, it's what I feel I must do. Reluctantly, I peer at him through my lashes and it's his undoing. He steps back from me, allowing me to slide down the wall as I pant from the heat of his body pressed against mine.

With the space between us, I can finally breathe.

Setting his jaw, it is Alpha who retreats. "I've got business to attend to. I expect to see you in the dining hall for dinner."

I nod, numb.

He leaves quickly, as if he couldn't get out of here fast enough, completely naked. I'm momentarily appalled by that, but I suppose it's a common thing when these men live as a giant wolf for half their lives.

Savages, the lot of them.

CHAPTER

Four-

I had fully intended on killing him, taking my life and his in a single moment with the small dragons I had brought forth from the water. It seemed like such a simple task, considering his crimes.

But I must have seen some sort of sincerity in him or maybe I do value my own life in some way, a strange revelation considering how ready I was to end this existence while I was in school.

I have a hard time justifying my actions to myself, my willingness to offer myself as tribute when I'd been so ready to take my own life. I envision Alpha before me, my face gripped in his palm. His scarred body left much to be desired as far as appearance.

I vaguely allow myself to imagine what it must have been like for him to endure such an injury but I stop myself before any sympathy can form. Sorting through the closet, I find a few robes in its furthest depths. Most likely set aside by my mother in case I returned, ever the optimist about my abilities. She was the only one who had written to me, not that I'd been allowed to read her letters.

I don't allow myself to feel her presence as I pull on the white long sleeve and intricately detailed vest. The variety of colored squares line the trim and the front. Sliding into the pale pants, I feel a little more like myself. Royalty, a Solomonari Prince, it was my comfortable default since returning.

As I open the door, I jump back as I am certain that I am face to face with Alpha only to discover the man who is before me is not him. He is tall and gray-haired but he is young, much younger. Maybe only in his early twenties, close to my own age.

His body is lanky, like that of a young man who hasn't quite come into his own yet. His dark eyes are peering at me shyly through his tangle of hair, he is afraid of me and I'm pleased by that.

He reaches up to brush his hair back out of his face, a long thin scar cuts through his eyebrow and goes straight down his cheek but the eye is undamaged. It only distorts his features, giving him a rather fierce look that his kind eyes can't carry.

"I'm here to bring you to dinner." His voice is low and deep but timid. He avoids eye contact, staring towards my hip instead of meeting my gaze. It would seem Alpha does not trust that I wouldn't allow my people to be slaughtered?

Perhaps he was checking to see if I was still alive or if I had conjured up more dragons. Rolling my eyes, I push past the tall man.

"I am perfectly capable of bringing myself. I wish for my people to not meet their demise at the hands of your leader." My voice is harsh. It's as if he wants to be shorter than me, which is difficult considering I'm not very tall and he's over six feet.

Is it part of the standard of the Lycan army to be gigantic?

"What?" I demand. The tension is putting me on edge, he flinches away from my cutting tone.

"I'm sorry for what happened here." He is cautious, the look on his face suggests he isn't happy with our situation either. His tone and sympathy remind me of Gena, briefly, I wonder where she is and if she's safe.

A frown is my only response as I try to play the diplomat. We walk wordlessly down the hallway into the dining hall and I pause as I realize the place is overrun with Lycans. We must pass through the throne room and in it; there is a stack of paintings and books.

My heart tears in half as I take in the scene. My books; history books, family journals, stories, and spellbooks. *Why? Why destroy them?* I look accusingly at the man beside me, "What the hell is this?" I demand and he looks ashamed.

Maybe this is what he was apologizing for?

"A cleansing." He watches the pile as it is set ablaze, and I ball my fists. *Was it a cleansing or a punishment?*

"Where is he?" I demand, the man pulls the corner of his mouth down in a grim expression. "Don't play stupid. Alpha. Where is he?"

"At dinner." He sounds as though this should be obvious. "At least he should be, sometimes he doesn't show up—"

I storm past him, charging into the dining hall to greet the vast expanse of Lycan presence filling the great tables. The smell of the woods and cooking meat combined with the heat makes my head spin. The young man leads me towards a table off to the side where I see my target. He gestures and I sit down roughly, chin elevated as I glower at my captor.

"A cleansing? Explain yourself!" My tone is not calm, I shame my breeding with my lack of control.

His expression is what I was expecting, frustrated with my arrogance but amused at my willingness to speak against him. "It's exactly what it sounds like. The paintings are a reminder of the slavery we have endured. You've been conquered, remember? You don't get to make demands and I must explain nothing to you."

I glare at the table, trying to comprehend what I've been told and run a hand through my hair to rein in my anger. I can't do anything about it right now, not if I want to keep my head and those, I'm responsible for.

A plate is set in front of me, and the other giant sits down—Alpha's mini-me. I mutter a thank you, confused because I thought I was supposed to be the slave. "Tonic is going to watch you until you can be trusted to do your job. Next time, the girl won't get off so easily."

"Who?" But then I realize it's 'mini-me' who he's talking about. *What kind of name is Tonic?* "If you did anything to hurt Gena—!" My voice raises and the overbearing weight of dozens of eyes fall on me, I force myself to rein it in, pulling the burning magic back from my fingertips.

He shrugs, indifferent.

I take a few bites of my food, instantly relieved because I know who made it. The staff must have been spared, the food tastes great and I'm grateful as my stomach pleads for more. I eat quietly as I listen to them talk, refusing to let the relief show.

It would appear Alpha runs a tight ship and some have been slacking with a temporary place to call home. There are talks of a rebellion and it piques my interest. A tall man sits beside me, even taller than Alpha. His long white hair goes down to his hips, and it's pulled back into a loose ponytail. He looks older, middle-aged, but he is muscular and fit under his shabby clothes.

His eyes are a startling yellow, much like the moon on a hazy night. I'm astonished that he only has one arm, the sleeve is carefully folded in his vest.

"The formations have been able to move pretty freely through the city, we have been met with little resistance. We have taken out over twenty magic users, they swore their allegiance to Lord Darrius and we have taken care of them. Any other magic users are now in hiding, I would assume, I don't think they will reveal themselves with so many of us in the city. The people have been cooperative, it won't be long before we figure out where the rebellion is hiding. We have left the houses intact, raided some of the libraries, and burned any magical books or art pertaining to the royal family." His voice is low, deeper, and tired sounding.

"Tell the Twins and Delta to go towards Ziduri and search there. We don't want to be spotted by any elves just yet, but I would not be surprised if we find the rebellion close to their borders. It would be easy to cross and reveal our position if they feel threatened. They did not make a move when Dezna fell, I'm imagining they are biding their time. We need to ensure that formations stay tight and that patrols are not missed. This young stock is useless, they need more training."

Alpha looks frustrated as he rolls his knuckles in his fist, the whole thing sounds barbaric to me. I'm still reeling at the fact the libraries I grew up in as a child are now empty.

How many of my friends were dead?

The white-haired man nods. "We have not seen any elves; I have instructed the men to not allow any witnesses. We cannot afford a leak. I will give Beta the order to double down on the training of the younger groups; they are not useful to us in battle if they cannot control the change. Besides, they can't cause trouble if they are exhausted." I realize that the yellow-eyed giant is looking at me now.

"So who is this and why are you playing with your food?" He sounds annoyed at my existence. "I had agreed the young son would be kept as a servant."

Alpha shrugs. "I have no idea what his name is. I didn't ask."

I don't like the look Ol' One Arm is giving me. "Nicolas." I offer nothing more.

"He's rude." One Arm doesn't approve. "Spoiled. Wealth wasted on the ungrateful."

I hear a chuckle; Alpha is amused but the glare from One Arm silences him; he looks unapologetic. "He is going to be useful when we find the spellbook; he is going to help us reverse the curse. Besides, it will raise morale in the city if they see that he is alive, we don't want to kill this entire city. We need something for the world to focus on when we finish. If there is nothing to rebuild, they will come searching for us."

I'm appalled at this; I can't hold it in any longer. "They will search for you anyway! I will command it!" I snap. "You killed the Lord Darrius! He ruled the entire magic community; you don't understand what you have done. What you have started!"

One Arm stiffens but Alpha raises his hand, and the man settles back into his chair.

"Patience Sota. He will learn. The magic community is grateful that your father is dead; we have done what nobody has dared to do in over one hundred years. Trust me; there is no remorse in the community for the death of the dictator."

My appetite is all but gone, despite my previously famished state. "I'm going back to my room."

Tonic stands with me and he follows me though I hear the tail end of the angry conversation behind us. I sigh and slow my pace as

I leave the throne room. The smell of burning wood and the smoke billowing off the burning books causes my eyes to water.

He looks afraid when I finally meet his face. "What's with the look? Somebody has to stand up to that asshole. I can see it on your face; you're trapped here just like I am." I don't know what gives me the right to speak to this man like this, maybe it's because he looks like a kicked puppy. He's easy prey to my anger.

I hear him sigh and he looks like he might not answer but finally, he speaks. "Nobody speaks to Alpha that way, it is... unnerving... to see." I roll my eyes.

"Someone needs to." I feel childish though; my inner self is sticking out his tongue and pouting.

"Speaking to him in that way puts him at risk; others might try and threaten his position due to your outburst. When we fight for rank, we fight to the death. If Beta had been there, you would have probably been killed." He looks haunted; maybe he has had a run-in with this 'Beta'.

"Is that why they call him 'Alpha'? It's a rank?" That seems a little ridiculous, I couldn't imagine going by anything but my given name.

"Somewhat. It prevents attachment since most do not hold the rank for long. Before the curse it was easier, we weren't forced to live in a pack but since the change, it's been hard to get used to the wolf side of things." He looks guarded; as if maybe he's saying too much. I find it interesting, so there is a chink in the armor.

"What is your rank?" I can't help but pry. He frowns and glances at the ground with his dark eyes.

"I'm an Omega. It's the lowest rank, the punching bag of the pack. My mother was a very lowly woman, practically a prostitute. My father was very prestigious, but it didn't carry over. I've never wanted to fight, never been good at it." He shrugs and I realize that I'm frowning. What a miserable life, this delusional man seems fine with it.

"I'm sorry to hear that." A slave who is 'free' to be a slave to his own people. A small smile comes onto his face.

"Really, it's okay. Alpha takes care of me; I've known him for a long time, since I was really little. He keeps me close by, so I live comfortably."

I decide that Tonic has a mental disorder if he is content with being the lowest of the low.

Offering a small smile, I bid him goodnight, rushing to my bedroom to flop on my bed.

Unaware of the time, the sun pouring in rousts me into stretching out over the plush down bed only to realize I'm not alone. Jumping awake, I find Alpha sitting in my windowsill. He looks clean; his vest clinging to his body over his pale shirt looks in better repair than the ones from yesterday.

Was that yesterday? I cleared my throat and he glanced toward me. Annoyed; there is no amusement this morning. I realize that his lower lip is split towards the corner and wonder if Tonic's suspicions were true.

"Well, you look pleasant. To what do I owe the visit?" My voice drips with sarcasm.

"You aren't holding up your end of the deal." He sounds restrained, as if being in my presence were uncomfortable. "Your back-chat is not needed."

"Well, your *plan* is ridiculous!" I retort and he stands abruptly.

Rage rushes into his eyes, his jaw set. "I did not ask for your opinion! Your job is to be a peacekeeper for your people and to serve me.

Need I remind you what is at stake? Do you need a demonstration to show you how serious I am?"

My throat tightens and I glare towards the ground, my chest heavy. "No. That won't be necessary." I manage, before I can look up, I feel that he is before me. The radiating heat overwhelms my senses. Shutting my eyes, I grit my teeth, leaning away.

"What was that?" He presses.

"I understand Alpha." I snap and he seems to accept that's the best I can do without cutting out my own tongue. I'm sick with myself, I'm betraying my own people.

"Good. Now get dressed. You will be going to the city with Tonic." It's hard for me to hide my surprise. So soon? I can only assume he wants to test to see if I will run. While the thought is tempting, I desperately want to see the city, my people, and check in on my friends.

Oh, that's right. I have a keeper.

"I'm not going to get dressed with you in here." I can't allow him to get close to me again, not after what almost happened. Rolling his eyes, he makes his way towards the door.

"Meet Tonic at the castle entrance promptly. He is waiting for you."

The ashes threaten to stain the bottom of my pants as I rush through the throne room, and I lift them to keep them free of debris. Scorned by the chuckles, if they had gone through what I had gone through to obtain these clothes they would lift them as well. I see Tonic and make my way over.

As we exit the door and leave the courtyard, I glance around, there's no carriage or means of transport. We are walking, I sigh in despair.

"Do Lycans just walk everywhere?" *That must be how they are in such good shape. They don't have the brain wattage to get tired.*

Tonic smiles a shy smile and my hope for a horse dwindles. It's a mile or so to the city from here, I curse my father for his attention to solitude and landscaping.

It is the beginning of fall and I'm grateful for the cool breeze. If it were summer, this would not have been possible. The path is more worn than I remember, I had just traveled through here and the land now feels foreign to me.

The heavy trees remain intact, but the path is widened from many foot soldiers going in and out. There are no Lycans on this path, at least none that I can see. "Where is everyone?" I dare ask. I expected to see the crawling horde that I saw yesterday.

Tonic appears confused for a moment but then shrugs. "Working?" I must baffle him. How could I possibly not know the ins and outs of his existence? It's the only thing he knows. "We travel in small groups, it's not safe to stay completely together."

I find myself anxious to see the city. How much had been destroyed? It's beautiful out, the mountains look especially clear, and the leaves are threatening to change colors. I inhale the scent of fall and embrace the crisp air. My own room might as well be a prison compared to the beauty of my country.

Chilled, I wrap my arms around myself, rubbing my forearms through my sleeves. It reminds me of my training, the discomfort of the outdoors brings back harsh memories of the climates we were forced to survive in.

"Cold?" He sounds sympathetic.

"No. Just lost in thought." My feet are already aching, he reassures me we are almost there. I can see the trees start to thin and as we crest a hill the city reveals itself.

I am struck with relief. It looks totally unharmed. I quicken my steps and I hear Tonic following close behind. My city. My home. I rush until my feet hit the stone pavement of her streets and freeze as I take it all in.

Tonic skitters to a halt at my side, surprised by my abrupt stop but I'm off again, making my way through the familiar streets and brushing my fingertips on whatever they can find to re-familiarize myself with a city I have so longed for these past few days. "How?" I ask Tonic finally.

"What do you mean? We said we weren't going to destroy the city."

What am I supposed to say? *I didn't believe you.* I give him a sideways glance and close my eyes as I lean against one of the stone walls of a building. I press my palms against the cool rock. "I thought it would be burned to the ground."

Tonic rolls his eyes. "The place is made of stone Nicolas, which would be quite a feat."

I laugh. A real laugh. And it rolls out of me until my sides hurt and I'm gasping for air. I don't know quite why it's so funny, but it hits me in such a way that I just can't help myself. It's something different. It's joy, for my people and me.

I decide to drag Tonic all over town; my people need to see me. I'm hit with a sudden surge of energy that had evaded me for weeks. Even before all this happened.

I make my way into the bakery and snag a loaf of bread to gorge myself on the sweetness. Hearing his sharp inhale, he shoves me back into the bakery as we exit which almost causes me to drop my bread. "What the hell?" I demand but he holds his hand up to silence me.

Tonic curses under his breath. "We are being followed."

CHAPTER

Five-

It doesn't surprise me to hear that someone lurks in the shadows, I'm the last heir to the throne and one of the invaders appears to be holding me captive. It would concern me more if people weren't concerned.

"Are you sure someone isn't just going the same way we are?" I feel ridiculous hiding in the bakery but it doesn't stop me from taking another bite out of my bread. I push past him, irritated, as I peer out the window. "Look, there's the book store. Let's go over there and if we are followed there, then I'll worry."

He doesn't look convinced but I walk past him, leaving the door to cross the street with a ridiculous amount of confidence. Behind me my puppy dog guard keeps a close watch, I can feel his tension and find it quite unnecessary.

In the store, I pace through the shelves and I'm disappointed that it's true that they have burned most of the spellbooks though I do find one thin copy of a healing book and slip that into the page keeper in my vest. It folds neatly away as I murmur the concealing spell, I slip some money on the counter while Tonic glares out the massive store-front window.

"They are waiting for us to exit." He reveals and I eye him, *how can he possibly know that?*

"What; are they talking to you?" My voice drips with my lack of faith in his ability to predict our situation. He doesn't notice, he's in full alert and I'm certain he will alert my captor if we don't solve this now.

"They are in that alley; I imagine they will approach when we are outside."

I struggle to see the threat. I truly lack the ability to comprehend one of my own people standing against a Lycan, especially considering they had just executed the royal family. They can't know Tonic as a pushover, from a distance he might even look intimidating.

"Let's go see what they want." I press.

Tonic's expression cracks and he gives me a nervous look. "I..." He's afraid. This is out of his pay grade. He's a babysitter, not a fighter and he doesn't want to risk his life for something that would assuredly get him in trouble.

"We can't just hide in here all day." He can. I will not. It has never been in me to value my own life and do what I am told. I was not bred and raised to listen to the likes of Tonic.

He knows that I will leave; I can see it on his face. I won't stay here and he can't allow me to go off on my own.

Sighing, he watches out the window. "Okay... Here's the plan. We're going to go out there and see what they want. If anything strange happens, I will change and you will climb on my back and then we head back towards the castle. We should meet up with one of the patrols there and that will keep us safe. Understand? I can take one or two but I'm not experienced enough to take on a whole group."

"How many did you smell?" Is that even correct to say? Could that be considered offensive? *Do I care?*

"Just one..."

One? What are we worrying about? I shrug and gesture for him to lead the charge. Huffing, he leads me out of the bookstore to the side alley where we spot our shadowy figure. They are hooded, in an oversized black coat. We can only see the lower half of their face and their hands. The remainder of the figure's body is covered in garments, meant to conceal one's identity. How did I not notice this person?

"What do you want?" Tonic demands. The figure smiles to reveal beautiful white teeth. No fangs. That makes me breathe a sigh of relief.

"I've been looking for you Nicolas, there's been talk that you were slaughtered. When we saw the smoke, we figured as much. The lycans must be brave to have let you out of the castle... Though I see you've brought a mutt. Have you turned sides so easily?"

I scoff. I didn't realize I was in such high demand. "Hardly the case, he is my guard. I am surprised there is room for gossip when the royal family is still fresh in their graves, idle tongues should spend more time in debt to their country rather than entertaining gossip."

I don't appreciate being followed but it must look strange that I'm in the company of one of the creatures who has put my city on lockdown and murdered my family. My chest tightens and I force the feelings down, I can't crack now. This person can't know I'm a captive. "I believe we asked you a question, what do you want?"

I hear Tonic growling and it makes me shiver as images of my father's death flashed through my memory. My mother is screaming and the blood—so much blood.

The figure takes a step forward and Tonic stiffens. I put my hand on his shoulder to assure him I want to hear what he has to say. "I'm with the rebellion. I'd like to take you there and show the people you are alive, we could use the morale boost. It's been hard biding our time; the Lycans have this place shored up pretty good. We are—" This voice is male. He seems to be looking towards Tonic. "Is there any way we can send this one away? The rebel leader urgently wants to meet with you."

Wouldn't that be nice? But no such luck would that bring. Tonic would surely return home and Alpha would tear this city apart to find me or worse, kill all of those who have ties to me in the castle.

"Tonic is with me... anything you say can be said in front of him. He is here to keep me safe. These are trying times, good sir, one can't be too careful." I reassure this hooded figure.

The man sighs and removes the hood to reveal long flowing honey-colored hair and dark eyes.

"You can see why I don't want to discuss matters with him?" He is an elf. His long pointed ears make it painfully obvious. The rebellion is made of elves?

A snarl comes from my wolf bodyguard. Maybe I should send him back? But I feel conflicted to keep him here, what would the others do to him if he lost me? I decide to revisit, later, why I'm so concerned for Tonic's life. I must vouch for him, I must insist. "Tonic is a good man. I know you don't want to give away your position but he doesn't want this either... he's on our side."

I hope Tonic has a good poker face or really, I hope that I'm telling the truth and that I haven't been wrong about him. He glances at me but then sighs and nods; I squeeze him in gratitude. The elf regards us both as I press on. "I need to be back before nightfall, I'm on a pretty strict schedule."

This appears to disturb the elf. "We need to get going then. Once night shift shows up this place gets a little—well, I'm sure you know." I ignore that; gesturing to him to guide the way. I feel as though something should be going off in my head, telling me not to follow this elf but I can't help but feel a sense of security in these familiar streets.

My watchdog stays close behind and I find myself growing used to the heat while finding comfort in it with the chilly air circulating in the shadows.

Arriving at the rebellion brings a whole new mixture of emotions. I am in a dead run before I know it. They're here, I'm not as alone as I had feared for these borders are filled with other magic users. I feel tears threatening to run over as I count in my head what faces I recognize. There are healers and shapeshifters; a couple of those with gifts have managed as well.

I'm thrilled and, at the same time, I'm devastated. I'm coming up short; there are some I don't see—a medicine woman, a few of the gifted and some spell casters. But the wolves have been mistaken, they have not killed nearly as many as they thought. While I'm broken for those we have lost, I'm so grateful for all who were saved. Everyone seems as relieved to see me as I am to see them.

Tonic appears painfully uncomfortable and they don't seem too thrilled with his presence either.

I see plenty of new faces, elves and even a few mortals are among them. There are more elves than I could have guessed. All in all, the rebellion stands fifty strong and I'm impressed but also I'm concerned, they stand no chance against this army. In an instant, the Lycans would destroy them.

I'm preparing my speech when the crowd begins to part and I'm greeted by a tall man who is in white silken clothes. His long platinum blond hair has the front braided into an intricate crown around his head while the rest falls to below his waist. It's so well brushed that it almost looks translucent as it sways behind him. His light eyes are locked on me and he pulls his full pale lips together in what could be a smile.

He watches me with an interest that I am, unfortunately, familiar with and it almost makes me squirm. Interest, he is practically drinking me in but I don't shy away. I extend my hand, boldly.

"Nicolas." I will introduce myself. He takes my fingers and bestows me a polite half-bow, bringing him down to my height. The motion conveys the heavy scent of perfume to my nose and I resist the urge to cough, he bears quite the odd scent of a man.

"Oh I know who you are. I've been dying to meet you once more." His voice is smooth like a fine wine, his hair slips from behind his back as he lowers and rises. His angular features make him almost look alien, too perfect, as if it was carved and polished onto flawless marble skin. I think of my own marred skin and retract my hand from his silken touch. This man has never known work a day in his life, much as I had lived a life of luxury, I earned my title as Solomonari.

"Haryek." He introduces himself. "Prince Haryek, son of Taryek."

I raise my eyebrows. "Son of Taryek? The Elf King?" Haryek doesn't give the shy smile I would have expected. He looks proud yet I'm not impressed, more so surprised he would be out of his cozy castle. "What finds you at the head of the rebellion?"

I knew of Haryek faintly, from a few dinners and parties in my youth. He was a political figure more than he was an heir to the throne. He handled most of the outside dealings in trade, wine, and slaves, his father must be furious at his absence. Without Haryek, how was Ziduri fairing for trade?

The elf shrugs a slow rise and fall of his shoulders as if he was taking a deep breath.

"I decided this would be a better route for me. What the three kingdoms have done to the Lycans was not something the whole of society agreed upon. It's time for change. I wish we could have spoken about this alone but I suppose now is as good of a time as any. I want to find a way to de-throne my father without murdering hundreds of elves.

"We do not have history books; we have certain people who remember these things and pass them down through the generations. Those would be critical losses for our society along with the other royals who my father will, no doubt, be hiding behind. With your abilities and my tactics, I feel we will have a fighting chance to get through this with little bloodshed."

I take this all in and watch him cautiously. What does he know about my abilities? Perhaps just what he's read. I'm not sure I want Haryek to be in charge of anything, let alone a kingdom, a close neighbor, and a valued trade partner. I think about Alpha sparing Elven lives and almost laugh but if nothing else; my royal training has taught me to stay serious.

I can't show him my doubts, I must keep him happy for the time being. "We have similar wants for our people; I don't want anyone else to have to die." This brings a smile to the elf's face but I don't smile back. I don't find this politician very sincere.

"My father will not hold back for long. The lycans have done the dirty work of removing your father, Lord Darrius; there is a chance at restoring balance to this world. I want to put good people in place, I want to form an alliance between the kingdoms once again and restore peace to this world. There is a time for the elite but where it stands, we cannot continue in this way. We must act quickly before someone comes and seizes this moment and destroys us all." His eyes flicker towards Tonic.

I glance at Tonic who looks uncomfortable. "I believe we do agree on that."

Who does he want to rule Dezna? *Me? Ha!* "I'm grateful for all you're doing for my people and I would love to repay the favor. I want to help in any way that I can." The answer sounds forced, how can I help? I don't know where my spellbook is. I'm under lock and key! "When I find my book, I will be of more use to you. I'm afraid right now I'm rather limited to what I can contribute."

Haryek allows a massive smile to come over his face and with a gesture, a small woman comes forward holding a bag. She hands it to me and I can sense it before it even reaches my fingers. As I shove the bag hurriedly out of my way, my book reveals itself and I clutch it to my chest as if I hold on to the very lifeline that is my true self. "How?"

"I saved it." Her voice is small. I stare at her; I feel horrible that I don't recognize her. My eyes travel over her burnt hands, my book is not meant for anyone but me to hold. I reach out and touch her hands, focusing my thoughts as her burns vanish. She smiles a small, grateful smile which I return. It's such a small gesture but it takes more out of me than I expect. I haven't used magic very much since I've been home, my energy reserve is low.

"So you will help?" Haryek presses. I know what he's hoping for. I lack excuses.

"As much as I can." I allow. We haven't been here long but I feel ready to leave. This is a lot to process and I was enjoying the day in the city. "I will return in a few days, I have a lot to think about and I need to build my strength." Haryek takes my hand once more and half bows.

"Till next time."

CHAPTER

Six-

His smooth voice sticks in my head as Tonic and I leave the rebellion. They live in meager houses far outside the city limits, what used to be the slums of our city, to be honest, it was not a part of the city that I frequented. I wonder what happened to its inhabitants but then I figure they must be part of the rebellion or run out by the lycan horde, I come to the halting conclusion that I truly don't know much about what has happened to my people.

My book hums in my page keeper, it seems happy to have me back and I'm thrilled that it was not destroyed for I really wasn't sure what would have happened if that had been the case. It was something I had handwritten in school, it wasn't as if I could just conjure another one.

"Thank you for going with me. You didn't have to, you could have just left." I don't know why I'm thanking him, he is being forced to babysit me. His dark eyes lock on my own and I realize we are no longer walking. He looks like he doesn't know what to say and honestly, neither do I.

"Are you going to tell Alpha what happened here?" He asks slowly. I frown.

"No. Are you?"

"No." His voice is short and he looks at the ground in defeat.

"Well, then that's settled. I'd like to keep visiting to keep an eye on Haryek, he might be useful but I don't believe we can quite trust him." I watch him flinch as if I've struck him.

"The more we visit here, the more scent we will leave. If Alpha finds these people, rest assured, they will all be slaughtered." He speaks the truth, no matter how much I fight it, it is the reality of my situation.

I'm a captive here and I'm no longer in charge. I have to find a way to help my people, to bring the kingdoms together. Alone they cannot defeat the Lycan army but united they very well could regain control. What if Haryek really was going to bring about change? I owed this to my people; for too long had they suffered at the hands of my father.

We walk in silence back towards the castle, I mull over what needs to be done in my head and as much as I'm dreading it, the only thing to do is talk to Alpha. I must appeal to his better nature. Was that at all possible? Was there anything about this man that was remotely human?

I notice Tonic has stopped, centered in the courtyard. Before me is a shorter man, the first short Lycan I have seen. He is a dark tan with jet black curly hair; Spanish in origin given his features. He approaches us, his golden eyes narrowed into slits, and his expression forming a scowl. Tonic swallows as he looks away, a harsh raspy growl rolls in the male's throat, and Tonic shrinks in submission.

"You must be Beta." I don't know why I assume this but the way he walks around as if he owns the place fits the bill. I see that I'm correct for he smiles at me brightly.

"I am." He responds, dragging his tongue over his teeth. "You must be the prince—oh, right you got demoted to a servant." He observes me, raking his eyes down my body. "How the mighty have fallen."

"Don't you have a job you should be attending to?" I retort sharply.

"You're rather rude for how small you are." His tone is accusatory.

"I've been told. Now if you'll excuse me I have my own matters to attend to." I walk past him but in a movement too quick for my human eyes, he has my throat. His fingers feel like iron cables. I gasp and clutch his wrist but it is as if I'm fighting with stone.

His grasp threatens to crush the very life out of me. "There is order around here. I don't know what Alpha thinks he's up to, keeping you alive like this, but I don't like it. So how about you show a little respect." I gasp as I fight for air. Suddenly, I'm released and fall to my knees as I wheeze and cough, my lungs blazing. I clutch my throat as if to remove invisible fingers and Tonic is at my side.

"Heal yourself." He whispers and I look at him through watery eyes.

"I can't." I rasp. My throat feels like it's an inferno.

I see the gray creature and my heart is pounding as I flashback to my father. His faded image takes the place of Beta, only Alpha doesn't attack him. Beta is spared where my father had his throat ripped out. "Having a little fun, Beta?"

The black-haired man shows his teeth in an animalistic threat. "Your pet is out of line." His tone is harsh, he wrinkles his nose. These aren't humans—these are animals.

Alpha flashes his fangs, hair standing on edge. All kneel in respect for the Alpha, save for Beta. Tonic's face is buried in my shoulder, I'm bewildered by the fear these people have for this man. Beta's body shakes and then distorts as the black wolf takes his place. I have never seen the change before and it horrifies me as I watch his human form break and shudder to become this massive wolf. Only magic could force a human to do that.

The black begins to lower his head and Alpha's muzzle is mere inches from his, pushing him lower until his head is practically in the dirt. He doesn't need to hold him there; the presence of the Alpha is enough to keep him there. "Next time it's your ass Beta."

I see a glimmer in the black's eye as Alpha releases him and he sulks off. I want to put up a barrier between us. I don't want to be here, not with this thing; this animal who killed my whole family. He must sense it because as quick as the wolf is there, Alpha is standing before us as a man—a completely naked man. I avert my eyes and, temporarily, my neck is forgotten. He extends his hand to help me up.

"Let me see." His voice is stern; I flinch away from his prodding fingers though he is surprisingly gentle. He frowns. "A little bruised. But, you will be fine."

I take a step away from him, I don't need his bare body so close to mine.

Tonic looks embarrassed, he should have stood up for me but Alpha makes no note of it. "Any sign of the rebellion?" He is talking to Tonic now and the poor man answers in a half-hearted shrug. Alpha rolls his eyes at the sullen male. "Don't let Beta get to you. His bark is worse than his bite. You know how he is, just try and keep this one alive a little while longer? We need him for now." He gives me an annoyed glance as he dismisses us.

Tonic breathes a sigh of relief and I rub my neck. "Does that happen often?" It stings to talk but my voice is returning quickly.

"What? The fighting? Yes but mostly with Beta. They kind of have a rivalry going on." Tonic shrugs and I decide I don't care enough to press. It seems that my home is, now, almost as dangerous as my school.

Can I not go a single day without one of these beasts trying to shred me? I didn't ask for this, I didn't want this. I'm tired and I want to go hide my book away from the wonderful ray of sunshine that is my captor.

"Can I have some alone time?" He watches me carefully but then nods. Maybe he has things to do or maybe I just give him a heart attack with how everyone seems so interested in me. He looks exhausted so I'm happy to give my watchdog a break.

I make my way into the castle and into my father's bedroom where it seems I will be staying. I take my book and mumble a few words as I enter, a secret panel opens from the wardrobe and I slide the book inside, along with the healing book, and then reseal it.

My mind wanders to my instructors, how I gained their favor. The only relationships I've ever had were in that school. I find my fingers trailing over my vest, outlining one of the many scars across my torso. Clutching my hand into a fist, I sit up and feel a little more certain of the path that I will need to take in order to help my people.

Donning civilian clothes, I make my way to dinner only to spot Gena on the way. "Gena." I greet, she curtsies quickly, stuffing the rag she was using to clean in her apron.

"M'lord."

"Are you alright? He didn't hurt you, did he?"

She quickly shakes her head with a gentle smile, "No, M'lord. I'm fine, I hadn't even known he'd seen me. Next time I'll be more careful."

Raising my hand, I dismiss the thought. "There won't be a next time, but if you could do something for me?" Nobody would notice a maid, nobody would think twice of her. "Could you keep tabs on Beta for me? Learn a bit more about him?" She parts her lips but finally, she curtsies with a nod. She would not deny me, "Thank you, Gena."

―――――――――

I sit with Tonic and notice there is a new man at the table but he is not talking, he looks embarrassed. His brown hair is short and shaggy. He has kind, chocolate eyes. "That's Delta." Tonic introduces. Delta smiles at me and then goes back to eating. "He's shy."

I offer a small hello to the strangely named individual. Maybe it's because he's practically sitting at the children's table considering I have so many babysitters. My gaze falls on Sota.

"So who are you exactly?" I question, "I don't feel like we have been properly introduced." Ol' One Arm smirks at me.

"I'm Sota. I'm the Alpha's advisor." He seems so nonchalant. As if it was obvious.

"He is one of the last Old Bloods." Tonic adds. Sota wrinkles his nose.

"M'not that old..." He grumbles and takes a bite of his food.

"He is the only Alpha to surrender the position and live." Tonic looks mystified but I feel like that should be a given, why should you have to die if you give up the position willingly?

Sota sighs at my expression, "I'm sure you've noticed pack politics are complicated."

"Tonic has told me a little." I don't know how much I care to hear about why they kill each other. I only wished they'd do it a little quicker; there would be fewer of them. Sota glares at Tonic and then turns his attention back towards me.

"Well, then I won't bore you. I'm glad he kept you. You will challenge him and he needs more of that in life. Why don't you bring him some dinner? I think he's gone to the library. He hasn't eaten today and he's cranky when he's hungry." I wait for the pun but then I realize they are serious and I sigh outwardly. I suppose I am his servant.

Tonic assists me in preparing a plate of what the Alpha would like, simple meats and bread. He instructs me to put on my best face. Pushing open the oak doors, he's sitting on the tile floor of the great library, surrounded by papers. Flat backed, as if the man could slouch, and calculating as he observes what he has created in the intricate paper display. The illumination of candlelight playfully dances across his tanned skin.

I slowly approach and my eyes wander over the papers, carrying the map of our country. Dezna, Ziduri, and then the massive expanse of the kingdoms of Man. There are a few question marks on the papers, but no marks indicating he knows about the rebellion.

"What are you doing?" I can't help but pry. He doesn't look at me.

"Planning. I was here looking for your father's book, I thought I smelt magic, it seems I was mistaken." I scoff at the thought.

"You can't smell magic." I retorted.

"You can't but I can. It smells like burning atmosphere. It's horrid." Sometimes I forget he has an accent. *How did someone from the England area get all the way out here?*

This is getting me nowhere, he shares nothing. "If you find it, it will destroy you. Very few people can actually handle it."

It's his turn to scoff but he doesn't entertain me and I roll my eyes at him. I hand him his plate, "Here. You need to eat something. You can't boss me around if you've starved to death."

His light eyes glance at the plate but he shakes his head, "Not hungry. Maybe later." *He's like a child.*

"You can destroy the world later, you can't not eat." It's frustrating; it's not a difficult task in itself but he, somehow, manages to make my life harder.

His body grows rigid with my meddling in his habits. "Wolves don't eat as often as humans do. I'm used to it; it only seems to be bothering **you**." His tone is becoming annoyed and I huff as I set the plate down on one of the tables to cross my arms over my chest.

He needed a dose of reality and it seemed it would be my job to give it to him. "You can't honestly think that you can do all of *this* on your own. Your people will be slaughtered, even if you can make it past Ziduri, there will be too many of Man's armies waiting for you."

"That is where good planning and battle tactics come into play. That is why your people were conquered and mine are preparing to march against Ziduri." My throat catches and I want to strike him. *How dare he! My people were conquered because he murdered their leaders! My family!*

"This isn't going to work!" I shout at him and he stands, I swallow but stand my ground against the overwhelming figure. In the dim light of the library, he looks absolutely menacing. He is soundless as he approaches on bare feet. "You can't win on your own. You're going to need help."

"That's why I have you. That's why your alive, to persuade your people—"

I shake my head, forcing myself to remain. "You need more! You need magic users. You need to find a way to partner with the rebellion." I know I've said too much.

As he approaches, I back away until I hit the table, placing my hands on it. His body pressed against mine, his hands resting beside mine, one of my hands slides up to press to his chest to distance him from me.

"Care to repeat that Nicolas?"

CHAPTER

Seven-

I have to turn this around.

It rolls on repeat in my head, I've said too much too soon. I had grown confident in my time with Tonic, concocting my plan to use Gena to spy on Beta, I had felt as if I were in control only to realize that I had only been playing with minor characters. The true mastermind, the true threat, was here before me.

I struggle for words; I can't breathe with the inferno that is his skin. "You're going to need to form an alliance." *Convince him.*

"With whom?" he demands.

I blink to clear my head. I've never experienced anything like him. My body threatens to bow in response to his presence, wishing to return to my coping mechanism, wishing to gain use of this pent-up male aggression. "The rebellion. You can help each other; they aren't here to kill the Lycans. They want the same things you do, to see the fall of Ziduri and order restored."

He takes a step back to consider this and I gulp in fresh, cool air. "Take me to them." The threat is real, his voice a terrifying amount of calm.

This is what I was afraid of. This is what Sota and Tonic had warned me about. "You can't hurt them. They aren't a threat to you but they could be an ally." I stay strong in my tone; I won't allow them to be slaughtered.

Alpha draws closer again, I smell the sweet scent of pine and lavender soap. His lips near my ear, his voice a sultry hum and he speaks to me in a tone that no man has any right to utter to another man. "I don't think you are in the position to tell me what I'm allowed to do."

He is so painfully close to me, I can feel his heartbeat and see the coils of muscle under his tanned skin. My hands slowly come to rest on his chest. The warmth is comforting to my chilled fingers; I gaze upon him with my own dark eyes, the familiarity of my position coming to the forefront of my consciousness.

My comfort had come from familiarity. I had dealt with plenty of powerful men, my school had been full of them, maybe this would be how I helped my people. "Talk with them. Hear what they have to say."

I carefully tighten my fingers on the thin material of his shirt as his body stiffens, wary of me. I keep my expression soft as my plan begins to form in my head, I know what is needed of me to bring him to my side. My mind races back to that moment in the bathroom, where he had asked my consent, where he had so passionately pressed me up against the wall with every intention of fulfilling his basic desires. The desire for me, the hunger for what I had to offer him.

Stretching up on my toes, I press my lips cautiously to his. He hesitates and I wonder if he will pull away. I'd been wrong before, there weren't many men who shared my unique perversion and if they did, it wasn't often they dared kiss with another man nor was it my preference.

The majority of men found comfort in the soft submission of our cultured, schooled women. Even if the forbidden desire was there, the inexperience and bravado often ruined the encounter once lips were involved.

With what appears to be great restraint, he meets my kiss and deepens it to invade my mouth with his tongue. Even when it's my idea, he is the Alpha and he fights for control of the situation.

The stubble of his jaw sends a shiver of excitement down my spine, I could pretend as though it was only in service that I perform these tasks, but the thrill of the unknown never failed to send me into an almost euphoric state. It is my disgust with the pleasure I take in the act that sends me spiraling when the deed is done.

I hold my own against him as my hand travels up to fist in his hair which elicits a low growl from him. My heart rate skyrockets as I loosen my grip with a gasp. I'm lifted onto the table and brought up to his height. His hips are between my legs and I feel his arousal pressed against me through the thin material of his pants. "What're you doing to me?" He murmurs against the junction of my neck and jaw.

The uttered words almost bring me to pause, I hesitate as my fingers trail through his thick hair and for a moment, he's almost human. I remind myself promptly that he killed my parents and any sympathy plummets. My body takes over and I'm fighting to get his shirt unbuttoned.

He's pulling my vest off my shoulders, hurried in his movements. I freeze and stop him as his hands find my stomach. My eyes shoot open and I hold my breath. "Leave the shirt on." It's not a request but a plea.

He regards me for a moment and I know he's filing this away for later but he leaves it, choosing instead to focus on the removal of my pants. I'm grateful, not all men are so courteous of my strange boundary. I shove his shirt off his body, fingers skating over his muscular abdomen, as he removes his own pants. His hard body captures the warmth of the dimming lights.

The darkness hides his scars well and I wonder if it would do the same for mine. I remind myself that this is my show as I stand, capturing his lips with mine. I push him back towards the structure, using his height to my advantage to make him sit on the edge. Taking him in my mouth boldly, I make an assertive amount of eye contact as he writhes under my skilled tongue.

I'm experienced enough to know the usefulness of preparation. We are locked in a silent war, fighting for control of this situation and succumbing to the other's desirable traits as if they were blows of battle. Little did he know he was dueling with a veteran in the art of temptation.

Satisfied with my work, I climb the table to straddle his hips.

Alpha places a series of kisses down my jaw and I flinch as he reaches my neck; a cold chill runs up my spine as he runs his tongue over my bruises. I groan, shoving my hand in his face in protest. "Don't." I don't need to be loved, I don't want to be loved. There's no need to pretend that he cares about me, that he longed to do anything other than taste my flesh for his own satisfaction.

I shove the offensive man back on the table and pin him beneath me. He's breathless and bewildered, I'm in my domain and he was merely my prisoner. Keeping my gaze firmly locked on his, I lower myself onto his length and groan at the fullness. I'm not used to him, I go slow as I wait for my body to adjust and shut my eyes. He writhes beneath me; I hear him growl a pleasurable sound low in his throat.

My confidence returns as I start to move, my nails dig into his chest at the mixed emotions of ungodly pleasure and shame that I'm once again using my body to get what I want. When I'm here, on top of a man, I feel powerful. I feel as though nobody can hurt me, I feel in control in a world that I seem to have very little say in.

I'd never felt attractive, never felt desirable, as many women have visited our home it had always seemed as if they knew something was wrong with me. Something alluded to my preferences, something gave away my hidden shame, that I was not only perverted but that I wished to lie with men.

Alpha startles me as he suddenly sits up and we are face to face once more, I watch him with wide uncertain eyes. My cheeks are hot; I pant and take in his piercing blue eyes as my hands fist in his hair. His arms wrap around me and I moan into his mouth as our lips find each other. I clutch him to me as I climb and increase my pace. He moves back against me, no longer battling for control, no longer fighting for position.

He feels so good beneath me; his warmth no longer suffocates me but draws me closer. I'm lost to what my motives were, my fingers tug at his soft gray hair and I manage a smile at the noise I'm rewarded with.

Why am I not surprised that he likes it a little rough?

Why am I not surprised that I do, too?

His stubbled jaw teasing my skin, the sound he makes driving me closer and closer to the edge.

His hand moves to my hip to encourage me, I know he's close and I'm chasing my release as his mouth finds my nipple. My body shudders, I cry out as I finish and he follows after me as he clutches me firmly.

I collapse onto him while I wait to catch my breath. My arms are loosely around his neck, my face buried into the side of his jaw. I carefully slide off and cringe as I'm sore and achy; the table has not been kind to my knees. I find my pants and pull them on, as does he, though he forgoes the shirt.

Adjusting my clothes, I fasten my pants with an airy sigh. "Now. As we were saying?" I press, unwilling to lose any of the momentum I had gained. Normally, I would have done this discussion during the act but, much to my surprise, I had found myself quite taken with the experience. It had completely slipped my mind to interrogate him.

He regards me suspiciously, as if I were fulfilling some judgment he'd already made long before I parted my lips. Annoyed by the assumption, I cut him off with a bold statement. "I will help you find the rebellion but you must agree to speak with them before you pass judgment. They could be helpful." Why should I care how he regards me, what he thinks of me? I already know his thoughts, he surely says them often enough.

His expression is unreadable, ever the steel trap of emotional distancing.

"Fine." Is all I get on the matter. "Take this plate back to the kitchen. It's late, you should go to bed."

I take the plate and move to leave, only to pause as I watch him return to his papers. "Would you eat some if I ate it first?" The hesitation would cause me to smile if I wasn't disgusted with my own caring for this man. It must be the after effects of getting a release that drive me to wish him to eat.

"Why does it matter to you?" His guarded expression causes me to sigh, running a hand through my hair in frustration.

"Why does it matter to you?" I retorted.

We are both unwilling to give up any information and I'm satisfied with that as he gestures towards a piece of bread and I roll my eyes as I snag a slice of the loaf and take a bite defiantly. The amusement glints in his eyes as he does the same only with a piece of meat as well. "Is the meat poisoned?" He questions, taking a sarcastic sniff of the offered meal.

While I wished it was, I don't think trying such measures would end successfully for me. "No. I don't eat meat."

Alpha regards me as if suddenly everything makes sense and I glare at him only to finish chewing down the bread and wishing I'd brought water. He hands me a burgled bottle of wine and while I'd like to be upset, I uncork it and take a heavy swig.

Sitting here in silence with the man who killed my family, after doing what I'd done, I'm met with the overbearing sense of guilt once more. "Did they suffer?" I ask finally.

"They?" The cold tone almost insulting, I wait, crossing my arms over my chest as I stare into the rumbling fireplace. The ever changing flame used to be so comforting, now it taunts me with its ability to be anything it desired. Why couldn't I change? Why did I have to have a default that most found so offensive?

Finally, I earn a moment of decency as I down another gulp. "No. I didn't kill your siblings, Beta did and he is not one to allow things to suffer."

Things. My family, my siblings, were things. "Oh."

He doesn't know what to do with me, it seemed fitting as I didn't know what to do with myself. I must have reminded him of whatever he saw in me that caused him to comfort me in the bathroom, while he doesn't touch me this time, I feel the relaxation in the air as he forces the calm to replace the heavy. "It's a pride thing for him. They went quickly."

I couldn't explain why he felt the need to reassure me, why he even thought to keep me alive, how could have known who or what I was? It wouldn't matter, none of it would matter, I couldn't use the book even if I did find it. But, as I stand here, listening to him, I did want to find it.

I could see the path solidifying, what I must do to get through this. If I found the book, if I found a way to use this, I could stop this and stop him. Sparing him a sideways glance, refusing to allow myself to succumb to the thought that he offered my siblings mercy, I stiffly nod and hand him back the wine bottle. "Well. Should we arrange to meet with the rebellion?"

Regain control, keep him following your lead, lead from the bottom. I chant my mantra.

"Tomorrow." His tone is final. It would appear I'm not the only one who wants to be alone. "We will discuss this more tomorrow."

CHAPTER

Eight-

I find myself looking over my shoulder a lot the next day. My night was plagued by nightmares of Beta ending my life the same way Alpha ended my father's. I toss and turn, jolting awake periodically.

My dream wolves seemed to take turns chasing me. Sometimes it was the gray, sometimes the black. I mull through breakfast and I notice Alpha is not here. In fact, he hasn't been around since that first day really. "He's not here."

I hear Tonic and startle, trying to appear as though I wasn't searching as I clear my throat.

"Excuse me?" I pretend to not comprehend what he's talking about but he sees through me and shrugs.

"Alpha. He went out on the patrol this morning; he, very rarely, is here for breakfast or any meals, really. You can relax."

Do I look tense? I feel drained; I need to find time to practice my skills. It's rainy and cold today; a good Solomonari might encourage the weather to find a different patch of earth to saturate but I feel no such inclination.

I'm not quite fond of the common knowledge that I fear these beasts, what I hold is not fear but malice. "I told you, I'm not afraid of him." I notice Sota is giving me a look and I frown.

With a heavy sigh, he angles his body towards me. "I heard you two went on an adventure the other day?" I feel Tonic shrink a little; it would appear I'm the only one who talked. I poke my food around on my plate; suddenly I'm not very hungry though I know I must eat. Out of the corner of my eye, I spot Gena who waves tentatively at me then disappears into the kitchen.

"Somewhat. It was quite informative; I'm hoping it will bring us one step closer to ending this nightmare." My tone feels colder than I hoped but it doesn't seem that Sota is reading too much into it. I need to find a way to excuse myself.

"And you hope to do that with... elves?" His drawn-out tone causes my eyes to shoot up and I open my mouth to speak but then I recall that Haryek touched my hand. He must have known the wolves would smell the rebellion on me, he wanted to be found.

Alpha would have no interest in conversing with humans but the fact that the rebellion was being run by elves could provide something interesting. I sigh and run a hand through my hair at how easily I'd been played by not only beasts of burden, but a pompous elf as well. Perhaps I wasn't as good as I thought at playing this game. It would seem everyone else was already quite a few moves ahead.

I'm no longer in the mood for twenty questions. "Well, it would be a start. I have no qualms with the elves." I keep my response short. "In fact, I might prefer them over some others."

Sota scoffs, unimpressed by my supposed confidence. "Elves only look out for themselves, they feel they are above us all."

Steadying my hand, I refuse to allow him to get to me. Some of our closest allies were Elves, it only made sense now that I would find comfort in their partnership. As I try to convince myself of Haryek's innocence of these claims, my blood begins to boil at the weight of the hypocrisy of such a statement.

"They aren't the only ones!" I snap back so quickly I astonish myself. Sota stares at me with those strong, yellow eyes and I know I'm getting on his nerves. I'm not cute anymore, I'm becoming an annoyance.

All warning signs urge me to tread lightly. "They know they can't stand against the pack, they want to create an alliance to stand against Ziduri. They want the same things we want, peace. Why does it matter if it's with elves and magic users?" I feel like I'm explaining myself to a parent more than an 'advisor', as if I need permission to feel the way that I do.

"You honestly think Alpha is going to stand with that logic?" Sota challenges me, causing me to pause and backtrack, confidence could only go so far when faced with harsh realities of true intentions.

"I've spoken with him about it. We have come to an agreement." I sound firm in my reasoning but Sota snorts out loud. The way in which he eyes me causes my cheeks to turn a few different shades of red. **He knows**. Oh god, he knows.

I look down and take a few bites of food, feeling that familiar shame rush over me in a tidal wave of regret. Someone who's been caught sleeping with their teacher, someone whose worth rests plainly on their sleeve, Sota's judgment is not wasted on my fragile self-esteem.

Did Alpha tell him? Had he heard? Could he smell me on him? My heart is pounding. I steal a glance around the table and Tonic is too busy talking with Delta to even notice us. Sota's eyes are locked on me and I swallow only to sit up straighter.

There is nothing to save me from my own choices, owning my most potent skill was the best I had to offer at times.

"Listen. It's none of my business. Alpha needs a way to blow off steam, you need *whatever* it is you're after by pulling this game. I'm not interested in getting into this bullshit. You need to make damn sure you know what you're doing before you put the lives of dozens of people at risk. If he is anything, he's absolutely lethal. Alpha will kill every last one of them if he feels it will help win this war. I would make sure my ducks are in a row if I was you, the lion spares the lamb... until it's hungry."

Sota stands to depart but I have no retort for him. I think he's an ass but I know I'm in control of the situation. I've seen firsthand what a horrible person Alpha can be. I know what he's capable of and haven't come close to forgetting his atrocities.

I take my guard dog away from his conversation with Delta and I force him to come with me.

It's time to figure this out; it is time to find my father's spellbook. It is the only thing powerful enough to stop this army of vermin and put an end to my continued torment.

I do some chores around the castle as a disguise to hash out a plan. Everyone else seems to have a job; it will appear no different that I want to neaten up my own home after they so kindly destroyed it. Perhaps I'm being ordered to do it? It was the best way to wait for Gena to come find me and I'm not waiting long. "Gena, this is Tonic." She curtseys and Tonic nods, awkwardly.

"This Beta doesn't often come into the castle, M'lord. But I did hear some men speaking about an alliance." This does me little good. "They were off by themselves, near the rear of the castle while I was tending what remains of the garden. I'm sorry, I tried to get more information. My English is not very good." He was smarter than I gave him credit for. Gena's wide eyes bring me back to the present and I offer a small smile.

"No, this is very helpful. Thank you so much for what you're doing, Gena. Please, take a rest for a bit in my quarters. You've earned it." I gesture for her to move down the hall and come to meet Tonic's bewildered gaze. "What?"

His lips part, unwilling to speak as I boldly stare at him. Finally, he finds his words. "You are spying on Beta?" He hisses, his tone hardly audible.

Shrugging, I begin to talk towards the library. "He surely sees it fit to spy on me." I keep my voice hushed, speaking through my teeth. "He's up to something."

"Of course he is! He's Beta!" Tonic spits, struggling to keep his voice down. "If Beta catches her, he will kill her brutally and there will be nothing Alpha can do to save her."

I don't want to think about that right now, I just want to focus on the next phase of my plan. "She won't get caught. Now. Are you going to help me or not?"

Entering the library, I'm surprised all of Alpha's papers are gone. I glance around but don't see them anywhere. Straightening out some books, I take the time to work on looking for my father's spellbook. I glance at Tonic, "Can you smell magic?"

"What?" He sets the copy of a romance novel back on the shelf and sighs as I hand him more books to hold. He's coarse, not ready to speak to me again just yet. I can't say that I blame him, it would seem Tonic might have better morals than all of us.

"Magic. Can you smell it when it happens?"

Tonic shrugs, "I don't know... I've never really looked for it before."

That was useful. I think for a moment and take the letter opener out of my pocket. Pulling the books out of his hands, I set them on the table before holding out my palm. There was only one way to find out, through practice. "Your hand." I command.

Tonic folds his hands behind his back. "Funny. No. I don't think so. Poke yourself."

"I can't heal myself. Your hand, please." He frowns and I groan outwardly at his adolescent behavior. "Don't be a baby! Give me your hand."

He groans back, only to growl as he places his hand in mine and I prick his finger. Wrinkling his nose in distaste for my cruelty, I ignore him as I say a quick few words and heal it. "Inhale." I command.

He rolls his eyes but does so. "I smell blood and... I don't know, something... burning? It's pretty faint. If I wasn't looking for it I wouldn't notice it. Why are we doing this?"

I grin broadly. "You have just been promoted to search wolf!" I tell him excitedly and pack up the rest of the books onto their shelves before gesturing to him to follow me into the hallway. "Come," I command and grasp his hands in the hallways. "I need you to look for that same smell in these halls. It will smell like the library and the magic. We need to find my father's book, Tonic."

"I'm not a tracker, Nicolas." The hurt in his voice is obvious, he's a little offended. I sigh, I don't have time for hurt feelings.

Softening my tone, I catch his eyes with my own gaze. "Tonic I need you to do this. I can't ask anyone else. Humor me, please? I need your help in finding it."

Watching me for a long moment, he takes a long inhale and nods reluctantly. "Alright, let's take a walk and see what we can find."

I'm hopeful that Tonic's nose is at least half as good as Alpha's though I'm not sure how all that truly works. How does one get better at smelling things? Is it a developed skill or something you're born with?

We walk down the familiar hallways, the large heavy curtains have been untouched and gather dust and cobwebs on their satin fibers. It saddens me to see the halls so bare. The walls are lighter where paintings used to be hung; I try to remember what was there and what it all looked like. Strange how one can know one's home so well until familiar things vanish.

It's hard to recall what it actually looked like, whose face hung in remembrance on our walls only to be forgotten once it was out of sight. We had spent weeks on those paintings, standing and posing so each of us could be immortalized in vibrant oil colors. I could have sworn I knew this place inside and out and now it feels almost foreign to me.

We seemed to be walking for almost an hour and I realized I had forgotten how big this castle was considering I exist in such a small part of it now. It smells unused; the lycans don't venture this far into it either and I can't say that I blame them. "We should tell everyone they're welcome to use these guest rooms. Might as well, the rooms are just growing dust."

Tonic shrugs. "We like sleeping outside, we feel safer. It's too easy to become trapped in here. Most lycans were kidnapped out of their homes so they don't feel comfortable in tight spaces." The sentiment brings back haunting memories, he suddenly freezes and inhales slowly.

"I think I found something." He sounds unsure as he walks and then pauses in front of a giant stone statue on a pedestal that is inset into the wall. I reach out to touch it and try to feel if anything re-markable stands out, but nothing reveals itself. I gave Tonic a glance, maybe I overestimated the ease of tracking. "It's here, the same smell only much stronger. Older."

Tonic takes a step back. "Nicolas, I don't think you should go in there."

I raise an eyebrow and now I'm intrigued. *In where?* Just when I'm about to start throwing spells at this statue, I hear footsteps and I see that I was wrong, there are a few guards that come back here.

I have no doubt in my mind that there is a hidden room behind the statue, finding it will be much easier than entering it and the thought of what waits for me gives me an uneasy feeling in my stomach. My father, surely, would have set up traps to prevent too much investigation.

The room was meant to protect the book, guard it against those who wish to use its power and that probably included me. He wasn't too fond of his children, why would he wish for them to gain the use of his book?

We would have to come back later.

Ushering him past the guards who eye us suspiciously, I know they can't possibly know what we were down there for and I'm relieved that magic isn't something that just anyone can smell.

Feeling stir crazy, I coax the timid lycan outside to do some work on the weather. I'm revitalized, pleased with our findings, it prompts me to feel good enough to manage some cloud control and at the very least, redirect the rain to move out of the city instead of looming over it.

It feels good to use, to feel it course through my veins as if it were the most potent of drugs. I feel alive; my body drinks up the familiar electricity as if it is my lifeblood.

At my school, they had such high expectations of us. We were expected to perform twenty-four-seven; at the drop of a hat, we could be forced to go somewhere, prevent something, or create something all while being hunted by bloodthirsty beasts. A Solomonari's magic can only become triggered by extreme stress. I had thought coming home was a break from that but, obviously, I was very wrong.

As the thought concludes the rain rumbles out of sight and over the horizon, I have made up my mind; I must go warn the rebellion that Alpha can't be trusted. I have a duty to myself and my people to uphold.

Everyone is riled up, the cold air has them all in good spirits and the rain was a welcomed relief to the heat we have been experiencing lately. The misty haze would hopefully shield my scent, preventing my ever prevalent captor from immediately knowing my wear abouts. It would give me time to get the warning to Haryek, if nothing else.

"Tonic, I want to go to the city, I have to talk to the rebellion. To Haryek. I have to tell them that we need more time to persuade Alpha to come to our side." Tonic gives me a long and hard look and I know I'm asking a lot from him but who else could take me? Alone, my people would be done for.

He signed up for this when he decided that he didn't want to fight!

"Tonic, I'm not asking," I tell him sternly.

He leads me hastily out of the castle towards the street. We walk in silence for most of the way; I can feel his tension at my quick pace. He is reacting to my energy, it must have him nervous, or perhaps it's the death march to our own demise if we're caught.

I feel him slow and wonder what sort of threats would motivate him to at least walk at the same speed as me, "What? Why are we slowing down?" I wheel around to face him and he looks concerned. "Tonic!" I snap, annoyed with him. Then I see what has truly caused his hesitation.

Beta.

CHAPTER

Nine-

The black beast lumbers towards us, a predator stalking his stunned prey. I take a step back, clutching my companion's arm. The fear strikes through me like a bolt of lightning, all at once my courage feels all but drained.

He looks at me like I'm something to eat, I'm a parasite invading his territory and he's come to end my existence. The black wolf bares his fangs as he stands between us and the city entrance. Beta must have been on night duty, he must have smelt us coming, or perhaps he had been waiting here all along.

"A little late to be out taking a stroll." He isn't asking, he's demanding a reason for our presence here. Tonic says nothing; he's stock still as if that would protect him.

It will be up to me to get us out of this. "I wanted to get here before the shops closed; I forgot something in the book store." I lied.

The wolf snarls and I slow my breathing. I refuse to show how it rips through my very soul. Flashbacks hit me like a slap in the face, I see my mother being torn apart. My chest throbs in agony, my soul bleeding for her. I feel light-headed.

"Do you find me a fool?" His tone is harsh, saliva seeping from his exposed jaws. "Do you know what I think? I think you are trying to escape. Your people are about to pay for your treachery. Wait until Alpha hears about this." His head tips back to howl and I throw up my hands.

"Stop!" I command. "I'm here to see the rebellion; to arrange a meeting with Alpha." He watches me in disbelief.

"The only use the pack has for the rebellion is to end it."

He's not buying it, it's not enough. "That's not true! Alpha wants to negotiate with them, I'm set to pick a time and place. We are going to make an alliance." I'm hoping the information will spare me the accusations that would cause my people to be slaughtered by their wolf overlord. Surely this beast must have a reasonable side? "Leave my people out of this, if you have a problem, take it up with me!"

I feel as though I have hit a nerve, for now, the black wolf begins to stalk forward once more. Tonic staggers behind me, I know what's about to happen, everything in my body tells me to brace for impact, for the death that is imminent.

The bark makes my blood run cold. I feel his breath hot on my face. "I'm sick to death of your pompous attitude. I'm sick of these pathetic excuses as to why you're still alive. You are nothing. You are worse than useless; you are a waste of good flesh. The fact that you have been kept alive for entertainment value is an insult to our kind, how can a whisp like you possibly command the attention of a man such as the Alpha? What kind of sorcery do you hold over him? What are you planning?"

Beta gets louder, more demanding. His hair stands on end and his muscles flex as he rolls back on his hind legs. I can feel it building, the tension of a spring coiling for launch.

I wonder what it will feel like, *will I be in too much pain to really comprehend? Will I be awake every moment of this short battle?*

He pulls his lips back to expose his teeth and parts his jaws in a deafening snarl. The echo stirs my hair and I shut my eyes.

"You're right. I'm nothing. I'm not a threat to you." I surrender to my imminent death. I've seen this play out before; I know I don't make it through this. I wonder if my father knew he would die that night; if he was ready. *Is anyone ready?*

I don't want to see it coming. I've seen enough to know what my murder would look like. I think back to my dream, the gray was the one who caught me, the black was never cunning enough but I suppose I wasn't ready for him this time. He did not have to chase me; I stood before him in acceptance. There isn't a trick or a cunning phrase that could remove me from his sights.

"You don't deserve him!" I hear the pain in his voice. I come to realize this isn't over my people or my position on the war. *This is over Alpha.* I open my eyes in disbelief just in time to see the familiar gray blur and at first, I think it is Tonic.

The roar that comes from Alpha shakes me out of my stupor. He shoves Beta across the path and the black wolf scrambles to get back to his feet. I cover my ears with my hands at the volume of the brawling wolves.

"Are you about finished making a fool of yourself?" Alpha demands, his teeth flash in a threat, ears laid back against his skull.

Beta snaps his jaws in a savage bark. "You are the fool, I am saving your life! They were running to the city full tilt, maybe you should ask your pet what he was up to!"

The growl coming from the gray beast in front of me resonates in my chest, rattling me. He's so close I could almost touch him. "That is not your job, your job is to do what you're asked and keep the pack in line. You are slacking on your duties to chase after the omega and a servant. Remind me, who should I be concerned about?" My anger twinges at the insult.

"He doesn't deserve you Alpha, he was about to turn you over to the rebellion. You are wasting your time with these feeble games! You know where you belong; to whom you belong..." Beta straightens his body and Alpha stiffens, even as a wolf, I recognize the hesitation that I continue to see when we are alone together.

"You think that person is you? Caspian, that was never a possibility and you know it." *Caspian?*

Beta glares at the ground and there is a long moment of silence.

He adjusts his stance, and decides. "Alpha. You are no longer fit to lead. You have been compromised, bewitched by this magical creature. I'm telling you to step down and I'll make your death quick and painless."

My heart twinges, catching me off guard. I think back to Gena's words and my heart climbs in my chest. "Alpha, it's a trap!" I shouted suddenly.

The large gray ears lay flat against his skull, "Come and take it if you want it."

Tonic pulls me quickly out of the way as Beta lunges and the two wolves crash to the ground in a heap of teeth, claws, and snarls. The ground gives way to their mass. The sound of teeth clashing and bodies crashing together makes me feel sick to my stomach.

"We have to stop this," I say to Tonic who shakes his head quickly, sinking to the ground.

"We can't! Beta has challenged Alpha! We have to stand aside, we can't interfere! It is against our laws." The gray wolf has the black on his back by the throat, clamped down and ready to go for the kill.

A white creature leaps out of the brush, with immense brute force he rams into Alpha's scarred shoulder which forces him to release Beta.

A yelp comes from the gray wolf and he grits his teeth as he staggers back a few steps, holding his paw up. Two against one? How is that fair?

"Tonic we have to do something. This isn't a challenge, this is a takeover. If you think we would be any better off with Beta as a leader, you are sadly mistaken." I command action from the shrinking male, I will not stand by and do nothing while my only lifeline is destroyed.

Tonic shakes his head again, putting his hands over his ears. "I can't, Nicolas! I'm not... I'm not strong enough! I don't want to die!"

I feel helpless to stop the fight as they close in on Alpha. My eyes drift to the beautiful sunset that is behind them, the blazing pinks, oranges, and yellows of the sky look like an inferno above this horrid scene. I hear the snap of jaws and I close my eyes, I figure it's over and that I must be next but nothing comes.

The fight continues and I can't believe that it's possible Alpha could be taking on two wolves by himself. When I allow myself to steal a glance, it's Delta who has come to help his Alpha.

Delta is not strong enough to fight the massive white creature and the fight is a losing battle. Soft, sweet Delta, his shaggy brown hair and his deep chocolate eyes, I see those same eyes reflected back on me as the white wolf pins him to the ground and tightens his hold on his throat.

I hear him gasp as life begins to leave his body and I see myself reflected in their humanity. He doesn't want to die but he will for a cause he believes in, for a man he believes in, for his family. Beta fights Alpha to the ground, his paw between the off-center shoulder blades, shoving him into the dirt with his jaws clamped behind his head.

His injured shoulder giving way, he collapses beneath the weight. I can't let this happen. I hate this man but I can't watch him die. Not like this.

My training begins to bubble to the surface. I am not powerless. I am more than capable. "No!" I scream a spell as it's revealed, anything that comes to mind and the wind throws Beta and the white beast towards the heavy tree line.

They begin to run at me, I've now become the main target. I shout again and this time they're lifted off the ground in a small vortex of wind. The sky begins to groan and turn black. The clouds pull together and I curse under my breath, I'm about to lose control of it. I belt out one more command as I shove my hands forward and feel the energy leave my body in a rush. I fall to my knees and suddenly feel very cold.

When my eyes open, I see that there is a wall of ice coming from the nearby creek, it has flown through the woods and crashed into Beta and the white wolf, encasing them in ice. The fingers of the cold water stretch high in the sky like a beautiful fountain of destruction.

Their whole bodies were surrounded by murky water, mixed with divine, shimmering ice cycles. I shiver, my hands feel frozen and I glance at my blackened palms before I press them against my coat. I feel weak, my body threatens to give out from the overdraw of magic. My head is pounding, fighting against the effects.

Tonic rushes to Delta.

"Delta please." He begs, pressing his cheek to the wolf's shoulder. He's gasping, fighting to stay alive. His chocolate eyes rolled back into his head. His membranes are pale; he's lost so much blood. I shamble over to him, my body feels almost wooden in its movements.

"Tonic, move," I command and press my hands into the dark red of his bloodied fur. I find the biggest wound and I mumble a few lines over and over until it begins to close. It won't heal him completely but it will save his life. He gasps, inhaling a full breath of air and lurching forward. Taking big gulps of air, he struggles to try to stand before falling over and going unconscious.

"Is he dead?!" Tonic searches my exhausted face.

"No. He's just out of it. It's hard to come back from being so close to death, he needs a warm bed and rest." I realize Alpha is standing over us because I can hear dripping. I look and see the artery on his neck has been nicked as blood seeps freely down his leg. How is he still standing? I approach and he bares his teeth at me, warning me to stay back.

"Cut your shit and let me help you." I snap, unwilling to admit to myself why the words surface. This is my chance, I could just allow him to die.

I'm so tired but if I don't stop the bleeding this would have all been for nothing. I can convince myself of that, I would kill him on my own terms.

Reaching out to touch him, in defiance, he snaps his jaws in my direction. I jerk my hand back with a look that suggests I may just allow him to die. "Listen here, asshole! I just saved your life. Cut it out! Just stand there and let me close these wounds on your neck or you're going to bleed out! Try that shit again and I'll freeze **you** in a block of ice!"

I'm answered with a growl but I shove my hand forward into his fur and murmur until the wound closes on his throat.

He shakes out his neck scruff at the sensation. I rested my hand there for a moment longer, the fur is so soft. I admire the various shades of gray and the richness of the color. My hand is completely gone in its density; I feel his hammering pulse beneath my fingertips.

I can feel his hot breath, hear his lungs expanding as he breathes much-needed air. The smell of the woods, of pine and cedar, fills my nose. I take a tuft between my fingertips and marvel in its smooth, silky texture. I forget I'm next to a murderous warlord and for a moment, I'm lost to the beauty of this massive creature.

One icy eye is locked on me; I realize it is not a human that is looking at me, this is not the eye of a man but a wolf that is watching me so carefully. The small pupil and the decisive look are a dead giveaway. I'm in the presence of the true Alpha, the wolf side that we cursed him with.

Tonic told me this was what made it so difficult, that inside them there was a creature wanting to get out. I see my reflection in that crystal clear eye, I take in the black rim and the way his coat turns to white around his eyes and muzzle. I find that I can't breathe, for if I do, the moment will end, and once more I'll be afraid of him.

The wolf steps away from me and I close my hand. I'm almost angry but then I realize I have nothing to be angry about. Alpha blinks a few times and I know he is back to himself. He approaches Delta and sniffs him, checking on him to make sure he is okay.

"They won't be like this forever; they will thaw out in an hour or two and be mad as hornets." I wish they were dead, that would make it so much easier.

Alpha sighs, flattening his ears against his skull. "That gives me enough time to go back and get Sota. Beta and John must pay for their acts against my leadership." I want to ask what that entails but I think I know, he's going to have to kill them and I don't want to be around when he does.

"If you're going to go back, let me heal your shoulder." I'm not asking as I approach and he takes a quick step back.

"I will heal on my own, I heal much quicker than humans do. You need to head back to the castle. Now." I'm irritated at the command.

"I don't think anyone is in any condition to be traveling. Look at Tonic, he's exhausted. Your men are fatigued. We should bed down here tonight and we can continue this in the morning. I'm drained and you're hurt." I'd love to be away for a night but Alpha sees things differently.

He narrows his eyes at my attempts. "Some of us have responsibilities to attend to. A leader knows no time frame. I have a job to do." He gives me a look that suggests he's disappointed with where my allegiances lie. I'm frustrated with his judgmental expression. I owe him nothing.

How dare he look at me with so much judgment? "I saved your life, the least you can do is thank me!" I feel bitter, even a little hurt. How could he look at me like that? If it wasn't for me he'd be dead!

"Thank you? You broke the rules! It wasn't your place, I was supposed to die. Delta was supposed to die. You have upset the balance." He sounds genuinely upset as if I had committed a grave crime.

I'm bewildered and I gape at him. "You wanted to die?" My voice is low.

"No. Nobody wants to die. But it was meant to be. It's what the gods wanted." He is insane. He must be.

"Fuck the gods!" I'm furious. I'm hurt. I'm exhausted. He is not amused with me but he gives me the look one gives a child when said child needs a beating behind closed doors. I don't care. I wish I had let him die if this is how he shows gratitude.

"Maybe in the future, you should mind your own business." With that, he dismisses us, limping slightly. I'm hurt by his lack of appreciation and that I am nothing but a slave to him, his words echo in my head.

"The omega and a servant."

Yes at times he treated me like a servant but it wasn't until now that I realized that was all I was to him. The words bring me to pause, *what am I even thinking?*

Tonic lifts Delta and carries him back to the rebellion, unwilling to leave his side. I find myself feeling painfully alone, there is nobody to comfort me. Nobody to reassure me of my worth. I wrap my arms around myself and feel the darkness of my self-loathing threatening to close in on me.

I hesitate when I realize I'm heading towards Haryek's cottage. I want to turn around, I know this isn't a good idea but I need someone, anyone other than the crippling loneliness that stands at the edge of my subconscious.

With a gentle rap of my knuckles, he pushes the door open and gestures for me to come inside. He gives me his warmest smile and I offer a small smile back before going into the warm cottage. I intend to tell him everything, perhaps Haryek could find a use for me.

CHAPTER

Ten-

Haryek returns with something I haven't seen much of since the Lycans arrived; a full plate of fruits and vegetables with warm wild rice soup. He sets the tray in front of me; I give him a grateful smile. I am quite famished considering that Lycans seem to take offense in regular meals, and I have been missing the sweet taste of fresh fruit.

I pop a strawberry in my mouth and moan appreciatively. *How could a strawberry taste so good?* I eat a few more and start on my soup. The warmth revives my chilled body; my hands start to return to their normal color. Haryek watches me with what one might consider concern.

"Are you okay?" He asks slowly. I eye him suspiciously and take another spoonful of soup. "I mean truly, are you okay? Not just physically."

I shrug and set my spoon down but refuse to relinquish control of the strawberries. Crossing my legs, I hold the bowl in my lap and take another bite as I watch the soup. "Is anyone alright anymore?"

I don't even sound like myself. I'm exhausted, frustrated, and on the brink of freezing to death. "My parents are dead. My kingdom is destroyed. My home is pretty much gone; every painting that ever held meaning to me is burned." *I'm a slave to a man I hate.* The words well up inside me and I close my eyes for a moment as my throat threatens to tighten, my eyes burning yet nothing is produced. I'm all cried out, there's not much left to cry about.

"No. I'm not alright but that's going to have to be okay for now. I can figure out how fucked up I am when all this is over."

My eyes shoot to him, this feminine man beside me who has never known any real hardship, I recall our previous conversation. "Haryek, how can you wish for your father's death? My father was a horrible man but I don't think I could ever wish ill of him, not even after all he's done. Not even after all I've been through. We don't get to choose our parents but I don't think we should kill them for their shortcomings."

I can only envision how I witnessed my father's death, I had almost watched Alpha and Delta die. It chills me to think I was stepping back into the world of my schooling. He scoots closer to me, I want to lean away and in an excuse to touch me, he pulls his robe tighter around my shoulders.

"My father has lived long enough, he is not good for the nation. He's sucking it dry, it's either him or my people and I fear I must choose my people. It's not easy. But, it's what we must do as the next in line. Dezna needed to be free of your father, just as Ziduri needed to be rid of mine." He sounds so sure, he's staring at the fire that is before us.

I track his gaze, admiring the freedom of the dancing flame. Glancing around the cottage, I feel like I've been in here before, maybe as a child. I wonder where the owner is. The man at my side looks so out of place here.

"Are you okay?" I ask him and his expression breaks.

"We are a lot alike, you and I. Completely alone in the loss that only we can understand. Two princes forced into this life, nobody asked me if I wanted this. Nobody asked if I wanted to become the savior of my people." His words strike me, how could Haryek and I have anything in common? I take another scoop of my soup, thoughtful of the web he weaves.

My only thought resonated with the fact that I was not the only one playing the game.

"I'm alright; I've decided this is the correct choice if we ever want to be free; if we ever want peace. That is why I did this, I fled from Ziduri to come here and start the rebellion once I heard the wolves were planning an uprising. I knew they were coming for your father. I, admittedly, allowed them to pass with no attack and then I took my group to follow behind them into the city. As they destroyed the libraries, I got as many out as I could and we came here, it was the first section of the city that was raided. They haven't been back this way since; we try to keep a low profile."

I absorb what I'm hearing. *Haryek allowed my town to be overrun?* I look at him, confused.

It would appear some wolves truly do wear sheep's clothing. I thought he was on our side. "You knew? You knew and you did nothing? My parents are dead, Haryek! My mother is dead!" This hurts more than I can stand. "My siblings. My life."

The tears threaten to run over now, just when I thought I had nothing left to cry over.

Haryek takes my hand in his, forcing me to look at him. "I did it for the good of **our** people. Nothing would have stopped the Lycan army. They were dead anyway, even if I wanted to stop them."

That was the difference between him and me, he had not wanted to help my people. "We needed this to happen; this paves the way to the future. We are now prepared to form the correct alliances, to put the correct people in place, and finally have balance. Neither kingdom could take on the cities of Man by themselves but together—we actually stand a chance."

I set my bowl back on my tray and push it away. My appetite is gone. I'm reeling from the thought of my parent's death being preventable, I'm not fit for this world of politics where life is expendable as not long ago, I was part of the 'throwaway' variety. "How do you plan to handle the Lycans now that they're in power? Their leader is a lunatic."

"That's where you come in. You'll do exactly what you did today, freeze them, burn them, and blow them away; I don't care! Do whatever you like to get your revenge on them, and then we move forward with our plans. Ziduri will be a piece of cake."

The plan doesn't sit right with me, how could he have known what I was capable of? It seems like a very convenient excuse to do very little for large gains.

"Worry about that tomorrow. We will discuss it at length, for now; eat. You must be famished." I obediently take another bite of strawberry, allowing for the perception that I am naive, that I can be so easily manipulated.

I feel his hand take my cheek as I swallow and I turn my head to see Haryek is very close to me, I recoil back a few inches. "The people are very grateful to you, Nicolas. I'm grateful to you." While I appreciate the flattery, I'm not an imbecile. This was a game I was well versed in, the art of manipulation.

I don't want him to touch me, I don't want his hands on me, but I do want his trust. "You deserve appreciation. You deserve to feel good." I offer a shy smile, a look I've mastered. Haryek sees what he wants, takes what he wants, "You are so beautiful, a rare gem with such complexion." He presses his lips to mine.

"Haryek..." I start. He closes the gap and kisses me once more. *What is one more diplomat?* What is one more time I bow before someone else to get what I want? I need his support and his crooked nature might not lend so kindly to much resistance.

"Let it happen." He encourages. His lips feel soft on mine; though his body is slender and feminine around his waist. I struggle with what little dignity I have. My hands press into his chest, keeping him at bay but he moves to kiss my neck.

Who am I to deny aid to my people at the expense of pride? A pride that I don't have, the pride that has never blessed me. "Let me make you feel good, Nicolas." My stomach curls and I swallow back the resistance.

My eyes catch his; I force a smile. "I'm just wrought with anticipation." It sounds false, a poor game of pretending. He chuckles and I avoid his lips to offer my neck as my eyes scan the surroundings and take in the warm room. I count the knick knacks on the shelf above the fireplace, admiring the little hand-painted figurines and their happy little faces. Among them, one porcelain vase, pale and tall, undeserving of the charm of the tiny men. His hands slip under my shirt and I jerk.

"Don't..." I tell him, he persists and I grasp his wrists, chest heaving. "Don't." I snap. He looks at me as if he doesn't know what to make of me. "I don't take my shirt off..." I explain and he arches a perfect brow.

I'm not 'simple', I never have been. I know the look of frustration well, there's not enough of me, not enough involvement or excitement to allow them to hide behind the veil that maybe I'm enjoying myself. I think of something else as he removes my clothes and falls upon my body in the throes of what can be considered passion.

When men feel inadequate, they make enough noise for us both. I allow this, for it's my responsibility as a servant to my people, to do what is necessary to guarantee them safety. Payment, in the form of my body, was an acceptable term for me.

I watch those little figurines, clutching this symbol of elven perfection, as I allow myself the liberty to think of anything else. Thankfully for me, it's over as quickly as it began, as his consideration for me ends the moment my pants were down and my body of access to him. As he finishes, he grins down at me, brushing my hair back out of my face. "My Romanian flower. I dare say that was quite the coming of minds."

I stare up at the ceiling before I sit up and offer him a small smile. "Yeah. It was. I hope to have a strong alliance in the future." I feel sticky and gross. He tips a wine glass to me as he pulls up his pants, taking a long sip. I excuse myself and make my way to the washroom; I dip a cloth in the basin of water there and scrub my body clean.

The liquid he used appears to be everywhere and I smell heavily of lavender. Once I'm satisfied with my cleanliness I come back out to find that the bedroom door is open and I make my way in there to see him in bed. He pats the bed with a grin and I clear my throat as I rack my brain for an excuse.

"I think I'll take the guest room if you don't mind." Any excuse not to be near him. He shrugs, indifferent, bidding me goodnight.

When I wake up, my body feels stiff and I stretch to alleviate my cramped muscles. I feel achy and sore but not as drained as I worried I'd be. Actually, I find that I feel pretty good as if I've been recharged. Using my magic has convinced my body it's out of retirement and it feels good to feel strong again. I glance around the room and wonder for a moment where I am. I realize I'm in the little cottage in the rebellion and I vaguely recall selling my soul for some strawberries and a hope of an alliance.

Running my hand through my hair, I can't help but roll my eyes heavily at myself. "Back to our old ways, hmm? I suppose things don't change. Good job, Nicolas. Just give it away on the street next to the bread cart." I belittle my ease of stepping into bed with men. Perhaps I had the wrong profession.

I spot Haryek as I enter the main room, his skin reminds me of polished marble and I question how long he's been awake considering his state of cleanliness. "Hungry?" He questions, "I think we have pancakes." He takes in my outfit and makes a disapproving face. A pair of wool leggings and a long sleeve shirt, coupled with a vest, will do for the chilly morning. Truthfully I was thrilled to wear civilian clothes. "Sorry for the lack of appropriate attire, the service around here is dreadful."

I shrug one shoulder, realize who I'm in the company of, and compose myself. "It's quite alright," I tell him, squaring my shoulders. I remind myself that I am a prince, even if my morals are lacking, I should act like one. "It's a novelty for me to dress in such a way. I've never been allowed to and it's quite comfortable."

Haryek almost looks disgusted but he laughs instead of acting on it. "Whatever makes you happy, baby. I have never felt the desire to dress as a peasant. Dirty and so unfashionable, I would get quite bored wearing a get-up like that every day!" He chuckles, taking a bite of pancake. While I'm dying to taste the sweet cakes, his tone settles wrong in my ears.

"What happened to the people who used to live in these cottages?" I don't know if I want to know.

"Most vacated to the city. They haven't returned or if they have, they've seen us and fled. The few that remained were persuaded to let us use their homes. One way or another." He shrugs. "We needed to have this whole area. It was for the greater good." I frown.

"Did you take some of these homes?" I press.

"Borrowed. Maybe one or two. The rest were abandoned." He catches my expression and sighs. Bringing me a plate of pancakes and some strawberries he sets it down in front of me. "How is it any different than what the lycans, that you are so quick to forgive, have done? Didn't they steal your own home?"

"Actually they all live outside my home so technically they have stolen my yard. I don't forgive them, I am biding my time so perhaps you should concern yourself with the matters here and the theft of Dezna land from her people." He doesn't look amused and after a long silence, he bows out and agrees with me. "You will be giving these homes back, we will make other accommodations for you."

"Nicolas...We need to get rid of the lycans. If we kill the 'alpha' then we stand a chance to run them off." He wishes to derail me, he wants to talk about something other than giving up his comfortable and burgled lifestyle.

"That won't work; they work on a practical point system. They will just put someone equally terrible in his place. Killing the lycans is exactly what got us into this mess so we can't just slaughter them all; something bigger and worse will just take their place. We need to find a way to make peace."

Those pale eyes remind me of that of a viper, staring down the rabbit as it waits for the poison to take effect. Holding strong, I set my jaw in defiance. Much as I was upset about what happened, I couldn't put my finger on what caused me to decide to save the man's life yesterday.

"These are my family's lands, it is my say, Haryek, and I say, we will do our best to make peace with the lycans." My voice is stern, firm in my reasoning.

With a smile, he bows and gestures to the breakfast before me. "I have a few meetings I have to go to today, we are discussing how to get supplies. You're welcome to visit with the magic users here, I'm sure they would love to hear of your story of how you *survived*." The hesitation makes my breathing pick up as if he questions the validity of my claims. "It might boost morale a little. We'll discuss this later, perhaps tonight over dinner?"

My lips turn down at the corners as I fight to keep the frown off my face. I need to go home and check on my people, I have my own missions to attend to. "I've got things to attend to at home; I'm a busy man you know. But I'll be back tomorrow, can we discuss more then?"

He nods and kisses my forehead before leaving me to my own devices. I wipe the affectionate gesture off my face with a grimace and I finish my pancakes in spite of myself. Taking my plate to the source of where the delicious smell is coming from, I find Delta and Tonic eating together in the dining hall.

A woman takes my plate and I note her to be human, in fact, most of the workers here are human. I hesitate that I call them workers. "I can do it," I tell her but she isn't hearing it, she grabs the plate before I can stop her. Her eyes don't meet mine.

"How're you feeling?" I ask hopefully as I sit down and Delta shies away from me.

"Nicolas isn't going to hurt you, Delta. Tell him, Nicolas." Tonic glances at me as he rubs Delta's back reassuringly. My heart breaks for this shaggy-haired young man who is looking at me like I'm a hell beast. One of his kind eyes is bruised and bloodshot; I remember looking into them as he was dying.

"I'm not going to hurt you Delta," I tell him calmly. He doesn't look like he believes me, he stays silent. I glance at their plates and

I'm glad they have eaten the pancakes though the fruit remains untouched.

Tonic purses his lips. "I told him you are on our side. You want
peace, you wouldn't hurt us. You were saving us last night?" He looks
at me to confirm, to play along just as I had looked at him. I come to
terms with the fact that Tonic fully believes that I am on their side
and I wouldn't betray them.

"I do want peace Delta; I would never harm either of you," I
choose my words carefully. *Don't trust me.* I will them to make a conscious effort to get far away from me. Exhaling slowly, I struggle with
my own self and my willingness to con those around me. Perhaps I
was no better than my father.

Delta's voice shocks me out of my musings. "That's what they all
say. That's what they told us when they rounded us up from our houses.
Then, they brought us to your father, they promised a better life for
us, a safer life for us and our families. Now, look at us! Housing with
knife ears and allowing our brothers to be slaughtered!" He shakes his
head and Tonic gasps at him.

"Delta!" He breathes.

"No, would you open your damn eyes, Tonic? Where was he? He's
been to see their leader; he's right buddies with them now, Tonic. We
need to get back to the pack, now. We aren't safe here, not with them,
and certainly not with him. We have jobs to do; I have a job to do.
There will be a decision made for a new Beta, we need to be ready
for the Ranking Ceremony."

His words cut me because he's right, it's as if he can see through
to the real me that hides beneath this facade of royalty with princely
mannerisms. Tonic gives me an apologetic look as he gets up with
Delta and I watch them disappear.

I have a job to do as well. I must get back to the castle and find my father's spellbook. I must gain back some leverage and stop this before it gets much farther out of hand.

CHAPTER

Eleven-

The walk home is long; it feels odd to be alone for once as it was not the norm for royalty to be without chaperones and accompanying parties. A welcomed reprieve from my sheltered life, walking in the cool morning air was a welcomed moment of peace. I shiver as I pass the dampened ground that housed the frozen wolves. I relive the attack, the snarling black creature claws for me and I shut my eyes and shake my head. *Why did he save me?*

I can only assume that Alpha figured I was worth more to him alive, he couldn't use me if Beta had succeeded in killing me. My feet are frozen, I realize I'm no longer walking; I watch the gray wolf appear before me and can feel his growl in my chest. I follow the foot-steps he took with my eyes, the indentions his paws left in the unworthy earth.

Following the scene, where they fell to the ground, my heart starts to accelerate as I watch Delta start to die before my eyes once more and as Beta starts to win I take a step back, shutting my eyes tightly.

"No." I breathe.

I feel my hands go cold, the power surges as I inhale sharply, fighting my way out of the scene. *"I was supposed to die."* I hear him say and I'm back in reality as I'm making my way to the castle again.

My pace is much more hurried this time, running from the vision and towards the safety of my castle.

As I enter the courtyard, I slow my pace as I see a pillar of logs, stacked together as if to form a log cabin. *Where did these come from?* Then I note that some clearing has been done to make the courtyard bigger. Nobody asked me if this was okay but then I suppose it's not up to me anymore. I slowly approach; the stack is taller than me. Touching the damp wood, I glance up as the branches are loaded inside of it.

There's nothing I can do, I pick my path through the multitude of wolves towards the castle, walking with as much grace and determination as my breeding allows me.

After what I've been through, and knowing that Beta is probably dead, I find that walking amongst them is no longer as terrifying.

Spotting Tonic, I seek out familiarity. "What's going on?" I touch his arm to get his attention and he gives me a side glance but tightens his mouth and looks as if he isn't sure he wants to talk to me. "Tonic." I mumble, turning his face to me, and I see the side of his cheek is swollen, busted just below his eye.

But Tonic looked fine this morning?

His lip is full and bruised. I reach to touch his face but he turns his head away, avoiding my touch. "What happened?" I demand. His eyes darken as he shrugs out of my grasp.

"Leave it alone Nicolas." He mumbles.

"No. What happened? Did he do this to you?" I demand, my blood boils and yet, I'm halted by my sudden desire to defend Tonic.

"I got what I deserved. I disobeyed orders. Nicolas, there are rules around here. We can't just keep going above it—" I cut him off with my hand and I reach up to heal his face. He shrinks away from me as

I insist upon him. I can't bear it, I can't think that I caused this to happen to him. Tonic wasn't like me, Tonic was good.

The subject appears to be closed, so I decide to move on to the real reason I wanted to see him. "What's with the giant log box?" I demand. He rolls his eyes, as much as he might be upset with me; we are friends for some reason and I might be the only friend he has.

"It's for the ceremony tonight. We are going to choose a new Beta and all the ranks will be challenged. I think it's why Alpha was trying to avoid having to kill Beta until all this was over, now all positions are open and the whole hierarchy has to be re-decided. It's a big... fight...? In the end, we will burn Beta and John's bodies and send them to Valhalla in a minor ceremony. Normally it's a big celebration but not this time."

My face pales as I cross my arms nervously over my chest, an attempt to hold in the panic. "All positions? What does that mean?" *Do I want to know?*

Tonic shares my concern.

"Alpha, Beta, Delta, and then a few officers and leaders." He watches me and he knows which one I'm focusing on.

A new Alpha could be quite troublesome for me, a change in position might not see me as any value at all nor would they share my interests. "How often is Alpha challenged?" I ask. Tonic offers me a small shrug.

"Nobody but Beta has shown any interest. Alpha made quite the impression when he took power; I don't think we have anything to worry about." He suddenly clams up and I notice someone is approaching us. He is short, shorter than me and his hair is thick and short with big, tangled curls. It's a strawberry blond and his honey-colored eyes look warm as he approaches with a broad smile.

"Tonic, who's this?" He sounds hopeful. His voice suits him, he's very fine-boned and feminine. His voice is soft and melodic with a heavy French accent. I instantly like him and relax a little. Is he a lycan? His thick lashes make him look almost childlike as he looks up at me; dressed in form-fitting, soft clothes.

Very carefully chosen to match, bracelets jingle on his wrists as he moves. He also bears multiple earrings and some rings; one big fashion statement. *How can anyone look so well dressed in the middle of a war?*

"Adriam, this is Nicolas. Nicolas, this is Adriam. A good friend."

Adriam extends his hand to me and I shake it, it's surprisingly firm but his skin is very soft. He's warm, smelling of a sweet perfume, foreign to my nose.

"Nice to meet you." He watches me with a guarded expression. "I've heard a lot about you." It almost sounds like a threat but his tone stays warm and I decide to play the role of the fool, oblivious to the scrutiny. "You're quite the talk of the castle, haven't had to pleasure of being in the company of a prince in quite some time." I offer him a kind smile in return. With a devious grin, he raises an eyebrow. "Should we go sit in on this morning's plans?"

I try to hide my surprise.

"Are we allowed?" I sound like a scolded child. He laughs and it's so musical that I almost laughed, too, as if there's a joke I'm not getting.

With a resounding giggle, he smirks. "Honey, I don't think there's much I'm not allowed to do. Surely you're not afraid of going to 'court'? Come on." He starts to walk and I glance at Tonic who gives me a shrug that says he just does what he's told. We follow quickly after this small man and he surely does part the seas of the crowds around us.

I remain beside him, finding familiarity in someone so similar to my own height. "So, you're a good friend?" I ask as we walk, starved for intel.

Adriam glances over his shoulder at me and slows his pace to keep up with my mortal gait. "An old one... Let's just say I've known the family for a long time." He smiles at a few men passing, everyone seems fond of our little tour guide.

"The family?" I press.

He hesitates, composing his thoughts. "Alpha's family."

"I haven't seen you here before." I challenge, even if they had been here for less than a few weeks, I was becoming familiar with the faces of the higher-ups around here.

He clicks his tongue in amusement, "Well. Maybe you just didn't notice me." After a moment, he sighs. "I was trying to avoid this war but—Alpha summoned me last night when Beta was killed. I have some-thing he needs, just as you do. Funny how that makes us quite valuable."

I can't help but raise an eyebrow. *I have something that Alpha needs?* I truly wonder what it could be that he could offer a force like this. A vote maybe if they voted on things but they try and kill each other so surely someone so petite wouldn't stand a chance in these rank wars coming up. "How long have you known Alpha?"

"Oh since he was but a thought. I knew his father pretty well. Not a fan but you do what you have to do. I liked his mother a lot more." He must see the hunger on my face and he purses his lips.

"Adriam is an 'Old Blood' Nicolas, like Sota." Tonic interjects. "They just live a lot longer than normal wolves; it's a different type of bloodline."

This could be an opportunity to gain insight, *ammunition.* "What happened to his mother?" I blurt out. A part of me hopes he knows my pain, I think back to the bathroom and I remember him telling me he knows what it's like to lose someone. The two men glance at each other and Adriam sighs.

"She died, giving birth to his sister. She wasn't like us. She was human."

I don't know why this surprises me so much but I'm shocked to learn the 'Alpha' was born from a mortal woman. I'm silenced and this gives me a lot to think about, I almost run into them when they come to a halt outside of the rear entrance to the castle.

We enter and I see the only man I don't recognize, I wonder if this is what Adriam was talking about. A truly massive man stands before me, and I almost back out of the room. He stands taller than Alpha, nearing six-foot-six if not more and his shoulders are so broad he overwhelms all around him. His hair is very short and pale blond, his complexion is light as well. He's one of the most muscular men I think I've ever seen and his eyes are so light they appear to have almost no color at all. He's dressed in dark clothes and they are stretched over his massive expanse of body.

Adriam approaches him and wraps an arm around his waist.

Alpha glances towards me; Tonic and Adriam smile broadly at him, he rolls his eyes so dramatically that I wonder how he manages to stay upright.

"As we all know, tonight we are having our ranking ceremony. I've called you all here because we need the support of the pack if we are going to make a move on Ziduri. We cannot afford a division of power right now and as we are all aware; Caspian had his loyalists, as did John being our commanding officer. The Twins have been running some surveillance for us and we believe we know the plan for tonight. A group from the upper ranks are going to try and take the Beta and Delta positions and push a move to attack Ziduri head-on.

We know this is not a move that will succeed, with the number of Elven archers on the capitol walls; we would not stand a chance once we invaded the inner cities. We would be forced to put them under siege and that is not something we are prepared to wait out."

"Any confirmed for the Alpha position?" Sota questions.

"Support is still strong for the Alpha." One of the twins speaks. "If there is an attack planned, it is a private one."

Sota doesn't seem convinced and rubs his chin.

"Which is why we have summoned Adriam here." Alpha proceeds.

Adriam is frowning as well. "You mean you've summoned Victor." He points out, squeezing the large man.

"Adriam, you know I would not have called you if it weren't serious. I know your opinion on this war, on any war and I know you want to protect what is yours. But we need Victor." Alpha's tone has changed. Suddenly, I feel as though I shouldn't be here. As if Tonic and I are intruders on something very private.

"I need Victor. You know we don't play with these political rules. The fact that you are family is the only reason we have come at all." Adriam sounds a little hurt; as if this call was insulting to him.

"Adam." Alpha's voice is softer. "Nothing is going to happen to him. He is an experienced combat veteran, you should be more worried about those on the other side..." He offers a small smile and Adriam stares at him for a long moment and sighs.

"You know it's cheating when you call me that..." He grumbles and looks up towards the towering blond. "What do you want, baby?" His voice is soft.

Victor, or so he's called, shrugs one shoulder. "I will fight as long as I can to kill knife ear." His Russian accent is thick and his voice is so deep it resonates in my chest. "Would be nice to stretch my legs, good workout."

Adriam sighs and rolls his eyes. "I guess we are in."

Alpha smiles in response and I try to recall if I've ever seen him smile. "Good. Victor, you need to move for Beta position. I'd like Delta to hold his position if possible and the twins can fill in for losing Commander John. I think that would have us sufficiently covered to regain control and have people we trust in the higher ranks.

"Once the ceremony is over, I'd like to start moving our smaller and more experienced groups closer to Ziduri to see if we can't stir something up to get an idea of how far they are willing to come from the capital. If we could get their army to fight us out here we stand a much better chance than trying to take the castle. As you all know, the deadline is tight. We must make a move before winter sets in. Once the leaves fall from the trees, all forms of camouflage go out the window. We will be easy targets."

"What if we used my magic to provide a cover?" I question. Everyone goes quiet and I see Adriam, my sweet tour guide, has a big smile for me.

"That won't be necessary." Alpha responds shortly, he waves me off dismissively.

Offended, I cannot hold my tongue. "Why the hell not? It worked with Beta, it would work in this situation too and everyone would be much less likely to get hurt this way." I can see he's frustrated but I continue. "I could make a fog to protect foot troops or I could be overhead on a dragon and provide cover fire."

I hear a low growl and I know my input was not requested.

His light eyes bore into me with frustration that knows no bounds. "Absolutely not. Magic is what got us into this mess." His voice is harsh and I want to roll my eyes—so I do. He's being a child.

I'm quick to point out how wrong he is. "Magic could save your life. Oh wait, that's not how things go here. It's an honor to die!" I cross my arms over my chest and I hear his fist hit the table.

"Get him out of here. Now!" He thunders and my tour guide appears beside me.

"Come on now, let's not poke the bear." He drags me out of the room and Tonic scrambles to follow us, not wanting to be left to deal with the rage of the Alpha. "I knew I liked you!" Adriam says happily, wrapping his arm around one of mine. I feel mentally drained from all this, I had thought court was difficult but the intensity of pack politics was much more irritating to unravel.

"You do?" I try not to sound surprised. "Why?"

"You're strong. You know, I always suspected him—" Tonic is looking at us both with a peculiar look and Adriam buttons his lips with a playful snag of his lower lip in his teeth, stifling the grin.

"Why did Alpha ask your permission to 'use' Victor?" I ask bluntly. Do all wolves have captives? How the hell does tiny Adriam secure Victor the Vast? Adriam smiles and for a moment he looks like his eyes are far away, like he's looking into the past.

"Because I own him." His tone is soft.

"What...?" I stop walking and stare, gaping at this tiny man.

"When we were young... Very young... There was a war going on similar to this one only it was Lycans versus Vampires. Tale as old as time right? I was a medic, fresh out of school, and seeing a lot more carnage than I was ever prepared for. The Vampires took a select few of us to use as they saw fit, mostly for entertainment. Victor was one of those. He came from Russia, he was pretty much feral. He spoke no English and he had been pretty badly abused. One day we rescued him in a raid and we knew he wouldn't survive, but I took him home and nursed him anyways. Hoping... I don't know what drew me to him.

"He did come around and boy was he furious. There was a language barrier; I spoke hardly any English, let alone Russian. I slowly gained his trust, through food and alcohol. There was no way to contain him, he was—is—massive. So little by little, we co-existed until the vampires figured out I had him. Victor had seen too much and they demanded his return in exchange for a few of our own men... I had to let him go." I watch the pain appear in his eyes.

How could you be so attached to someone you couldn't even understand?

"I tracked him, eventually he ended up at a sale. Victor had no family, no friends, nobody to say that he deserved freedom. So I purchased him, it took almost everything I had but it was worth it. I offered him his papers but he never took them. He came home with me and he never left, it took a long time before it became what it is now." His words drift off.

"What is it now...?" I question, caught up in the mystery of it all. I glance at Tonic and he seems enthralled too.

"Love?" Adriam asks and laughs so innocently, almost shy. "We protect each other. We are all the other has, I never thought Victor would share my 'interests', not when I bought him and not when I helped him. Something drew me to him that I couldn't explain and over time we grew together, I won't go into the gory details but this works for us. I make the decisions; he likes to be the muscle. He allows me to be who I am and indulges in the things that I like." He shrugs and runs his hands through his hair. "It comes in all forms."

So he fancies men as well? "I can't believe you're so open about it." Tonic mumbles and Adriam and I are both surprised. Tonic flushes and clears his throat.

"Well would you, or anyone for that matter, call Victor out on being a homosexual? I sure wouldn't." Adriam smirks and we all agree.

CHAPTER

Twelve-

While I'm more confused now to the inner workings of the pack politics, I'm relieved that putting the capital under siege doesn't seem to be an option as that would simply take way too long. Of one thing that I'm certain, I cannot go to Haryek with the information pertaining to the fate of Ziduri.

While he claims to be on our side, I don't trust him not to warn his father to get the upper hand on the lycans. An attempt against the lycan horde at its current size and strength would prove quite difficult and our society could not afford an all-out war that could very well attract the attention of the armies of Man. We needed to resolve this peacefully, if at all possible.

My people had been left at a very vulnerable point, with no King in place, we were now at true risk for a second hostile takeover. One where we might not fair so lucky, the lycans were allowing my people to live. Would Man do the same?

I've found my way into the kitchen, enjoying some alone time. Decided on cooking myself a dish of nostalgia, lamb and curry over a bed of seasoned rice with some pasta on the side. I chop absently, preparing the herbs. While meat was not my preference, the taste of home was welcomed to my troubled mind.

Adriam had selflessly saved Victor with no motive behind it other than a gut feeling.

I doubted my ability to do such a thing. It seemed impossible to trust a feral man into your home in hopes that he wouldn't kill you in your sleep but, on that same thought, my mind drifts to my current predicament. A feral being did live on the outskirts of my home and it didn't bring me much pause.

Sighing, I toss the herbs onto the pan and decide I need to ask myself what I'm doing with these men in my life. It wasn't in my best interest to entertain so many interests. I don't get too far into my thoughts before I feel him and I glance up to see Alpha.

"Alpha." I greet slowly. I'm still pissed with him; he's been an ass, but I am a servant, and respect is due if I want my subjects to survive.

"In what world do you speak to me in such a manner? I expected better of someone who claims to have such noble blood." He snaps; his tone harsh.

I was foolish to believe I would get away with that, the man had an ego larger than our tallest building. "I'm upset with you. I saved your life and you threw it in my face. I didn't have to, I could have let you die then your whole pack would be at risk." I throw the lamb in the pan and the sizzle satisfies my mood.

He takes quick steps towards me, "I think you're forgetting how the chain of command works. I'm the master, the leader, your Alpha. You don't question my decisions; now, apologize for your horrid behavior." He sounds serious and I scoff at the whole situation.

His English accent makes it difficult to take him seriously, as I'm quite unfamiliar with those from that side of the world. He's quite lucky that I taught myself to speak English, I'm sure plenty of my subjects were not enjoying the guessing game of his demands.

"In case you haven't noticed, I'm not the best 'servant'. I'm not apologizing to you for saving you and I'd do it again unless you keep being a complete ass then I might think twice." I hear the rumble but I don't entertain a glance in his direction.

I feel strong, seeing my people are alive and well has spurred me to strive for boldness. As much as I hate to admit it, I'm a glutton for punishment. When I glance up he's gone and I realize all too late it's because he's beside me. I take a step back before stopping myself and standing my ground. In comparison with Victor, I find him less frightening. "Yes, Alpha? Can I help you?" My voice drips with sarcasm.

"You've gotten bold in your time with the rebellion." His hand comes up to catch my throat, his thumb pressing into my jaw to elevate my chin. The warmth of his hand is welcomed to my cool skin, I meet his icy gaze with my own and I can feel myself challenging him.

"Maybe I'm just not afraid of you any longer." I breathe, while it wasn't exactly the truth, at the moment I did not feel as though he would harm me.

His teeth graze my jaw and my eyes practically roll back into my head as I melt. "You should be."

I'm embarrassed at my response to such a simple gesture but I realize this is why I was provoking him. I knew what I'd get. He backs me against the cool stone of the kitchen wall and tilts my head to expose my throat, stubble dragging over my skin. The roughness of my back hitting the stone, his hard body imposing his will on mine, I reach up to tangle my hands in his hair and get a groan in response. But suddenly he stops. I'm panting against the wall as he straightens.

"What?" I can hear the plea in my voice, my hands slide out of his hair and rest on his toned biceps. He feels rigid.

"What is that god awful smell?" He questions, frowning.

A smell? I find it hard to believe that he judges my scent when he often smells like exertion and woods. "Oh, it's lamb and curry. It's a family recipe. I probably need to turn the stove off." Flustered, I slip away from him and head towards the stove but he grasps my hand and pulls me to him once more, this time partway. Taking my wrist, he brings it up to his nose.

Suspicion begins to creep onto his expression. "It's you. You smell like lavender... cologne?" He frowns and drops my hand and I feel myself pale a little. "Visited a suitor, I see." His voice is cold.

He couldn't possibly know what I'd done and honestly why would it matter? "Yes, after you left me at the rebellion I had to stay at Prince Haryek's dwelling." I tread lightly, careful not to give too much away.

His expression is unreadable, "What poor company you keep." I turn away from him to cut off the stove, suddenly I'm not hungry.

My entirety in school had been a flurry of gentlemen, in and out of my life and bed. "It's none of your business what I've done, you don't have a claim on me. I'm supposed to obey you, not serve only you when it suits you. You're not innocent." He is silent, I glance over at him and for a second I wonder if he looks a little hurt. It takes the wind out of my sails. I was expecting a lot of things but the pained expression was not one of them.

"Clean this up and run my bath. Maybe that is a task you can handle." He turns on his heel, I curse under my breath. I pick at a few bites of the cooked lamb, I don't have time for my other plans now but this stuff was pretty much done. After a few forkfuls, my appetite is officially gone and I pack it all up for later, leaving a note for Gena to find me.

I feel as though all the walking and protein are making me stronger. My body had always been slighter in build for I took after my mother more than my father, a life of leisure had not gifted me with much for bulk. As was the nature of our community, magic usually catered to our whims. I heat the tub and almost on cue, he appears though he is tight and tense, he doesn't want me here.

"You can go." He tells me sternly.

"Is it not my job to bathe you?" He doesn't answer as he pulls his shirt over his head. The scars never cease to take my breath away. I trace them with my eyes as they tangle over his shoulder blade and down his back then I fixate on his neck. *How I want to taste that neck...*

I walk over, grab a cloth to dip it in the bathwater only for him to grab my hand before I can touch him, his face hard. "Don't." His tone is rough.

I have to fix this, I can't allow him to slip through my fingers and lose the trust that I was working on creating. I need him to trust me, I need him to desire me. "This is my job, to show appreciation for my Alpha. I'm just doing what I'm told." I press the cloth to his chest and he stiffens to my touch as I scrub circles. The rigidity in his body is not from appreciation but discomfort.

After a moment, I go ahead and remove his pants considering I don't want to deal with wet clothes as well, averting my eyes to appease the seething male. He cautiously steps out of them and allows me to continue scrubbing him.

"What happened?" I ask him, feeling bold. He's already upset with me, what more could he do? I run the cloth over the scars on his shoulder and pectoral muscle. His whole body is taut under my hand.

I take my finger and trace one of the long scars down towards his abdominal muscles and he snatches my hand. "Stop." He sounds tired as if he doesn't want to put up with me right now.

I need to know more about him, I need to prove myself of value. "I've been told it's a pretty good story. I'm surprised you don't want to tell me." I press. With some coaxing, I slide my hand out of his and return to scrubbing him, watching him patiently.

"If I tell you will you leave me be? I wish to be alone." The request surprises me but I nod and he sighs once more.

"My father was the Alpha before I was. When our pack was captured, we were mostly sent to the same master as laborers. My father gained the favor of the master's wife, he got comfortable with the way things were going. More and more of our people were being sold off, families separated. Our conditions were horrible, people started getting sick and, as I'm certain you know, there isn't much for care when it comes to lycans.

"My father said it was our job to follow this new order, being the Alpha we could only obey him. But I wanted freedom..." He is looking off into the void of the room, his voice sounds strained as if this is difficult for him to talk about.

With a heavy sigh, he continues. "I figured out how to shift, to call our wolf forward. I went to my father with the discovery and told him we could overthrow our master, we could be free. But he wanted no part in that, that would mean war and he was perfectly content living a good lifestyle as the house pet. He used the change to threaten the pack, to back them down. It takes a lot of concentration to change the first few times; nobody was willing to put themselves at risk to try it. I knew that I would be killed before I could complete the change, myself."

I inhale sharply.

He was willing to sacrifice himself for his people, just as I was. "So that's why you fought him like this. That's suicide." I couldn't imagine thinking that any being would've thought they would win in that sort of fight.

His eyes meet mine, searching my face. "A leader does what he has to do for his people. I did not intend to live through that fight, I made my peace and challenged him. I knew I would not win but if I could kill him before I died it would be worth it. He had gotten sloppy from living indoors but human bodies are no match for the power of the wolf. So I gave him an opportunity and he took it."

He tilted his head to the side so I can see the full view of his neck and shoulder. The jagged scars of fangs decimating flesh, from his neck, down to his pectoral muscles. "I'm not sure where it all started or came from. I just remember the weight of him on me; it didn't hurt at the time. I recall shoving my hand through his chest and ripping out his heart."

Absently, my hand comes forward and I trace the long scars on his pectoral muscle. His eyes are locked on me, guarded.

"The rest is history. Adriam rushed to my aid. He was a long time loyalist of my father. My shoulder was pretty bad off, the healing had already begun. I recall the sound of him setting the bones in my shoulder, thinking I wasn't going to live. Being told I wasn't going to live. Adriam fought pretty hard to save me. Once I healed up enough to be mobile, I taught the others how to shift and the army was formed. Now I have this reputation that follows me for some strange reason."

"Can't imagine why..." I try not to be too sarcastic. I slowly walk around him to his back and I trace my fingers over the scars that trail from his shoulder all the way down to his lower back. I run my cloth over them and then work on his shoulders for a moment. I can feel the tension threatening to melt away and it brings a small smile to my face only to have it fall as he steps away from me.

He keeps his back to me. "You can go now." My arms wrap around him from behind, holding onto him in defiance. I could not explain what in me caused me to linger, what brings me to remain here when he's asked me to go. "Nicolas, don't." He tells me firmly and I feel like a scolded child.

I don't like being rejected, I don't like being treated as if I was in the wrong. "What is your problem? I thought this was just sex? That's what I want. Why does it bother you so badly?" I demand.

I feel that loneliness creeping in on me. "Don't tell me you don't take advantage of every man that comes to your chambers. You can't honestly tell me I'm the only one you're currently fucking." I feel ridiculous for having to point out my own lack of worth just to get sex but, I'm desperate to feel something.

This is how I cope, this is how I feel in control.

He would not be so easy to manipulate, removing my hands from his sides and holding them between us as he turns to face me. "I'm not and I don't." He says slowly. "This is not something that I've ever done before."

"Maybe if you were less of a jerk—" I hesitate and still once more as he waits for me to stop making a complete ass of myself. "You've never been with a man before me?" He shrugs in response. That doesn't make much sense. "Why not?"

"You're just full of questions today." He grumbles. "I don't know. I'm not attracted to men. Or at least I wasn't. It's been kind of an interesting experience for me as well." My lips fall open as I consider his words, and he squirms under my judgment, potentially even embarrassed. "In that light, I feel we should stop doing this. It's immoral and a distraction."

I, of all people, should know what it feels like to be used. Though in my defense, he was using me too. I stand up on my toes to reach his full height and knot my hands in his hair before pulling him down to kiss me.

I'm pleased that he doesn't hesitate, he trespasses my mouth with his tongue and I arch against him. I pull off the long sleeve shirt I'm wearing and I'm relieved I put on my silk undershirt beneath it. He makes quick work of my pants and I step out of the leggings as I throw myself at him, putting my arms around his neck and relishing in his strength as he pulls me close. I go to defend my undershirt but he doesn't offer to remove it.

Capturing his lower lip in my teeth, I bite down to incite a more aggressive response from him. He growls low in his throat and I know that I have brought forth exactly what I was hoping for. He breaks away from me and spins me around, shoving me towards the tub. "Heat it." He commands.

Obediently, I warm the tub up. "Bend over." He tells me as I lower my chest though I'm caught off guard by a sharp smack to my ass. "Is that how you bend over for your Alpha?" He questions, I gasp as I change my tactic, pushing my ass out against him and spreading my legs. "Better." I'm rewarded as he trails his fingers down my back. He runs his length against me and I groan, writhing beneath him. I can't handle the slow torment right now, I need to be used. I press back against him desperately.

"Please."

"Hmmm... apologize to your Alpha." He rubs against me once more and I groan in response, bowing my head.

"I'm sorry, Alpha." I breathe.

"That's a good boy." He grips my hair and pulls me sharply back against him, slamming into me. I cry out, it's more than I can take and everything that I've been craving all in one. He uses me, relentless in his pace as he takes me. I grip the tub and babble obscenities mixed with his name as I take everything he's willing to give me.

"Remember who you serve." He tells me in between thrusts. I moan in response as I climb, panting, desperate to find the release I've been looking for. I rock back against him, chasing my climax. We finish together and I cry out incoherently. He moans my name and finishes inside me; riding out the aftershocks. Before I can comprehend it, he'd climbed into the tub and pulling me to get in with him. The water spills out around us but thankfully it's a wet room and there's a drain. I sit in his lap, facing him and crushing my lips against his.

He tastes like Alpha, his unyielding jaw, his stubbled chin. My fingers tangle into his hair and I pull hard. "Fuck." He moans and rakes his fingers down my thighs. "You're asking for trouble." He warns me and I smile against his lips.

"Am I?" I purr innocently, I got what I was after and I feel his arousal between my legs. Reaching down, I position him and lower myself onto him. He inhales sharply and I brace my forearms on his shoulders as I ride him. My hands clutch his hair; forcing his head back as I attack his neck. "Remember who keeps you coming back." I challenge him and he chuckles at my boldness.

I lose myself in him, getting lost in the sensation. It isn't long before I'm calling his name once more. I'm coming again and he's following close behind me. We're both spent and I collapse into his neck, panting. He holds me for longer than I dare to count before I finally sit up and brush his hair out of his face. We are both sweaty and sticky from the steam of the tub, the sex causing me to go a bit wild with my magic and making the tub too hot. My skin looks pink from the heat.

Taking the washcloth, I start to scrub his chest once more. "What are the chances of you dying tonight?" I have to know. These fights don't end in handshakes, they end in death.

CHAPTER

Thirteen-

Alpha's expression tells me he wasn't expecting my question and he falls silent. "Really? You're not going to tell me? Why—are you worried I'll freeze your challengers?" My hand slides up to his neck as I massage and clean at the same time. Being close to him, I feel more comfortable testing the boundaries, treading on the edge of how far I can prod.

I marvel at the muscle beneath me, the man doesn't have an ounce of fat on him. But I suppose neither would I if I exercised for a living. What I truly find interesting is the similarities I see in our marred frames, even given my smaller stature. We were both damaged, he might be one of the only people who know my pain though I can only assume he's not as self-conscious about his injuries as I am.

We were cut from the same cloth in that someone had mutilated our bodies beyond what was socially acceptable.

"Not quite. I'm not intending on losing, I might be broken but I'm a skilled fighter. It's kind of my job, in case you hadn't noticed."

I find a small hint of amusement at a touch of sarcasm. I see the faint hint of a smile curl at his lips, I offer a smile back. "So what do you do with this? Are we going to start braiding it?" I reach up to push his thick hair out of his face and take note of how soft it is, curious I had never stopped to marvel at such a small detail.

I imagined it would be more wiry and dense considering the color. But, it's just as soft as his pelt. As our gaze centers on the other, I retract my hand and clear my throat.

"I'm sure Adriam will find a way to cut it soon enough." His tone leaves something to be desired, the warmth between us quickens my pulse and I make the decision to introduce chaos as I wring my wash-cloth out over his head to wet his hair. He startles as I do so and splashes me in the process, I can't afford these moments between us to expand, I can't be allowed to feel anything beyond malice towards him, my people deserve better.

The steamy water soaks my chest, the thirsty silk undershirt drinks the fluid greedily. "You've soaked me, you brute." I pluck at my now clinging white shirt and feel suddenly very self-conscious. His hand sweeps his hair back out of his eyes with a curse to the gods, blazing with rage at my ill-timed behavior, only when he spots my vulnerability, the inferno simmers.

We are wary of each other, untested, this was becoming a trend that neither of us was comfortable with and yet, I couldn't find it in me to regret taking full advantage of the sinful man. "You haven't really answered my question." I remind him, hopeful for a better answer. I want to think of anything other than my idle fingers.

"There is an officer that I personally trained. I know him quite well, I'm not concerned."

It seems egotistical to excuse someone because he knows them. "If you trained him then he knows your weaknesses too." My eyes drift and end up on his shoulder, the lingering gaze pulls the corners of his mouth down as he slips out from under me to stand.

Exiting the tub, I devour him with my eyes. His tanned skin con-trasts against the white fluffy towel he uses to dry himself. I start at his chest, the spattering of hair there, and follow the trail before he catches my attention by speaking.

With a tight jaw, he squares his shoulders. "You'd do well to remember that even with impairment, I'm quite capable of doing what needs to be done."

He wasn't my usual patron but I could appreciate his form, what was left of it at least. "I'll say," I mumble, startled by the laugh that my response provokes.

Alpha raises an eyebrow, "Are you saying you're using me for my body?" He looks genuinely amused; I'm embarrassed as I hop out of the tub and tug at my shirt. But, what do I have to be ashamed for? The man murders for a living. Toweling off, I feel my boldness growing.

"Perhaps. We all have needs, Alpha." I tell him and wrap my towel around myself, covering my torso from curious eyes because I cannot bear the thought of revealing my own scars. "When does this ceremony begin?" I ask, "Should I dress a certain way?"

He keeps his amused look and I decide I like this version of Alpha. Playful, witty, and willing to take my commentary. "Naked. Absolutely naked." He says seriously, his tone bordered on sultry.

I pale as I stare at him before coming to the conclusion that this was his attempt at humor. "Ass," I scold him and he slaps mine as he walks past me into the bedroom. "What are you wearing?" I can only compare it to court and the way of dressing was quite important to a first impression.

He hesitates, considering his words. "My wolf. It will mostly be wolves in attendance; it's not safe to be in our human forms when it comes to ranking battles where anything goes and the only rule is the competitor must die."

I shake my head in response.

It sounds barbaric, it's nothing as I had hoped. "How is this right? Why must you die? Why can't you just step down should you be bested in a duel? I'm sure Delta doesn't want to fight in his condition." It seems ridiculous that this superior species decides rank by killing each other but then I suppose it has a lot to do with their ass-backward religion. "What is Valhalla?" I ask, irritated.

He pulls on a pair of pants and glimpses over at me out of the corner of his eye. "It's how the old bloods wrote it, as instructed by the gods." He tells me, he doesn't look like he really wants to delve into much detail but he should know me better than that by now.

"Old bloods? Like Adriam and Sota?" I press.

He's guarded, "Not quite..."

"Alpha. Please. I'm just trying to understand." I approach him and grasp the hem of his pants, buttoning them for him, tempting him with the only thing that seems to bring him out of the depths.

Watching me suspiciously, he exhales. Once more he yields to my temptation, once more he reveals more than he wishes. *Why?*

"The old bloods are descended from the original lycans, such as my father and Beta's. They are progeny instead of created. While there are plenty of secondary lines, the old bloods come from the purest strains."

I stare at him. "What, so, you're from some ancient line?" I almost laughed. *How old is this guy?*

Alpha purses his lips. "In a way, yes."

"That's why you're gray then?" I tease and he rolls his eyes dramatically.

Stepping away from me, he grabs his shirt and pulls it on as well as layering his vest over top of it. The top few buttons of his shirt remain open and I resist the urge to button them for him. He probably won't remain in these clothes for long, it'd be a wasted effort and I won't entertain my unreasonable urge to touch him.

"My wolf is gray, in case you hadn't noticed. It's actually a very uncommon color; it's said to decide the purity of the soul. The darker the coat, the darker the intentions. Grays are neutral and undecided. They can change to white or black depending on fate or some stay the same."

This interests me and I stare at his thick, tangled locks. Does it look more white or black? *Which is he?* He smirks at me, "I'm neutral, love. Not much to do about it either I guess. Too much of my father in me."

Sometimes I forget he's English. I move to look out the window, feigning indifference. We aren't so different, he and I. While I didn't murder people's families, I did care greatly for my people and our heritage, it would seem he treaded on much the same principles. The large difference between us was mere sophistication, I was not descended from barbarians. The sight below startles me; the courtyard is crawling with wolves. There has to be over a hundred, nearing two hundred.

He joins me, looming over me with his substantial height compared to my own. "I've got to get down there, it's starting soon. Tonic will be behind me with Adriam and Sota; I suggest you join them there. The men get a touch overcharged and it would be dangerous to be on your own." This is not a suggestion and I just nod, absently. "I'll send Tonic up to fetch you."

His Alpha face is on and I know that the charming man I just spent the last few hours with has been replaced by the warlord.

I dress in my robes to prepare for the evening, making my way back to the kitchen to finish my lunch though I suppose it is dinner now. The halls are empty, everyone is outside and the air feels electric; unsettling. They mobilize, not in a war against me, but against their own men. All in the name of some gods they don't even know exist, to claim rank in some ancient society.

How totally pointless, I shut my eyes tightly as I close the kitchen door and take a few deep breaths before I seek out my only source of comfort I can think of, wine. I pour myself a glass and take a deep drink. The taste is so familiar and I welcome the warmth it brings. It reminds me of my mother and suddenly I'm completely shattered as if the drink were poison to my subconscious.

I feel the tears threaten to spill over as I clutch my cup. I can almost hear her voice as she pours her own glass and tells me that wine is the only thing holding her together some days. "Me too, Mama..." I breathe, taking another drink with a shaky exhale. My mourning is interrupted by Tonic.

"Are you okay?" He asks; his voice small but concerned. He seems embarrassed to have caught me having a moment; as if he thinks maybe I'm hiding in here. Sniffling, I rub my eyes with my sleeve and nod.

I am royalty, I am a prince, I must hold myself together. "Yes, I'm fine, just remembering my mother. Do you drink?" I offer him the bottle, and he holds up his hands.

"I'm okay. I'm just coming to bring you to Alpha. It will be starting soon; you and I are unfortunately targets." He regards me as if I might be some drunk who needs to be babysat when I've merely had one glass. I down the rest of my wine and nod.

"Alright, let's go. I'm ready." I follow him out of the dining hall into the main courtyard and we are overwhelmed by the sounds of drums. The sound is deafening, rhythmic like a heartbeat. The sun is starting to set over the tree line and as we walk, multiple fires are being lit to surround a place that was once grass but is now dense sand.

I feel like an invader to an alien world. We are surrounded by naked men, partially clothed or shifting into wolves. Their shadows cast eerie figures across the walls of the castle. My heart throbs and I clutch Tonic closer, it's too much for my fragile state. Hearing the drums and the snarls, it sucks me right back to that moment where my life was forever changed. Some are already brawling, preparing for this massacre.

Is this what it was like before they entered my castle?

I can see Alpha, standing in the main hall of the throne room, soaked in blood and teeth bared. I watch his stalk, the determination as he approaches my aged father. His words are muted, all I can see is his bloody prints on our marbled floors. He leaps and my father is clutched in his jaws.

Ducking my head down, I follow close to Tonic and we mount a set of stairs to climb up to a large boulder that overlooks the new sandpit. At its peak stands the Alpha, the fire cascades light down his coat and illuminate his startling eyes, casting shadows across his large body. Adriam is sitting in a chair that is backed up to a rock face and I notice that we are in a modified version of the garden. I sit beside him; uncomfortable with what a spectacular view we have of the sandpit.

Alpha's whole body is vibrating, his large head lowered as he watches his pack gather. The noise consuming all else, my whole town must think they are being invaded again. *How could no one hear this coming?*

I can only remind myself this is who they are, *what* they are, the thought is sobering considering I was tangled up with their leader not an hour ago. *What is wrong with me?*

Stepping away from me, Tonic allows his wolf to come forward and I realize I don't think I've ever really even seen his wolf. Maybe once? He's darker than Alpha and I find that hard to believe after hearing Alpha's theory though Tonic's dark chocolate eyes play on the colors in his coats. I find he is much more of an off gray than he is the silvery color that the Alpha possesses.

His wolf is not interested in the activities; he lays down and curls his body around my chair, resting his head at my feet. I'm grateful for him because, on this cool night, I find I'm chilled and I wish I had dressed more warmly.

Oh Tonic, how is this fair for him? He wants this to end as much as I do, there have to be others that feel this way. What happens when this war is over? Do they just continue to conquer the rest of the world? Though it doesn't seem like they have any interest in staying in the lands they take control of, just liberating their own people.

I feel as though I stare at Tonic's forehead for hours, counting the hairs and examining how his coat melts from one color to the next before I hear Alpha speak, startling me back into reality. "Silence!" He commands and a hush falls over the crowd, the entirety of the pack avert their eyes in respect for their Alpha.

"We are here to carry on the traditions of our people. Tonight, a position has been opened and as you all know, we must have a full hierarchy. The Beta, Caspian, has been killed for committing an assault on the Alpha. The officer, John, was in conspiracy with him, and his life was also forfeit." There is mumbling through the crowd and I hear a snarl come from the large gray wolf as the group falls silent once more.

"As always, all positions are open for discussion and attempt. Any challenger must accept that the penalty for attempting a position is death. The survivor may claim the rank as his own and will go by the name of that rank; a rank can be questioned as many times as there are challengers. Each fight must be fought one on one. There is no surrender, so choose wisely. Our announcer tonight will be Sota."

I realize I've only just noticed that Sota was not sitting with us. He had been so quiet and off to the side, the look on his face shows concern. Sota lifts his hand to silence the crowd; I focus on his back and his long, flowing white hair. "Everyone clear the square." He commands and the group backs away from the sand, giving it plenty of space.

"Go." He mumbles and Alpha hops down from his perch into the sand. The front line trembles as some wolves fight to get to the back and some fight for a better view. "Does anyone challenge the Alpha for Alpha rank?" He calls. Silence. I glance at Adriam who is very focused on the event. "Don't be shy, anyone at all?" He taunts.

My heart leaps when I hear a voice. A deep, familiar one.

"Would maybe like to try for Alpha? Might be better pay grade." Everyone's eyes snap to the absolutely massive white wolf that steps into the ring. My heart drops and I quickly look at Adriam who is smirking. What is this? "Come now, I don't want to break other shoulder. Step out of ring and I let you live."

His Russian accent rolls thick. Victor?

"Adriam, what on earth?" I breathe, battling the flurry of emotions from concern to shock.

I'm about to watch Alpha die.

He doesn't stand a chance against this creature. People that he thought were his friends, people that I thought we could trust. I can't see his face, I can only see Victor's, his expression appears smug. My eyes shift to Sota and I squirm in my chair, I want to run to him and tell him to call it off, to tell him that this couldn't have been the plan.

At this moment, nothing else matters save for preventing the slaughter of my only lifeline.

The drums are forcing my heart to race to try and keep time, their fast pace must have everyone's adrenaline up. I watch as the two begin to circle each other, sizing each other up. Victor moves first and I cover my eyes with my hands. I can't watch, I was not trained for this amount of brutality in what should be a court system.

On bated breath, I don't hear any contact. Again I hear the lurch but once more, I hear no contact and I split my fingers to find out what's going on. Alpha was correct, he's skilled. He aptly avoids Victor, at one point even jumping over him but it doesn't look like Victor is really trying to hit him.

Before I know it, there are a few chuckles exchanged and the mood seems to have lightened a little. Adriam is glancing at me out of the corner of his eye and I glare at him.

Sota calls for the two to stop and Victor gives Alpha a playful shove, "Can't fight when you can't catch, eh?" He comments and looks at Sota. "I guess I just accept Beta position then?" Sota rolls his eyes at both of them, displeased with the pair.

"That's not usually how this works. Do we have any challengers for the Beta position?" A hush falls over the crowd once more and I figure they have the same problem I have with Victor. He's unrealistically huge.

Victor goes unchallenged and both of the males hop back up on Alpha's perch. Next, comes the Delta position and I find that I think Delta looks sore. Somehow I struggle to think that Delta has fought for anything, he's so gentle and soft. I watch his sandy pelt and all I can think of is watching him die.

I wish I had healed him more but it wasn't as if he was being very cooperative. Delta, unfortunately, does get a challenger.

The fight begins much less artistically. The rival male is very strong but not very fast. I feel as though Delta is using Alpha's technique because he's scrambling around trying to avoid these world-ending blows that the rival is trying to put on him. The rival begins to wear down, finding it harder to chase him. Delta takes his shot and moves in for the kill, gripping the rival by the throat but it seems to have been premature because suddenly Delta is on the floor in the jaws of the rival.

The larger male shakes him, trying to disorientate him and cause more blood loss. His paws lose their hold; if he lets go, it's over. Suddenly his claws find the rival's eye and he takes his opportunity, he digs his hind feet into the other male's stomach, kicking him strongly and twisting his body to try and free himself.

The male is forced to release and the crowd cheers. Delta moves quickly, grabbing the other wolf by the top of the muzzle, he expertly tosses his head and snaps the male's neck.

The crowd roars with approval. I see no reason to cheer; as they tend to him ringside, I must disconnect myself from the worry that clutches my throat. I have my own people to think about, my own path to follow. Delta would be on his own tonight.

I turn my head to see that Tonic is in the ring and all over again, my heart sinks. My eyes fall on Alpha's face, this is not part of the plan.

Fourteen-

How did this happen?

Tonic is a grown man and it wasn't like we were babysitting him or that he was famous for doing these sorts of things.

Tonic was probably one of the most decisive and non-risk-taking men I've ever met. I don't think the man buttered his toast without regretting it afterward so I don't understand what prompted him to step into the slaughterhouse that was this sandpit. The drums echo my heartbeat, pounding in my ears. I almost feel dizzy.

What can I do? I'll be killed if I follow him.

"What position are you competing for? You understand the rules… any fight is to the death if you wish to climb in rank." Sota asks.

I can hear the strain in his voice. Alpha's face is composed, yet I note by the distance in his eyes that he is stunned as well.

"Officer." Tonic responds almost too quickly. He's nervous. I wish that I had questioned him more on his opinion on this. How had I not noticed him slipping away? How had I not realized he was gone long before this moment when it was already far too late?

"What is happening? How did he get past us?" My voice is close to hysterics. I can't allow this. I can't watch Tonic die.

Adriam's eyes slide towards me, the man has been so still. Maybe he's just as tense as I am; he just doesn't rant and rave about it. "Honey, I think you need to take a seat and let Alpha do his job. I didn't know that's where Tonic was going; maybe seeing Delta fight encouraged him to make an attempt?"

I stare at him, sit down? *How?* But somehow I manage and it seems like it takes all my restraint to hold me into this chair. My body rigid, my throat dry as I think of exactly what I will say to him if he survives this.

"Do we have any contenders for the officer position?" I hear Sota call, there is no response and maybe the pack has taken pity on this poor man. I watch the gangly youngster, he looks so brave. His long, lean limbs cast thin shadows, making him look even smaller in the dimming light. My heart does gymnastics against my ribs and lungs when I hear someone respond.

I know that we won't make it out of this night unscathed. I will lose someone. Today. Right now. Another person I love will die. It comes out quicker than I can stop it, I love Tonic, I love him as if he were my own brother. He was my only friend in this cruel existence.

The tears threaten to spill over and I reach over to grip Adriam's hand and I find that he clutches me just as hard as I'm holding him. He isn't as weepy as I am but he's seen so much more death than I have. Maybe he's just accepted that Tonic had some kind of suicide wish?

"Are you ready?" Sota asks. Victor and Alpha crowd at the peak of the rock; leaned forward and intense like two gargoyles at attention. The fires flicker off their coats, casting harsh shadows against the grays and whites, sending a shudder down my spine as I force myself to look away from those intense eyes.

This fight starts similar to Delta's and I'm seeing a pattern. Maybe the little display at the beginning of the night was a good show of defense skills, showing that there is no shame in not going head to head with a much larger foe. That and a show of bravado and strength on Victor's part that gained him the much-hoped-for position of Beta.

Does that mean I can't call him Victor? I quiver at the thought of anyone but the black beast holding the title Beta.

I jump out of my thoughts when I hear scrambling, Tonic had tripped.

He lacked the poise and strength to effectively maneuver in the deep sand. The crowd is in a frenzy as the contender grabs him by his hock and throws him across the arena. I flinch and I realize it's partly because Adriam has me in a death grip.

Tonic rolls like a log back across the arena with a swift kick from a hind leg. He's toying with him, he isn't fighting. The rival knows he will win. My gray friend cries out as a paw comes down on his back, knocking him back into the sand. He's not biting him because he wants him to last, he wants him to suffer.

"Is there nothing we can do?" I plead with Adriam who doesn't answer me. I feel as though I know the answer, his silence screams at me that we are about to watch the end.

Tonic attempts another stand and once again he's kicked over, he tumbles across the arena and lands on his side in a daze. Sota raises his fist and the fight halts for a moment. "Stand Tonic." Sota commands him.

Slowly he gets to his feet only to be dealt another blow. It seems so unfair, *why did he do this? Why did he decide to enter the ring?*

"You're pathetic." I hear the rival taunt and my blood boils. I stand and I try to make my way to the stairs but Adriam has my hand. He forces me back into my chair with an amount of strength that I didn't expect from his small form. My back hits the chair with an audible thud, earning a glower from Alpha over his shoulder at the disruption.

"He'll kill you too. He's on his own in the ring."

"Stand Tonic." I hear Sota command again. This time my gray companion doesn't stand, my sweet chocolate eyed friend. He lies with his ears back, looking like he's tempted to curl into a ball and give up.

"Get up Tonic." I hear another voice and this time it's Alpha. "You cannot just lie there, get up!" The rival begins his approach, running his tongue over his lips because he knows this will be swift and easy "Tonic, I'm ordering you to get up!"

I can hear the desperation in Alpha's voice. The male is hovering over him and I can't look. I wonder if it will be quick, I hope that it will be quick. I hope that he is afforded all the mercy my parents were not. Would he be afraid? I hear a snarl and the snapping of jaws, in the echo of death the crowd is completely silent.

"He's dead... I just know it." I bury my face in Adriam's shoulder but he's silent as well. Slowly I look up and I see why nobody has said a word.

Alpha is standing over Tonic and he has broken the lower jaw of the competitor almost completely off with a swipe of his front paw.

The dark male staggers backward; the noise he makes and the blood rushing from his wound are quite a sight. He flails and falls to the ground, no doubt going into shock from the pain of such an injury.

A murmur starts in the crowd, the rules have been broken. Alpha looks different, his coat is standing on end, his tail erect and his ears fully pricked. His fangs totally exposed, he doesn't look afraid as it seems that his pack is deciding whether it should turn on him or not. Multiple wolves step into the ring and the onslaught of accusations begins.

"The laws have been broken!"

"Tonic was meant to die!"

"Who pays for the life that was just taken?"

"An Alpha should not interfere with rank!"

"He's just an Omega!"

They circle him, ears pinned and teeth exposed, but he doesn't meet their gaze. He stares straight ahead, he's patient, skilled and he knows better than to panic. I can't help my marvel at the calm resistance, they have him where they want him. "Move Alpha." I whisper, willing him to do anything but stand there. Yet, if he moves, Tonic will be slaughtered. Two silvery coats slowly become swallowed by the growing number of darker coats that surround them. Browns, tans, blacks, and gold, all swirling in the sand.

Victor leaps down into the circle and I hear Adriam's breath catch.

"Do we really want more broken jaws? Is one not enough? I'm too sober for this bullshit." The snarl that rips through him resonates in my chest.

The circle widens as the angered wolves consider their options.

I can't recall who it was that started the fight or maybe it was just a mutual decision. I remember the fight between Alpha and Beta in the courtyard. I think back to when I would go hunting with my father, how the grizzlies would stand on their hind legs and slap each other with their paws.

I can feel the ground shake as I close my eyes; I remember hiding behind my father's protective shield as we watched them battle it out. He would pat my shoulder and tell me it was only natural, that this was supposed to be a beautiful thing. Only now, there's no shield and it's all too real. The clashing of teeth and the sounds of battling titans bring me out of my memory and I glimpse over to see Adriam is hiding his face as well.

Neither of us can handle this, can stomach this. It does make me feel better to know that Adriam is just as sickened as I am though maybe it's because Victor is in the middle of this. Sota has called forward his wolf and he throws his head back and he lets loose a commanding howl.

Everyone falls silent once more. I take inventory and I can't tell whose blood is whose. Bodies litter the circle, bloody and battered, muzzles gaping in the eternal surprise of their demise. Their reddish coats tinted with fresh blood and gnarled wounds.

Alpha has hardly given up any ground, Tonic remains firmly underneath him and Victor has his back to him. His beautiful white coat is stained and soaked through. The pearly white sand bears the bloody scars of battle, pools of murky ink in the darkness. The morning would show the true colors of what had occurred here, the bloodshed could only hide in the dark where evil lurks.

"That is quite enough. We are done with ranking for the night. The Alpha has spoken; the fight was an unfair advantage. We do not question the Alpha!" He reprimands the remaining brawlers and they all avert their eyes.

"Get back to your groups; we have bodies to send to Valhalla... Pray to Oden that they are welcome at the gates with the conduct shown here tonight. An absolute disgrace. Ready the fires, light the stack, and load these bodies into it. The night is almost over and the smoke pillar must reach the clouds before the sun rises."

They scatter and I see Sota limp down the stairs. I steal after him, breaking away from Adriam.

"What the fuck were you thinking?" Sota snaps to Alpha who lays his ears back in frustration.

"Of all the stupid, immature, ridiculous things you could have done, **Verando**, this was one of them. Tonic made his choice and you put us all at risk to defend him. To defend the Omega! These men are already on the edge of their rope, we've been on this mission for months and we are no closer to taking Ziduri so allowing them to blow off a little steam would be beneficial. Do you understand what this does to our support? What this means for us?"

"It was an unfair fight," Alpha responds, his tone cold.

"For fucks sake... This is **WAR** Verando. We don't have the luxury of fair! The men are doubting our abilities to conquer the elf nation and you are showing your weakness by defending the lowest form of life in our ranks. We cannot appear weak. Not now. Straighten. The.Fuck.Up." He turns his yellow gaze to Tonic, his eyes blaze like lanterns in the dark. His body grows, a former Alpha against dust in the wind, a dead man walking.

"Are you happy? Is this what you wanted? A whore's son ruining our only chance at preventing an uprising, I hope they come for you in your sleep you worthless dog. Get training or get the hell out."

Tonic averts his eyes, looking towards the woods. Victor raises a brow but Sota has little to say to him. "Learn English. You sound like you're fucking five..." Sota is fizzling out, regaining control of the immense heat emanating from his body. Sota charges into the distance, murmuring about a drink as Victor glances back towards Alpha.

"I think I speak the English pretty good."

Alpha rolls his eyes and helps Tonic to his feet.

Verando? Is that Alpha? I slowly finish my trek down the stairs and approach the trio. "Are any of you hurt?" I try not to sound so timid but I did just watch them murder multiple people. For the first time since that first night, it was very real to me exactly how lethal this witty, charming man could be.

When did I forget that? When did that become foreign to me?

Victor shrugs, "Is a scratch. Will heal a good scar. Not as good as one on face but will have to do." He departs, he knows he's in trouble with Adriam and he doesn't want to deal with it.

Before he can disappear I see he's a naked human man on his way to find alcohol. I look towards Alpha and Tonic, of the two Tonic just seems like he's more banged up than bloody. Alpha, on the other hand, has seen better days. I sigh because I know he won't want my help, much as I feel compelled to help him. I can only convince myself it's for my own benefit that he survives. If nothing else, his physical company has been enjoyable.

"Anything serious?" I feel helpless; he shouldn't be punished for saving Tonic's life. The urge to thank him climbs into my throat but how will he receive it?

"No." His voice is short. He's upset.

"For what it's worth, I think that was very brave what you did." I walk over to throw my arm around my friend's neck. I had truly thought I was going to lose Tonic and I glanced at Alpha to see if my words affected him but he's already walking away. I'll have to go over him a little better later and see if he truly does need my help. I'll have to heal him in his sleep, most likely, though it's rare he sleeps around me.

"How are you?" I ask Tonic, looking him over.

"I've been better." He's obviously a little shaken up. His wide chocolate eyes searching around like a frightened feline, his body crouched as his fur attempts to settle.

"Tonic what were you thinking?"

"I just was sick of how things have been going. I was hoping if I could win; if I could get into the upper ranks? Then, I would have a say and could maybe start to change things. I don't know... It was stupid. If Verando hadn't jumped in, I don't know what I would have done." He sighs and shakes his large head in disbelief.

There it is again. **Verando**.

Much as I don't want to derail from my disappointment in Tonic, I have to ask. "Is that Alpha's name? Verando?"

Tonic looks at me with a look of pure terror. "Erm... No. His name is Alpha." The look on my face says I'm not amused. I wait patiently. "Nicolas I really can't say more, I'm already going to be in trouble."

"Hey, Sota said it first." I try and encourage him. He just groans in response, he knows he's trapped.

"Isn't almost dying punishment enough without you prying into the life of our leader?" All empathy goes out the window when the man holds onto something that I desire. "Yes... okay? His name is Verando."

I smile at him and hug him once more. I don't know why the information means so much to me but it does and I'm happy to know it. It's just one more piece into the puzzle that is my captor.

CHAPTER

Fifteen-

I take Tonic into the castle and bring him into the dining hall to get to work on his injuries. My magic is limited but simple healing is something I'm quite capable of. I'm thankful for the fact that when wolves transform back to their human forms, they're naked. Spying Gena, I flag her down to come to assist me in the cleaning of this battered male. She flushes, averting her eyes at his naked form.

Tonic and I are too shy around each other to have ever gotten to the part where he needed to take off his clothes should he have had another option. I sit him on one of the tables and start at his head, his black eye and his busted lip mixed with his swollen jaw. Gena scrubs him, refusing to look at either of us.

"How many are dead?" she whispers. Her voice carried a different tone, relief. She wants them to be dead, much as I should.

I decide to just heal the jaw but leave the superficial stuff. He needs to still look beaten up to prevent reoccurrence. "I'm not sure. I think I counted six."

She frowns. "I'd hoped for more. I feel like this nightmare will never end."

I run my hands down his neck and over his shoulders, cataloging every flinch and cringe. His blackened ribs worry me with the massive bruising on his side. He much resembles a scolded child, ashamed and possibly upset by Gena's words. I sigh and I heal his ribs, they don't seem broken but I decide I have a new agenda that he can help me accomplish if he wishes to repay me for healing him.

"Don't beat yourself up. You were doing it for a good cause." I offer. Even if I think his cause is ridiculous, I have to be a supportive friend. He really is one of the only friends I have right now.

Shrugging one shoulder, his lower lip threatens to protrude as he glowers at the aged wood of the table. "Alpha is very upset with me. Sota wants me to leave... I'm not really worried about my injuries, Nicolas."

Gena steals a glance in my direction. "Shall I get some herbal pain killer, M'lord?"

I shake my head. "Perhaps just some water, Gena. Thank you."

My gaze falls on the male as she quickly skirts out of the room. "Tonic, Alpha is not upset with you." At least I don't think he is, I've seen that look before and it didn't look like hatred to me. "He's upset at what could have happened to you. You scared him, you scared us all."

His nose wrinkles, rejecting my kindness. "I'm not a child, Nicolas. I don't need you worrying over me. I want to help; I want to be a part of this. I'm just not a skilled fighter. I suppose it would help if I ever went to training but I figured if Delta could do it so could I. I've been working on my confidence. I just want to help, Nicolas."

A good person would comfort their friend. A good friend would not see this as an opportunity to gain leverage. Unfortunately for Tonic, I couldn't even be sure if I was one of the good people anymore. "Well, do you want to help me?"

I try not to sound too hopeful. His eyes flicked upward, confused. "Do you want to help or not?"

Rolling his eyes, he slowly nods.

"Good! Meet me by the statue we found when everyone goes to sleep. We'd do it now but I worry what would happen if we got caught. Nobody is in their right mind right now." He seems to agree, and I kiss his cheek which causes him to flush. "Please be kind to Gena, stay with her for a while? She might like the company." I twiddle my fingers at the maid as I leave her to tend and dress his wounds, her reddened cheeks satisfy me that I had thought correctly on her timid glances.

Perhaps this would change her affections to someone else as they would never work for me and, much as I could be cruel, I didn't like hurting her.

I look out my bedroom window and see that the last of the logs are burning, the crowds begin to separate into their dwellings for the night.

Pulling out my spellbook, I scan through revealing spells as surely this room would be riddled with traps to prevent the reveal of the book. I would have to be ready for the worst, that this book was meant to destroy me, never to be read by anyone else.

My fingers trail absently over my own scrawled writing, wrought with stress and stained, smudged, with tears. When I had learned the revealing spell, I was sure it would cost me my life.

We were locked in a maze, told by our instructor that a revealing spell was unique to each Solomonari and that some of us wouldn't have one at all. It would come to you when you most needed it and with that, they released a starved dragon at one end and told us to find our way out.

It hunted us by our magic, hungry to get back to its own realm and not under any sort of control. We all would have died if it hadn't been for me. I think of the desperation as we ran as a unit in our stark white outfits. There was nowhere to hide where we wouldn't be spotted, no room for errors.

Thinking back, I could still hear the ragged breath and smell the sulfur haze that followed the creature as it sought us out. We had rounded our final corner only to discover it was a dead-end, our navigator had lost track of the turns.

We were hopelessly lost and losing precious daylight, not that the crazed beast cared for the cover of darkness. Without fire, it was known we would not have survived a night in the maze. When all plans of escape failed, they had turned to me, the prince of Lord Darrius, and I had little to answer for them. I was the banished prince, the one deemed to not return. My instructor had been tutoring my lust, not my mind.

We were just leading the dragon to us with all our clambering around. A particularly hot-blooded female in our group melted down, I remember seeing that she had ripped her fingernails off trying to claw a hole in the stone walls strangled by brush. As the dragon rounded the corner, we all made our peace with our gods, only mine spoke back.

I pressed my hands through the wall and created a door just big enough for us to squeeze through. It couldn't have come a moment sooner for the dragon was upon us. It didn't stop it from flying, coming over the wall, and trying to kill us from the other side. We fought our way through to the end of the maze with minimal casualties thanks to my revealing spell and a few others my classmates had managed to conjure up to keep us alive.

Thinking back to that day, I relive how afraid I was, reminding myself that my father had only sent me there to kill me. I would be better than him. I had to be, just as I was in the maze, I was my people's only hope.

I'm stronger now.

As my resolve knows, my mind begins to darken. Maybe it was a good thing that Alpha ended him? I find myself missing my brother, my sisters, my mother, and my freedom more than I ever even pondered the existence of my father. A shudder rolls through my body, disgusted by my own dismissive thoughts.

I come out of my daydream with a start when Alpha pushes the door open and I gasp and close my book and cover it with my pillow. What was he doing here?

His busted lip, his scratched up arms, neck, and sides. Blood streams from various wounds, coating the glimpses of tanned skin. He's completely naked as he walks over and sits beside the bed with his back pressed against it. "I've had... a little too much... to drink." He admits and closes his eyes as he tilts his head back.

I wonder if he's passed out.

"So you come here?" I question and I slide off the bed, sneaking my book into my robe.

"Of course, this is where I come when I want to forget, when I want to feel good!" He slurs.

I hesitate and roll my eyes. Well, at least I shouldn't feel so bad for using him now. He's using me too.

"Where's Tonic? I must—I must speak with him. Prompt-tily. I know you're friends, where are you hiding him? With your wizardry and... I dunno... whatever it is you use to hide people."

Oh god. He *is* drunk. I slide my book into my wardrobe, conjuring a retort with something cutting and witty when he starts to stand, only to almost fall onto his face. I rush to him and help him stand. **God he's heavy!**

"Alpha, you need to stand up. You're covered in blood and honestly, in your condition, I think drinking was pretty stupid." I sigh as I take him in. "You've messed up your pretty face," I mumbled, reaching up to heal his lip and sliced cheek. He pulls away, almost falling over once more. I sigh, grabbing his wrist to stabilize him. "You are drunk," I mumble. His face was one of his few redeeming qualities, without that this might not work.

"Don't use your sorcery on me! Where's Tonic?"

"Don't worry about Tonic just... Can you sit here while I go and fetch some water so I can get this off of you? You're going to stain my robes and then you'll see some real sorcery when I dismember you." I push him back towards one of the plush chairs and try not to get my body too close to his with its current state.

Alpha gives me almost a goofy grin, dimpling his cheek, "I like it when you talk dirty to me." He teases, leaning down to kiss me, only, I'm ready for him. I easily put my hand up to cover his mouth.

"Down boy... I'm not interested in a bloody, half-conscious war-lord." My cheeks flush as he parts his lips and takes two of my fingers into his mouth to suck on them. My body erupts into flames, wishing to partake in every piece of this sinful man.

He's caught me completely off guard and he knows it. "Okay, maybe a little. But not like this. I need to rinse you off." His hands come to pull me closer and I retract my fingers from his mouth to slip out of his grasp. "Stay," I command him strictly. He gives me a wary look before sighing and sitting down in the chair I'd been trying to guide him to. "I'll be right back."

When I return I half expect him to not be there but I am pleased to see that he still is. Only he's found a way to occupy his time and it involves touching himself. He gives me a wicked smile and I swallow before gesturing to him to follow me into the bathroom. I don't allow myself to steal a glance, one of us has to be in control and it would seem that today it would be me.

"Be still," I command him as I get to work scrubbing him.

"So bossy." He grumbles. I'm not used to relaxed Alpha, it's quite a change and it's a little unnerving. He stands as still as he can as I go over his cuts and heal the deeper ones. I make quick work of scrubbing him; it's something I'm getting used to doing.

The plains of his body are becoming familiar to me, each coil of muscle, each beautiful piece of sculpted flesh under my twitching fingers. I bite my lower lip as my cloth goes over his stomach and towards the object of my desire. I try to not dwell too long on any spot, he watches me too intently to give in so easily. How I long to taste that tempting flesh.

"Let's get you to bed." I take his hand and lead him towards the bedroom only to quickly realize this isn't going to work. He pulls me into his grasp, only to meet my lips with his own. I melt against him.

How can I be attracted to someone like this?

Maybe the fact it's forbidden is what keeps me coming back, what keeps me interested. I can't think clearly with the way he's pressing his body against me and tangling his hand in my hair. "This isn't the bed." I try to get some form of control back; he grins against my lips and kisses me once more. I yield, taking in his scent, dragging my tongue over his lower lip.

"Someone's in a hurry." He murmurs, catching my lower lip with his teeth. I force myself to put my hands against his chest and put some distance between him, my mind rages with the desire to surrender to this battered man.

"I think you know I'm ***putting*** you to bed, not taking you to bed."

"I don't think that's part of our deal." He pushes me back towards the wall and pins me against it as he fumbles with my pants and attacks my neck. My fingertips rake against his chest as my body writhes and betrays me.

This is what I was missing with Haryek, *the domination.*

The animalistic nature; the way he attacks my body. "I want you to beg." I'm ready and willing but he starts to slide down my body before I can respond. Yanking my pants down, he takes me in his hand and I inhale sharply.

His fist slides up and down my length before he takes me into his mouth and I moan as I tangle my fingers in his hair.

No one had ever serviced me, no one had ever taken my pleasure into their own hands. I had always been the pawn, I'd always been the one to yield and please. He rolls his tongue against me and I curse under my breath, my legs threaten to buckle as I press my free hand into his shoulder. He chuckles against me, bringing a heated gasp from my lips.

Sucking hard, he glances up at me. I meet the startling light eyes, it's almost my undoing to see him gaze at me as if I mattered, to see him revel in my pleasure. "Gods Alpha, please!" My body shakes as his slow, torturous tongue teases me. His gaze holds mine, he hums in appreciation for my ragged breath as I bite my lower lip to stay in control. "I want you to take me. I need you to take me."

But he is merciless and as he applies his teeth I come undone and explode in his mouth. I'm out of breath, incoherent, and dazed as I ride out the waves. I hardly have time to remember my name as his lips find mine, his tongue commands entrance to my mouth. I taste myself, throwing myself at him as I cling to any part of him that'll have me.

"That's more like it." He purrs as I'm shoving him back towards the bed. My hands are jumbled and shaky as I fight to get my pants off and in my rush, I rip both my shirt and my tank top off.

He throws me to the bed and I pull him with me. Wrapping my legs around his waist, I dig my heels in to encourage him and he grazes my neck with his teeth.

Any sense of volume control is lost as he loses himself in me, his breath hot against my ear as I take in his glistening body. He's braced on his elbows and my arms wrap around his neck, my legs around his waist. For a moment we make eye contact and he leans down to kiss me, his lips grazing mine yet it's not enough. I crush our lips together as I climb, dangerously close to release as he chases his own.

I plead for him, begging him, calling for him, as I meet his lips we find our release together. My fingers knot in the hair at the base of his neck, this man seemed to be unraveling everything I'd come to know about myself. I have never enjoyed sex, not like this. It was physical currency for me, if this was what it could be, then I had never tasted something quite so extraordinary.

In all our passion, I had slipped. I'd called him by his real name, the one I'd learned not hours ago.

We are both out of breath as we lay tangled on top of one another. He lies on his back and I'm cuddled up to his side. I watch his scars as he breathes, watching them expand and contract with his chest and I run my fingers over them absently. "I like drunken Alpha," I tell him.

I wonder if he's asleep since he's been so quiet. I'm surprised he's still here as I glance up, finding that he's staring at the ceiling.

"So I'm Alpha again?" He questions, his tone is careful and I freeze. I think back to our moments together and frown.

"For now." I respond, just as cautious. "I don't mind Alpha when you're not being horrible."

"Well, that's good to know." He's guarding his tone, it would seem release had sobered him.

Sighing, I prop myself up on my elbow and look down at him. His eyes shift towards me and he looks conflicted. "Look. I didn't mean to call you that, I heard Sota say it... It just kind of stuck with me. I like it, it's an interesting name."

I bite my lower lip, why am I shy all of a sudden? This man has been over every inch of me but we aren't on a first-name basis. We don't trust each other.

He looks back up at the ceiling. "I... liked... hearing you say it."

This catches me off guard but I feel the smile spread over my face. "Maybe I'll keep calling you by it?" I offer.

He scoffs. "Only when you're good. Can't have you thinking that I've gone soft. You know, my friends used to call me Randy."

This brings a giggle from me that I didn't know I possessed. "Randy?" I ask, somehow I just can't see it.

He shrugs and offers me a boyish smile in return, dimpling his cheek. "Randy." He repeats back and I snuggle back up to him.

It isn't long before he's asleep, he's exhausted and I knew he would be out like a light. Though now, I'm conflicted about leaving. Here, in his arms, I'm the happiest I've been in months. But, I know I must go.

Slipping out of his grasp is easy enough, apparently, he had more to drink than I thought because he sleeps like he's dead. I carefully walk over to pull on one of his shirts and a pair of shorts and slide my way out of the room.

Tonic is impatient when I get to the statue.

"Where were you? I've been here for almost an hour! The sun will be up soon." He looks confused at my outfit and I'm instantly regretting my choices for clothes. I must reek of Alpha.

"A meeting," I tell him in a guarded tone and he doesn't question me as he straightens his body.

"Well, what are we waiting for? Let's get this door open and steal a book." I try to sound optimistic but I suddenly feel as if getting out of bed was a horrible idea.

CHAPTER

Sixteen-

The statue seems to almost hum as I near it, as if realizes it's close to a magic user.

I feel as though it might feel as though I stand a chance at opening it, my magic courses through my fingertips at the ready. It's not going to just respond to any simple revealing spell. I put my hands on the pedestal and the statue groans as I chant, the wall shudders and shakes as the statue slowly starts to move.

It's taking almost everything I have to just slide it. The stale air from the passageway threatens to gag me as it finishes its pass and comes to a rest. My hands are clammy; I feel drained as if the statue itself sucked the very essence out of me. Lord Darrius was so much more powerful than me, it was foolish to think my own meager magic could stand up to such a force.

"Stay close to me, Tonic. We don't need to get separated." I honestly don't know what could be down there. It could be a maze, a room, or even a realm. My father was the most powerful wizard the world had known, everything he did was meticulous and for a greater purpose. Or, so he said. It would make little sense for this task to be quite so easy.

We make our way down the passage, and it's dark and rank, the smell of dust and dead air make breathing difficult. The air feels heavy, each step feels weighted. Tonic crowds close to me and the cavern feels very cold and lifeless.

My father probably hadn't been down here in some time, not like he was known for his good housekeeping. We can practically hear our heartbeats in the eerie silence and ahead, I can see a dim light.

I try not to race towards it, the dark is eating away at me and I feel as if it might consume us. I feel watched, as if there are eyes bearing down on us, looking over our shoulders and just out of the corner of our eye.

I practically gasp for air as we reach the light and I realize it's a skylight but I can't picture from where in the castle it resides. The roof must be charmed. The air feels lighter here and we are surrounded by stone shelves and books.

Tonic groans. I know from experience that he loathes the dust and dander of leafing through titles. "How are we going to search all these before everyone wakes up?"

I know none of these are my father's spellbook. "This is all history and lore, some are spellbooks but nothing like what we are looking for. Take a good smell. Where is it the strongest?" I watch him patiently as he inhales, only to cough, then tries again.

"There?" He doesn't sound sure but there's an iron gate that is latched with a piece of rope.

Cautiously I approach and extend my hand. The rope turns into a snake that writhes and hisses, snatching at us in quick, sharp bites.

I mutter a few quick words and it returns to its rope-like state. The gate screeches open and I take a few steps inside. There, I see my ax and I quickly reach for it only to have my hand stabbed through by the tip of a giant spear.

I try not to scream as I retract my hand, clutching it to my chest. The towering stone guardian pulls back his spear to stab again and I jump to the side to narrowly dodge the jab. Tonic allows his wolf to come forward but his teeth are useless against the stone spear.

"Mutt." The guardian garbled as it swats him aside carelessly.

He yelps as he hits the wall but it gives me time to grab my ax and I swing it with everything I have to strike the stone beast's leg. The electricity jolts through us both, with a crack of light, the leg sloughs off the giant with an audible groan as it slams to the ground.

The creature screeches as it crawls toward me, its stone helmet cracked and I can see the glimmer of red eyes beneath as it pulls itself.

Tonic leaps onto its back and digs his claws into the crack on its helmet. The guardian roars and swings at him. He stays low, pulling, trying to dislodge its head. I use the last of my strength to swing my ax for its neck and somewhat hit my target. The head dislodges and rolls away, red eyes dimming as the stone begins to crumble.

I shudder and my hand is screaming. I can see the floor as I look at the top of my hand and I feel sick, I dry heave and hold the offending limb as far away from me as I can. My fingers refuse to respond as I try and flex them. The muscles have been torn, the bone shattered.

Tonic limps towards me and he also looks sickened. My chest throbs and I feel like I'm going to throw up but it doesn't stop. It throbs again and I reach for the wall to support myself as I vomit. Blood seeps from my lips and I put my busted hand over my mouth and I'm sick once more when I realize my blood is sliding through the hole in my hand.

"Nicolas?!" Tonic is desperate. I can feel the panic on my face as I look at him. This isn't just nausea.

"I... I don't know... I think the guardian was cursed." I wipe the blood from my face on my shirt.

"I'm going to be okay," I assure him but I really don't know. I'm unsteady on my legs, I cling to the wall like a lifeline. I've used too much magic, I can't fight this.

My eyes fall on the spellbook. I go for it and I can feel its invisible fingers reaching for me; pulling at the remains of my magic. If we leave it here, it could revive the guardian. I look at Tonic. "Tonic... when I pick this up, I don't know what's going to happen. You need to take me to Stefan."

Tonic watches me as if I've lost my mind. I can't afford to doubt him now.

"Tonic!" I snap and he nods. "You have to take me to Stefan! Do you understand?" I command him and he nods again. "You will take me into the city and there is a large house at the heart. It will smell like the dead, you must bring me to him and do what he says. Exactly what he says. Do you understand?" I repeat it because he must, my life depends on it.

"Nicolas I'm scared." He breathes and I touch his furry head.

"Me too." I clench my teeth as I touch the book and everything goes black.

The book siphons as much magic as I can muster and clings to my hand as if I'm cemented to it. I can't release it as it searches for my father and finds only my unworthy body. I can hear someone screaming and I realize it's me. It's like I'm watching from another body as I crumble.

This is it. I'm going to die. I hear my father's voice and I blink at the brightness that surrounds me.

"Found it did you?" His voice is young, not like I remember.

"No thanks to you." I spit. Why do I hurt so badly? I look at my hand but there's no reason it should hurt so bad. I flex my fingers but they refuse to move. My father draws me back to him.

"You would have enough magic to meld the book to you if you hadn't wasted your time in school." I laugh and he looks impressed. "You've grown bold." He comments. I find it humorous that even in death he mocks me.

"You continue to lie. I would never have been strong enough to meld your book and you made sure of that."

"Nicolas, you are stronger than all of us. You are one of the Solomonari. You can do things I only dreamed of doing—"

I cut him off. "Don't. Do not justify what you've done to me." I feel the emotion well up in my throat. "You sent me *away*! You knew I would die. I wasn't strong enough."

His face holds only patience. "You needed guidance I could not give you; you are not like me or your brothers. It made you stronger; it made you who you needed to be. Who your people need you to be." He sounds so sure and I feel myself sinking into darkness. Why is everyone else so sure of who I should be? "Or you could just... stop."

I stare at him and blink away tears. "Stop?" My voice is almost a whisper. I wince and clutch my chest. *Ow. It hurts.* I touch my mouth and see my hand is bloody. "Are you doing this to me?!" I accuse.

"Yes and no. A past-self set this trap for you. But you could stop. Just let go. Give in. It'll all go black, no pain, no discomfort. Just that, the end." He watches my face and he takes a few steps towards me.

I think about it and I wince again, I notice everything around me is getting darker as if my path is already decided. "My chest hurts," I tell him.

"So give up. Do what you've wanted to do for years now. You don't have to keep fighting. There will be others who will fight." He shrugs, indifferent to my demise. That's how he's always been, indifferent.

"You always expected me to do that, you always knew I was weak. You couldn't believe that I lived through the training, you didn't want me to. You wanted to be rid of me!" I straighten as I stare at him and he shrugs once more.

"I expected you to be more grateful. I gave you a purpose, now I'm giving you a way out."

I shake my head and I feel anger welling up inside me. "It was not your life to decide for! It was mine! *Was!* It will never be the same now because of you, all of this is because of you!" I'm screaming at him, tears streaming down my face. "I'm not ready for this to be over, I have to fix this. I have to fix what you have broken, I have to save my people!"

"Then wake up, Nicolas!" He shouts back at me.

I jolt upright on the table and inhale sharply. Clutching my chest, I heave and gasp for air. I was dead. I was actually dead. I take in my surroundings and I see that I'm in an older style, castle type home. Everything is done in mahogany, black and deep red.

My eyes stop on a familiar face, his pale, angular features look horrified and relieved all at the same time. I take in his long black hair and sharp nose, his deep brown eyes, and his proper attire. I throw my arms around his neck and relish in his cool skin. "Stefan!"

Tonic did it, he brought me back. He kisses my cheek and I squeeze him as hard as I can and realize how weak I am. I feel like I weigh a thousand pounds and I almost slump back down but he wraps his arms around me.

"Easy now. It's hard to come back from purgatory. You've been gone for almost an hour." His voice is so smooth, almost song-like. It sounds so good to hear, I haven't seen him for what feels like a lifetime.

It's so good to see my friend, my oldest friend in name and in truth.

"Well, maybe you should thank your friend." He gestures to Tonic and I realize he really did save my life. I scrabble across the table to hug my naked companion and he wraps me in a warm hug. His skin feels amazing against my reanimated corpse but I notice that I am not lifeless and cold so I must have just been restored.

"How?" I ask, unwilling to let Tonic go even though I can feel he's uncomfortable, wanting to be free of my grasp. I hold him tighter and adjust myself to see Stefan.

"I sent your friend with the golden nose here to find a couple of herbs and, thankfully, it's a full moon so the moonlight flower was in bloom. That did the trick; else we would be trying to figure out if you would turn into a better werewolf or vampire." He smiles a fanged smile and I feel Tonic's skin crawl.

"You're not a 'vampire'... you're a Strigoi. There's a difference." He rolls his eyes at me and I smile and kiss Tonic's cheek. "I'd be honored to be either."

"Thank you Tonic... Thank you so much." I nuzzle into his neck, he pats my shoulder awkwardly and it brings a giggle from me because it feels natural. I realize that not everyone is having as good of a time as I am. The air is heavy and I frown. "What? Can't a man be happy that he came back from the dead? What's with this heaviness?"

Tonic sighs. "Alpha came into the room… he saw what happened. He knows."

I don't know how to feel about this. I glance around and see that we still possess the book. "Well, he needs to get the hell over himself. We did what we had to do." Stefan smiles but I notice that Tonic is not smiling.

"Nicolas, We thought you were dead. You went cold, your heart stopped. I got you here as fast as I could but your eyes were rolled back into your head and this book was stuck to you, sucking the life out of you. I don't think him seeing that has helped our cause; we were all a little freaked out. Stefan didn't know if he could save you, you used so much of your magic. There was very little left."

I come to realize that they're blaming me. They feel I've been reckless, that I made a mistake.

"Baby, you can't do that to yourself! You spread yourself too thin, you know how you get. You can't save everyone, if Tonic hadn't been there that would have been it. Lights out." Stefan's voice is calm but reprimanding.

The offense is heavy in my tone. I was the only one who could do this, without it, we wouldn't have the book. "I did what I had to do to get the book. I had to try; it could have the answers to the curse." I reach for it but Stefan slaps my hand, I can't help but marvel at the fact it's almost healed. I haven't regenerated yet, I'm still dangerously low, too weak for much other than casual conversation.

"Can I go to bed?" I demand. I don't want to be lectured.

They exchange nervous glances. "Alpha is outside." Tonic informs me.

"Of course he is…" It shouldn't surprise me but it does, bringing to me a tiny thrill that I dare not evaluate.

"I didn't know if you wanted to see him." Stefan looks guarded because he knows me but he is also very curious as to why the warlord looks so distraught. I know I'll have to explain that one tomorrow. The sun is almost up and it's time for Stefan to retire for the day.

"Let him in," I tell him weakly and a small spirit flashes to the door and opens it. His entrance is enough to take my breath away and furrow my brow all at the same time, the brilliance of his hair against the darkness of the room causing me to momentarily forget that I was waiting for the onslaught.

"Can I talk to Nicolas alone?" His voice is strained. With a sigh, Stefan leads Tonic off into the house. Alpha stares down at me, expectant, menacing.

"What?!" I demand in annoyance.

"Don't start Nicolas…" He sounds tired.

"Me?! You storm in here demanding explanations! Looking at me like you care! I did what I needed to do." I had to do it for nobody else could. It was what he asked me to do, what he'd kept me to do. "I did what you asked."

He scoffs and shakes his head, pinching the bridge of his nose. "You died." He sounds accusing.

The double standard wasn't fair. "You have almost died many times. I thought we had a deal that we weren't supposed to save lives." I retort bitterly. "Or is it just me that that doesn't apply to?"

"Did you just think you could hide the book from me? What if Tonic hadn't been there?" He turns the tables on me because he knows the other is a losing argument.

"I thought it was understood that this whole thing is one big, what if? You wanted the book; I had to find it so I did. If you had been there you would have triggered the guardian yourself with your brutish antics and then there would be no bringing you back. It had to be this way. I needed *Tonic*. You were incapacitated anyways! You were drunk off your ass, celebrating a ceremony that almost got that sweet boy killed!"

My words must cut him because he doesn't have a retort. I damn him, damn him for caring for me, damn him for rushing in here as if I might matter to him in some form. He had no right to me, no right to worry for my safety after all the pain he caused me.

Damn him.

He was too drunk to help me, he couldn't have done anything to save me and in the end, if it hadn't been for Tonic, I would have been dead. We're at a stalemate, I expect him to lash out but it would seem I've got him pinned.

I'm too tired to deal with these emotions, to deal with him and his complicated messages. In a rush of anger, I shove off the table yet my body threatens to drop to the ground in a heap. Moving quicker than I can blink, he catches me, my hands grip his biceps in surprise. I can only stare at his chest before glancing up at him, we both look conflicted.

Why do I have to chase people away?

I don't like the hovering, the scolding. I'm not a child. But I am currently acting like one. I deflate a little; if I'm going to continue with my plan I have to fix it. I have to keep telling myself that's why I don't turn him away.

"Verando. I had to do it. I couldn't allow you to be involved, and before you ask, I'm not giving you the book. But I'm still going to help you." With a heavy sigh, I close my eyes, pressing my forehead to his chest. "I also don't want you to go."

He flinches at my words. "Don't call me that. Not here."

Of course. One step forward, two steps back with us.

"I want you to stay," I say again.

Alpha battles with himself but he nods.

I stand up on my tiptoes and he bends to meet me. I kiss him, needing him. He takes my cheek in his hand to pull me against him and I deepen the kiss as I curl my arms around his neck. "I thought I lost you." He breathes against my lips.

My eyes flutter open, inhale his need for me as my lips hover over his. I realize he's supporting most of my weight and smile a little. "You're not getting rid of me that easily." My body forms to his, meshing to his hips, clinging to him in every way possible to close the gap between us.

I'm suddenly very aware that Tonic and Stefan are staring at us. Tonic immediately averts his eyes and flushes three different colors of red. Alpha kisses me once more before scooping me up into his arms.

"Is there a room he can sleep in?" He asks Stefan, his tone strained. Stefan looks curious about him now.

"Up the stairs, the third door on the right." He purrs.

Alpha rolls his eyes and takes me up the stairs, ignoring the other two.

"They saw." I sound shy, feigning innocence.

"I know." I can't read his expression.

I don't say anything as he sets me on the bed and climbs in behind me, putting his arms around me from behind. "Go to sleep. Some of us have work to do." He grumbles, his tone softer than before.

"Yes Sir," I respond playfully and cling to his arm. Thankfully sleep finds me quickly.

Seventeen-

I don't know what time it is when I wake up. I resist the urge to leap up when I wake in an unfamiliar room yet the smell of the woods, the warmth brings me back to the events of yesterday. I realize I'm in Stefan's house.

How many days did I hide out here in my youth?

He is one of my oldest friends in the realist sense. I glance carefully over my shoulder and see my warlord is still asleep. He must be worn out as he never was one to sleep in. I can't help but wonder how much sleep he got last night, summarizing that it couldn't have been much.

Slowly, I slip out from under his arm and stand up.

My whole body hurts, my hand is bandaged and I'm glad because I don't want to see it though I vaguely remember that it looked better than it did in the chamber. My stomach flips and I stop my thoughts as I go to the closet and raid it for clothes.

Finding a nice long sleeve, vest and some trousers, I pull them on, grateful for Stefan's fashion sense. For the first time in a long time, I didn't scramble into my shirt, assuring myself that no one noticed. Even in my lonesome, I couldn't bear to see myself but today I find I'm either too tired or too overwhelmed by my situation to care.

There is a lack of mirrors in here, maybe that's it.

I steal a glance at the sleeping man, he hasn't moved. His tangle of gray hair shields his eyes but he's too still. There is no chance he's awake, I wonder if I have ever seen him asleep and if I have, it's only been fleeting moments.

I resist the urge to go and touch him; I need to let him sleep because I know when he wakes up there will be more discussion about what happens to this book and what that means for all of us.

Sighing, I make my way downstairs and find that I feel so much more comfortable here than I do in my own home. I grew up here, I would ride from my home and in exchange for some blood from my horse I could remain as long as I liked. Stefan was always so intriguing, he had the best stories and he never treated me any differently for he was a prince as well. Or at least, at one point he had been.

I start when I see Tonic is already awake and he's wearing only a pair of pants though I see that he's a bit too tall for them. I smile, my savior crammed into pants like a boy who has outgrown his clothes. I walk up and sit silently next to him and find that he looks different. Relaxed, tired, and older.

"I wouldn't be here if it wasn't for you." I break the silence and cross my arms to rest my elbows on the table. He shrugs, his cheeks redden. "Tonic, I don't think I can ever thank you enough for what you did for me. For what you continue to do for me. I hate that I put you in danger but I wouldn't have wanted anyone else there beside me. You truly are one of my closest friends."

"I was just doing what was right Nicolas, it wasn't anything special." He has always been the most humble.

"It was for me," I tell him firmly but gently. It was my life. Something that my own family didn't even care about. I wonder if anyone has really, truly, saved my life with nothing to gain. I can only think of Tonic.

He offers me a shy smile and I smile back, unfolding myself to hug him. "How did you sleep?" I ask him, how often does one get to have an idle conversation in this world?

Tonic flushes deep to his core and immediately looks down. "I um. Fine. Fine. I slept fine. Better than—well not the best but fine. Just fine." His stammering takes me off guard, which is strange even for Tonic. I blink a few times and straighten.

"So it's fine then?" I question with a small laugh. He nods almost too quickly and I feel the urge to pry. "Where did you sleep?" I gestured around the house, it wasn't down here.

There is no evidence that anyone has been down here. He shrugs and glances at the stairs; flushes again only to look down once more. He almost seems to shrink before me and I frown. I don't like this; I want my happy confident Tonic back. Then it begins to dawn on me all at once. "Or... Who did you sleep... **with**?" I test the words and he freezes like a statue. I gasp; he panics and looks away.

"Tonic!" I breathe. But then I feel like a mother bear protecting her cub, **Stefan**! My blood boils, *playing with a young boy's heart!* "Tonic, I'm sorry Stefan is very... he could have charmed you or seduced you. You don't have to be ashamed."

He pauses and glances at me and straightens a little. "I um... He didn't seduce me. Not really that is. He invited me up for some clothes, I just—" He stops and I wait patiently. "I've never felt like I belonged. I always felt like something was wrong with me, like I was defective. I've never *liked* girls, I mean—there are girls who I think are beautiful and who I've liked but nothing like this. When I saw you... um... Kissing... Alpha I just... It clicked for me."

He works his way carefully through his words and I drink them in. *Oh, Tonic.* "How I've always felt, why I've always been so shy around men, it made sense. So I just asked Stefan if I could try it, I have never kissed anyone before."

I gape at him. "Not even as a lad?"

He shrugs.

"The omega is denied comforts of the flesh and as I said, I probably could have but it just wasn't clicking for me. I just couldn't love a woman that way; I couldn't see myself with anyone and I figured it was because I hadn't seen the right one but I realized yesterday that it was because I was looking at the wrong people."

I frown, it's something I thankfully didn't have much trouble in. I knew when I was very young exactly what caught my fancy and that was never something I had been ashamed of. My mother had been very accepting of my choices, as was my sister. Now finding someone to *love* was a different story that I didn't even want to touch the edge of.

My self-loathing had nothing to do with my sexuality. "Tonic, that's wonderful. I just wish you had done it with someone who was less... promiscuous. Don't get me wrong, Stefan is one of my dearest friends but he definitely has never been denied any comforts. I just don't want you to fall for someone who isn't going to reciprocate those feelings."

Tonic's chuckle surprises me. I really didn't even know Tonic could laugh but I instantly love it and it makes me laugh too. "Nicolas, I'm not falling in love with him. I just found a part of myself that had felt unobtainable, I want to explore it. I'm not stupid."

It makes me smile, I knew Tonic had sense.

"So. How long has this been going on between you and Alpha?" He turns the tables on me. I blink a few times and clear my throat. What? The mind-blowing sex and going from hating each other to throwing ourselves at each other from one minute to the next? I shrug and hop up to go make some tea. "Hey, I told you mine, now it's your turn." He prods and I sigh. I liked the quiet Tonic better.

"Since it, all began. That first day. Well. We just kissed at first." I tell him. Let him soak that in. I pour water in the iron kettle and set it on the stove. I set the little burner ablaze and lean back against the counter.

Tonic looks surprised.

"I never would have thought of Verando in that way. He just doesn't seem, I don't know—The type?" He sounds confused and I frown at him.

"What's the type? You can't help what you like Tonic. I didn't bewitch him. He came on to me." I sigh and run my fingers through my hair. I remind myself that I probably need a haircut soon. "Look at Victor, he blows 'type' right out of the water," I grumble and glance at my pot, willing it to be ready now. This was not the conversation I wanted to have this morning.

"Do you like it?" He asks bluntly. I blink.

"What? Sex?" I ask, raising a brow and almost laughing. "Um. Yes. Sex is great. Did you not like it?"

"I did. I'm just curious, I don't have anyone I can ask this stuff with so I—I hope that's okay." He looks shy and I offer him a small smile.

"Ask away."

"What's it like?" He boldly questions like a teen hungry for knowledge. I wrap my arms around myself, uncomfortable with delving into my own thoughts.

"Overwhelming. Degrading. Amazing. Mind-blowing." I sigh. I think of his mouth on me and inhale sharply before pouring myself some water; then taking a teabag and dip it in the cup.

"Wow." He mumbles like maybe it was too much information. I shrug once more, I knew that Tonic and I had gotten close but I was unwilling to entertain this as anything other than surprise.

"Yeah. It isn't like that for everyone though. It's a preference. It's what I like." I don't want him to feel like he has to have the same screwed up kinks I have.

Tonic looks surprised. "You want to feel that way?" He raises a brow "I get the last bits but you want to feel degraded? You picked the right person..."

I grimace. No. That's not it.

"I *need* to feel that way. It's not something I can help. It makes me feel alive, to lose yourself to someone and trust them. I've faced a lot of pain, hurt, and regret in my life. Being able to control it, to thrive on it, it's the only way to stay alive for me. There's some other head trash that goes along with it but I like it. It's like positions or methods, everyone likes something different. I just like to be dominated."

I feel my cheeks flush. I've never said this out loud before, told anyone this. Honestly, it's a realization to me even. The fact that I crave it, that I secretly like to defy and face the consequences.

"I wouldn't know, I've got limited experience. To each their own, I suppose." Tonic shrugs and I smirk.

"Don't knock it till you try it." I challenge him. He looks almost afraid for a moment but he comes back with new confidence. I take a sip of my tea and glance up to see that Stefan is in the stairway and I almost spit out my drink again but I force myself to swallow it and look away. Oh lovely.

"Having such a wonderful conversation without me?" He purrs and floats soundlessly over to sit at the counter with us. Tonic flushes as Stefan kisses his cheek. It warms my heart just a little but I'm going to have to have a conversation with Stefan later about this.

"Oh you know, just talking about dicks and what to do with them. Nothing out of the ordinary." I tell him which causes Tonic to practically evaporate from embarrassment. *That's what you get, rookie.*

"Tonic knows exactly what to do with mine. I trained him well." He smiles and Tonic gets up.

"I'm going to go see if I can catch more sleep. Glad you're alright, Nicolas." He departs quickly and Stefan watches him like a love-drunk school girl as he goes.

"Okay. When you get hot friends and don't tell me, I start to think you're mad at me. What the hell? These creatures are gorgeous." Stefan instantly pries at me with his eyes and it brings a frown.

"They aren't really accepting of what you are. Well. Tonic is but not Alpha." I gesture up the stairs to where the warlord still slumbers.

"Mmmm... save that one for yourself. I don't blame you. But come on, well-endowed men who walk around naked and take care of themselves? Sign me up." He reclines back onto the counter, dipping his head back to look at me with a look of restraint. I roll my eyes.

"Yeah, give that a go. He'll bite you in half." I pull my shirt down at the collar to expose my bite mark scar. Stefan chews his lower lip and waggles his eyebrows at me. "It's not what you think." But I'm smiling and he can see through me.

"Please enlighten me then." He purrs.

"It's just sex," I tell him. I take a drink of my drink and glance at him out of the corner of my eye.

"Overwhelming. Degrading. Mind-blowing was it?" I don't flush, I just stare at him and he grins at me so wickedly that I almost giggle.

"All of that but just sex," I reassure him.

"'Just sex' looked pretty worried about you." He points out. That makes me frown because I know that's true but I can't allow myself to go there.

"He needs me if he wants to win this war."

Stefan straightens and gasps. "*That* is who killed your parents. I was so wrapped up last night I didn't think about when Tonic called him Alpha. Nicolas!" I frown a little deeper and glance at my drink. "Bad boy." His purr returns and I groan and walk away from him to go sit on one of the couches.

"Stefan, I really don't need a lecture. It's complicated."

"I'll say. Complicated is pretty damn good looking though. A little busted up for my tastes but I know you have your issues with your own appearance." He frowns and plucks at my shirt as he floats over me on his side as if he was laying on the ground, propped up on his elbow. I swat at his hand.

"He's more than that. He can be good, he loves his people. He is totally dedicated. Something that some of us know little about." I roll my eyes and Stefan pretends to look hurt. He vanishes then reappears in the chair across from me.

"Now you're defending him. Interesting." He ignores my comment and I stick my tongue out at him, casting a pillow at him which he easily catches. "Well, who am I to judge? You know what I've done, who I've done. Just protect yourself, baby. You know how I worry about you. I'd hate to have to find out what Lycan tastes like. Oh, wait. I already have. It's pretty damn good." He reclines back onto the couch and it fires me up to remind him about Tonic.

"Hey, he was a virgin you asshole. If you hurt him, I swear Stefan, I'll burn you at the stake. He's a good guy. Too good for any of us really." Stefan holds up his hands in innocence.

"I'm just coasting, baby. I'm not trying to find love. It was his idea."

Much as Stefan's promiscuous nature irritates me, I can see Tonic's point of view. I don't have anyone to gush with and talk about this sort of stuff to either. Almost as if on cue, Verando makes his way downstairs and pauses when he sees Stefan. He doesn't hide his scowl very well as he stretches and makes his way into the room. I wish I could be so comfortable with my body.

"Sleep well?" I ask, hoping to avoid yet another lecture.

"Surprisingly. Tell your little spirit to leave me alone, by the way." He glares toward Stefan who looks confused, tilting his head.

"Pavel?" He questions.

"I don't know what its name is... it came up there asking me questions about—" He stops himself and sighs. "It doesn't matter; just tell it to fuck off." I blink and stare at him; Stefan raises a brow and gives me a look as if I could do better than a foul-tempered dictator.

"Sorry, didn't realize that he was in there with you. I'll tell him to mind his own business, perhaps." Always the gracious host. I give Stefan an apologetic look and stand up.

"Are you leaving?" I ask because he hasn't sat down yet.

"Yes, I've been gone for too long and Victor isn't experienced enough to start rotations. It'd be different if we weren't venturing closer to Ziduri today but we have seen elf tracks so we need to get ahead of this." I frown and he takes my chin in his hand.

"I'm glad you're okay. We aren't done discussing this, not by a long shot. But for now, I do need to go. Try and stay out of trouble until I see you again, the list is ever-growing and I am pretty old. It's hard to keep track."

I'm caught off guard by his playful demeanor. I throw my arms around his neck and kiss him.

He kisses me back and smiles against my lips. "Get some rest." He commands me and I nod, we both know that's not going to happen. He says nothing to Stefan as he quickly departs. By the time he clears the front yard, the giant gray wolf takes his place and he's in a full sprint back to his people. I'm only now aware of my heart pounding in my chest.

Stefan is very close to me, watching my face.

"Just sex, huh?" He pries. I swat at him and step away.

"Do I have any healers' robes left here? I need to go see Haryek."

CHAPTER

Eighteen-

I decide to leave Tonic with his newfound friend. It isn't often that Stefan makes a new friend and honestly, I didn't need Tonic more involved in my plans than he already was. I needed to speak with Haryek about the plan and gauge his reaction on my own without worrying about being revealed to Alpha.

Besides, I don't know how many more questions about my relationship with Alpha I could take.

I ponder this as I walk. I think about his concern, leaving his people with little notice to come and check on me. The fact that he stayed in the home of a Strigoi was mind-boggling to me, the two were natural enemies since the great wars of vampires and werewolves, even if a Strigoi was only a subgenre.

I know better than to deceive myself with romantic thoughts that this brute might actually care for me, but it does feel good to ponder. People didn't often care much for me, I found that I was often lacking in what made people likable. My mother had put it that I marched to my own rhythm, I had never fit into the pieces that made for polite society.

My piece was bent, broken, and misshapen. It was easier to toss it to the side than attempt to make it fit with the other rounded corners,

I was pointy and hard-edged. People found me difficult in that I had a peculiar habit of speaking whatever was on my mind, despite the reaction it might bring. It would seem it took a dictator to find someone I had things in common with.

With some extra pep in my step, I make my way through my familiar city towards the outskirts where the rebellion lay hidden, passing the haunting carcass of a destroyed building. Yet, it looked burned, not looted as many of the lycan claimed buildings

For a brief moment, I wonder if he's safe, concerned over that stark coat color, and his lack of ability to hide. I know that none of us are safe in these times. I remind myself that it would be wise to gather a dragon for my own protection, that there are far more foes than those that surround my castle. In fact, among them, I feel the safest I'd felt in many years. Much as I like to forget, my father had his enemies.

I arrive at the rebellion quicker than I remember, figuring I must be becoming fit within my time with the lycans. All I do is carry water and walk, it would make sense. Much to my chagrin, Haryek is the first to meet me.

Unfortunately, he has not forgotten about my last visit as he stands too close, hungry. Haryek is my opposite, the monster others saw me as. I did sexual favors as a means of survival, Haryek did them as a way of control. "Haryek." I greet them coolly.

He smiles at me, a beaming white beacon of perfection reflected back. He swoops in to hug me but I offer my hand instead. "I'd like to update you on our current situation, alone if we may." I don't need anyone hearing me confront him, his type never went quietly. I want to confront him about our last meeting, he seems too keen for me to avoid the topic.

"Eager are we? Well, can we adjourn to my cabin if that suits you?" He offers and gives me an inviting gesture to his residence. I frown and take a step back, rolling my shoulders back as I access my breeding and status. It begins to dawn on me that the reason I reached the rebellion quicker, today, is that it had grown. They had taken hold of more homes.

"How about a walk?" I suggest, my tone short.

"Of course." He offers me his arm and I reject it, though he's quick to attempt to snatch it anyways. "Don't be a tease, Nicolas, dear." His voice is tight beneath his teeth, raising the hair on the back of my neck as his arm snakes around my waist, fingers twisting painfully into my hip. Suddenly I feel as though this walk is no longer voluntary.

We make our way towards the gardens and the smell would be intoxicating if my anger wasn't in full swing. There must be an earth mage among those here. He plucks a rose and offers it over; I take it with a look that says I'm not amused as I force myself out of his grasp. "Really? Do I look like someone who likes hearts and roses?"

I smell it casually, playing with fire. He could be so alluring, he could so easily suck me back in with a smooth smile and his over-confidence. Maybe a part of me does like it? To be doted on and courted is so novel, something I've only really heard about and never experienced myself.

As easily as it crosses my mind, I toss the rose over my shoulder. Too bad for him, I'm not an idiot. I just make poor choices.

"So what news do you bring?" He questions, annoyed with my dismissal.

"I've found my father's spellbook."

The elf freezes and stares at me as if I've grown a second head. "My god. Well, where is it? Is the lycan leader dead?" The wicked undertones appear like horns on a devil, the mask slips and the beast underneath is revealed. Haryek wants way more than my alliance.

"Safe." I tell him shortly.

"Safe?" He repeats back, frustrated.

"Yes. We can't use it because it's too powerful. A lot of people had to die to make that book, Haryek, I don't think its purpose is to save people. It's best to find some other way." I dare not reveal my near death, I don't want to give him any more ammunition against me.

He doesn't seem to understand my logic, "We had a deal, Nicolas. You would use the book to help us win the war. We were going to do this together."

My throat feels dry yet I hold my ground. I was not scared of a monster, though there would be little I could do to defend myself in my condition. "I have to think about everyone involved. These negotiations didn't involve the book turning out to hold a curse. Besides, there are more pressing matters on the terms of your involvement." I turn to face him and put on my own politician's face. "We must side with the lycans if we want to win this, you must give back all the lands and homes you've taken from my people."

Haryek laughs, out loud, at me only to frown when he spies that I'm serious. "This is not the same conversation we have had so you'll understand my shock and honestly, horror at the thought? These are not humans, or elves, or magical beings Nicolas. These are wild beasts. We cannot trust them, how can we fight alongside them?"

"They aren't beasts Haryek—"

He's quick to interrupt, his eyes wild with his bewilderment. "They're what, Nicolas? Just the murderers of your family!"

There would be no room to yield, I couldn't give an ounce. "I think I have a connection with their leader, I think if I play my cards right I can get him on our side which means we stand a chance at making it to Ziduri without massive casualties."

Haryek runs his hand through his hair, carefully adjusting the carefully carved hair crown. He isn't pleased with my decision making, his face contorted with disgust. "A connection? Is that what this is? What, do you plan to seduce him? Suck his dick and then we'll all be one big alliance?" He snaps at me.

I gape at him, "That might be how you do things but that certainly is not what my intentions are!" I snap. He's too close to how right he is; only I go a step further and frequently bed this man.

"Please, I see through you. You and I are very similar; we fuck to get what we want. You were too easy to convince to join my bed. That wasn't the first time you had done that and it certainly wasn't the last. You're an experienced whore alright." The steps warn me to retreat as the gaze of a different kind of predator bears down on me. My body rings alarm bells.

"How dare you! You took advantage of me! You came on to me!" I remind him, spinning it, any way to reflect the way he looks at me now.

I can smell the heavy dose of cologne covering his white silks. "Ha! Took advantage!" He laughs at me, amused. "You practically begged for it." Closing the distance, his hand grips my jaw. Swiftly, I move to slap him but he grasps my hand. His body is on mine and he shoves me against one of the stone pillars. Petals rain down all around us from the overhead tree, shedding its colored leaves.

Those white teeth near my ear, full lips close enough to feel their smoothness on my skin. I wrench against him, trying to twist again, pleading with my magic to do anything to protect me. "Now listen here. I'm sick of this little game. I thought you were my equal and you still could be if you stop with these ideas that these beasts can be reasoned with. A relationship between us could be good for our kingdoms but..." His tongue pops, his hand slips to tighten on my throat. "I don't know if I want that if you're going to be so accusing every time we fuck." He drags his thumb over my lip and I jerk my head away, glaring at him.

"Trust me, it will just be the one time. I think we are done here." I shove his chest but he bears down on me and I feel like I'm suffocating. "Let go of me Haryek." I search for his groin with my knee yet in the heavy robes he dons over his suit, it's difficult to find such a minor piece of anatomy.

"No, I don't think we are. I think I deserve an appropriate apology for your horrid accusations. So why don't you turn around and show me a little gratitude for giving you a kingdom when I take over this hell hole and turn it into something useful? Lest you want me to reduce this place to a pile of rubble the moment I get the opportunity." The bitterness rings through his voice, threatening me just as Alpha did. Shaking my head, I fight to dislodge him, I fight to get away. It doesn't occur to me to scream, nobody answered my screams before.

Temporarily, I'm halted as I feel his hand firmly strike my face. "This is going to happen with or without your consent so I suggest you decide right now which it will be. One will be much quicker than the other. There is still a chance for us, darling, to be together as the power couple. You'll see in time that this is what needs to happen. That it will happen."

I will my magic to return, pushing towards my fingertips as I feel my world threaten to go dark at the attempt. I'm defenseless, at his mercy. I'm not strong, I have no claws or fangs, my body is too depleted to fight back.

"Do your worst." I spit at him.

He smirks and presses his lips against mine. He invades my mouth so suddenly with his tongue that I practically gag on the taste of the coffee from his breakfast. What I know to do is to retreat back inside myself. *This will be over soon, just find your happy place.*

I think about my mother teaching me to braid my sister's hair. I think about my first spell, how proud I was. Of long nights awake with Stefan; I think of Alpha, telling me that his friends call him Randy. I could almost giggle. Suddenly the weight is lifted and I slide to the ground, my ears are ringing as life rushes back into me.

I inhale a few desperate breaths. My vision is blurred as I blink a few times, trying to figure out when my impending rape will happen. Is this part of his game? But nothing happens. *"Nicolas."* I hear a voice and blink once more. I hear it again and my eyes start to focus. It's Adriam who's before me.

"If you ever touch him again…" The threat lay heavy in the air.

"Who's yelling?" I rasp. My eyes focus in and out but I can make out the shape of a man. A tall, large man. He has Haryek by the throat, the elf dangles in the air.

"Who do you think?" Adriam responds disapprovingly, "Are you alright?"

I nod but my throat is sore and I wince as I reach up to touch it. When did it become common practice to clutch one by the throat?

"I think there has been a misunderstanding." Haryek garbles as his windpipe is slowly crushed.

"I saw you, bloody knife ear!" He throws Haryek to the ground, the elf cries out at the impact as the lycan is quick to follow his rolling body. A sharp kick is delivered to the elf's ribs, flipping him. Haryek coughs and sputters, clutching his ribs as blood seeps from his perfect lips.

It's almost beautiful the way the red contrasts against his pale skin.

"Please stop." I try but it's hardly loud enough. "Stop him. Stop him!" It's Alpha who I want to stop. Alpha is the one causing a scene, Alpha is the one drawing the crowd.

"Honey, there's not much that could stop him." Adriam murmurs, defeated.

I can see him fighting with himself; Alpha is no longer a man. He's a wolf fighting to get out, pure animalistic rage. He cries out in agony and drops to his knees, clutching his body. The wolf rips through him and his clothes lay in an explosion around him as the gray beast stands where there used to be a man.

The wolf bares his fangs, he roars as he takes shaky steps forward but I watch his pupils enlarge. This is what it looks like when they lose control. This was what everyone had warned me about it, the hair-trigger could not be stopped.

I stare at this beast and I expected to feel the same pain I felt when he ripped my father to pieces but that feeling is gone. The pain remains, the loss, and the grief but I no longer feel violently ill. He looks magnificent, his coat has begun to change to a lighter gray and his startling eyes are locked onto his prey. *What a creation.*

I marvel at him until I realize he is going to kill Haryek. He approaches more confidently now, I can see the intent because I've seen it before. Before I know what I'm doing I leap to my feet and run. He retracts, poised to protect himself from me and I stand in front of Haryek.

"Stop!" I tell him firmly. "You've done enough; you have made your point."

The wolf bares his fangs and barks at me. His ears are flat back against his skull, lips curled back so that I can see every exposed fang.

This is not Verando before me, the charming man from this morning was buried deep beneath the consciousness of the wolf.

"There is no reason for you to kill this man. I'm-I'm okay." I soften my voice, using the only power I have over him and that's this strange desire to keep me alive. He snarls at me and snaps his jaws, moving to step around me but I hold out my hands to cut him off. "If you kill him, it will ruin everything. You must stop."

Slowly he starts to relax, I see him starting to contemplate his thoughts. The rage and hatred are leaving his eyes, I take a deep breath and reach out to touch him. He stiffens and his ears become erect, I can feel his hot breath and the warmth radiating off of him. Alpha watches my hand, his whole body tense, and his muzzle tight as the breeze teases the long tresses of his plush coat.

I'm inches away from him when suddenly I'm pulled backward. His jaws snapped shut where my hand had just been seconds before. "Get away from that creature!" Haryek yells at me, pulling me against his side.

Rebels. Locals. Wolves. We're surrounded by a captive audience that can only see the savage beast trying to remove their prince's hand from his body.

"He wouldn't hurt me!" I yell at him, fighting out of his grasp.

Any ground I had gained is lost, the beast lowers himself to spring, to remove Haryek from my side.

"Victor!" I nearly scream and the white wolf has read my mind as he grabs Alpha by his scruff, using every ounce of his brute force to drag him away.

I shove Haryek, my eyes burn with my mounting frustration. "What is wrong with you?! You attacked me first! He was protecting me."

"I was saving you! You could have lost your hand!" He responds, loud, announcing to the world that Alpha was the culprit, not the esteemed elf. I feel tears welling in my eyes; nobody saw what Haryek had done. They had only seen the attack that Alpha responded with.

My body begins to shake, if it was my last act, Haryek would never get the best of me again. "If this is your idea of forming alliances, you are sadly mistaken." The venom drips off my tone, as real of a threat as I can promise.

I retreat to Adriam who puts his arm around me, a growl rumbling in his throat as he glowers at Haryek. We mount Swift and Fleet, retreating to the safety of my castle.

CHAPTER

Nineteen-

Self-reflection isn't something that I'm good at. It isn't often that my poor decisions come back to haunt me in such a real way, I must admit to myself that I'm out of my element. At the time, sleeping with Haryek had seemed like the best way to bond us together but now my lines feel more crossed than ever.

I underestimated the elf, a fatal flaw. My lack of anticipation had cost us not only the support of the community but had soiled my relationship with the pack. Much to my surprise, my angle towards my unwelcome house guests seemed higher on my priority list. More and more I was drifting away from the rebellion, towards the group that wished to conquer the planet.

Maybe I'd gone mad, perhaps this was my problem and I was truly a traitor to my nation. But, when my eyes glanced over to see the small group walking together back to my home, I knew exactly what had begun to draw my loyalty.

I wanted so badly to belong to something, anything. Knowing that these beasts had come for me, come to my aid, had struck a chord in me that had been left untapped.

Much as my mother had loved me, even she had turned me over to my father's command when the decision was made to send me to school. No one had ever come for me, no one had ever wondered where I was or how long I'd been gone. I might be their captive but they had prevented something that I, myself, had accepted as fact.

At least in my own twisted logic, I was indebted to do something of a kindness for them.

"Is he okay?" I ask.

Adriam shoots me a hard look. "Would you be?" He snaps, his harshness surprising me after my own self-reflection. Did he not see my gratitude?

"I don't—"

Adriam holds up his hand and cuts me off. "You really need to figure this shit out, Nicolas. Because this is getting old. Sneaking around, talking to Haryek and then we find you tangled up together? Were you going to sleep with him?"

Quickly I shake my head. I had fought for myself, one of the few times I'd done it but I'd tried. I truly had tried. "No! He was forcing himself on me!"

"And why the fuck do you think he would do that?" Adriam almost yells but he stops and closes his golden eyes for a moment as he attempts to collect his thoughts. When he opens them, he's calmer.

"I'm not saying rape is something that is acceptable but Haryek probably wouldn't have tried to get in your pants if he hadn't already been there once before. This bullshit where you fuck anything that moves ends today.

"We have mere months to get this shit done before winter sets in and life gets a hell of a lot harder. I want to go home, Nicolas. We all want to go home. This is not a game; this is real fucking life with real fucking people! My people! My family!" Now it's Adriam's turn to cry, his tears spill over and he chokes back a sob.

As the silence overtakes us, as I refuse to respond due to my own hurt, the real reason for his pain becomes obvious. With a shaky breath, he shakes his head. "He's not Alpha to me. He's Randy. I've raised him. I've held him, watched over him, cared for him, and guided him. I love him, Nicolas. Don't fuck with someone that I love."

We ride back in silence. There's nothing I can respond to that with. I don't love Alpha, not as Adriam does and the thought that I'd intentionally hurt someone makes me sick. Adriam's accusations are cutting, it isn't often someone sees me for who I truly am. This side of myself had never been public, much as many often suspected.

When we get back to the castle, I see that Alpha is still front and center. He hasn't shifted back. He's stuck.

"We cannot get shift back to human. Wolf is too strong. I have tried reason but holding on." Victor tells us and I hop off Fleet and try to go to him but Adriam grabs my arm.

"Don't you think that you have done enough?" He snaps. He's still hurt. Victor looks questioning.

My fear for Alpha is minimal, he needs me, I'm the only one here who can break the curse. "Then let him kill me. I did this to him." I yank my arm away and go to him.

Like a wild animal, two wolves hold onto the thrashing beast as he fights to get free. Savage, wild, in pain, the creature is beyond what the two can handle and I know that releasing him could easily be my death. Much as I don't understand it, something in the gray creature wanted to protect me.

"Let him go." I tell them, earning a startled look. As the wolf settles, they obediently release him and step away. I'm face to face with the creature who killed my family, the wolf who wanted nothing more than to avenge his fallen race. "Here's your opportunity." I challenge him, holding out my arms. "I'm right here."

But, he doesn't move. Much as his fangs are bared, his muscles taut, his ears flattened against his skull, he regards me with an amount of uncertainty. It would appear my second assumption was more so the correct one. Finally, I exhale down, lowering my hands. "I'm okay." I told him.

Adriam's words resonate with me. Alpha is acting out of protection for his human counterpart, doing what the human side of him isn't capable of. Eliminating the pain in his life and that pain, unfortunately, is me. "I'm done. I'm not going to run off anymore, it's okay. I know I've been hurting you and I don't mean to. But it's done now. No more games." I speak slowly and hold up my hands to show him I'm not a threat. I might be the only thing who isn't a threat to this creature.

He regards me and snaps his jaws at my hand, threatening me to back away.

"You protected me." I reassure him, a dry attempt at humor for it sounds so foreign on my tongue. He starts to relax and deliberately, I reach my hand out to touch his neck. Alpha tenses once more, his ears suddenly erect. I can feel it, he's about to rip my throat out as the wide blue eye settles on my face. But I push through and I press my hand into his hair to touch his skin. He's so soft, like velvet under my fingers. He watches me just as I watch him, breathing in unison, feeling his heart beating so strongly under my fingertips.

"Let go." I exhale, for both of us. We both need to let go.

Alpha lowers his head and brings it around to look at me; I try not to show my nerves. Cautiously, I reach out to touch him as I rest my hand on his forehead to brush up towards his ears. The silky, dense texture tangles in my fingertips. My heart pounds for this creature, as if he were meant to be mine, as if he were for me, alone, to appreciate. It's an unfamiliar amount of comfort that disturbs me.

Once more, we breathe in unison, a collective sigh.

Suddenly he steps back from me; his pupils shrink back down. His body contorts and the human side returns to us. Alpha is on his hands and knees, gasping for air. His body trembles with fatigue. Every available pack member rushes to his aid, surrounding him and pushing me out of the circle. I'm vaguely aware that he's lost consciousness as they carry him off and I vaguely hope they put him back in my room for I don't wish to search for him later.

Adriam puts his hand on my shoulder, he says nothing but I know he's grateful.

I don't want his gratitude. I just want to understand what emotion I'd felt, what had drawn me to this wolf so strongly in that one moment of contact.

Gena slips past the group to meet me, two horses burgled from the stables walking alongside her. With their leader incapacitated they wouldn't notice the absence. It wasn't often anyone cared what I was doing, nor did they notice. "My Lord. Please..." She hands me the reins and I climb into the saddle without thinking.

We ride down the street, and she veers me off the beaten path down a more hand carved trail. We raced through the woods, my civilian clothes blended into the scenery much more naturally than my robes would. I found that, today, I didn't even wish to wear them. I felt foreign in my own body, as if I didn't even know who I was anymore.

Finally, after what feels like an eternity, I begin to recognize the path and yank on the reins to bring my bewildered steed to a stuttering halt. "What on earth are you doing?" I demand of her, reining in the prancing animal.

Gena's expression is pained, she blinks back the emotion as she wheels her animal around to face me. "Prince Nicolas, I am begging you on behalf of your subjects. You must retreat while we have a moment's time. You will surely perish if you remain here, My Lord. Please, I've spoken with the staff and we all feel it is a worthy sacrifice if it would mean that your life be spared."

Clutching my horse's reins, she directs it back down the path but I jerk them back out of her hands. "And leave you all to die? Do you find me that cold?"

Shaking her head rapidly, she rubs her eyes with the back of her hand. "My Lord..." Blinking it away, she finally looks at me. "I saw you in the kitchen, where he forced himself upon you and he spoke of you sharing Prince Haryek's bed. It's no place for a prince to be taken as if he were a common street wench, for your dignity, Nicolas, we are begging you to go."

My dignity. The castle echoed quite a bit and I wasn't used to volume control, they must have heard my dealings with Alpha and wondered if they were involuntary. Why wouldn't they? While I didn't hide it, it wasn't necessarily common knowledge. Be it my own people to turn against my preferences where Lycans so openly accept what I am. Hurrying her breathing, she watches me, wide eyed. "You must cast away this sin and step back into grace. We cannot damn you to suffer such a fate for the sake of our lives. This is the path to market, merely two towns over. On the horse, it would be difficult to follow you."

For a mere moment, I considered it.

She was right, it would be hard to track me even with their noses. I was dressed as a civilian, I was covered in the scent of multiple different lycans. Nobody might even know who I was should I not tell them, I could just be a boy, find my aunt and live with her until this all blew over. They would move on, burning my city to the ground but I would survive to rebuild.

Clutching the reins so tightly, my fists threatened to turn white from the weight of my grasp. I had run from so much in my life, I had skirted by and trialed and begged for my life, it only made sense that the universe would finally offer me a hand to ease my distress. "What Prince would I be if I left you to such a fate?"

Gena's eyes shut, she bows her head, knowing my answer. Her palm holds the sack of gold coins as she holds it out to me. "Please, My Lord." She begs once more. I take the coins from her, retrieving a few before placing the bag back in her hand. Her fingers dare not close.

"You've done well for me. It's time for you to go." Sharp, her eyes flick to meet mine. "That's enough to get you started, more than enough. You've served my family your entire life, you must go. My work here is nowhere near done but I can't continue to tangle you up in it. Thank you Gena, for all you've done for me." Carefully, I close her fingers around the sack and push it to her breast.

"Nicolas, I can't accept this." Quickly she attempts to hand it back but I drop my hand.

"You will, I command you to. As your future king, you might actually have to listen to me someday." I attempt humor as her eyes film over. Directing my horse, I guide it to stand beside hers. "I'm sorry that I couldn't be more for you, I know that you've always hoped..." Hoped what? That I'd enjoy her company? She was a common servant, I couldn't even if I did find women appealing but at times, it would seem that the young servants often hoped to be laden with a royal child.

It was a lavish life, purchased to raise the bastard in solitude, they would live comfortably under the protection of the crown in exchange for silence. Lone heirs might even inherit power. While it seemed callous to think that of her, I knew too well not to expect any less from those surrounding my father's court. "I'm just glad that we were friends. I... your mother told me a long time ago that you weren't quite a fan of the ladies."

I can only shrug. I wasn't a fan of anyone if it didn't benefit me, it suited that she never fell into my trap. "Be safe, Gena." I bid her goodbye as she rides the path that I could have taken. Rolling the saved coins absently in my palm, I slip them into my pocket and turn my steed to ride back into the city. If I allowed myself to think on it too strongly, there would be nothing to stop me from riding after her.

There was no convincing myself that there was a life there, I don't even entertain it with the picture of me hiding at my aunt's. My place was here, atoning for all my family had done to wrong a culture of people and a society built around that wrong.

The cobblestones clack loudly against the horse's shod hooves as I hop down and quickly stride to the shabby building where our measly police force resided. Knocking firmly on the door, they all leap to their feet, feigning attention as they struggle to come out of their sleepy stupor.

"Gentlemen." I greet.

"Prince Nicolas." The leader bows. "To what do I owe the honor? Good to see that you're in fine health after this morning's events."

The fear in his eyes is clear, he's terrified I'm going to ask him to go after Alpha and remove the lycans from the city. Was my father truly that unreasonable? Pursing my lips, I collect myself into my perfectly formed 'prince' carriage. "Were you aware that Prince Haryek resided in the outskirts of the city with a rebellion force?"

Exchanging glances, they reluctantly nod. "He told us he was acting under your account. He's a royal, My Lord, there wasn't much—" My narrowed eyes stop him in his tracks and he tightens his jaw. It confirms my suspicions, yes, my father was as brutal and ruthless as I had been told.

"Please see to it that Prince Haryek is served with papers that demand his immediate removal of any and all patrons living in Dezna homes that were previously occupied. They may harvest wood and build their own structures, they may use abandoned homes, but they must return to our people the ones they have taken for rebellion use. If any rebels are caught creating a disturbance in our borders, please detain them and bring them directly to me."

Once more, the eyes switch back and forth between each other. "Would that mean the castle?"

"Of course." My sharp tone causes a flinch and I set it back a notch. "Bring them to me in the castle. Put up notices. Rebellion forces are to be monitored but we will not tolerate any destruction of Dezna land. That is an act of treason. Understand?"

He nods quickly and I dismiss them, marching out to climb back onto my animal before I can lose my confidence and take it back. Haryek would not be happy but I wanted him to be uncomfortable.

It was time to start making counter moves.

CHAPTER

Twenty-

Arriving back, I smell of horses and the woods and find it more comforting than any of the stale scents pushed upon me by my home. Never before had I given so much consideration to my own scent and yet now, I found it calming.

I force myself to go and have dinner, much as I'm not hungry, I'm pleased to see I'm alone in the dining hall as I cross to the kitchen only to find my staff shocked to see me. They blame themselves for my appearance, rough as it might look, I'm not much in the mood to deal with their concern.

"Oh yes, I promise I'm fine. This is all actually from negotiating with the other side!" I try to show some humor but they are horrified. I realize I've been dealing with brutes for far too long, I'm not good for polite company any longer. I clear my throat. "Can I scavenge some dinner?" Tea just isn't doing it anymore, besides that I feel the startling urge to consume my feelings.

As the food is prepared, I remind myself that it's my job to feed my captor.

"Make that two dinners?" I ask hopefully. For once I'm pleased that it's a simple chicken sandwich. I stand a chance at him actually eating this, for someone who lives outside and eats dead animals he sure is picky about what 'human' food he will touch. The thought makes me shudder as I turn down the sandwich for something more leafy and less 'flesh'. My diet grew more and more vegetarian by the day.

I give the woman, who once was my nanny, a hug as I take the plates and decide to try and find my 'master'.

I'm too pleased to find that he resides in my bedroom. Entering, I shut the door behind me. He is awake, thankfully, sitting on the window sill looking out. He must have heard me coming because he doesn't move, "You're awake." I try not to sound too surprised.

Alpha reminds me of a child in time out, pouting. "Adriam has me on lock down until the evening run. He has prescribed a 'break' though I don't know how restful he believes it is to have me sitting here watching the day progress without me." It shouldn't amuse me so much that tiny Adriam has this place wrapped around his finger.

"I like Adriam." I told him. I walk over and set the plates on the bed.

"He wouldn't allow it any other way. Everyone likes Adriam."

I can't tell if he's happy about that or not.

"Do you want some lunch?" I sound hopeful but he doesn't respond. He resembles a cat with the intensity in which he watches the scattering forms, watching the bird on the window sill. Only the bird is his subjects, potentially doing things that aren't to his standards. I clear my throat, "Would my Alpha like some lunch? It's hard to conquer the world on an empty stomach."

"Were you going to sleep with him?" He questions, his voice low.

"Him who?" I almost smile but I stop myself when I see him bristle. "For god sakes... No!" I snap and huff in frustration.

"Then what were you doing there?" He doesn't look at me.

I'm not playing this game. I had passed on my chance for escape, I didn't do it to simply return for interrogation. In fact, I wasn't totally sure why I came back at all. "Food in exchange for answers." I tell him sternly, only to be answered by a low growl. "Or I can leave and there's nothing you can do about it. I'm not the one on lock down."

"There is plenty I can do about it once night falls." The intensity of his voice causes my heartbeat to quicken. I inhale and stand my ground. Slowly, he stands and approaches me. Sitting on the edge of the bed across from me, Alpha grabs the sandwich and takes a deliberate yet annoyed bite. He gestures for me to speak.

I smile sarcastically at him and sit down as well. "I went to tell him that I found my father's book." I know he won't be pleased by this and I'm correct. In a fit of rage, he moves to put his sandwich down but I purse my lips and glare at him. I can feel the heat radiating off of him as he contemplates my worth, deciding to answer me with another bite.

"We had made a deal the night that I spent with him, he wanted me to use the book to help him conquer Ziduri himself. He feels as though the lycans would not be careful to not destroy their histories, since all the history of the elf kingdom is remembered and passed down through story tellers." I wait for him to swallow because I can see that he wants to speak. I take a bite of my own food, nibbling on some lightly dressed lettuce and toasted bread pieces.

"He is correct. We would destroy any loyalist to Taryek."

I want to shake him. *This kind of talk is what makes people think wolves can't be reasoned with! Maybe they can't.* "That is the whole history of a people lost, Verando!" I'm exasperated. How could he not care?!

"Don't. Call me. That." His voice is low and harsh, it hurts me.

I set my jaw and look away. "Alpha." I correct, my voice dripping with sarcasm.

"A history built on the backs of slaves, not just my people but others before them. History repeats itself, there is nothing to be remembered."

He sounds so sure and I don't know how much convincing I could do at this point so I just sit in silence and take another bite.

"What were you doing with him?" Alpha demands. He sounds like he doesn't want to know. I glance at him and say nothing. "Damn it, Nicolas, this isn't a game!" He practically shouts but I wait. He knows my terms. My job is to feed him and take care of him, I wouldn't be blamed for him wasting away, too.

He takes a manful chomp and I know I'm running out of bargaining power.

"I wanted to confront him about the night I spent with him, I wanted to tell him he must give back Dezna land to the citizens as the rebellion has taken some of my people's homes." I can see that he's seething. "I tried to fight him off but I just... I don't know. I panicked?"

I leave out the part where he saw through me, where he called me out on my secret.

"Why didn't you use your magic? Like you did with Caspian?" Alpha doesn't see that side of me and it breaks my heart. He doesn't see me as a horrible man who is using him to fill his sick need for companionship and domination. I could almost laugh at how low I've sunk; a murderer is more honest than I am. *He couldn't possibly realize how fucked up I really am.*

"There was no water around. It's the element I'm the best in, like I said, I just panicked and didn't think. My magic isn't working well right now." I want to remind him that I didn't fight him off, either.

We stare at each other in silence for a long moment. He's concerned and conflicted. "Were you going to kill him?" I ask him, my voice low as if I don't want anyone else to hear.

"Yes." He is blunt. There is no hesitation.

I swallow. "Alpha, that would have ruined everything, they would have had you killed."

"They could try." His tone chills me to my core. They would not have succeeded. The wolf is in there, he welcomes them to try. The Alpha fears nothing.

"If we are ever going to have an alliance, we have to stop killing each other and focus our efforts on the enemy and that's Taryek and his army. We are going to need numbers if your eventual goal is to reach the cities of Man."

He almost scoffs. "What's this 'we'? This is not your war."

I stare at him. I hadn't thought that he wouldn't bring me with him. I'm his servant? But I do suppose he had been telling me that he would leave me to run my city when he was done using it as a fortress.

I think of Adriam. *"We want to go home."* We included Alpha.

"When we go back to the rebellion I will be having a discussion with Haryek and I intend to finish what I started. Haryek cannot be allowed to continue like this. He must be punished for what he's done if what you say is true. We can't have a rapist ruling Ziduri, he is no better than his father."

While I agree with that, I don't see this helping the cause. "You can't kill him." I tell him sternly.

"We'll see how the mood strikes me."

He's so defiant! I watch as he sets his stubbled jaw, the way he runs his fingers roughly through his hair in frustration. I can feel his eyes locked onto my reddened cheek and my bruised throat. I'm hit with the overwhelming pain of the realization that he's going to leave.

He's going to leave and never come back, probably because he will be dead. There is no winning this war, even if by some miracle it happened—he would return home and that would be the end. I shove our plates off the edge of the bed and throw myself at him. My lips meet his and my jaw protests as I deepen the kiss and cling to him.

I can feel the tears welling up in my eyes. I'm going to miss him. He's not even gone yet and I know that I will miss him. I catch him off guard, he stiffens against me. After a long moment, he breaks the kiss and presses his forehead against mine.

We are both breathless; my heart is pounding in my chest. I instinctively move to kiss him again but he blocks me with the side of his face. "Nicolas..." It sounds like an excuse. I can't help but feel every time is supposed to be the last time. I feel as though I'm a drug to him and he keeps trying to wean himself off of me.

I should respect that. The only problem is I'm addicted to him too and I'm a hell of a junkie.

I rake my teeth over his jaw as I move down to kiss his neck. I'm learning him and he tilts his head to the side to expose his neck as I run my tongue up and catch his ear between my teeth. My nails drag over his chest through his shirt, answered by a rumble low in his throat as he pushes me back onto the bed. "You are awfully disobedient today." He tells me, his voice low and rough.

He's between my legs and I can see his arousal straining against his pants.

"I'm sorry Alpha. I'm just trying to do my job." I responded. I'm breathless, I clutch at the pillow above my head and grind against him. I'm desperate for friction, anything. He's on his knees, his hand resting on mine. Glorious, the way his shirt is stretched over his chest and his parted full lips, I'm intoxicated by him.

"Your job is to serve me, I don't think I invited you to kiss me. You've been awfully bold lately." In one swift move he flips me over and I'm on my face. He yanks my hips into the air and smacks me sharply on the ass. I cry out and clutch the sheets, my libido sings, the domination that I crave sends my pulse skyrocketing. "Do you feel as though I'm not worthy of your time?" He smacks me again.

"No Alpha!" I responded. I'm a junkie getting his fix.

"Your Alpha requires your immediate attention. I would waste away if I relied on your service!" He smacks me with the other hand and my body shudders, the anticipation is pure torture.

"I'll do better, Alpha." My body craves punishment. When I bow before him, I don't have to think, I can just exist, shut off, and serve. It's liberating, a high I'd been chasing since that first night.

He takes his hand and squeezes my ass through my pants. Shoving his hips against me, he grinds his bulge against my backside and I can't help but groan as I press back against him. Roughly, he yanks my pants down and reaches between my legs to skirt his fingers over my erection. "Look how hard you are." He sounds pleased. The thrill that I please him sends tingles up my spine.

I bite my lower lip, rocking my hips. "Be still." He commands. "I'm going to fuck you, Nicolas. If it pleases me, you may be allowed to finish after I'm done with you." His husky tone causes my lips to part in anticipation, I shiver as he grabs the jar of oils from the night stand. I know exactly why I returned, I was unable to help myself.

I, defiantly, shove my hips back against him, I desperately need a reminder.

He pulls his pants down and enters me completely. I moan loudly and arch my back, relishing in the feel of being at his mercy. Alpha grips my hair, reclining my head back so he can hear me and I'm happy to oblige. The sensation is almost more than I can take; I grit my teeth at his relentless pace. He uses my body and I completely surrender to him.

My legs tremble as he takes me, I can feel my body building and I struggle to contain it. This is what I've been craving, someone else to take control. In this single moment, I belong to him and only him. My body serves its purpose and does it well, pleasing this man who doesn't judge my perverted nature.

To be as totally helpless as I feel, my body is an inferno as he quickens and I know he's getting close. I rock back to meet him, wanting to please my Alpha. As he finishes, I'm left with a feeling of desperation. We're both panting but my body feels electric. Obediently, I await instruction. "Get up." He commands and I raise my chest, looking at him over my shoulder. He bites his lower lip and I know I've achieved what I was after.

His hands feel like steel vices as he jerks me up so my back is against his slick chest. He kisses me deeply, his hand exploring my body as I melt against his lips. "Take off your clothes."

I hop up almost too quickly, nearly falling over. He smirks at my clumsiness, bringing color to my cheeks.

I pause. "I want to take off my shirt but you can't touch me..." I told him. He looks like he wants to argue but this is a hard limit for me. I couldn't take it, this was difficult enough. "Lay on your back."

I pull my pants off followed by my over shirt, leaving my silk undershirt. As I climb up onto the bed, I wait for him to do as I say. Pulling off his pants, I begin kissing down his abdomen as I slide down then return to straddle his waist. I take our erections in my hand to slowly stroke, the sensation making my breath ragged and I get the response I wanted as he springs to life in my hand.

"Do you trust me?" I ask.

Alpha looks wary but he nods. I bite my lower lip and slide my hands up his shirt, rolling it up his body and he lifts his arms to oblige me. "I'm going to put this around your elbows behind your head. You need to keep your hands up behind your head. Understand?"

His lips part but he simply answers. "Yes."

I lock it around his elbows. He grabs it in his hands and keeps them behind his head. I look down at him and I flush, his flexed biceps and abdominals almost send me over the edge. I scold my previous self, thinking that he was anything but created to be appreciated when we first met.

My mouth waters, "My god..." I breathe. To my surprise, he looks just as turned on as I do. I run my finger slowly down the line of his abs, past his navel and up his erection. He moans and flexes against my hand, the sound is a symphony to my ears.

I cautiously remove my shirt. My torso is revealed, its olive patchwork standing out against his sun-kissed skin but we aren't so different. My body is covered in scars, lines and bite marks. Each one telling a story, lines over top of lines from claws and teeth. My body had been ravaged by every being I'd given myself to, each a painful reminder of why I can't let go.

I was broken, there was no fixing me. I couldn't be put back together, the pieces wouldn't fit.

"You're incredible." I hear him say and I steal a glance, he's not looking at my chest. He's looking at me. With new confidence, I mount him and we moan together.

I put my hands on his chest and lose myself in him, "Randy." I gasp, I'm already so close. Seeing him like this, at my disposal, is almost more than I can bear.

"Nicolas..." He responds, watching me come apart. I sit up and tangle my hands in my own hair. He raises his hips to meet me as I quicken my pace. I become incoherent, at my own mercy as I relish in the freedom of acceptance. I finish with an intensity I hadn't known, feeling the world threaten to spin as my body shakes. It takes everything I have not to collapse as I ride it out. I bring one hand down to catch myself, resting it on his stomach.

It takes me a moment to catch my breath and he watches me as I slide off of him. Feeling bold and empowered, I lean down to lick my completion off his stomach. Alpha inhales sharply and I come up to kiss him deeply, offering him a taste as I deepen the kiss.

When I've had my fill of him, I pull his shirt off the rest of the way and he stretches out his arms. I take the opportunity to cuddle up to his side and kiss his chest.

"I need to be disobedient more often." I tell him playfully.

"Oh you're plenty disobedient. You'd be punished more often if you weren't always running off." He responds, his eyes are closed and he looks relaxed. A rare sight.

I roll my eyes and toy with one of his nipples. He grasps my hand immediately and his eyes are blazing. *Oh.* "You're insatiable." It's a warning. I note that for later.

"Do you like being tied up?" I figure, why not pry?

He hesitates. "If the mood strikes." His response is guarded.

"Noted. I like tying you up." I pause, is he going to ask me why? I glance at him but he's not looking at me, he's looking at the ceiling. Alpha doesn't pry. Not often at least. Maybe it's because he doesn't want to know. "Does it hurt? Turning into a wolf? You were practically screaming back at the rebellion." The thought causes me physical pain. I cuddle closer to him.

"Yes. Adriam has done some dissections on the dead. Our bones must fracture and re-bond to create the wolf. It happens so instantaneously it's not a prolonged thing. It feels like your entire body is being ripped apart then shoved back together. It is worse when it is not happening willingly because then it starts happening from the inside. Your ribs start cracking, your pelvis, your collarbone..." He trails off and sighs.

How horrible. *I've got to fix this.*

"It's about on par with the change when we were actual werewolves only this happens so often you kind of get used to it after a while. Some people even think it feels good. My wolf really wants out so that can be problematic. It rushes the change and can make it more painful." He shrugs.

I reach up to brush his hair out of his eyes. "I'm sorry." *For everything.*

"Yeah. Me too." He offers me a small smile and kisses the top of my head. "We've got to go visit Haryek tomorrow and you're not going to like it."

Little did he know I'd already beaten him to it. "You've worn me out too much to speak about battle tactics." For now, I'd deflect.

"Go to sleep, I've still got a couple more hours of lock down... Then you need to clean up this mess." He yawns, I knew he would be just as tired as me.

"Make me." I challenge sleepily.

"Gladly."

Twenty-One-

I'm jolted from my sleep because I realize I'm covered in sweat. It'd been a long time since I'd been awakened in this manner, yet my body doesn't feel as though it's performing the correct response. I feel good, my body is sore and aches, but I feel refreshed. As my eyes drift, I come to realize it's Verando, he's dreaming.

He flinches in his sleep; his teeth clenched tightly shut and his face contorted.

"Verando." I try and keep my voice low. Slowly I sit up, "Verando." I tell him again and press my hand to his chest. "Randy!" I raise my voice.

He sits bolt upright, panting. My poor wrist is clutched in his hand and I resist the urge to cry out. Looking around frantically, his eyes settle on me and then my hand. A murmured apology passes from his lips as he quickly releases me, I test my fingers, assuring myself that my hand wasn't broken.

"Bad dream?" I ask him, a little bewildered.

"Something like that..." He mumbles as he buries his face in his hands, attempting to catch his breath.

"Well? What happened?" I couldn't help but wonder if this was the source of his wish to sleep alone.

Reluctant to entertain me, he changes the subject. "Did you call me Randy?"

I hesitate. "Yes. You wouldn't wake up."

Alpha regards me for a moment but surprises me with a small smile, dimpling his cheek. "It helped."

"You're welcome," I tell him boldly and he shakes his head as he scoots to the edge of the bed. I groan and reach for him, crawling over and draping over his shoulders. He was so warm, the chill of the castle invited me to appreciate lycan warmth. "You weren't supposed to leave. Tell me what you dreamt of."

"Just a nightmare, is all. No need to fret about it... They happen so often I couldn't even tell you anymore."

Changing tactics, I'm hungry for information. "Are you from England?" I ask, wanting to get my playful warlord back.

Cautious, Alpha raises an eyebrow at me. "I was born in London. I grew up in Spain."

I sit cross-legged like a child and wait for him to continue.

"What, have you got nothing better to do than root around in my past?"

I nod. One of my favorite looks returns, the frustration mixed with amusement, and I wait patiently.

"I want to trade. Mine for yours, you tell me what all this business with your shirt is about. I'll tell you about where I grew up."

Oh, he doesn't play fair. "Hmm. I don't think I want to play this game." I move to stand but he wraps his arms around me, pulling me firmly back into his lap.

"Come on. Out with it." His good mood is infectious. I lean back into his chest, giving myself permission to enjoy someone holding me. It was as if he were holding my pieces together, he had to be so strong, there was too much for one normal man to hold.

"When I was in school, my instructors favored me. It was very difficult to stay alive, so many of my classmates were killed or even devoured. You see, my instructor was a dragon who could shapeshift into a man. He thought I showed promise but when I got there I was little more than a pretty face to him.

"I didn't have the training, I've never been a fighter, I've always been better at solving problems with magic and reason. But that comes with a cost if you want to stay alive so in exchange for my safety I did whatever he asked." I frown at the thought and curl my arms around myself. He watches my face.

"I guess I felt like it's what I deserved for being so weak. It worked." I shrug. "Even men who aren't attracted to men took my 'participation' in exchange for my safety. It was only my final teacher who decided I needed to actually prove myself. I learned a lot from her. But the first did most of this, I was so inexperienced. I didn't know how to say no or when to tell him it was too much. So I just let it happen and he certainly did a number on me."

It was the first time I'd told anyone about what happened to me. When I'd come home, I'd been a shell of my former self and my parents stood aside while I wasted away. They were proud, the parties felt endless and the praise only saw to lessen my self-worth as I knew exactly how undeserving I was. I bore the marks to prove my perversion.

His hand slips to capture my chin, startling me at the contact as he tilts my head.

"You have nothing to be ashamed of." For a moment, he's no longer Alpha. He's a real person, feeling my pain and trying to comfort me. I offer him a small smile as he kisses me.

"Okay! Your turn!" I manage. I can't think about this. I want to hear about his existence.

"It's pretty boring."

"Try me!" I try to sound enthusiastic.

"My mother died giving birth to my sister when I was very young, five or six. She was human and it was too much for her body."

"What was she like?" I interrupt, his eyes go distant as he remembers her.

"Soft. Warm. She had red hair a lot like the color of yours. She was too good, really. She wasn't meant for this life."

I think of my mother and I lean against his arm, *you're warm too.*

"When she died, my father had no interest. He handed me off to a man named Marcus Senior. Marcus raised me, alongside his son Marcus Junior. The accent just stuck, though I do speak Spanish."

"Is that where you met Tonic?" I ask, hungry for knowledge.

"Yes. I was probably sixteen when I met Tonic. This whole thing was just starting to unravel. He was pretty small when it began." Sixteen-year-old Verando... I ponder what he was like.

"How old are you?"

"Does it matter?" He raises an eyebrow, sliding out of my grasp, he stretches.

I flop onto my side as I watch him. "I have a thing for older men; I've got a bet with Stefan."

Thinking for a moment, he shrugs. "I think I'm over forty. I haven't aged much in the last ten years. The gray doesn't help."

I don't know why that surprises me so much, I sit up and go to get dressed before he questions me about my own age. At the ripe old age of twenty-five, I really need to think about my daddy issues.

As the day progresses, I'm drawn to following Tonic around and contemplating a visit to Stefan. I convince Verando to join me for dinner and that ends up being more frustrating than anything. I discover that the man has the attention span of a gnat and can't sit still for much cooking. He, unfortunately, has little interest in anything that I'm cooking though he does humor me by tasting it before making a hasty retreat to go on the run he was promised.

I'm left feeling slightly deflated and I feel like I did when I was in school. *Does he like me? Was I too forward?* I roll my eyes at myself and pack up my food to go find Tonic. I hand it over to him and he brightens my spirits with his embellishment of how good it smells. Tonic can be my boyfriend. "Thank you! At least someone likes my cooking!"

I watch him as he runs off to be with Stefan and I hug myself quietly. It feels weird not having my bodyguard around, especially when I have to cover for him considering that nobody knows where he is off to.

I'm more disappointed than I'd like to admit when Verando doesn't show up that night. I find myself feeling abandoned, I roll my eyes at myself as my mind wanders. *This is not a relationship, he killed your family. He is a murderer, he is an animal.*

I sigh and bury my face in my pillow. *He's taking over your whole city; he's planning to murder hundreds if not thousands of elves. He hates what you are. What the fuck am I doing?*

But I think of him and I can't help but smile. What am I doing? "Get a grip." I tell myself. "You have a country to save. Your people need you; this isn't a time for letting your emotions get the best of you!"

So when the next morning comes, I have a newfound determination. I march with determination down to breakfast and plop down with Sota, Swift, Fleet, Adriam, and Victor.

Adriam looks amused. "You look to be in a good mood."

"I'm determined to make these negotiations happen," I tell him firmly, taking a bite of my biscuit and gravy.

"Good luck with that. Wolf and knife ear don't usually like each other." Victor looks amused. "I hope you save the girly looking one for last."

Adriam swats him. "I think Haryek is beautiful... that skin. If only he weren't disgusting." He sighs and Victor rolls his eyes.

Swift and Fleet look like they would throw up if it wasn't rude.

"Where's Delta?" I question.

"He's with Alpha, getting in some extra training." Sota seems pleased with this.

"Does that man ever eat?" I demand.

Sota shrugs. "Nicolas, most wolves eat raw. 'This' is just to appease the human side. Some are more human than a wolf; some are more wolf than human. A good deal of the pack hunts for food instead of coming here."

"We are just civilized." Adriam adds but frowns as Victor shoves an entire biscuit in his mouth.

"Most of us... Old habits die hard." He hands him a napkin and sighs. "I would hurry. He will leave without you."

I choke down the rest of my breakfast and leap to my feet.

"Good luck!" Adriam chimes hopefully.

I quickly march out to the courtyard where I see my warlord standing there.

It's a chilly fall morning and yet he's in a short sleeve with a vest and thin pants with his tall boots. *How is he not freezing?* I march straight past him. "Coming?" I ask stiffly.

He raises an eyebrow and follows after me. It's easy for him to keep up with my pace and I realize I've never actually made this walk with Alpha. The man has a huge stride and I notice I'm actually holding him up but I refuse to walk faster on principle.

"So, I asked the police force to give Haryek a cease and desist on his encroachment into Dezna." I want to keep this professional, show him that I'm capable of doing these things on my own.

"You did?" He questions.

"Yes. I'm the victim here. I feel I should approve of the punishment." He gives me my favorite look but I refuse to smile. The frustration is clear but he's amused at my business-like conduct. "He's already under heavy restrictions, I feel satisfied with that."

"Well I'm going to put him in the dungeon until this is over and then maybe I'll let him out on good behavior but he's going to be stripped of his titles. I'm going to appoint a new leader for the rebellion." He sounds absolute.

I almost choke. "Are you kidding? Verando that is not going to go well!" I can't help it, I test the name. But he doesn't correct me. "After that stunt yesterday, the rebellion will probably shoot you on sight."

He scoffs. "I conquered this place, remember? If they have a problem with it, they will meet a similar fate. This isn't your decision, Nicolas."

I stop and stare at him. "We need to give him a chance to improve his behavior. He is a politician; he is the face of the rebellion. We cannot just go in there and start making demands."

"Watch me." He challenges me and I set my jaw. "Did you forget who's in charge here?"

The way he glowers down at me puts me on edge, threatening to boil over into outright rage. "You're being an ass!" I tell him in frustration, crossing my arms over my chest.

Before I can take it back, it's reached him and I know that I'm done for. "Excuse me?"

I stand my ground. "An ass!" I snap. As much as I enjoyed being dominated, I was not a fan of his mistreatment of my position. If we were going to do this together, then it had to be together.

"In what world do you talk to me this way?" He snaps and takes a step towards me.

I can feel the inferno and I take a step backward as my back meets a tree. In a quick motion, I put my hands against it to brace myself. "In a world where you are doing this wrong. You need my help. This is my fight, you are just there as the muscle."

His eyes blaze as he puts one hand against the tree to block my escape. My chin juts out, I inhale to fill my chest as I glare back at him. I was unwilling to yield, these were my people. "You've got some balls, Nicolas. I'll give you that." He's trying to control it; I can feel that he's vibrating. The heat is overwhelming.

"Glad to see that you can control yourself." I breathe.

"You're playing a dangerous game." He practically snarls.

"I needed to see, glad to know I'm right." I'm breathing hard; his presence sends my body up in flames. I don't know if it's him or the heat radiating off of him.

He feels it, too.

I swore myself off this stuff last night when he left me alone. I told myself I wouldn't do this anymore. My body wasn't a weapon, my emotions were too fragile. I had found a piece of myself that I was desperate to hold onto. "You left me alone last night." I accuse him.

"Is that what this really is?" His expression burns, seething under the surface of control. "Need I remind you we're in the middle of an active war?"

"I worry about you, asshole." I snap, only to be answered by his lips grazing the healing bruises on my neck.

"On your knees." He commands me.

"You're kidding! We're in public!"

"Get.On.Your.Knees!" He snarls, resonating in my chest. What would he do if I didn't do it? Would he actually hurt me? I slide down his body till I'm resting on my knees before him, cheeks burning hot with embarrassment as I frantically search for anyone who might be passing. "Since you're so inclined to use your mouth, maybe you can put it to good work. If you please me, I might serve you after."

It disgusts me and excites me all at the same time. I shake my head, pressing my lips firmly together. This is too far, beyond what I'm willing to do. If someone saw, we'd both be ruined. "I'm waiting." His voice rolls, amused with my position before him. "I'm not a patient man, Nicolas."

My body shakes with excitement as my hands slowly grasp the hem of his pants. My lips part as his hand tangles in my hair, pulling my head back. "This is your punishment. Do not keep me waiting."

I take him in my mouth and I wrap my fist around the base. Sucking hard, I clutch his thigh with my free hand as I sigh in submission to the task. The sounds of appreciation he makes lull me back into the realm of comfort, the world melts away and there is only him before me.

With newfound vigor, I attack him. It's not an apology or an acceptance of punishment but the thrill of releasing control and accepting a task that brings me an equal amount of joy. I worship him with my tongue, chasing his release as he pants. Dutifully, I swallow and wet my lips as I meet his gaze.

"What're you doing to me?" He exhales, dragging his thumb over my lower lip as I graze my teeth over the offending appendage.

Helping me to my feet, I snake my fingers into his hair as I pull him down to my level and kiss him. My body melts against him as I hook my leg over his hip, relishing in the taste of him.

"Insatiable." He grumbles at me, delivering a firm smack on my ass as he pulls away to resume our path.

I shrug as I tangle my fingers with his, determined to maintain contact. As we near the city, I force myself to release him. There would be the walk home to resume any previous activity, I was not nearly done with him yet.

Showing him to the rebellion, I'm not surprised when Haryek is waiting for us.

"It's rude to keep someone waiting." He tells us as we near.

"I didn't think you'd be waiting." I try not to sound too bitter. Much as I wanted Verando to allow me to handle it, a part of me would love to see the man dead.

"Of course he is, he wants to make a scene," Alpha grumbles but he doesn't add anything further.

"I'm just ready for the onslaught, you never know with you brutes." Haryek taunts him but he doesn't respond, much to my appreciation. I'm ready for this, I'm ready to deal with Haryek.

"Haryek, Alpha is just here to ensure my safety. You'll be dealing with me today." I tell him, straightening a little. Haryek grins, a sly fox who'd found the door to the hen house. He won't be smiling for long; I've had all night to think about this. The moment I decided to remain, I knew the course of action I must take.

With careful poise, Haryek performs a half bow. "Can we have this conversation in private? I'm just not comfortable around your friend here after yesterday."

"Absolutely not!" Alpha snaps but I touch his arm.

"If we can't trust him, then he just proves your point. I'll be okay. There is plenty of water in the city. I can do this." I assure him, wishing to smooth the line between his eyebrows yet knowing it wasn't my place to soothe this man. Especially not in public. My hands remain at my sides, doing this alone didn't worry me. It would mean Haryek and I could have an unaltered conversation, without fear of the gray-haired male's retaliation.

It physically hurts him and I refuse to look into it. He couldn't possibly care about me, he dare not show it or allude to it yet I can see it in his eyes that he's in pain at the thought of relinquishing me to this pale devil. "I'll be right outside the door. You have ten minutes before I come in. If I hear a single harsh word—"

The threat is very real.

Haryek holds up his hands innocently, grinning ear to ear. "I am the one who wants peace, remember?" The elf opens the door to the cabin, inviting me into the pyre. I give Alpha a reassuring look, touching his arm, giving myself the slightest permission. The lycan nods to me, jaw tight.

I follow Haryek into the cabin.

Twenty-Two-

I struggle to explore why it bothered me so much to leave Alpha outside. It'd be easy to pin it on simply not wanting to be alone with Haryek, I stop the train of thought in its tracks. I can't allow myself to get sidetracked while riding the high of punishment.

Haryek leads me to the table and pulls me a chair, I block his hand, taking the back of the chair in my palm as I sit down abruptly. I'm not quite in the mood for taking any sort of offerings from such a sleazy character. "Tea?" He offers.

"Trying to poison me?" Tea is not something the Lycans see a need for, my taste for anything other than water and ale had been clawing at the back of the throat for nearing on a week now. While I wouldn't put it past Haryek to slip death into my cup, it seemed like a move that was beyond him. If he wanted me dead, I'd imagine he would have done it by now.

Haryek feigns anguish, "You wound me. I just want you to be comfortable."

"Cut the shit, Haryek. Did the Chief of Police meet you with your papers? You must give back those houses you took." I would just stick with business, I would refuse to play his games, I would remain in control and I would get the answers and the results that I needed.

"Of course." Haryek goes over to the stove and pulls down two cups, the porcelain tea cups glint in the light falling through the cracked window. I spy Alpha, arms crossed, staring into the woods with what I imagine is longing. I was removing him from some important task to have him here, I was sure. Would he suffer more backlash for this?

"Haryek, we have to figure this out. I haven't told the entirety of what went on but I can't ignore your behavior. I would very much like to give you a second chance but you must prove to me your worth. I'd like a full report of exactly who is in the rebellion and documentation of everyone's abilities. Then, we can begin to discuss your punishment." I begin.

I note the rigidity in his shoulders. My time with Lycans was slowly turning me into an expert on body language. The cup trembles as he rests it on the tiny saucer, heating the water over the stove. I know that this is not from fear, one does not stand quite so hard when faced with fear. He was angry, so angry with me. "I was just caught up in the moment, Nicolas! You know how it is, I can't help that I'm attracted to you."

His voice is light, soft and melodic. He chuckles, carefully adjusting his woven crown in the mirror. The corner of his lip threatens to turn down, threatens to twitch ever so slightly. Much as he wants to smile, I know that I'm getting to him.

I am not like him. I have my dignity in that I would never force myself onto someone. I would never force someone into a physical relationship with me if they didn't want it. "No, I don't, Haryek. I've never tried to rape someone." And if this is what he does when he's attracted to someone then Alpha is right.

Haryek brings over the cups and sits down across from me, pouring the tea carefully so as not to burn himself. The smell wafts to my nose and I could almost groan in appreciation. Perhaps I would partake, I watched him make it, it wouldn't seem like he'd done anything to it. Snatching the cup quickly, I take a deep, slow breath. "If this is how you choose to behave then I feel I must warn you I will happily turn you over to the lycans to do with as they see fit. This is a non-negotiation, Haryek. I was hoping to see some remorse from you."

With large, glimmering eyes, he smiles so widely that it almost frightens me. It looks unnatural on his pristine face. Awkwardly, I glance away, for looking horrified by someone's natural smile might not be the best for polite company. I steal a sip of the tea, sighing at the delicate flavor and the sweetness of it.

"Look, I've learned my lesson. Your boyfriend, or whatever is going on there, made it pretty clear that you're off limits. There will always be people like us Nicolas. You need me." He takes a drink of his own beverage, a careful sip. Tilting his head casually, he observes me with careful regard, dragging his eyes over my slightly unkempt appearance. "Honestly Nicolas, are you happy living like this? Look at you, you're a far cry from a royal as of today. You look right to be a beggar on the street, they obviously are not caring for you."

I sigh and stir my drink before taking a sip. Little did he know this was the healthiest I'd felt in a long time, this was the most like myself I'd been since my return home. Haryek had no desire to know me, he only wanted what he thought was rightfully his. "I think you should be much more concerned about what I'm not showing you than my appearance." I warn him, bringing a crack to that careful expression.

"If this is going to work, you're going to have to make a public apology. I will spare the people the details of the attempted rape but you will publicly, openly, accept the lycans and announce your partnership with them. Do not think I don't know it is the rebellion burning community houses, making them look like Lycan retaliation." I tell him firmly, catching him off guard by the way his eyebrows raise and he clears his throat.

The thought brings a grin to my lips, pleasing me to see him sweat. Maybe I was cut out for this? Maybe this was something I could do?

"I don't think that will be necessary." He almost growls, his expression slowly shifting to menacing.

I open my mouth to argue with him but instantly, I feel strange. Frowning, I rub the side of my head as the cold sweat drifts over my brow. Sniffing the tea, I catch the heavy scent of mint and wrinkle my nose. It was so strong, something I hadn't noticed before, perhaps it was just overwhelming my senses. Taking another sip, I wrinkle my nose and banish the tea from my side, pushing it to the center of the table.

This seems to displease him but I'm fine with being rude. "It is absolutely necessary Haryek. You will apologize. Today. In front of everyone." My stomach begins to flip and twist, I resist the urge to vomit as I put the back of my hand to my lips.

His smooth voice comes out of the depths of the spinning room. "Nicolas, look at me." His voice is so soft, alluring to my failing consciousness. I open my eyes and stare at him. My anger begins to melt, my resolve crumbling as I feel the overwhelming pressure of intoxication clouding over my vision.

How could I be angry at such a sweet man?

"I would never hurt you. Honestly, I think I acted the way I did because I'm completely in love with you." Haryek watches me through his pale lashes. I quickly stand, shoving away from the table as I stagger. Disgusted, violated, feeling as though I might succumb to whatever has been done to me and yet, I can't look away from him. My body reels and I quickly reach for the counter to hold myself up.

"You love me?" I can't comprehend it, it's as if I'm not even speaking. Someone else forms the words, someone else speaks for me and I begin to fade into the background.

"Of course... And you love me too. Don't you? So you're going to forgive this. All of this." He stands slowly, approaching me like a wounded animal.

I feel like I've been sedated. When my eyes reach his, it's as if I'm seeing him through a film. My words come out filtered, altered to mean anything other than what I'm saying. "I do. I love you. I'm so sorry Haryek." I breathe, making my stomach wrench and I almost double over in agony.

"It's okay, baby." He pulls me in and kisses me. It seals my fate, clouding over whatever remained. The world takes on a new color, tinted and splotchy as I search for the beacon of light that is Haryek in the haze. "It's okay, just sit. It's a lot to take in."

The door swings open as Alpha storms in, our ten minutes are up. Why was I here? "We are done here, have you said what you need to say?" His harsh gaze falls on me though it quickly changes and I tilt my head as I struggle to see him. Did he look worried? I quickly turn my gaze to see Haryek's throat, sore and bruised. He had hurt Haryek, he was the one who had beaten him.

My head swims as the words force themselves out, someone else pulls the strings as I fight to keep them in. "Alpha, how could you hurt Haryek so badly?" I'm suddenly overwhelmed with anger all over again. My chest hurts, burning deep in my core, my body feels as though it's failing with every word. I shake my head, staggering as Haryek tries to hold me up. Alarm bells ring all over, warning me, pleading with it to stop.

He looks stunned, staring at me. "Excuse me?"

"You are so much stronger than him! You have an unfair advantage; look what you've done to him! It's not Haryek who should be punished, it's you." My mind is riddled with disgust, *who am I?*

So quickly he turns on the object of my obsession, the beacon of light in the haze. Alpha descends on the elf who makes no move to defend himself. "What have you done to him?" It is me who jumps to his defense.

My outstretched hands land on Alpha's chest and I crumble, he grips my arms and I yearn for the contact only to twist out of his grasp as if he'd electrocuted me. "Do not touch him! I think you've done enough here with your behavior. Haryek was right about your breed. You are an animal, you can't control yourself! Look at what you've done to my home, to my family, to me." I'm shouting and tears are streaming down my face.

Why does this hurt so bad? I'm broken, being torn apart from the inside. My body begins to shake, I want him to leave, I feel as though I'm burning alive and resist the urge to scream at the pain. Clutching my stomach, Haryek steps to support me once more.

He looks shattered. "Nicolas…" He breathes. Did he feel it, too?

"Leave, Alpha. Now. We need to think about how we are going to punish you. You are at fault here. Not Haryek." I can hardly breathe as I tell him this. I feel weak. A piece of me walks out the door as he turns and departs, before I can call him back, before I can beg him to talk me out of this. He must have seen how much pain I was in, he must know this is his doing. It didn't hurt like this until he walked in.

The marble hands of the elf cup my face, gathering me to look up at him. Foreign eyes rejoice and I feel like I'm drowning. "You were incredible baby. A true leader. I'm so proud of you!" He encourages. I smile weakly up at him, a faux happiness clouding over like a sedative.

"I don't feel well... I think I need to rest."

He frowns. "No darling, we need to go and spread the news that the prince is on our side! We have some announcements to make!"

I sigh, my legs feel as though they're made of sacks of mud. *Anything for him.*

We leave the cabin and I glance around, Alpha is gone.

We walk amongst the people and my heart flips as the rebels surge through the city. The police chief questions my intentions but doesn't go much further when he gathers the look on my face. It feels like a loss, it feels as though this was not how it was meant to be.

Civilians stare as vacantly as I do as the rebels flood into buildings, partaking in food and drink, robbing from their own neighbors at the command of Haryek for a celebration that I felt was a slap in the face to the hard working citizens of the rebuilding town.

Any time my resolve wavered, I merely had to look at Haryek to get another dose of sedation. My brain would numb, my body would grow colder and I would slip back into the stupor of acceptance of this reality just as I had before I'd come home from school. Just when I'd thought I'd gotten rid of this side of myself, it was as if I'd woken up from a dream only to realize I'd never found that light at all.

My heart now belonged to Haryek, I could only watch as the rebels flooded the streets of the city and wonder who the real villains were.

CHAPTER

Twenty-Three-

"That was good of Nicolas to cover for you." Stefan pours some hot chocolate into a mug and hands it to Tonic. "I certainly have enjoyed having you here."

"I've enjoyed being here. It's been very eye-opening." Tonic takes the mug and inhales the sweet aroma. He takes a long draw and settles back into the couch. It's night once more and he's had to adjust to a more nocturnal lifestyle if he wants to keep up his nightly escapades. Stefan had been a welcome break from pack mentality, it was nice to escape to a more civilized lifestyle if only for a moment.

"Eye-opening?" Stefan drifts over to rest on the couch, resting his head in Tonic's lap. The warmth of the lycan male transferred into his undead body, almost warming him to near human-like temperatures.

"Mmm... I feel more like myself than I've ever felt. I feel whole." Tonic slowly runs his hand through Stefan's hair; the long locks trace over his lap and threaten to spill like an inky waterfall over the edge. The Strigoi hums in appreciation, shutting his eyes if only for a moment.

"Happy to be of service." His voice sounds a little distant, his eyes hiding his emotion.

Tonic offers a tender smile, bending to kiss the chilled forehead. "Don't worry, I'm not going to be moving in. I know you like your lifestyle, don't feel as though you will have to change your address. I'm not really the commitment type..." Tonics' reassurance brings a laugh from the Strigoi.

"How would you know your type, little pet?" Stefan teases, sitting up with an amused expression.

This takes the younger male by surprise and he considers for a moment, gently sipping the drink. "I-I really don't know. It's just how I feel. I want to have fun with this. I don't even know if I'll live to see next week. I couldn't be with someone, knowing they wanted more, only to die... I just want to enjoy whatever time I have left." The laughter leaves Stefan's eyes and turns to something much softer. He reaches up to brush Tonic's cheek with the back of his hand.

With gentle admiration, the Strigoi floats to press his lips to the younger man's. "Nicolas is right. You are too good, for any of us."

Tonic carefully places his mug on the end table, returning the kiss with a sigh of appreciation for the chilled, smooth skin. Exploring his mouth with his tongue, Tonic breaks the kiss to breathe as Stefan captures the corner of his mouth. "Tonight I'm not." He encourages the pale male, trying to distract him from the thought that he possessed some kind of purity that needed saving. "You've already robbed me of my virtue, might as well enjoy it."

Stefan couldn't help but laugh, tangling his fingers in the gray locks. "Your delicious, sexy virtue. My my, what a treat..."

Much as he was enjoying the attention, a distant rustle outside catches his ear, pulling him from the sensational Strigoi. Tonic pauses, straightening. "Do you hear something?" He asks.

Stefan moves to kiss his neck, running his fangs lightly over his skin. The salty taste of athletic, young lycan sending a shiver down his spine. The symphony of a warm, wet heart pulsing just under the skin driving him mad. It nearly makes his mouth water, he presses a cool kiss to the flickering skin. "Only this delicious heartbeat, baby." He breathes.

Tonic's eyes practically roll back in his head and he fights for control. "No, no. I really think I heard something." He bites his lower lip, arguing with his judgment. The temptation of the experienced man is enough to pull him from any distraction, be it real or false.

"It's probably Pavel. He's a crafty little thing; he's been so in and out lately. I don't think he quite likes to share me with you." Stefan traces his tongue over the tanned skin with a groan. "You are a naughty, naughty man. How dare you smell so divine."

"I suppose you're probably right." The gray-haired lycan exposes his neck to indulge his hungry vampire host. "Yet you keep talking..." he challenges with a low exhale.

With a chaste kiss of gratitude, the Strigoi bares his fangs. "I never thought a lycan could taste so good." He sinks his teeth into his neck, Tonic's breath pulls sharply through his teeth. Stefan's cool hand caresses the side of his face, the other finding one of his nipples as Tonic squirms beneath him; he shudders as Stefan retracts his fangs.

"I could get used to this." Stefan's voice is silky, his eyes brightened and his skin looks almost alive. "Here, taste." He grins wickedly as he kisses the younger man with his bloodied lips.

Tonic returns the kiss hungrily, clinging to the more experienced male. "I'm yours." He pants against his mouth, deepening the kiss as his arms wrap around the pale neck.

Both men startle at the sudden rap on the door, strong and loud, echoing through the halls. Stefan sits up, frowning. "That's odd. I never get company. I wonder if it's Nicolas, I told you that you should have gone back this morning."

Rolling his eyes at the scolding, Tonic sits up to attempt to steady his breathing. He wipes at his mouth with the back of his hand and presses his palm to the bite on his neck. His heart pounds wildly in his chest as he leans back into the overly plush couch cushions, unable to think clearly with such a host so ready for the taking.

As Alpha's form appears in the doorway, Tonic begins to shrink back. *Oh no.* This was exactly what he feared would happen; these few days of paradise will surely cost him his life. He begins to devise his speech, hoping that some convincing words would somehow spare him, but the expression on Alpha's face stops him dead in his tracks.

He looks haunted, broken.

"He's practically incoherent. He just keeps saying he wants to forget." Stefan mumbles, displeased with the interruption but concerned for the normally stoic male.

Forgetting the wound on his neck, Tonic jumps to his feet and approaches Alpha quickly. "Alpha, What's wrong?" He tries to keep control of the tone in his voice, not wanting to add stress to the situation or overstep his boundaries.

Stefan strolls around the room, cautious, to join the pair as he crosses his arms over his chest. Not one to forget, he still hadn't quite forgiven the lycan for his rude behavior the day before. "Don't forget my warning to you, lycan. Did you hurt him?"

The disturbing silence, the vacancy on the Alpha male's face, pushed the young lycan to his breaking point. The silence was overwhelming, sending a chill down his spine. Something must be horribly wrong. "Alpha, say something!" Tonic prompts.

After a long moment, his light eyes lift and he finally speaks. "I want you to make me forget. I want you to remove this, all of this fucking shit. Take it away." His voice is hardly more than a croak, devoid of emotion yet fractured as he pleads for mercy from the Strigoi.

Exchanging glances, Stefan switches to a slightly more serious posture. "Take what away?" He asks, patiently, to encourage Alpha to elaborate.

"Nicolas. Everything to do with him, I want it gone." His voice is hollow, empty, a simple plea for a reprieve from an agony that had never touched him before.

Scoffing, Stefan flips his hair in what could be considered offense. It was his duty to his friend to pursue every avenue, he knew me well enough to know that I was quite smitten with the odd male. "Why on earth would I do that? You were right as rain last time you were here; it's been only a few days. Who fucks up this bad in a few days?"

With a harsh snarl, Alpha slams his hands on the stone kitchen island. "Does it matter?" He looks up with a grimace, "I just want this… pain… to go away." He says through gritted teeth, clutching his chest as if he'd thought about ripping out his own heart. It was beyond anything he'd felt, anything he'd ever wanted to feel.

Tonic raises a hand to calm the calculating Strigoi, his own silent plea for some empathy for the man who'd helped raise him. "I think you need to sit down, take a breath, and explain to us what is going on before we talk about taking away parts of your memory," Stefan instructs him and he numbly allows the men to lead him to an armchair. "Explain." Stefan coaxes.

Alpha looks as if he's made of stone. He's too still, his eyes are unseeing. "We went to speak with Haryek, Nicolas wanted to speak with Haryek, by himself of course. He wanted to decide the punishment for Haryek's crimes against him."

Stefan scowls, resentment was a language he spoke quite clearly, "Yes, the rapist elf. Tonic told me."

Alpha blinks for a moment and looks towards Tonic who looks as though he could crawl in a hole and die, all over again. "What are you doing here, Tonic?" Of course, he would not allow that to go unnoticed.

Desperate to keep his toy, Stefan quickly deflects. "Hey, focus! Then what?" Stefan snaps his fingers and regains Alpha's attention.

"We... disagreed—and had some words but it was resolved by the time we got to the rebellion. Haryek wanted to speak with Nicolas alone, they both were dead set on it and I allowed it." Hearing it out loud now, the error of his ways was front and center. There was no escaping it, it was his own mistake which led to whatever had happened to me.

"What makes you think 'that' was a good idea?" Stefan snaps.

Alpha glowers at him. "You've known him for longer than I have, you know what he's like when he has an idea in his head. It was poor judgment, I was too relaxed. I should never have allowed it to occur. It was like he was a different person and when he looked at me, all he could see was a monster. He said that they must decide what to do with me, that I should be punished, and then I left."

"And he just let you leave?" Tonic pipes in, shocked.

"I just want this to go away. I can't go on like this, feeling this way. If he comes for me, I won't be able to—" He trails off.

"To kill him?" Tonic breathes.

Alpha sets his jaw and closes his eyes, disturbed at his own weakness when it came to me. Time and time again he had wondered what had changed, what had happened to make him suddenly so involved in whether I lived or died.

"This doesn't add up. I know Nicolas, almost better than myself. Something's not right here. We must be missing something." Stefan begins to pace the floor, glowering at the ground.

Alpha runs his hand through his hair. "Does it matter how right or wrong we think it is? He's gone, he's chosen his side. I'm accepting the facts. He was completely flipped; it was like he was changed somehow; as if I didn't even know him. I've got to do what I need to do to protect my people, no matter how I feel about it." Even if that meant killing me.

Stefan holds up his hand. "A different person." He breathes. "Surely it wasn't a shapeshifter, you probably would have picked up on the spell..."

"I'm positive it was him. My smell was all over him." Alpha looks like he regrets admitting that and glances away. "If anything it was like he was drugged. Maybe Haryek got a hold of some of the bullshit your creepy mist creature was going off about."

Stefan appears in front of Alpha very suddenly, catching him off guard. "What bullshit? What did Pavel offer you?" He demands, frantic.

"Spells for obsession and whatnot, I didn't pay it much attention. That shit isn't real—" The whole room seems to be coming to the realization the Stefan had. Tonic gasps and Alpha picks up a lamp and throws it, enraged.

"He wouldn't dare!" He snarls.

Stefan swallows the heavy lump in his throat. "Alpha—If this is the truth... Nicolas is in grave danger."

"Reverse it!" Alpha commands of Stefan, the thunderous roar of his voice causing Tonic to nearly drop to his knees and the Strigoi hold up his hands in defense against the enraged man.

"I would love to but there is no reversing a love potion. They are temporary; they wear off in five days." His voice hangs, there's always a catch.

"We don't have five days." Alpha snaps. "Haryek is going to bring the rebellion to my doorstep, demanding my head and I can't—" He trails off.

He can't hurt me.

"Of course we can't, there is more at stake here!" Stefan snaps "I wasn't joking when I told him he needed to use less of his magic; we just brought him back from the dead not days ago! He is drained dry. A normal human would just fall into a comatose state if the potion was too strong or if they tried to fight it. But if Nicolas tries to fight it, in his weakened state, it stands the chance to drain his magic dry and that's it. He will go into a comatose state but he won't wake up. It will continue to drain on him; these spells aren't meant to be used on magic users. Let alone one who has just died!"

As the mood of the room begins to drift into darkness, it's Tonic who steps above it all. With resolve, he clears his throat. "So we just need to keep Alpha away from Nicolas for a few days? Haryek is a charmer; surely he can keep up the charade for five days until it wears off." Tonic chimes in.

Alpha falls silent, thinking it over. "You're assuming Nicolas would be triggered by me. Nicolas isn't in love with me."

Stefan frowns, seeming to agree with Tonic as he drifts closer to him. "Baby, do you honestly think Haryek will let this opportunity pass? Any flaw in Haryek's façade, even if we can make them avoid Alpha, will cause him to fight the potion. Seeing Alpha, alone, could tip him over the edge."

After a moment's silence, Alpha takes a deep breath. "Tonic, to-morrow you will go to the rebellion and you will tell him that I'm doing horrible things. Tell him I'm burning down the homes of anyone who I feel is assisting the rebellion; tell them that I'm executing loyalists in the streets. If he thinks I'm destroying the town, he will have no reason to question Haryek."

The younger male's jaw drops and he quickly shakes his head. Even if it did work, what would be the consequences, what if I never forgave him? Before he can answer, the chilled hand rests on his shoulder. "It might buy us some time, though." Stefan chimes in. "If we can hold him off one more day... we might be able to arrange for a recharge. I have a friend who is also a Solomonari. If we can get him to come here, he can summon a dragon and we can siphon the magic off of it and put it into Nicolas. That would give him enough magic to break the potion's hold."

"Siphon the magic off a dragon? I'm assuming they don't particularly like it when you do that?" Alpha wrinkles his nose in disgust.

Stefan chuckles weakly. "No, they don't. A dragon's magic is very precious but there is a stone table that the Lord of Magic has hidden in the castle that he used for these sorts of ceremonies. How do you think he became so powerful? Once the dragon is on the table, we will be able to complete the spell to finish the transfer. Nicolas just has to be near the table."

Tonic shudders. "And if your friend won't come?" He sounds reluctant to ask.

Stefan grimaces, while that possibility was high, he couldn't consider it right now. My life depended on it. "If he won't come, there is little we can do, I'm afraid. Nicolas won't survive the five days it takes for the potion to wear off. We will have to act quickly if we want to see this happen." He turns his attention to Alpha. "I can only work at night so I'm limited in my ability to help. I need you to get every person in your pack searching for this table, I can probably get my friend here by tomorrow night and we can fill him in on what needs to happen. We should be able to enact the spell by the third day if Tonic can keep up with the bad press about your misdeeds."

"I can do this." Tonic assures them both though his confidence in his ability to lie to me ebbed by the moment.

"You must do this. There is no room for failure." The somber tone in which he tells Tonic makes the omega shudder, stepping away as if it would somehow lessen the pressure.

Stefan rolls his eyes, "You'll do great, baby." Tonic offers them both a weak smile.

"I'm going to get started looking for this table. I'll try to make myself scarce and communicate to you both through Swift, Fleet, and Delta." He turns to leave, wanting to be far away from this place, wanting nothing more than to leave this behind him yet knowing it was far from over.

"Alpha, we will figure this out. He's going to be okay." Stefan calls to him. Alpha doesn't hesitate, he shifts the moment he's out the door and he's racing back towards the castle.

Tonic feels a strangled sob trying to come through and wraps his arms around himself. "Stefan, what if we can't do this?" His voice is hardly above a whisper.

"We have to, Tonic." He sounds so sure as he whistles and his spirit creature appears. "Pavel, I've heard you've been mischievous." Suddenly he pulls a silk handkerchief out of his pocket and snakes it over the spirit who hisses and rolls, trying to get free. "Listen here, you slimy husk! Did you give the elf a potion?"

"*Yesssss!*" Pavel hisses. "*Lycans bad! Lycan dirrrttttyy.*" Its raspy voice makes Tonic's skin crawl.

"That is very bad of you, Pavel! Now listen. You must go and gather up Loan. He looks very similar to Nicolas. Do you understand?" He shakes the bag and the creature chatters and hisses.

"Yeesssss masterrr." Stefan throws the cloth and the spirit springs free, it's gone in an instant. He turns to Tonic and frowns, taking the younger man's face in his hands and kissing him firmly.

"To be continued, my sweet... we both have a lot of work to do. I need you to take good care of Nicolas. Don't let him use his magic and keep an eye on him. Keep him fed, make him rest. Everything is going to be okay."

"Thank you Stefan." Tonic wraps his arms around his cool waist, leaning his cheek into one of the chilled hands.

"Don't thank me yet." Stefan frowns. "We still have two more days to make it through."

CHAPTER

Twenty-Four-

Haryek wastes no time in pulling me from group to group; announcing my alliance. It's difficult to see why this comes as a surprise to anyone.

I love him. Don't I?

The whole concept still feels so strange to me. Are they judging me because they didn't suspect I'd be with a man? Or because I'm not good enough to be next to this perfect being? I glance at Haryek and frown, feeling inadequate and nauseous all at once. There was an entire portion of our lives together that was vacant, an empty void of voices, and nothing more. The familiarity of this kind of emotional connection would surely come from years of companionship. Yet, I could remember nothing.

Visions of our one night together flicker before my mind, I stabilize myself, pressing my palm to my temple as I try and make sense of the jumbled emotions. There's a veil over the memory, shimmering as my body reacts to the thought, yet it feels incomplete. I shake my head, focusing on the object of my obsession as Haryek explains my allegiance to the local police force.

"We will begin the search tomorrow, it's time to put an end to this murderous cycle. We can no longer tolerate lycan activity in our country." Haryek commands, earning a timid nod from the police chief. The group around us cheers, it would seem the patrons of the rebellion were the only ones happy about this news. My own joy was sullied, I didn't want to confront the lycan horde any more than they did.

I pull my lips into a thin line, my thoughts warp until my eyes settle on Haryek, and then all at once, everything feels right with the world if only for a moment.

I must remind myself that I'm in love with him, as that's what my inner self commands me to do. We make our way towards dinner and the more conversations I have, the more I feel as though I'm not fooling anyone.

How are we going to capture Alpha?

I sit down with Haryek and I suspect I must be starving because the beginning of this morning refuses to register in my mind. Nibbling on fruit and avoiding any of the meat products, I watch wearily as metalsmiths forge new weapons in the hollowed outbuildings that were once homes. What should enrage me only proceeds to make me feel exhausted and I sag down onto my elbow. "Weapons, Haryek?"

The elf dismisses me with a casual wave. "We must protect ourselves, when is there a better time than when one is hunting an animal?"

The sharp pain aches in my chest. I shoved my plate away, pressing the back of my hand to my lips as I stifled a heave of my stomach. As a prince, I've been taught to conduct myself. I feel like I'm in the middle of war negotiations, not talking to the man I'm so desperately in love with. "What are we going to do with Alpha once we have a hold of him?" I need to hear that there is a plan, fifty rebels don't stand a chance against a lycan army but maybe he will come willingly?

"Well, if I had my way I would have him executed for the murder of your family." He shrugs as he bites an apple. The crisp sound of the bite into the fruit snaps into me and all over again I'm watching my father's death. I see, before me, the wolf, and as the sting of juice runs down Haryek's chin all I can see is blood. I hear my father laughing.

Dying.

My mother is screaming and crying.

He takes another bite, I register that he's talking but it sounds as if I'm underwater. My mother dies in front of me as the memory fades back into the haze. Instinctively, I slip closer to him, wanting the warmth in my chilled form. I feel as though I am dying. My body refuses to warm itself, I feel like a reanimated corpse.

"Nicolas." She's speaking to me but I know this isn't real. In her death, she had no words for me. "Nicolas!" I hear it louder this time; I'm being pulled out of the water. Someone is gasping for air, is someone drowning with me? The breathing sounds like a snarl, the wolf is in front of me and his fangs are bared. They drip blood red.

Red everywhere.

He pulls air through his teeth and poises to strike. "Nicolas!" Someone yells.

I blink. Haryek is in front of me, he looks almost embarrassed by my reaction to his suggestion. "What was that?" He questions. I realize I am the one breathing so heavily, my chest heaves, and I feel as though I have been holding my breath as my body fights for air. "You were completely gone; you looked like you'd seen a ghost." He takes another bite and I flinch.

I'm hallucinating. *Why am I hallucinating?* Vacant, my hands travel over my body as if I might find answers in my shivering form.

I don't want to bring light to my lack of control, I try to focus on the task at hand. "We would never get to that point with his people backing him. We will be lucky if we can capture him and contain him. The castle is the only place with the dungeon and it's filled with lycans."

His arm wraps around me, I welcome the sedation that his presence brings. I wish to sleep, my eyelids droop as I lean into him. "Details. We will figure that out tomorrow. Trust me; you're a master negotiator. I have a feeling taking him prisoner will be easier than you think." Haryek gives me a knowing grin and I force a glimpse of a smile, I like seeing him happy.

"We will discuss this tomorrow." He squeezes me, kissing the top of my head. My world begins to brighten, I don't feel quite so nauseous as he pays me this crucial piece of attention, feeding my starved self-esteem. "Come, I think it's time we go to bed. We have a long day in the morning."

As I follow him back to his cabin, my arm wrapped around his waist, his around my shoulders, I find myself not wanting to go in as I hesitate at the door. Haryek pauses and offers me a sweet smile. "Coming?" I close my eyes for a moment as my head pounds, thrumming loudly against my aching skull.

"Mhm." My body is at war with itself, fighting with some imaginary beast that keeps pulling me from these segments of numb contentment. Clinging to him, I could plead for relief if I knew what I was asking for. Pressed firmly against the elf, it eases the ache. "I love you." I tell him, testing the words, hoping they would hold some sort of power that would soothe my turmoil. "Did something happen? I feel like... I don't know how to describe it."

Slipping out of my grasp, he drifts into the kitchen to pour himself a glass of wine. "It's been a long day, you've had a lot of trauma these past few weeks, I don't expect you to remember anything. Maybe you hit your head?" Offering me the glass, it tempts me but I refused.

Haryek shrugs, taking a sip. "I figured you'd want to consummate this victory?"

In my current state, sex was the last thing on my mind. "There's always tomorrow?" I offer, my limbs feel too heavy to even carry me to bed, let alone perform any sort of duty.

Blocking out the disappointment on his face, I seek out the bed as I wriggle out of pieces of my clothes, leaving a trail of fatigue behind me. Grateful for the opportunity, I follow him to bed and watch as he undresses only to flinch when I see his bruised ribs, marring his beautiful skin. "Does it hurt?" I ask with a frown.

His expression turns sour, slighted by my rejection, "Only when I breathe."

Feigning humor, I retort with a slight grin. When he's speaking I feel better, when we're close I feel almost normal. "Doesn't seem to have slowed you down."

"It is very painful, Nicolas." Haryek's harsh tone takes me back, returning me firmly to my place.

"I'm sorry." I breathe. His arms curl around me yet I receive little comfort. There's not enough warmth between us for the chill that overtakes me, even under the heavy down blanket, I'm at the mercy of the cold.

"It is somewhat your fault. But, we will sort it out in the morning." Much as he holds me, I find little comfort in the darkness of the room. Not wanting to disturb him, I lay motionless for most of the night.

It was quite possibly one of the worst nights of sleep I've had in a long while. I wake up and feel as if I've only just shut my eyes. I feel chilled and briefly wonder if Alpha has gone on his run before sitting up to see Haryek beside me. My stomach sinks and I almost feel as if I could be sick once more. The headache betrays me; I leap out of bed to rush out the back door of the small cottage, though there is little to expel it doesn't stop my body from violently trying.

When I come back inside, I settle for a glass of water. Swishing it in my mouth, I spit in the sink to banish the taste from my lips.

Haryek stumbles his way into the kitchen. "Don't look at me. I'm feeling a little ill this morning." He takes the hint and keeps his distance. Haryek is not a morning person and it puts a damper on my mood. He looks more human, despite his ears, when he first wakes up. Scrutinizing him, I accept his flaws much better than I do his attributes. My head swims for my obsession with this being, yet my pulse murmurs along at a slow roll.

"Enjoying the view?" He purrs.

"I can't complain," I responded, though, my inner self could find plenty to fault. "I'm going to go get breakfast?" I offered as he waved me off to go do what I needed to do.

I feel terribly alone as I walk to the dining hall. Everyone greets me, bids me good morning. I'm embarrassed when I realize we are one of the last ones to wake up. But there are warm pancakes and fruit waiting for me, I instinctively grab enough for two before moving to sit by myself.

In silence, I chew. The empty seats draw me as if occupied by patrons I just couldn't see. Why did I feel as though I should be surrounded? Why did I miss that feeling that I couldn't even place?

My mood is dropping like the temperature; shrugging at the cold despite the warm air of the makeshift dining hall. I glance through the large stained glass window and I feel as though I should see snow but the sun is bright and shimmery through the colored glass.

The heavy hands rest on my shoulders, instantly I know better than to suspect it could be Haryek from the weight of the large palms.

Tonic sits beside me and I feel my first true spark of happiness since yesterday. "What're you doing here? Did you not see the posted notice? Haryek wants to ban all lycans, it's not safe for you here."

He chuckles, eyeing my companion's pancakes. I passed him the plate, an apology for what we were about to do. With the vigor of a young boy, he eats the pancakes with great appreciation. "I'm not afraid of Haryek or the police force, I have bigger things to worry about."

"Oh excuse me, your highness," I responded sarcastically, leaning my cheek into my palm. "Enjoying Stefan?" I ask hopefully.

He just nods, taking another few bites. His appetite is contagious and I take a few bites as well. My headache feels pity for me and ebbs just enough to be bearable.

"So... siding with the rebellion I see?" He asks me, timidly.

I don't know what to say to him. *Yes? I think your leader is a psychopath?* "I'm siding with Haryek, not against the lycans." I explain but it doesn't sound much better.

He makes a face and straightens. "What does that mean?" He asks slowly.

"It means that we need to have a serious conversation with Alpha... today. I want to keep working with him; I just need to know he's on our side." My body aches for something that I can't place, I want to be away from this place, even if it means leaving Haryek for a short amount of time. Everything in me screams that I have to warn them that the rebellion is planning an invasion of my home.

"Alpha's not in today..." He looks guarded.

"What do you mean?" I question.

"Well. After yesterday, he went into the city, rounded up all the rebel loyalists, and executed them in the streets. He—erm... Has gone towards Ziduri to hunt for any runaways. If you meet him head-on in the field, there will be nothing stopping him from finishing what he started with Haryek."

"What?" My voice is barely a whisper. "How? How could he do that?" I want to scream but my throat is tight.

Tonic's dark eyes refuse to look at me, ashamed. "Well, you threatened him, Nicolas. What did you think would happen?" Tonic gives me a look like I should have expected this to happen.

I should have, Alpha isn't human. He has no conscience; all he cares about is that he gets to Valhalla and destroying an entire race of people.

"Haryek was right, we can't let him live." But I can't kill him. Tonic stares at me wide-eyed. I cling to the vision that is Haryek, I cling to the sanity of someone of noble breeding.

"I think that's a bit extreme. There will be riots in the pack, don't forget Alpha has his own loyalists." He's backtracking. He has to protect his leader but I know he does speak some truth.

Glancing down too, I know it's a fleeting thought. "I could never kill him myself, I don't know why. I guess it's not in me to take a life. No, I won't stoop to his level. But I can make sure he stays in a cell and thinks about his decisions for the rest of his existence." *Then, I wouldn't have to lose him.*

My consciousness feels like a wave, drifting in and out of reality. I almost sag and Tonic grabs my arm, righting me. "Nicolas! You've used a lot of magic, maybe you should go back to Haryek's and lay down for a while?" he offers.

Sleep sounds like a good idea and I nod.

We get up and leave the dining hall; he has his arm around my waist. I stop in my tracks when I see a man who looks just like me. His deep red hair, we even share the same roman style nose. He's dressed in his robes, his skin is a deeper complexion than mine and his eyes are more golden than they are deep brown. He looks alive where I feel like a walking corpse, I know him because we went to school together.

"Loan?" I ask, surprised more than anything. Tonic looks appalled, as if he weren't supposed to be here.

"Loan, you're early." Tonic's voice is strained.

"Well when I heard that there was another Solomonari around, I had to come and see!" His voice is so smooth; he could almost be attractive if I didn't remember him being such an arrogant ass.

"Did Stefan invite you?" I'm instantly annoyed. If this is a game, if he hurts Tonic, I will throw him into the sun myself. It was no mystery to me that Stefan and Loan had entertained each other on a physical level.

"He thought it would do you some good to have more friends." He gives me his best smile and I roll my eyes.

"I have plenty of friends." I feel like a child who doesn't want to share his toys.

"C'mon Nikki!" He complains and I scowl.

As if on cue, Haryek saunters in with an amount of appreciation for the healthier-looking man that doesn't go unnoticed by my fragile self-worth. My chest throbs, I resist the urge to clutch for my heart. "Who's this?"

Loan extends his hand. "Loan, I went to school with Nikki here."

"Don't call me that." My mother called me that. Nobody can call me that. "My name is Nicolas." They exchange casual glances, sizing each other up. It feels as though I'm losing connection with my thoughts, they flicker in and out in a disconnect.

"Nicolas, don't be rude to our guests." Haryek paws at me like a schoolgirl in front of her new crush. Does he not see that I'm suffering? That my magic is slipping away and I can't even explain why?

"He's not our guest, he came here unannounced and I feel he should be going."

Tonic tightens his grip around my waist.

"Same old Nic." Loan shakes his head and Haryek chuckles. I feel sick.

"Haryek do something." Tonic hisses at my elf lover, the man who is supposed to love me. The man I'm supposed to love. *Why does this all feel so wrong? Am I just jealous?*

My chest begins to heave, I feel like I can't breathe. "What? It's just harmless fun. Nicolas, you know I only have eyes for you." He reaches for me and pulls me into his side. The funnel of my vision spirals rapidly, their shapes threaten to mix together as my body sways under the weight of my own conscious thought. Voices swirl, a life I can't remember leading flashing before my eyes and I'm with another man.

Not Haryek.

I want to push away, to be anywhere but here. "I want to go home, Haryek," It's hardly a whisper.

"Your home is right there, baby." He gestures to the cottage.

I shake my head, pressing my hands against him to shove away. "No. I want to go home. Take me home."

Tonic grabs my arm. "Nicolas, you have to stay here. It's not safe for you out there, not with Alpha on the loose."

Of all the people I fear, Alpha is not one of them, not in this new reality. "He won't hurt me!" I finally blurt out, absolute in my resolve as my brain lights off in a fest of colorful explosions behind my eyes. Some-things not right, I've been poisoned. I can feel it now, tasting it on the back of my tongue as the spell tries desperately to regain control.

"Uh oh. Looks like this party is about to start early." I hear Loan's voice.

"No, it can't happen now! We are over sixteen hours ahead of schedule! —Not even awake!" Tonic's desperation drags me to the surface. I realize that I've fallen, someone holds me so close yet their body provides little comfort.

"Nic!" The words sound like an echo

"Stay awake, Nicolas." I hear Haryek and I focus on that. "Stay awake."

Twenty-Five-

I briefly hear conversations happening around me. I feel like I'm sinking, falling deeper into the abyss. A part of me is fighting, telling me that I'm going to want to stick around for this but a part of me is swimming for the bottom. It would be easy to let go, life has not been kind or easy. To rest, to truly rest, would be such a gift at this moment. Everything hurts and I feel as if there is no end.

A roar rousts me as I swim for the surface. My eyes pry open, I'm aware that I'm being held by Haryek, my body swings gently as if I'm being rocked to sleep.

He's running.

I crane my head to see a larger dragon than I would ever have dared to summon. Her five heads twist and curl, she arches one to the sky for she's suspicious of us and our trickery. The others are interested, the forked tongues flicker and taste for magic as Loan stands before her.

I weakly roll my eyes; of course, he could summon such a dragon. He was always a good student. But I suppose he did actually try. From what I remember, he was someone who actually wanted to learn our trade so he could help people. I just spent most of my time trying to survive.

Loan was *thriving*.

Her inky black scales reflect the light beautifully. She is sparkling, her hide fresh out of the lake she had come from. "Climb on!" Loan demands of our troop.

Tonic hesitates. "I'm going to go on foot. I have to try and get there first. I don't know if we've even found the table yet!" He calls over the beat of her mighty wings. His body trembles, and she roars at him, forbidding his presence. For as long as time has existed, the dragon's opposite has always been the wolf.

"GO!" Loan yells at him and the boy is suddenly a gray streak running towards the castle. "We have to get on, she wants magic and I can't hold her for long." The strain in his voice is clear; she will kill him if he becomes too weak to send her home.

One of her inky tongues curls over her muzzle and her other heads taste excitedly. Only one of her necks wears the gold band to bind her to this world. She must be a greedy beast to agree to such terms. I wince as Haryek shuffles onto the back of the creature, seeking out the warmth of his clothes and searching for the pull that had held me to this realm.

Loan hops on the front and digs his heels into her sides. She roars and twists her necks as she ascends. The beat of her wings is exhilarating and it stirs me. I've always loved riding dragons and I look down over my beautiful city, now decimated from recent rebellion activity. With newfound anger, I feel more concrete in my position. I can't allow this to continue, I must stop the rebels from using my city as a playground.

This black beast is hard to control; she swerves and sways haphazardly in the sky. "Come on, ya bitch!" Loan snaps and digs his heels in. Her body rumbles and fiery lava drips from her lips at her disdain for her commander.

I can feel the tremble in Haryek's body and my eyes drift towards him. "Don't be worried, flying dragons is supposed to be fun," My body sways back and forth between the Nicolas that the spell wants me to be and the one who fights for my salvation. Nothing good comes from this state, in the back of my mind I catch glimpses of my death and lying on Stefan's table. The potion fights against me, crushing the memory back down and presenting me with Haryek.

He looks at me like I've lost my mind. "I don't think I'll be doing it again anytime soon."

"Keep him talking Haryek, we are almost there."

I'm too exhausted to worry about it. My world goes blurry around the edges and I glance down at the ground where I can see a gray wolf running.

"Alpha." I breathe. It feels like an electric shock, I cringe and clutch my chest as a cry leaves my throat.

Haryek looks frantically to see what I've seen. "No, baby, that's Tonic." He tells me hurriedly. "See? The coat's different. Can you see the black?" He tries to bring me back and I force myself to look again. It's hard to see from this height but I focus on the size difference most of all. Tonic was not nearly as big as the wolf I'd become familiar with.

"Yes. He's a good friend." I snuggle into Haryek's chest to focus on his heartbeat. It's so much faster than mine. "I'm cold," I complained. The wind billows, whipping my skin with its chilled lashes that sting as if I were made of the finest silk. My body surrenders to the onslaught, accepting its fate. Even with the dragon's blazing body, my own refuses to produce heat any longer. Haryek wraps his jacket around me, I catch his gaze and note that he looks horrified.

"If he dies, it's on your hands, elf." Loan grumbles and Haryek holds me tighter.

Dies?

"Who?" I ask, *surely not me?* I think about the darkness and I can see a piece of myself standing in the blackness, gesturing me to come down with one ghostly hand. I blink the image away and look at my own hand. The paper skin stands out in strong contrast against the black of the dragon. The ghostly hands tremble as my fingertips blacken. The magic receded from the ends of my body, fighting to keep my heart beating.

"Nobody, darling. We are almost there." The dragon lands in the courtyard and I grunt at the abruptness. She snaps her jaws at any wolf that dares come close.

"Have we found the table?" Loan calls as Delta rushes towards us.

"We believe it's on top of the castle. In the middle of the pillars, there is a flat spot but it's on a glass floor. I don't know how well it will support the weight." He looks unsure, just as they all do every time they look at me. When someone begins to die, it's common for those around to feel uncomfortable. They might act like it won't happen, to provide social anesthetic for the person whose life is nearing the end. A cruel herd mentality, really.

"It will have to do. Does it smell like magic?" Loan ushers the information out of him.

"Everything smells like magic right now but currently all we can smell is the sulfur of this beast!" Delta scowls towards the dragon and she hisses at him in response. Maybe the fact that they are both animals gives them a common hatred of each other. Her black teeth are exposed and her black eyes flicker white as her third eyelid swivels back and forth. Delta shudders, visibly.

All I can think of is the desire to speak to Delta, to confirm the stories I've been told.

Before I can greet him the dragon leaps back into the air and she's climbing again. The sharp angle causes us to slip, with no saddle her scales bear little purchase. Haryek holds me tightly, "Loan!" Haryek's desperate voice pulls me back from the edge, the potion that was killing me now the only thing holding me to this world.

My red-haired companion fights with the beast, mentally forcing her into submission. She screams her displeasure and thrashes her neck as she circles the castle. Fire belches from one of her mouths and rolls down the side of one of the tall pillars. She lands hard and Haryek slips. I realize I'm not even holding on and Loan grabs me as Haryek scrambles to right himself on her back.

"Just go! If I fall off, I'll be okay." Haryek calls over the popping and scraping of the dragon's claws as she travels from pillar to pillar. Debris and brick fly from the castle walls as she wrenches her claws into the old cracks and crevices, the aged rock groans in displeasure at her weight but thankfully it was built to withstand dragons.

"We need you to keep him alive. You're the only thing holding him to this plain. His magic is almost gone!"

So I am going to die. I had hoped that I would at least go out with more purpose than this. I never pictured a lack of magic would be what ended my life. The memory of lying on Stefan's table flashes again, my life flooding back into my consciousness as the potion begins to fail.

A normal person would have rallied; they would have sat up and forced strength from within. But I've never been normal and I feel, almost, okay with this. No wonder I've felt horrible the past few days. I've been dying. It seems only just that my last days would be spent with Haryek, whom I love but don't all at the same time.

With Alpha nowhere to be found and my city in shambles, a war on the horizon, I can't think of a reason that I should suffer alongside these people any longer. I want to tell them to stop going through the trouble but the words don't come out. A side of me is ashamed of my weakness.

What would my parents think? Or really, my mother. She would be disappointed in my disinterest in saving my own life. She would have had some motivational speech, she would have called to my better nature and assured me that it doesn't have to end quite so dramatically. I can hear her, chuckling at me.

"Oh Nikki, always for the drama. Wouldn't a normal death, of something as boring as age or illness, be so much simpler?" It makes me smile.

The creature jumps again and we land on the false floor of the castle. The glass screeches as her claws drag across it. Her one rebellious head screams and wraps around the other necks, it recognizes the table. One head curiously pulls forward and she bellows as she fights with herself.

Quicker than we can stop her, she begins to bite at the head with the collar. Dragons don't need all their heads, they can regrow them as they absorb magic and age. She decides, now, that it's time to be rid of the collar.

Loan's eyes widen. "They're killing the control! Quick! Victor!" He calls as the large blond hops off the edge of the wall, holding a chain.

"I did not have a dragon, had to take long way." Victor glances at the dragon and grins. He rolls his shoulders and pops his neck. "So need to get dragon from there to there?" The Russian gestures to the table.

"Yes. Quickly. If they eat that head we will have no way to control her."

Victor nods and runs forward, he dodges heads as he leaps onto the dragon's back and one of the heads snaps at him. He delivers a powerful kick to the dragon's muzzle and it bucks violently as all heads turn to face him.

He grins wickedly, thrilled to be faced with certain death. With a thunderous snarl, his arms spread as an open invitation for the full force of the dragon's charge. Wrapping his arms around its muzzle, he begins to bind its mouth closed with the chain. One head's mouth leaks lava and he thrusts his hand up to shove its mouth towards the sky as it bleeds fire.

It screams in defiance as fire rains down on us. Haryek and Loan violently pat my clothes to put out any embers, I'm vaguely aware of the little tufts of flame as they land. They dance in the darkness of my vision like little embers of life flickering away.

Victor lands back on the ground and uses his weight to pull the chain taut, pulling the dragon towards the table. She screams at him, fire blazes from her mouth, and Loan yells out a spell, putting a protection layer between Victor and the beast. "I can't hold this and her, Victor!" He calls out and flinches at the effort.

"Taking one moment! Can not perform magic!" He yells and bears his full weight on the chain. He yanks hard as her feet scrape the glass. His massive muscles ripple beneath his clothes, tearing his shirt over his broad shoulder blade from the exertion as he pulls. The veins on his arms bulge and his cheeks redden, he grinds his teeth in defiance.

She bites the shield and thrashes her head, taking turns snapping at it. The glass begins to groan. Sulfur fog leaks from her mouths, threatening to suffocate us.

"Fuck..." Loan breathes. "Now Victor! Get her there now!"

Victor is suddenly no longer a man, the white wolf holds the chain in his teeth. Her feet move quicker now as he bears his full weight on the chain, pulling her closer to the table. The glass begins to ping and pop. It shudders with each step. Her eyes glimmer as she sparks a plan and with a mighty heave, she crashes her tail down on the fragile glass with a sickening snap. Shards and fragments of glass leap from the surface, glittering in the air like the shimmering sheen of her scales.

"She's breaking the glass!" Haryek cries.

One scaly claw rests on the table and she roars. One of her heads bites the stone, chipping it and her teeth which cause her to spiral against the chain. It shortens it, yanking Victor closer but also entwines around her long necks.

Loan is forced to drop the shield to try and regain control of the one half dead head that wears the collar. He falls to his knees, gasping for air much like I was. She parts her jaws and draws off of him, siphoning his magic.

"You can do it Loan." Haryek breathes, putting his hand on Loan's shoulder.

She breathes fire, burning Victor's shoulder. He snarls and with one violent jerk, her claws reach the table. Loan leaps to his feet and runs, he slams his hands on the table and cries out as one of her heads latches on to his side and tries to force him away. Victor's fangs find her neck and her screams bring my hands to my ears. Releasing Loan, she clutches Victor with all her heads and prepares to tear him in half.

"No!" I cry. The table erupts in light and she releases Victor, her body spasms, and the table groans under the weight. As Victor hits the glass, it cracks and bursts. The dragon shrieks as the table crashes through the floor.

We are all falling.

CHAPTER

Twenty-Six-

The dust fills the ancient library and I feel like I'm suffocating but not for the same reasons as almost moments before. My body feels different, stronger. I feel rejuvenated; better than I felt even when I was using magic every day in school. As my eyes adjusted, I came to realize that we'd fallen into my father's library. Laying haphazardly on a pile of aged books, rocks, and massive, heavy curtains, it would seem we'd been lucky enough to land almost entirely on the dragon.

The smell of sulfur is strong, I'm briefly aware that we are all now trapped down here with a massive dragon but I realize I'm the only one scrambling to my feet.

I slip, losing my footing on the glass chunks surrounding us and I briefly remember wondering where the roof of this room was. This was certainly not the way I wanted to find out. The table is broken in pieces, resting on top of the dragon who, unfortunately, did not survive the crash.

Dark, red blood surrounds her and her body has shrunk to half its original size. Loan is close to her, his breathing shallow. At first, I feared that he was dead. I rush to him, slipping and stumbling over the rubble, and kneel down beside him. Pushing some of the rocks and debris from him, I check his pulse. Still with us but he's used a lot of energy.

He looks similar to how I looked, his tanned skin ghostly pale. His hair lacks the familiar sheen. His light brown eyes are looking at me, he's awake and I'm grateful that he's coherent enough to look at me with such malice.

"I'm going to give you some of my magic, and then you need to tell me if you need healing okay?" I tell him, in a low voice. As if the dragon were still lurking, I murmured a few words over and over, holding my hand to his back. His heart rate quickens back to a normal pace and he inhales sharply and slowly raises himself out of the gravel.

Loan slaps my hand away, giving me a scowl. "Thanks." His voice is hardly above a grumble. It's not much but it will keep him alive. He cringes and grips his bloodied side. The bitemark oozes blood and debris, packed with dust and grit from the impact, it would help with the clotting but not do much to prevent infection and the pain he must be in.

"Let me heal you." I reach for him but he glares daggers at me.

"Maybe we should make sure everyone else is alive before we are back to square one with this overuse of magic?" His tone is harsh and slowly he stands, holding his hand to his side to slow the bleeding. His robes are stained on his side, streaking red down his leg and over his hands. The torn tatters of clothes remind me that I'm down to my last robes as well.

My eyes scan the room and I find Haryek by his translucent hair.

He's fighting his way out of the rubble and I rush to him, Loan close behind me. I expect to feel attachment, the pull, but there's nothing and I slow my pace. Loan reaches him first and starts to move rock pieces from his legs. "I think your leg is broken." He tells him and Haryek groans, shutting his eyes and looking away.

He's filthy, covered in soot and stone dust and dirt. Down here, he looks less perfect, and maybe now I'm just seeing him clearly? "A little help?" Loan snaps at me.

I jump and rush to help them, careful not to hurt Haryek's injured leg that, I can confirm, is broken by the way it twists in two different directions. *Victor.* I look around but he's nowhere to be found. "Where's Victor?" I demand. Both men look at me like I'm an invalid.

"Sorry, forgot to keep an eye on the lunatic." Loan gawks at me, a reminder that I've been a large inconvenience to him.

"Victor." I raise my voice just slightly, hoping to hear an answer. I hear the rubble grumbling and I prepare myself for whatever might still be down in this magically cursed cavern but I begin to relax when I realize it is only our Russian companion.

He is completely naked and covered in blood. His body is littered with bite marks, his forehead busted so blood runs freely down his face and over his startling eyes. From ear to ear, he grins quite savagely with a booming laugh that echoes of the walls, trembling the cavern as if it fears for its goods.

He has a glass shard in one hand and he, in one motion, pops a single dragon fang from a puncture on his shoulder. He holds it up like a gory trophy and laughs, hysterically. Holding his fist up in triumph, he turns his attention to us and throws the bloodied shard of glass into the pile of rubble.

"Look! Souvenir!" Putting his foot dramatically on the dragon's neck, he belts out a war call that chills me to my core. I remind myself to never upset Victor.

Flushing, I look away suddenly and clear my throat when I come to the conclusion that he's very much naked. "Glad you got a prize," I mumbled, holding my hand up to block his genitals from my view. I don't know why it feels so disrespectful to look at this man. Maybe it's my respect for Adriam or the fact that I don't know if I want to know how large Victor truly is.

"Well, that makes this almost worth it." Loan says appreciatively of the naked form before us and Haryek clears his throat.

"Excuse me, gentleman, but I'd kind of like to get this whole fucking leg thing remedied? Today, if you will?" He snaps impatiently.

"Right." I look at him and stoop down to help him up, Loan grabs his other side though he isn't much help considering his side is busted up. All three of them had seen better days; it's only me who is unscathed due to my bout with dragon magic. Loan slips away from us suddenly and makes his way over to the dragon. He frowns and kneels down to put his hand on top of one of her heads.

"I'm sorry girl..." His voice is low and I feel as though I might actually see some remorse on his face. He touches her so gently, his hand skirting over her scales and stroking down her snake-like head. His shoes collect her blood but he doesn't seem to mind ruining his already destroyed healer's robes.

Saying a few quick words, a mist-like substance leaves her mouth and her body reduces down to the size of the small dragon I pulled from the servants' quarters. He carefully picks her up, his eyes brighter. "We will return her to her world. Maybe she can be reborn there." He doesn't look at me as he storms past and I follow, supporting Haryek. Victor is close behind, admiring his fang.

We navigate into the hallway and as we shamble our way to the front doors, I start to recall the last few days. Once we enter the courtyard, I freeze. The entire pack is here and I realize I had no idea how truly large it was. Hundreds of wolves. Two? Three maybe? They surround us, crammed together. Loan doesn't even hesitate but Haryek and I are in uncharted territory. Loan glances over his shoulder and scoffs, "They're not here for me." He explains his ease and strokes his dragon's corpse.

As Victor appears, everyone erupts in applause and I realize Adriam is running towards us. He throws his arms around the brute's neck, hanging from him like a necklace due to his height. He wraps his legs around Victor's waist and clings to him. The Russian puts one arm around his French lover and shows him the fang.

"Worth it." He tells him with the most ridiculous grin and Adriam just laughs and kisses his bloodied cheek and neck.

"I thought you were dead, you big idiot!" He sobs, burying his face into the large man's neck. "Don't ever do that again."

"Next time in a life or death situation, I remember to ask permission to fall from the ceiling?" The heavy sarcasm would make me laugh if not for the hundreds of eyes bearing down on us.

Adriam nods and Victor kisses him in a way that every man might wish to be kissed, with every ounce of adoration that a feral Russian male can spare. As he breaks the kiss, Adriam hesitates and turns to face us.

"Hold on baby." Even Loan pauses. "You. All of you. We aren't done here. I'm going to go hug my husband and thank the gods that he is alive to be with us but then, we are all having a discussion. One hour, in the dining hall. Understood?"

We all nod, even Haryek. He wraps his arm around Victor's and leads him away. I can still hear Victor's thundering voice as I turn my attention back to the very lame Haryek, who is still suffering from a broken leg.

"I should probably heal you, though I feel you kind of deserve it. It's starting to come back to me. You drugged me, didn't you?" I demand from the elf.

He shrugs, disinterested. "I did what I thought was necessary, I didn't think you'd go and try to die." He looks at me as if it's my fault.

I gape at him in disbelief. "I know plenty of men who get by just fine on a splint."

Loan pipes in and glances down at his dragon. "I've got to go return her, I'll be back shortly. Try not to be too entertaining while I'm gone." He smirks as he wanders towards the lake. I admire his dedication to the lizard.

As much as I don't like him, he didn't have to help the dragon and she certainly will remember him in her next life, if she gets one. It's such a selfless act, I envy his commitment.

Haryek is watching me, uncertain. I sigh and kneel to feel his leg. Without asking him, in one quick pull of his ankle, I reset the bones. It was much like tending to our young livestock, I'd reset quite a few legs in my time playing with the sons of our local dairy farmer. I never liked to see things suffer, much to my aversion to meat, watching the young calves limp after being stepped on had always compelled me to try and heal them.

Haryek, now, reminded me of one of those calves. In pain and naivety, he wasn't nearly as useful as a calf.

"I think I'm going to splint this and let you deal with it." I guide him back to the dining hall and turn the table into a makeshift workspace. I grab some boards from the throne room, where they have destroyed so many of my heirlooms, and compare them until I find two the right length. Then I take the inner sheet of some of the curtains from the hall and grab my knife and get to work cutting them down till I have quite a few thin strips to fashion the boards together with.

I get to work setting his leg and he cringes. "I'm surprised you're helping me." I toy with not answering though honestly; I'm so disappointed in myself it's good to talk about anything at this point.

"You tried to help me in the end, I should return the favor." I want to be angry but I'm not. I use people all the time; I shouldn't be so upset that Haryek used me. "Why did you drug me, Haryek?" I finally managed.

He thinks and flinches as I pull tight on the strip to set the boards. "I wanted you for myself, you were something I couldn't have. I'm not sorry, not really anyways. I think it was a good move politically. It broke the ice, got us all working together. It's unfortunate you almost died but it would have worked out either way." I want to be angry. My blood boils.

"Glad it didn't fuck up your plans," I mutter and finish wrapping his leg.

"We could have been really good together. I almost had you convinced that you loved me and that you would help me get rid of that 'Alpha' but it seems as though you are too into him to be persuaded. Put on a good show though." He regards me, raising a perfectly arched eyebrow.

I slow my hands and glance at his leg. "I'd like to think I worked my way out of it myself," I tell him stubbornly. "And for what it's worth, it was your complete disregard for anything but yourself that convinced me that I could never actually love you. I don't think even a love potion could convince me to care for you."

He laughs at me in that condescending way that only he knows how. I yank the bandage tighter and he gasps. "Keep telling yourself that, darling. I'm not stupid; I spent two whole days with you. You're fucked up but you're not exempt from feeling something for someone. Your 'thing' for him is what almost killed you when I gave you the love potion."

It does make a little bit of sense but I push it to the back of my mind. I've got too much going on to worry about how I feel for someone. "I guess I am messed up, huh?" I sigh and help him slide forward on the table.

I'm taken by surprise as Tonic runs across the room and throws his arms around me, the first person that looks happy that I'm alive. I'm still pretty sore though I feel great otherwise, almost restless.

"I'm so happy you're okay. I knew you would be, we had things set too well for you to slip through the cracks!" He sounds so cheerful and I truly believe that Tonic never doubted me for a minute.

I hug him back, so tightly that I worry I might hurt him but he soaks it in and I stay there for a long moment, as long as he allows before he wiggles uncomfortably. "Thanks, Tonic. You've saved my life again." I tell him, will this one ever stop saving people?

He flushes and shrugs. "It was a group effort. Stefan called for Loan and Alpha found the table."

My heart skips a beat and I frown. So where is he then? "I'll have to thank him later." My tone is half-hearted.

"He was pretty worried about you, you know." His words cut me and I offer a small smile. Of course, he was. I'm his ticket to winning this war.

I feel like I'm just about to break down and go looking for him when the entourage enters the room and I can feel the heavy tone this is about to take. Sota, Adriam, a clothed Victor and Loan enter the room. Adriam is seething, on fire. His eyes blazed. If Tonic could fall to his knees he would but instead he takes a step back from Haryek and me.

"Tonic, leave us," Adriam says firmly. My only friend scurries out of the room. All eyes are on me, I feel like a child and I squirm under the pressure. "What. Did. I. Say?" Adriam's voice is low. He's no longer my sweet gay friend, he's Adriam the Old Blood. The medic. The lover. The family member.

Victor is patched from head to toe under his clothes. He's the only one who looks happy to see me.

"Where's Alpha?" I need to speak to the man in charge, not Adriam.

"Is that really important right now?" Adriam's tone is harsh. "What did I tell you? What did you then, immediately, go and do? For two days our pack has been at a standstill looking for this fucking table!" His French accent rolls strong. "To save you! Again!" He gestures at me. "What did I tell you about him?" He gestures at Haryek now. "Elves are nothing but trouble, you were supposed to go and negotiate terms to put this rapist in a place where he couldn't hurt anyone, any longer."

I don't know what to say, I just wait for it to be over with. He's hurt; I can see it in his eyes. He trusted me. They all did.

"Alpha came back—" He stops and takes a deep breath. "Verando. He tells us that you are dying and for some reason, we are supposed to save you. You have not held up your end of the deal, you have done nothing but sabotage this entire mission. My husband is expected to fight a fucking dragon to revive you and for what? I find you, in here, mending this elf." The hurt is revealed, he almost lost Victor. For all he knew, Victor was dead after he fell through the roof.

"This game is done. We are not ready for this war, at this rate, if Ziduri was to launch an attack on us we would be met unprepared. I will not risk my family's life because you can't seem to get your shit together, let alone pick a side. I get it, I really do. We killed your family, we've taken your home. I'm going to tell you this once. Suck it the hell up.

"We have all faced hardship. You either need to decide to stand against us or you need to get it together. We are all fighting for the same thing and that is freedom of our races. We have two months until we are marching on Ziduri and I can't have you screwing with his head anymore. Do what you have been spared to do or I will end you myself. Do you understand?"

I don't know why I'm surprised. What did I expect? My continued disobedience wouldn't be tolerated for much longer. I was constantly pulling Alpha away from his pack, his job, and his duties. I was hard to manage; I took a lot of time and effort to protect and it seemed to be that I had my own agenda. After all, I was their prisoner and they had put a lot of trust in me that I honestly didn't understand. But, that wasn't the question today. "I understand."

"Good. Have Tonic take this Elf home and leave him there. You will discontinue visits to the rebellion, you are returning to your role as a *prisoner*. Haryek, you will be hearing from us shortly." With that Adriam turns on his heel and storms out.

I glance at his entourage and see that only Loan seems to be in agreement with him. Victor and Sota are stone-faced and that surprises me, I figured Sota would have had me executed but there he is, looking unsure of these commands. I find myself wondering where Verando is, why is Adriam making these decisions? Tonic scrambles back in, as a wolf and lowers himself for Haryek to climb on.

The elf looks at me. "When you are done letting people boss you around, let me know. I'm not prepared to lay down for a Frenchman, let alone this one." He tells me, rolling his eyes at me as he slides onto Tonic and they are gone. I'm all alone and for once, I'm happy about it. I feel conflicted.

I see what they are saying but this isn't me, it's not in me to fall in line and mindlessly obey any order. But who am *I*, truly?

CHAPTER

Twenty-Seven-

It is strange to be shaken from your norm. I'd become used to having free reign that now that I'm back on restriction, that I'm a prisoner, I'm reminded that I'm an adult who's being put into time out. Only, this time it's for real. Adriam would not see my worth as Alpha did.

I sit in my window sill because I hope I'll see him but I don't. I think about how I would be dwelling, how I would be thinking of a way out but right now, I'm just questioning where I was in my head while I was dying on the back of the dragon. I think of how I felt like I was sinking, I check myself and I don't see the same images.

It's like I'm watching from the outside. I tell myself that it isn't my fault I'm feeling this way, my parents were brutally murdered in front of me. It's normal to ask yourself what there is to live for. Isn't it?

I watch them out there, they're so busy and they remind me of ants. The cool air is beginning to change the colors of the leaves, their multi-colored coats are starting to blend with the trees. I watch their formations, the way they travel like one unit. It would be optimal if I could do that but I try to envision it and I can't.

I've never been able to fall in line, follow the flow and do what was expected of me. I suppose that's truly why I was sent off, instead of my brother. He was a good 'ant'. He could follow orders; he could make the hard calls. I always allowed my emotions to get involved, I always looked for an easier way and to avoid the root of the problem because I didn't want to be hurt when I, ultimately, failed. Failure was something that I was used to and I hated disappointing people.

I rest my cheek on the glass and go back to that first day. I think of myself, face to face with the man who murdered my family. I press my hand to the glass; it's cool to the touch. I think about falling, sailing to the ground. Would it hurt? I smile, I wasn't afraid then. I'm not afraid now. So what's changed?

Him.

My opposite. Someone who knows with absolute certainty who he is and what his purpose is. Maybe Adriam is right, staying away is probably the best for all of us.

But can I do what is expected? Be a mouthpiece? Smile and wave while I stand in front of a lycan wave of destruction? That's what my father would have done if it meant survival, what my brothers would have done. But what would I do?

Maybe that's what Adriam meant when he told me I needed to get it together. We share the same in that we've all lost people, yet, could I truly forgive people who killed my family? It made little sense to me, my intentions had been to side with the rebellion and end the Lycans just as Haryek had proposed. But, when it came time, I couldn't side with him.

I feel a tear slip and I take a deep breath. I realize that all I really want right now, desperately, is to talk to my mother. I can see her soft face, sitting on the ledge with me and looking out the window just as I am but she's not seeing the view I am. She was always so positive, so uplifting. I sniffle and crane my head back, "I miss you." I told her. Her loss, needing her and knowing I'll never get a response, perhaps it's cripplingly loneliness that causes me to wish to help these murderous beings.

The mother in my head doesn't look at me because she knows that's not what I need. I just miss being around her, being near her. My mother never offered me great words of wisdom or guidance, she just loved me unconditionally and that was all I needed from her. I allow myself, for the first time since the first few days, to really break down for the loss of my mother and when I think of my siblings it opens a whole new door of pain that honestly scares me.

But I absorb it; I sob and let myself work through it. I don't feel better but I do feel more like myself and maybe I can finally start healing from this. I will never be my old self but that's not what this world needs right now. I must grow and change, for my people. I start thinking of my father and it brings on a fit of whole new anger and determination. I can't do things their way but I can do it my way and that will have to be good enough.

With new gusto, I stand up and grab a new set of clothes. Just a long sleeve and some pants with a vest. I head down to the servants' quarters and make use of the servants' showers, they are operated on a pump and so much easier than hauling buckets.

I scrub the grit and grime from my hair and cringe at my sore muscles. The running water feels amazing on my stiff body. I scrub myself clean from the debris of the fall and the past few days. Allowing myself to stand there as long as I can take the heat, I force myself out and scrub my hair dry. Pulling on my clothes, I take my robes to my room to clean them later. It isn't often I get to look like a civilian yet more and more, I'm finding comfort in this identity.

Before the takeover, I was either dressed completely for court or, most recently, donning my robes. This 'new' Nicolas didn't fit into either of those roles.

Heading outside, I glance around to first make sure Adriam isn't around. I make my way cautiously around, avoiding anyone from the trio and try to seek out Alpha. But everyone seems to be avoiding me or they're too busy to talk to the Alpha's servant when he's been nothing but trouble. They've all seen what happens when you try and help me and they want no part of it.

I have little luck finding Alpha so I decide to venture into the city. If Adriam wishes to kill me, I might as well make it worth his while. Secretly, I hope that Alpha will fear I'm making an escape and reveal himself.

I visit the bakery and nab a loaf of bread, everyone here is always so happy to see me even though they hardly know who I am. It feels so fake, at least with the pack I know I'm generally disliked. Here I think people like me because it's practically the law to do so; I'm no longer lulled into the false sense of security that it brings. After experiencing a full dose of the love potion, I know exactly what that false affection breeds.

Wandering the streets, I give the casual wave and finish my loaf of bread before a new shop catches my eye. The sparks flying off the anvil surprise me. We never had anything like this before, I make my way over and the clinking of metal gets louder and louder until I'm standing in front of the workshop and realize they are doing metal-working. It's a blacksmith shop. I'm surprised to see some of my own people in there, minimalistic magic users who had not lifted a finger to do anything other than a farm in generations. I blink and the man swinging a hammer smiles at me.

"Prince Nicolas." He greets. I try not to wince.

"Hello. What is it that you're doing?" I ask curiously.

"Well currently I'm making a knife, My Lord. Not doing a good job of it but I haven't been at it long." He laughs and I smile. He looks happy enough. A few other men are in here as well, none that I recognized.

"That's great. I er—who is doing this? We never had a metal worker in Dezna before." I wonder what wolf knows how to metalwork. I admire their coal forges, I watch the man crank the handle as the flame roars to life. Then I realize who is helping.

Alpha comes out of the back with a shining sword he's wiping off with a cloth. He looks happy, truly happy. I smile until I realize it's not me he's looking at, he's happy here. Away from everyone. Away from me. For when he sees me, he looks conflicted.

I hold my breath as he weighs his options but he sighs and hands the sword off with instructions to finish grinding it to a polish. As he approaches me, I feel as though we are in the same space. We both are unsure what to do with ourselves, for his conscience speaks to him just as loudly as mine speaks to me. The other is dangerous, we should avoid each other at all costs for it is in our fate to wish to kill each other.

He smells like coal, it's odd. I'm so used to the smell of the woods on him, his skin is tarnished in black. Inky, dark streaks of grit mark his skin and brighten the already icy eyes.

I walk away from the workshop towards the outer edge of the city and he follows me soundlessly. As I come to a halt, I take him in, it feels like I've not seen him in years but it's only been two days.

"Hi." Is all I can manage.

"You're alive." He sounds relieved but there is a hidden tone behind it. He keeps his distance.

"I am. The table worked, Victor was able to pull the dragon—"

He interrupts me. "Is everyone okay?" He asks with concern.

Everyone else must come before what we want, it's a painful fact that I'm slowly molding to. "Yes. Everyone is fine..." My voice is slow, I bite my lower lip.

We stare at each other for a long moment, wary of the other. The air is heavy with the weight of the crossroads we continue to confront, how much longer could we pretend that this was normal? "Well, I'm glad you are okay." Alpha offers me.

"That's it? I mean... Thank you for your help. I know you helped but—" I take a breath, how do I say this? I cross my arms over my chest. "Where have you been? We just fought off a dragon. I was dying not hours ago." I know it's foolish to expect anything other than dismissal but I must know, it would help with my clarity to see that he values me just as Haryek does, to hear him say the same words that Adriam uttered to me. If he would banish me too, it would make my decision to act against them much easier to swallow.

"Here. I wasn't allowed to go home, if you had seen me you could've died." His response is short, almost accusing.

I hadn't expected him to care. This would be the second time he had saved my life. "Well, I appreciate you doing that. I know that must have been hard for you." I allow

This is killing me, he gives nothing away. I take a step forward and he takes a step back. "Randy—" I start and he holds up his hand.

"Stop." He tells me firmly. I stop and drop my hands.

I need something, anything. In my mind, I plead with him to convince me to remain in my home and not continue on this path, to not rejoin Haryek, to not demolish this alliance.

"I can't. Not now. This has been a lot. I don't—" He sighs and pinches the bridge of his nose, we mirror each other, as if he's pleading for the same thing. "I thought I had lost—I went to Stefan to—" He stops and puts on his Alpha face. "I went against everything I believe in and stand for."

I don't understand. I take another step and he takes two steps back. He's pulling away from me, I can see it on his face. Perhaps this is the difference in our ages, that he understands siding against me would be the best for his people. In reality, Alpha was a victim to his advisors as much as I was at the mercy of his will. He would have received a similar speech that I had, he would be faced with the same harsh lines.

My heart twists, "I was under a spell!" I try and reason with him, I just want him to believe me if nothing else. There is a pull here; I remember feeling it when I was drugged by Haryek. That need. I take deliberate steps, moving towards him and warn him with my eyes. He stays this time but his whole body is rigid.

"All you do is defy me..." It's an excuse, a reason to keep his distance.

"You like it when I disobey you," I responded back, slowly. That burn hits me, the urge. His presence intoxicated me, without any potion to encourage it. I'm within feet of him. I'm convinced if I could just touch him; he will come back to my side and I realize I've come not to convince myself that I need to stay but simply to satisfy my need to see that my grandest addiction would still participate in my favorite pastime.

"Nicolas." He warns me, the restraint in his voice clear.

"Randy." I pleaded with him. I reach for him and his growl surprises me. He takes a big step back and flinches. The growl rolls through him again and he groans, clutching his stomach, stooping over for a second.

"Fuck." He hisses through his teeth, the inferno is more intense than the coal forges we were just surrounded by. He pants as he slowly straightens. I watch his eyes; I can see he's fighting for control. "This isn't going to work Nicolas." He sounds so sure. I want to fight back.

"It wasn't my fault!" I yell at him, I feel the tears threatening to come on again. He stares at me; I can see the pain he's hiding and know this is hard for him, too. "Is it your wolf? Is your wolf doing this?"

Those light eyes tell me all I need to know, the presence of the wolf glowers from inside those eyes. "If you get any closer to me—I can't control it. He will kill you." He sounds tired, like it's an extreme effort just to stand here.

"You won't hurt me. You can fight it." I take another measure towards him, watching him. His pupils dilate and he sets his jaw on the edge of an eruption as his body shakes beyond his control. I can't hurt him, I step back up, breathing for the first time as I give him the distance. I can't be selfish anymore. He grimaces and my frown deepens. "You can't fight it, can you?" It's not a question, though.

"No. The wolf has decided. It's just not safe for you to be around me. So I'm going to be spending time in the outer ranks and Victor will be controlling the inner workings on your end. We won't have to see each other. You're free."

"I don't want to avoid you. I want to see you. I don't care if you hurt me, your pack needs you! Victor isn't even running things, Adriam is!" I snap, angry, that the person who was supposed to be so secure in his beliefs would dare give up on me now.

"Adriam is more than capable."

I shake my head, balling my fists as magic surges to my fingertips. The threat tests my own control, my body resists the urge to defend myself. "He's not you! You're going to turn your back on your pack? I didn't have a choice, you do! You have controlled it this long. Go beat up Victor, run, and train with Sota, there has to be a way."

"Not this time." He tells me slowly, glaring at the ground.

I can't. I can't absorb this. I knew it was just sex, which I knew would end. But I didn't think it would end with him giving up. "I can't believe you are giving up."

"You haven't given me much choice, have you?" Alpha turns it on me, his tone harsh. "I can't hurt you, I won't allow it to happen so I'm stuck running things from here. Those are my options. I didn't ask for this!" His temper flares and he clenches his teeth. The blaze coming back, he cries out and drops to his knees. "Nicolas, you have to go. Right now."

His clothes shred as he changes. The gray wolf stands before me, his ears laid flat back. He snarls at me, fangs bared. *Why is this wolf always so angry?* I think of the few times I've seen him happy, or even still. *How is that fair?* My inner monolog is interrupted by the coiling of the spring before me. His body prepares for launch, he was preparing to kill me and I couldn›t fathom one reason to move my feet.

But once again, I'm in the way and being protected. His jaws clamp on Swift's shoulder. Fleet is in front of me. "Get on."

"Get him back home," Swift says through clenched teeth as Alpha tries to shove past him to get to me. Swift sweeps his bad shoulder and knocks him to the ground. The snarl that follows makes him look like he regrets his decisions.

"Just run till he changes back, brother, he'll come to his senses." Fleet looks sympathetically to his brother and runs back towards the castle. I feel the tears coming freely.

"I'm sorry... I know this is exactly what Adriam was talking about. I didn't expect him to be there but when he was, I had to see him." I'm explaining my emotions to this man who has been forced to sideline my entire relationship with his leader. He's probably pretty sick of my crap.

"I'll tell Adriam you just ran into him by accident, just don't do it again. I rather like my brother and don't want to see him get killed by Alpha." I'm surprised he's talking to me; I don't think I've said more than ten words to either of the brothers.

"I was hoping he would change back," I mutter.

"Well, that's not the one to do it with. Alpha has never had great control over his wolf but these past two days he's been on a hair-trigger. I would stay pretty far away from that if I was you."

When he drops me at the castle, it's Sota who greets us, the telling expression on his face assures me that feigning cluelessness would not help me here. So, I opt to stand stubbornly as I wait for yet another speech or some onslaught of threats, "Tell Swift I'm sorry." I murmur. He rolls his eyes and he's gone.

"Did you see him?" Sota asks, his voice stern.

"I did. He tried to kill me." I tell him softly, not looking at him.

"He did or his wolf did?" He raises an eyebrow.

"His wolf." I refuse to acknowledge the burn that this brings to me. Thanks to Haryek's selfishness, I feel as though my relationship with the beast had been forever tainted.

"Then you can see why we need to fix this..." Sota speaks slowly.

Twenty-Eight-

I'm skeptical of Sota's request for an alliance. Any indication that the man was looking out for Alpha's better interests were tainted with the heavy feeling of suspicion that loomed on this man's every word. Sota seemed too opportunistic to make for a trustworthy ally. Much as he had been truthful in his threats, he seemed all too willing to allow me to sneak off and be consumed by the creature.

"You're a part of this, like it or not. I'm not going to pretend like I understand it or that I particularly care for you but we need our Alpha and right now, he's avoiding you. We have to get him back and there's only one way to do that." He watches me carefully.

His words drip with malice, contempt for me, and all the irritations I'd caused him. My time in court had made me wise to the wicked ways of older men, while I'd never spoken among the men I had witnessed many squabbles and it was always the lame and the incapacitated who spoke the softest and spun the most deception. "Which is?" I coax.

The devil beckons me. "Are you willing to do what it takes to get him back?"

Was I?

I hardly knew the man, I owed him nothing, I was indebted to him in no way as it was I who continued to save his life over the atrocities he'd committed taking my home from. Still, I suppose he had been useful. I couldn't do this on my own, I couldn't continue this quest without the help of Alpha. Reminding myself that loyalty spoke volumes among these people, I swallow my pride. "Anything," I answer immediately.

Sota grins, creasing the leathery, worn skin on his tanned face. "You're quite a good liar, I must say, I'm impressed for how young you are. Playing with the big boys and managing to keep up, if you could keep your cock in your pants it would suit you fine to sit on the throne. Too bad that will never happen." He feels as though he's wounded me somehow, little did he know my desire to sit where my father sat was almost shamefully low. I wanted no kingdom, I thirsted for no forms of power.

Like a good servant, I play the fool and offer him a puzzled glimpse, unwilling to hide the glint in my eye that warned him to keep his suspicions of me. With a shudder, he continues. "Every morning, the entire pack goes on a run in two groups. Victor leads the second but Alpha leads the first. It's a bonding experience, wolves in the mid ranks shift positions daily. This is how it's decided."

At least they weren't trying to kill each other any longer. I can see where this is going, my lips turn down into a frown.

"I can't keep up anymore, not missing a leg but I do ride on Delta's back. I think you need to ride Alpha."

I wait for the joke. *Ride the wolf who wants to kill me?* So soon my suspicions of this man had been proven correct, he wished to eliminate me himself. "Funny. I thought you said ride Alpha. Much as you seem aware of my preferences, I'm not quite fond of public indecency so I'm afraid I'll have to pass." Crossing my arms over my chest, I turn my back to him, I wasn't insane nor was I suicidal.

His response to my lude suggestion doesn't disappoint. It was one thing for him to suspect, another to confirm it for him.

"Vile creature... laying with men and speaking about it like a common whore." Sota grips my arm and I threaten him with my free hand, my fingertips darkening in a very real threat. "It will make him respect you and I think that's the push he needs to come off this bullshit. It's not easy; I don't think I've ever even seen you sit on Alpha. Can you be an adult for five whole moments and do what must be done?"

I consider it, attempting to wrench my arm from his grasp. "He never just lets me ride around on him but you know, it's not something I really ask him either. Alpha is not exactly one for generosity." I vaguely picture if this was something that could be proved in the bedroom. "How do you know it will even work? I'm not a lycan."

In a firm jerk, he pulls me to him as he regards me. "You're too pretty to be so naive. Are you going to do this or not?" With a firm shove, I push him away, leaving icy handprints on his chest. My skin crawls, my chest heaves for only a moment as I show my fear of yet another being finding me any sort of appealing. Sota was not interested in me, he just wanted to get under my skin.

"Fine. But don't ever touch me again."

We decide it needs to happen sooner rather than later. I leave him to do whatever it is slimy old men do when they're not imposing themselves on the younger generation.

Desperate to avoid Adriam, I steal Tonic and we, once more, head to the city but this time it's to see Stefan as it's getting close to the evening. He needs to know I'm alive and I could use some time away. Propaganda litters the walls of the city as we walk, the small town of Dezna has erupted into a social divide overnight.

Those who wished the lycans to stay and for salvation paired against those who wished them to go and the monarchy restored. My face, painted and slashed through coupled with calls to arms. A man stands on a shabby wooden crate, screaming into a crowd that the rebellion was the only truth. The crown had abandoned them, I had abandoned them. I pull my hood tighter over my head.

Taking the opportunity, I sit on Tonic's back, trying to get used to the feel of the movement beneath me. Much as I'd like to focus, the man's voice rings true in my ears. I felt conflicted, with Alpha out of the way, it might be the best chance I had to restore my kingdom. It would seem, much as Sota wished he were in control, that the entire structure truly did wish for his return.

We don't say much to each other on the way over. My fingers trace through his thick coat, as we pass a building I snag a paper and read its scrawled Romanian, it begs for justice and liberation from the rule of my father. I didn't know my people well enough to know what they would wish, it would seem Haryek and even the famed dictator himself knew them more than I ever thought to.

Heading to Stefan's house, I try not to think about it. I want to relax, not worry about saving a city.

We enter Stefan's house, for a moment I'm content until I spot Loan. I could almost turn around and leave; he's not my favorite person and even less so after he had to save my life. He holds a smug grin for me and I attempt to pretend I hadn't noticed. "How're you Loan?" I ask, cold.

He rolls his eyes and takes a drink of whatever alcoholic beverage is in his glass. With a cast of his middle finger in my direction, he downs his glass and I wrinkle my nose at his behavior. "Peasant," I grunt under my breath.

Loan had come from meager beginnings, one of the only villagers to ever attend the school and survive. Plenty were born to humble beginnings, few had the temperament and the will to survive the trials.

"Loan had quite the story for me." Stefan wraps his arms around Tonic's waist and kisses his cheek. For a moment, I long for that, someone to love me and look at me the way that Stefan looks at Tonic. Yet, Tonic does not share that adoration.

"I'm sure he embellished quite a bit," I grumble but Stefan frowns.

Crossing his arms over his chest, he faces me squarely. "You almost died on the back of a psycho dragon and if it weren't for the white wolf you would never have gotten her onto the table which then crashed through a glass floor?" He doesn't sound amused.

I shrug. "Something like that." I begin to make myself some tea but then pause and decide on water instead. After my experience, I'm not touching tea for a long time.

"How do you feel?" He knows me; he knows that I've already kicked my own ass.

I shrug once more, a lazy rise and fall in my shoulders that I can hear the discipline for already. My mother would be disgusted as such a response, my time with these brutes sullied my good breeding. "Better than I deserve. Better than I've felt since I've been home." I admit.

"You're damn right. The rest of us feel like shit." Loan snaps.

Tonic looks like he agrees, he's exhausted.

"I offered to heal you," I responded sharply.

"Not everything needs magic. It's users like you that are the reason we are in this mess." He tells me in frustration and I just scoff at him. *And I'm dramatic?*

I shake my head and take a sip of my water.

"We never would have needed these bloody creatures if we could do for ourselves as we did in the past." He gestures towards Tonic who holds up his hands in defense. "It is this elitist bullshit that caused this. We are at war because our kind uses magic to excess, we can't even defend ourselves against three hundred slaves."

Stefan returns to Tonic's side, wrapping his arms around the quiet lycan. "I think it's a good thing, Loan. It'll bring about change, we have been so desperate for change. It's about time Taryek felt the tremble of war on his doorstep."

"They aren't natural." Loan says, lowering his tone. "These creatures aren't here to liberate us."

The words spill out of my mouth before I can stop them. "It's not their fault. That is the root of this, why this is happening. They didn't ask for this." I know this hits Stefan personally, he didn't ask for his curse nor did I. We were both victims in a way.

"Most of us want to be cured, to go back to how things were." Tonic speaks, but I can tell he struggles with that statement. The wolf is a part of them, a conscious side of their lives. How did they feel about this?

"Don't we all? Your kind isn't the only one suffering at the hands of others." Loan takes a large drink and Stefan pinches the bridge of his nose in embarrassment at his intoxicated friend. "The only good your father did was protect things that were important. Like the elders, those with special gifts, and the borders of his territory. Those underlings, the ones who live outside the capital, live under this blanket of protection but get no help from the 'Lord'. We didn't all grow up rich and privileged, asshole." He practically spits at me.

I don't have much to say, I'm not versed in what happens outside Dezna. Sure we checked on them when we trekked to Ziduri but it really was the job of the mayors and the lords of the towns to keep them in check. "You're a Solomonari. They are pretty respected by everyone, even in the elf and human worlds. I think you're speaking out of turn, Loan."

Laughing, a burst of humor that almost makes him fall over, he slams his fist on the table. "I speak for those who suffer every day from lack of work since these beasts came into our lives. You haven't had to have a job so I suppose that doesn't mean much to you but the ones the Lycans replaced? The ones who were doing side work to feed their families? The ones who have little magic? They are actively hunted by witch hunters, magical thieves, and racists from all the lands.

"Your father was a piece of shit but at least on his lands, we were somewhat safe. Now it's open season. I didn't realize the capital had no other defenses. We are sitting ducks out there as Elves move down the border." Loan downs his drink, scowling at the empty cup. "If you think Haryek is here for anything other than claim on this land, you are sadly mistaken. They are vultures waiting for the beast to die."

"We would have smelled if there were more elves." Tonic interjects.

"Why on earth would they come near your side? They are coming in from the back door, we have enough to hold them back but we are taking major losses. We can't keep up, I can't keep up. That's why I came here; Stefan said I could make my case." He grins towards the Strigoi, who looks like he wishes he had better friends.

Well, then why hadn't he said so? "If this is your idea of making a plea, you're doing a horrible job with your string of insults."

Waving a dismissive finger at me, he shakes his head. "Not you, pretty boy. You're a pawn now; I'm talking about your captors. Their job was to defend, it's time to defend!"

I frown at the drunken Solomonari. "Good luck with that, Alpha isn't fond of magic users. I'm afraid it is me you'll be dealing with."

With a hearty scoff, Loan scratches his stomach and reclines his feet up on a nearby chair. "Is lycan cock so good that you must publicly defend it? Are your daddy issues so horrible that you defend a man who murdered your family? Take sides for him? Really, I'm dying to know, Nicolas."

His insults bring me back to the days of my schooling. As he sizes me up, waiting for that scorned rebuttal, I know better than to feed into the taunts. It was nothing I hadn't heard before, when you used your body, people tend to notice. I bear the marks of someone who had been used on my very soul, I was easy prey for a man as inwardly worshiped as Loan.

"It's not like that." *It kind of is.* «He›s not who we think he is.»

Stefan readies to defend me but I stop him, Loan would say whatever he liked to me, he felt he'd earned that right. "Bullshit. I've been distracted by a pretty face before but I've seen the guy and I'm not impressed, given half of his body isn't even there. Have you considered women? Not bad if you can get past their wicked tongues." He shrugs and tips his empty glass longingly.

I hear Tonic growl. "He got the injuries protecting his people. Everything he does is for his people." The gray-haired young man steps forward and Stefan grips his wrist. The room erupts into an inferno as his body emits mass amounts of heat.

Leaning up on his seat, Loan eyes the young man. "Good! So you can help me make my case to the brute. Our leader wants to come and talk, you see there's a giant magical rebellion in the city of Cluj-Napoca. We have pretty much taken it over." He gestures with his hand lazily.

Those dark eyes turn to me. "We would very much like some of this Lycan brute force since they are the ones who messed things up so royally. Since you know him so well, maybe you can put it into better words and persuade him. If he's truly this valiant man and if you truly want to help your people." He looks me up and down and I feel disgusted by him.

Much as I want to cast him out of my city, I allow Loan to enlighten me on the situation. They have gained control of the large city of Cluj-Napoca which impressed me, considering the elf presence was strong in that town.

They are suffering attacks from elf and human lines on an almost weekly basis. Since Cluj-Napoca was surrounded by mostly flat farmlands on half of its territory, it's been easy to prevent most of the attacks but when they do come through, they lack the fighting ability since most of their residents are women and children.

They have a good system of magic users but nothing like we have here. It's a two-day walk from there to the bordering cities of the Elf Capital but he feels as though a large force has shored up in the town of Brasov which puts them very close to the magic rebellion and even closer to our doorstep than we had thought.

This information would come at a dear cost but I couldn't allow it to slip through my fingers. If it was true, then aid for my city might be only a falcon's flight away. Or, it meant protecting the lycan army would involve getting Alpha to side with us.

"And all you're wanting is the support of the Alpha?" I question, raising an eyebrow.

"We want him to provide some protection and for his people to do what they have been raving about. We need to get this war started. My people. Our people won't survive much more of this brutality. I think the elves intend to conquer Dezna and claim all this land for themselves. If that happens, there will be no room for any of us unless we want to serve under Taryek and I think I would rather be chewed up by the Lycans. Our people are ready."

Haryek's descent on the magical community would come as little surprise to anyone of importance in our cities. There had to be someone to replace the lycan slaves, magic users would surely suffice.

Composing my face, I nod. "I think it's worth talking to him about, he is not in a good place right now but we are working on remedying this situation. Right now, if you want to prove yourself useful to our cause, you could work on Haryek. Maybe scare some sense into him, he is going to single-handedly ruin this whole operation with the stunt he pulled. The lycans are ready to skin him alive. If you can handle that problem, I think we would probably have a deal."

"At least he's pretty." Loan shrugs.

I roll my eyes and enjoy the change in topic.

We talk of everything from Haryek to what kind of men we like, to Loan trying to convince us that women could really be a lot of fun if we could get over the lack of a penis. Tonic was the most interested in that topic and I couldn't help but laugh at the twinge of jealousy coming from Stefan at his questions. It was good to feel normal, if only for a night.

Twenty-Nine-

That night, the walk home is particularly lonely as I leave Tonic to do what he must with Stefan. I can't bring myself to separate them given that Stefan looks at him as if he'd found some new purpose. Ever the hopeless romantic.

The thought truly made my stomach flex, my palms sweat, to be so smitten with someone so quickly was dangerous. *What if they didn't love you back?*

Surely he could see that Tonic wasn't nearly as infatuated with him as he was with the younger man. Yet he pursued, chasing the young man so eagerly like a lovesick puppy. I couldn't help but wonder if anyone would ever see fit to look at me in such a way, even if it were just a longing sigh or a simple recall of a time when I made them happy. In all my escapades, I couldn't recall a single person who might think back on me fondly.

As I make my way into my room, I spy myself in the mirror, running a hand through my hair as I twist and turn to look at my slim body. I couldn't even find it in me to look at myself that way, how could I expect it of anyone else? I was slight, there was no mass of muscle underneath my civilian clothes. Nothing redeeming in unique features save for blood-red hair that felt more like a curse and a beacon for trouble.

I can't help but laugh at my own assessment. My siblings had often teased me, when we would pass a man on the streets with red hair they would claim my parentage was in question. My mother always came to my aid, the villagers would gawk and regard me with uncertainty as if the taunting children had brought it to light that I looked little to nothing like my father. I was shorter, smaller, more refined than my siblings.

"Sota thinks you're pretty," I tell the man in the mirror, capturing my own chin and dragging my thumb over the lower lip as if to incite any sort of seduction from my deep dark eyes. A lover of men, an abnormality. Pressing my fingers to my lips, I offer the captured kiss to the moonlight peeking through the windows. "Good night, mama. I miss you more every day."

My back arches as I stretch and inhale. The smell of the woods fills my nose and I smile. So many mixed emotions follow that intoxicating aroma. I roll onto my side and my hand comes into contact with something warm. Very warm. "Tonic?" I breathe, who else would it be? It's been days since I've seen my captor; nobody else would come in here.

I figure he might be afraid considering there is a large storm rolling in tonight. I cuddle closer to the warmth, finding comfort in it.

"Not quite." A smooth voice returns, the low baritone and English accent make my eyes shoot open.

Alpha.

"You're here? Wha—How?" I demand, stammering for words as I roust from my sleep. I sit upon my hip, looking down at him and drinking him in. His bare chest, the smattering of chest hair, and his scars, my eyes rake over him as I check to see that he is here—really here. He looks calm, not like the Alpha I saw in the town; the one who wanted to eat me.

"Have you been calling Tonic to your bed now? I've been told we look alike." His tone is teasing, though he is questioning me. While I attempt to find offense in it, there's a part of me that is just grateful to no longer be alone. My inadequate nightly anxiety tended to cause me to seek companionship, I was going through withdrawals in his absence.

Instead, I opt to find his jealousy amusing. "No. I figured he was afraid of the storm. I haven't seen you in days." I run my hand over his warm skin, tracing the lines of his abdominal muscles with my fingertips. His eyes darken and he grabs my hand, I click my tongue in amusement. "Jealous, are we?"

There is no amusement in his eyes, yet his hand softens against mine. "I don't know how long I can stay in control." It's a warning, I watch him for a long moment and he narrows his eyes. "I'm not jealous of an omega. I could have you whenever I want you, you belong to me. You. Are. Mine."

My throat dries, my lips part as my heart rate accelerates at the words. "Then what are you waiting for?" For someone who leads an entire army and feels as if he could single-handedly rule the world, he seems so unsure around me. He's vulnerable, I feel as though there is a hidden reason behind his words.

The risk isn't just his lack of control, the risk is the fact he doesn't know if he wants to get involved with me all over again. An addict called to the flame, he yearns for me as I do for him. We are broken, but together, the pieces don't seem to matter so much.

I think back to the times we tried to quit each other, every time we came together seemed like the last and each time, we came back with an intensity that frightened me in its consumption of my every thought. We are poisonous and that's what sick, twisted beings do. I remember thinking that I was a selfish creature, and I find that I agree with my past self, I'm too selfish to allow him to slip through my fingers again.

"What are you thinking about?" He asks, reaching up to smooth the crease out from between my eyebrows.

I smirk at him, I can't let him see that I'm not in control of this game. "I'm admiring how someone of your age can be in such incredible shape."

We don't share with each other. We don't tell the truth or express our feelings. He doesn't address that I need him, I can silently see that he needs me too because he stays as if drawn to me. Rolling his eyes at me, I laugh at his response because I realize how much I miss him. Leaning down, I snuggle up to his side and kiss his neck, warm under my lips, smelling so divine in the heavy scent of woods and uniquely Alpha.

He inhales and I smirk at the reaction I have on him, encouraged at the response I elicit. I graze his jaw with my teeth and rake my fingernails down his chest as I marvel at the feel of his density under my hands. A body had never mattered to me before, the attraction had never been at the forefront of my mind, and yet this man drove me to the depths of my desire. I called him my Alpha because I worshiped this unholy form.

He reaches for my chin and drags me to him, meeting my lips with his own. I break the kiss, breathless.

"I should go. You weren't supposed to wake up."

"And yet here you are." I remind him.

His lips crush against mine and I climb to straddle him in a feat of desperation. I'm pleased to find that he's naked beneath me.

My body erupts into flames as my skin finds his warmth and I react to his sheer presence. I'm practically shaking with anticipation as we tangle, his hands explore my body, shredding my clothes. Alpha slips his fingers into my underwear and with an easy maneuver, he splits them, ripping him from my body as I gasp down at him.

This is what I've been craving. This was what my tainted soul yearned for, what no other man had been able to give me. This dark man, this alpha male, met me in depravity and managed to raise me above the shame and into a euphoria where I finally felt witnessed.

Scrambling for the nightstand, I grasp the rubbing oil and apply it hurriedly to him. I had learned better to have such lubricant on hand if I wished to have any sort of comfort tomorrow. I lower myself onto him with a shaky sigh, my hands rest on his chest as I ease myself down. I shut my eyes, taking in the sensation of allowing this man to claim me.

When I open them, he's watching me, I inhale sharply at his piercing eyes and his expression.

The moonlight plays against my form, hiding my scars just as I had hoped it would, yet his glisten at the beam peeking through the heavy curtains. His eyes glimmer, charged by the light, "You're beautiful." He breathes and I pause, avoiding eye contact.

I find myself deflating a little, *is it even right for a man to be beautiful?*

"Bloody hell, take the fucking compliment!" He tells me, bewildered. In one quick maneuver, I'm on my back and he's between my legs, I'm left disorientated from the inhuman speed.

Swallowing my moment of fear, I grip the pillows above my head in a silent challenge. "Make me, Sir." I command him, in an act of defiance, and he fills me. I cry out and arch my back off the bed, biting my lower lip to control the volume.

"Watch me." He growls as I attempt to shut my eyes, to relish in the overwhelming feeling of his pace. He's relentless and it's exactly what I've been craving. What I've needed.

Suddenly he stills and my eyes flutter open. "Now. Apologize for your rude behavior and maybe I'll let you finish. Your Alpha paid you a compliment."

I gape at him and curse under my breath, shaking my head, toying with a grin as he takes me once more. I writhe, desperate for friction yet his unyielding hands hold me as he stills once more. "Apologize." He commands. Once more he takes me and I'm almost undone.

"Okay okay!" I plead and he fills me once more, I can't take it. My body trembles with need for this brute. "I'm sorry! Thank you, Alpha! Thank you for your compliment!" Glimpsing him through my eyelashes, I allow my lips to part in a sigh of a need fulfilled. I needed to be dominated as much as he needed to claim me.

I can hear the grin on his voice. "Good boy." He leans down to kiss me and I attack him, my hands knot in his hair as I yank his face to mine. Our teeth clash as I taste him, wanting all of him. He responds by giving me what I want and I moan into his mouth as he starts to move. I find that I relish at his slower pace that he rewards me with.

For once, I don't hurry for the end, I want to last in this moment for as long as I can stand.

Alpha rolls onto his back and pulls me on top of him. I brace my hands on his chest once more. One of his hands comes up to run down my chest and I shiver at the touch but don't pull away from him. He pushes me up into a sitting position, drunkenly I support myself with my palms on his chest. "I want to see you."

Who am I to disobey my Alpha? Proud of the request, I straighten and tangle my hands in my hair as I lose myself on him, chasing my release. I hear the words in my head, his smooth voice telling me I'm beautiful. My words drag together as he encourages me, I'm undone at his command and slump onto his chest as he follows behind me.

"I love you." He murmurs, his arms so snuggly wrapped around me.

My eyes shoot open and I blink a few times.

I'm completely alone. I look around and see that the room is empty; the sun is just starting to peek in through the curtains. I rub my eyes and then stare at the bedsheets.

How? Was it just a dream?

I feel all over my body, I'm numb and chilled since I kicked my covers off the bed. I feel exhausted; I must have thrashed around all night. As I slide to the edge of the bed, I can't help but feel the pain of disappointment. It felt so real; I could feel his warmth and smell him. My mood plummets as I go to get dressed and make my way to the dining hall for breakfast.

The castle is alive with wolves, it's unnerving but I think to myself that I'm usually not awake this early. I grab the familiar breakfast and sit down with my usual crowd who seem surprised that I'm awake. I roll my eyes at them, briefly wondering if there was a closeted gay man I could take my frustrations out on.

Picking at my breakfast, I distract myself with thoughts of Gena and if she was happy; if she made it to the next village. "Do you all just sit here until I wake up?" I ask, taking a bite of some of the hash-browns.

"No, we actually have jobs. This is the morning briefing, we were actually about to go on our pack run. I'm just surprised to see you, we've been expecting you for a few mornings but you hadn't shown up so I just figured you weren't interested." Sota arches a snowy brow at me, measuring my mood.

"Nobody told me to come? I figured it was something you get invited to..." I mumble, taking another bite as I don't care to meet his suspicions. It's not in me today to bait him, my mind swims with my vivid dream and, truly, I'd rather just be alone.

"Well, I was hoping you'd show some initiative. But better late than never I suppose, you have good timing. We haven't really been able to convince him to come back until recently. I think the bastard was enjoying his vacation." Sota shrugs in annoyance.

I blink, lifted from the depths. "Alpha is here?" I ask. *Maybe it wasn't a dream.*

"Came in last night with the night crew." He raises an eyebrow at me, I guess I'm too excited for the news but surely that validates my dream? Maybe I could just sense his presence and dreamt about him or perhaps, in the smallest of chances, he truly had visited me last night?

"So what does that mean?" My voice is small, am I ready for this?

Sota grins. "It means the boss is back and the boys are in for a real wake up call."

Tonic sighs; he looks like he might have been enjoying his time off.

"And?" I press.

"And today, you ride with us."

I gulp. Today will make or break us. Today I will decide if I can overcome the wolf or lose my life to it.

CHAPTER

Thirty-

I take as long as I'm allowed to eat my breakfast. Nobody really rushes me though I can tell that Sota is getting impatient. I start to notice fewer and fewer people have their clothes on, I suppose because they all, very shortly, will no longer be human.

I cling to Tonic as we make our way out of the main hall and into the courtyard. I don't think I will ever be used to being surrounded by dozens of naked men though that theory is quickly pushed aside by the fact that I'm now surrounded by over a hundred wolves.

The pack is alive and vibrating though surprisingly the volume is little over a dull roar. The city is probably peacefully sleeping with no idea a pack of beasts is about to go running around her. Hell, they live outside my window and I was none the wiser that this was going on, the silence and precision in which the pack could maneuver astounded me. How did the rebellion have any hope of standing against them?

Needing a distraction, I turn my attention to the Alpha look-alike, Tonic seems just as on edge as I am. "Where will you be?" I ask him hopefully.

"Up front today," Sota answered. I noticed the look of concern on my companion's face. "Tonic is the only one fast enough to catch

Alpha. We are all pretty impressed that he outran that dragon. If something goes wrong, you'll have to jump off of Alpha onto Tonic."

I blink. What do I look like to these people? I can do magic but I'm not a miracle worker nor am I particularly skilled at extravagant maneuvers that shift of wolves at high speed would take.

My only hope in this was that Tonic would be my support system. "You're okay with this?" I ask him, watching his kind brown eyes. Sometimes, I wonder what he would look like without the scar but I can't seem to picture it.

Reluctantly, he nods. "Yes." But I can see the concern.

I squeezed him. In other words, he'll do it for his friends.

"Delta will try to stay as close as possible but I weigh him down. We won't have Victor to muscle him down, as if he could catch him anyways. Swift and Fleet will be there, as well, for back up if we need them. I think you can do this, I have confidence that you can do this." It's the first kind words the Sota has said to me and for a brief moment, I can see why Alpha respects him so much.

Feeling a little better, I nod. "Okay. So how does this work." *Surely it can't be too hard?*

"Delta, shift," Sota instructs and Delta is suddenly a brown and honey-colored wolf before us. Smaller than Alpha but still substantial, he doesn't look as young as Tonic. He lowers himself obediently and Sota climbs on, I watch as his eyes become focused and unfocused as he adjusts.

Clearing his throat, Sota seems quite cocky that it is him I would be forced to answer to. I must swallow my pride, this isn't about me, this is about making a decision that I still haven't come to a conclusion on. When faced with so many options, choosing the ones who slaughter my family seemed cowardly, and yet, seeing them now I couldn't imagine standing against them.

"I've been testing this theory a lot lately, your father programmed some sort of instinct into us when we were created. We were built to be ridden; it's inside of us to obey the person on our backs. I started with the lower wolves and worked my way up to Delta. The human side goes away when someone is seated on the wolf, it comes and goes but it seems that for the most part, this is when the wolf is at its purest. Delta's wolf fought me quite a bit but he was pretty manageable. The most important fact is don't fall off. Once you fall off, that's the end." He grabs a hand full of Delta's scruff and pulls back.

Delta obediently backs up.

"They are much like riding a horse, they don't seem to have much feeling in this scruff area. I hold on with my legs, I lean back when I want to stop. The scruff helps steer, it gets easier the more you do it. But I wouldn't kick him like a horse." He's trying to lighten the mood; he must see the stress on my face. "Are you ready?"

No.

But, I nod. Sota hops off of Delta, he blinks a few times and shakes out his coat. Sota motions with his hand, Swift and Fleet approach with Alpha squeezed between them. He looks concerned, his coat a startling gray compared to the hues of the twins surrounding him. He lays his ears back and stops short.

"I don't like this." He tells Sota, not looking at me. For a moment, I almost allow myself to believe it was a concern for me that stopped him. I knew that if I died, all his leverage would be lost.

"It's the only way. The pack needs you and I can't allow you to do this to yourself. This is the life you have chosen, it's time to do what has to be done." Sota sounds absolute; for now, he is the only one the Alpha bows to.

The light blue eyes settle on me with an agonizingly long pause. "He will die." Alpha's voice is hard, hardly above a murmur. Wrought with what could be a concern, I square my shoulders, I don't need anyone to fear for me. I'd faced much more challenging foes.

"He won't. He's stronger than you think." Sota speaks softly as he approaches, he grabs Alpha's scruff and pulls him forward. The gray creature shuts his eyes, fighting for control as he gets closer to me until we are mere feet from each other. I can feel his warmth. I'm envious of Sota's strength but I quickly push the thought away. I don't wish to handle such a regal beast in such a disrespectful manner. It makes me uncomfortable, not the thought of being killed, but the thought of dominating such a valiant man.

I take my mind off the task by focusing on the way the light is currently hitting the gray coat before me, how it turns to an almost stone white color as it nears his chest and belly.

Extending my hand to touch his shoulder, lost in thought, I pause and glance over. The cool blue eye is watching me and I can tell it's the wolf. The low, raspy growl rumbles through his body but Sota surprises us both when he bumps him abruptly with his palm on the shoulder. Alpha snaps at him and Sota responds with an elbow to the nose. Alpha and I, both, stare at him in complete bewilderment.

"Are you done?" Sota asks, patiently.

The wolf huffs and looks away in offense.

"If he does manage to get you off, he's going to try and kill you. As I'm sure you've seen already. You're going to have to grab him by the ear, like this, and stay as close to him as you can until we can get to you. It doesn't take a lot of strength. The ears are pretty sensitive." Sota demonstrates by showing me how to grab the creature's ear and twist it in my palm, lowering his head below the level of our chest. It elicits a whine and instantly makes me wonder if this is the right thing to do.

I feel like my father would be smiling down on me and it makes my stomach turn. When I was a boy, my father took me hunting for bears. With no guns, we hunted the lumbering beast for miles, it seemed to understand long before it stopped running that something about us hadn't been right. Like a master puppeteer, he took hold of the beast, contorting its body into positions and in ways that were unnatural to the creature. Ways that caused it to howl and moan in pain, the panic in its eyes bore into me as he shredded it in a display of power.

It was a blood sport, to do nothing more than practice magic that I did not possess. My brothers had returned victorious, I had sworn off meat from that day forward save for dire situations.

I'm about to fulfill his plan, to ride these animals he created. "Doesn't really seem fair, does it?" I mumble, glancing at Sota as he directs Swift and Fleet to position them around us. I carefully touch the soft coat, watching him out of the corner of my eye, though I'm not surprised that he is watching me too.

"Life's not fair. He's an animal, Nicolas. In this state, he's no more than a dog. It's the nature of our design. If you don't like it, help us get through this war and break this curse." Sota's yellow eyes lock on me and I look away.

Can I? Can I help them? How could I possibly fix this? In my mind's eye, I see the bear all over again, mirrored in this glassy eye.

"It's time to get on."

Before I can answer, he stoops down, practically seats me on his shoulder, and throws me onto the creature's back. It feels different than sitting on Tonic and I try to remember if I have ever sat up here. He's taller and broader. The muscles are tight under my thighs, he adjusts his stance to make up for my weight and his ears practically touch. For a moment, we breathe in unison.

"That wasn't so bad," I told Sota, attempting to calm my nerves. *What right did I have to sit on this creature?*

Sota laughs, amused by my optimism. "You haven't moved yet." He climbs back onto Delta and moves him to stand beside my larger wolf. I feel like I tower over everyone, Swift and Fleet hang to my right and Tonic walks behind us, with his ears low, head down and tail tucked. He's not used to being front and center.

I can see Swift and Fleet bickering out of the corner of my eye, they snap and shove at each other. As we walk, the pack falls in line behind us and the sound is rhythmic as their paws march towards the outskirts of the city.

It's strange how beautiful my city is and how I've never noticed it before. I watch the rolling farmland, the blue haze of mountains in the distance catch the morning sun. It's peaceful out here, as we pick up the pace and begin to cross the open terrain.

We amble along; I'm impressed at how smooth it all feels. Riding Tonic had always felt so bumpy before but this is something that is maintainable. As a boy, we had been banned from playing so far from the castle, banned from doing much of anything a young child might do for fear of embarrassing the royal family.

The ground is crunchy with frost, as we get farther from the city I start to see a few of the mountains have snow caps. Winter surely is mere months away. I'm enthralled in the beauty, from inside a carriage I had never truly witnessed the city come to life under the morning sun.

I scan the horizon with my eyes and I see the path we are headed towards. It's an open expanse of land that travels between the capital and the outside cities. It goes on for miles, a type of highway for us to travel to one another and now, apparently, a place for the pack to get its exercise.

"How fast can a wolf run?" My heart beats for a whole other reason. I want to run, to get away from this place that had been a prison for me.

"We are pretty on par with most horses. Alpha is a little faster due to his breeding but the shoulder has slowed him down."

We round the corner and Sota warns me to prepare myself. I tighten my hands in his scruff and grab onto him with my legs. The sensation makes him jump forward and pin his ears. He growls at me and shakes his body in irritation at my presence. I tug the fur under my fingers, "Cut your crap." I grumble at him in annoyance.

He barks at me in response and bolts forward. It almost unseats me and I hunker down closer to his neck, at first I feel as though I might fall off from the leaping strides he takes. His paws stretch out in front of him, propelling him faster.

I steal a glance behind us and see that Swift and Fleet are trying to keep up but Tonic is close behind us, coasting along like a scared puppy though he seems to be relaxing as we get farther and farther from the pack.

He starts to smoothen out, hits his stride, and surges forward, I can feel the awkwardness in his gait coming from his left front leg, how the stride is not as long with the limb. I can feel the weakness on the left side of his back.

In my distracted state, he breaks free of the pack and leaps over a fallen log. I yelp with surprise, grabbing hold of him. The bastard has gone off the trail, he blazes through the trees. I cringe as we are whipped and slapped by vines and branches. Tonic comes up alongside us and helps me slide back into position with his muzzle.

Alpha snaps at him and we nearly run headlong into a tree with the attempt.

"Control him!" Tonic tells me.

"Oh right, as if I can!" I responded back in frustration, this was ridiculous. I'm going to die here. I couldn't do this, I didn't want to do this. I didn't own him, nobody did and nobody should!

"Just do it!"

I dig my fingers down to his undercoat and pull hard. The gray creature comes to a screeching halt and Tonic blazes past us.

Reason with him, I command myself.

"Listen here. Wolf. Alpha. Whatever the hell you are. I know you can talk. I've heard it before. People make mistakes, okay? I didn't hurt your human half on purpose! Shit happens, the only one hurting him right now is you. So you need to lighten the hell up! Do you understand?" I'm yelling at a dog.

He sets his teeth and looks like he's actually going to respond but something catches his nose and he cranes his head to the sky, sniffing.

"Oh don't play dumb, I saw you! You can talk, now talk damn it." I whack his shoulder and he pins his ears and kicks one of his hind paws.

"Stop talking." The voice is rough and gravely. He sniffs again, his ears scanning the woods.

Tonic frowns and sniffs as well. "I don't smell anything." He looks towards me in confusion.

"Omega." Alpha rasps in disappointment and suddenly turns his head back towards the pack. "Elves." He breathes. "There." He points out of the trees towards the tree line across the clearing.

I frown. "Okay, so we need to stay here until the pack catches up," I tell him firmly.

"No time. Now." He takes a step and I pull his scruff.

"No! Not Now. We will be slaughtered!" Here I am again, arguing with a dog.

"Trust. Me." He looks over his shoulder at me and I sigh. Everything tells me this is not going to work. But I do trust him, even this side of him. He bounds out of the woods into the open and Tonic scoots close behind, he pauses and throws his head back and howls.

The sound is deafening, I put my hands over my ears. If I wasn't so close to him, I would think it was beautiful. Tonic instinctively howls as well. I can hear the barking in the distance and the first arrow zips over our head.

"We need to go. Now!" I tell him and dig my heels into his side. He leaps forward and we are racing towards the pack. Lone arrows zip past us, over us, and in front of us. I can faintly see Sota, I can't believe how far ahead we got. Swift and Fleet are nearing us.

An arrow hits Fleet in the chest, his outstretched paws miss the ground and he tumbles in a flurry of legs as he hits the ground and rolls. Swift's eyes grow large and he skitters to a stop. "Fleet!" He screams and Alpha hits his side with his shoulder.

"Get to the trees. Warn the pack! We are being ambushed." I can see moments of clarity where my Alpha is returning to us, the wolf can't handle this on his own and must have called for reinforcements. I fell sick, glimpsing back over my shoulder to confirm that Fleet was no longer moving. Alpha jerks his shoulder, bumping me back into place. "Don't look back." he snarls at me.

"Randy..." I breathe, hugging his neck. Fleet is dead, in a twisted heap with his mouth hanging open. Swift fights with himself as his wolf begs for his brother but his rational side knows he needs to get to the pack. Tonic is pressing as close to the surviving twin as he can manage, using his own presence to force him to keep running.

"Get to the trees!" Alpha yells as a flurry of arrows fills the air. Their sharp sounds become ear splitting as they hit the ground around us. We dash for the trees and I hold as tightly as I can to my wolf, to protect him from the onslaught.

I hear yelps and cries behind us, everything goes dark for a second as we hit the woods to hunker down behind the trees. The trees sound alive as the pack shuffles in and hides low in the underbrush though, with the lack of leaves, no one is doing much hiding.

"Nicolas." I hear Tonic.

I glance up and realize my small group is staring at us. My eyes drift and I see that Alpha has two arrows embedded in his shoulder. "Shit! Randy!" I slide off and cry out in pain. I've been shot through my thigh. I could be sick, I shield my mouth and turn my head away, I'm just relieved my pants are dark. I can't see how much blood is truly there but it has stained his coat and that's enough to make my stomach want to flip.

I jump down and guard my injured leg. Sota holds his hand up to stop me. "Stop! There's an artery in your leg, you could have nicked it!"

I blink at him a few times and look at my thigh, it seems to be on the outside, meatier layer. "I think I'm okay." I breathe, though the pain is searing. I look towards Alpha and pale as Sota yanks one of the arrows out of him. I could almost blackout as the second one is removed. "Fleet." I manage, "Someone needs to go back to get Fleet."

Swift makes a strangled sound, hiding against Tonic's shoulder.

"Thank the gods they were in your shoulder blade, arrows couldn't get through the bone that dense. It was just in the skin and muscle."

Sota pats him and he cringes before walking over to me to inspect my thigh. "Fleet's dead, nothing for it. Our only job now is to survive this ambush and you're going to help us."

Thirty-One-

"Take cover!" Delta yells and everyone puts their back up against the surrounding trees and arrows rain from the sky once more. I throw my arms around Alpha's neck, holding him tightly. He sits, rocking back on his hind legs with his back against the bark of the tree. I can hear a few chuckles here and there as the arrows slowly begin to die down, a few yelps and pained cries but mostly laughter and disbelief.

"Cheeky fucks!" Sota scoffs. I take inventory of everyone that I can see. Nobody is dead, except for Fleet. They pull arrows from each other like it's nothing unless they look particularly deep.

"The pack had to have heard that howl. I suspect Adriam and Victor will be here any minute to aid us." Delta reports.

Alpha scoffs, laying his ears back. "We don't need bloody aid. We can take care of these ones ourselves. They are in the woods, their arrows are useless in short-range unless they've taken to the trees and we will see them if that's the case. We need to chase them out into the open." His response is absolute, I'm still reeling from the death of a beloved twin.

It's Ol' One Arm who comes to the defense of the pack against their bloodthirsty leader. "These are elves; they are some of the best in the world with a bow. Don't think some dead leaves are going to muck up their aim." Sota reminds him, uncertain.

With a harsh growl, the gray wolf bares his teeth. "Got any other suggestions?" Alpha snaps back in response, bringing the surrounding wolves to heel as they lower their heads in respect. The Alpha would have his blood.

"Yes. Stay here until aid arrives." He tells him sternly.

Alpha doesn't look amused. "We are vulnerable in this position. There are too many of us to just hunker down with so little cover. We need to move forward and take them out. Drive them out." He stands up, determined. The pack readies itself as they rise to their feet, they would follow their leader, they would die for him if that's what it took.

Desperate to prevent any more bloodshed, I quickly speak up. "I can help. I can provide a fog and that will give us some cover? I don't want to kill anyone but we need to get out of this alive." I plead with him, it's his turn now. He must trust me; if only he could. Wasn't that the point of all this?

Alpha watches me for a long moment, considering his options before he nods, much to my surprise. "Okay. Let's see it." He allows.

I can't believe what I'm hearing. But I limp away from him, putting my hand over my pierced thigh to support it. I take a deep breath, I don't have my book so it makes things a little more difficult but as I chant, I can feel the mist pulling in from around me. Thankfully our home is located so close to bodies of water. The fog rolls in thick and heavy, the damp air leaves a fine film on the fur of the wolves surrounding me.

The castle is going to smell of wet dog tonight, I just know it.

"I don't know how long this will last, I'm pretty charged up but I have to focus on this if I want to keep the cover as heavy."

Impressed, they regard me with whole new respect. All save for the Alpha who appears unjustly suspicious. I'm sure, in his mind, he can't help but wonder if I'm behind this attack in the first place. "We don't need long," Alpha assures me and he addresses the pack. "Move forward! Push them out of the woods!" He commands and the pack begins to move.

I put my arm over Tonic's shoulders and limp alongside him as the pack soundlessly moves out in front of us. They hunt, heads low, soundless in the leaf litter as their natural coat colors blend seamlessly into the forest.

Shutting my eyes, I see Fleet, he didn't have to die. "Tonic, am I doing the right thing?" I ask him with a frown, because it feels like I'm helping to murder a group of elves who never stood a chance before I surrounded them with fog.

Tonic saw things much as I did, he did not have the thirst of their leader, he did not have an eye for war and a talent for producing death. "Yes." He finally murmurs. "This is what needs to be done. You are saving lives. The lives of my brothers, the life of the Alpha." He tries to reassure me and I offer him a weak smile. My leg is in agony.

Suddenly I'm shoved to the ground and Tonic dives. "They're above us!" He yells. Arrows rain down on us; I pull myself along as I crawl on my belly towards my companion who is hunkered down next to a fallen log. A wolf jumps on the tree beside us and Tonic cries out in surprise. I press my back against him and grip my leg. It's killing me, blood seeps out of the exit holes.

"I have to get this arrow out." I groan through my teeth.

The wolf in the tree rips down an elf and the poor man screams in agony as he's chewed on. Finally the wolf finds his throat and the sound of his neck snapping causes me to pale. I can only focus on my breath, forming a cold cloud before me as my magic charges to my fingertips to come to my protection.

The wolf glares at Tonic before sprinting off and I scoot towards the dead elf. I search his pockets; the smell of blood is overwhelming. Finally, I find a knife and I pull it out of its holder. "Tonic. I need you to shift into a human and cut the skin off the top of this arrow. I can't do it myself." I tell him firmly.

Another scream sounds from behind us and Tonic presses back against the log. "I can't." His eyes are wide. This is probably his first battle, much as it was mine. School had prepared me to handle stress, it was in stress that my magic thrived. I increase the fog cover, doing anything to block out the screams.

I don't have time or patience for Tonic's fear. "Tonic I'm not asking you! I need my leg. I can't run around with this arrow hanging out of it!" Like I needed another scar.

After a moment he nods and suddenly he's human again. He crawls towards me and takes a deep breath as I rip my pants to reveal the wound. "You're going to need to bite something." He glances at me and I vaguely wonder how it felt to get that scar over his eye. Arrows fly all around us, I clutch him closer to me, pulling his head down to protect him as a wolf leaps over top of us. I blast an icy shield to cover us, protecting us from the onslaught.

"Just do it!"

He inspects it for a moment, it's just the edge. I had been so worried it had grazed the bone but it seems like it's just pierced the flesh. In a careful slice, he rids me of the arrow and I feel as though I'll blackout from the pain.

It's as if someone has run a red hot blade down my leg. The arrow being removed brings a whole new relief and a whole new pain but at least I don't have to worry about snagging it. This is going to be a horrendous scar. I rip one of the sleeves off my long sleeve and tie it over the cut; blood seeps quickly into the material and drenches it.

"Look out!" Tonic yells and I glance up to see a bloodied elf towering over us, knife in hand. Without a second thought, I grab my bloodied arrow and plunge it into his foot. He shrieks in pain and Tonic leaps over my head, as a wolf, to grasp his throat in his jaws. I lower my shield, trembling from the shock.

This is war. This is madness. The fog dissipates since I've been distracted, it reveals a bloody picture. A large party of elves runs into the clearing. The pack chases them out, circling them, surrounding them. Arrows fly through the air as the few remaining sentries are plucked from their trees.

The sound of the screeches of dying men surrounding us is like a horrific symphony. There's never a moment of silence, only lulls in the choir of death. I see him, Alpha, as he tears the throat from a man who was in the wrong place at the wrong time. He is merciless, he is absolutely lethal, he is a dictator on a rampage of blood lust that proved true everything I'd been told about him.

I conjure up more fog, I can't watch this. As the mist rolls in, my eyes travel over the scene. So many bodies litter the floor but not all of them are of elvish descent. I wish for Haryek to see this, it's a warning to me, that this witty, charming man was exactly who he was promised to be.

I blink a few times when I realize someone is talking to me. It's Adriam, of all people. I want to beg him to take me out of here, to bring me back to my home, yet the words won't come. I'm a pawn, an accessory to murder.

"We have to get out of here!" I can finally hear him.

My body feels heavy, I stare at my bleeding leg. "I can't... I have to control the fog." I tell him, numb.

He checks my pulse, frowning. "We can get you a safe distance away. I have to stitch this now before you go into shock." He gestures to my leg and I grimace.

I realize I'm sitting in between the bodies, my hands bloodied, kneeling in a pool of my own blood. He's checking me, to see if I'm alright and honestly I'm not sure that I am.

Adriam grips my face, his hands are hot and wet, covered in the sticky substance. "Come on, I've brought reinforcements. They can spare you for a minute. The fight's almost over."

I scramble onto Tonic's back, as does Adriam. We race out of the kill zone, towards the source of the mist. Deeper into the woods and towards the creek. It surprises me that the woods can hide so many secrets, back here you can hardly even tell that not a few hundred yards away there are people killing each other and fighting for their lives.

I watch as Adriam removes my bandage and my stomach twists at the pain and the sight of my leg.

"Oh god. Did you cut this?" He asks.

"No." I lie then sigh. "Tonic did."

Unimpressed, Adriam carefully prods the wound. "For the love of the gods. Okay. Well it's going to be ugly."

I shrug in response. It was only fair they got their pound of flesh.

He wets a rag and squeezes it out over my cut. I cringe at the burn; it reminds me of treating the wounds of my chest but only on a larger scale. Taking a bucket out of his bag, he fills it with water. "Heat this." He commands me and I obediently do so. He dips the rag and turns the water red.

Draining it on my cut again, I clutch the ground and struggle to remain still. I wonder if Alpha screamed. Did he endure or did he writhe as he was put back together? "You don't have to be brave for me; I know this must really hurt. I am a doctor you know, nothing will surprise me."

I try not to look embarrassed by my thought process. I had never been one to react to pain, no matter the torment. It brings me back to my childhood once more and I try not to dwell on how this forsaken day had made me think more of my youth than I had in the past ten years. I remember breaking my finger during a fencing lesson and continuing on, only to be told later that it was an odd thing to hide the pain. At the time, it had felt less burdensome than allowing them to fret over me, as they quickly did.

"I'm not big on expressing pain." I actually get off on it sometimes. "You were the one that stitched Alpha back together right?" I want to take my mind off this as he breaks out the needle and thread.

Glancing up at me, he nods and then splashes some alcohol on my gash.

I gasp and tense up. "Did you think he would live?" I coax.

"Is this the time for this?" He mumbles, but he sighs because he knows I'm due a good deal of stitches so maybe it is. He takes a salve from his bag and packs it into my gash expertly, it burns at first but it slowly starts to feel better. Then he takes out a syringe and gives me a few small injections of what I'm assuming is pain killer because I feel like my leg is being opened up again at first but then I feel nothing.

I'm relieved because I was not looking forward to the stitches.

Just when I've given up hope for my answer, he speaks. "No, I didn't. But I promised myself I would fight as long as he did. When I got to him, he was so pale. There was blood everywhere, he was choking on it. Sota told me to let him die, there would be no quality of life for him with a mangled shoulder like that.

"But, I knew I could fix it and I knew he wouldn't allow it to hold him back. Sota has a hard time seeing past the present sometimes. I think he compared it to his own loss, not one he would have chosen." He pops the first stitch and I marvel at his expert work with the tweezers as he ties a few knots and begins the process of closing this thing on my leg.

"I asked him if he wanted me to save him but he couldn't speak, his father's fangs had torn his neck apart as well. I remember watching, with every heartbeat, his life slip away. But he just stared at me, you know that look. He wanted to live. So I worked on him and he made it through. He's tough, I'll give him that. It took everything I had to reset that shoulder, it was so badly broken." He sighs and I'm so caught up in the story, I realize that he's almost done.

I'm compelled to like this tiny, feminine man all over again. His gentle eyes, his thick heavy curls, and the amount of gaudy jewelry donning his neck, ears, and wrists. Much as he had been miserable to deal with, I could see him for his true self. He wanted people to live as badly as I did. "Adriam? I'm sorry." I tell him finally.

The honey-colored eyes spy me through heavy strawberry lashes. Behind those large, innocent pupils, I saw a flash of a murderer that rivaled Alpha in death tolls. Adriam was just as lethal as the warlord, himself. "I know. Thanks." He responds with a weak smile. "Let's get back before they finish killing each other and we miss the good parts."

Climbing back onto Tonic's back, we race back towards the scene to find that we are coming in on the tail end. The last few elves are surrounded and the stragglers are being picked off from the woods. I can't say that I'm upset that we missed this part.

"Stop. We will take these ones back with us for questioning." Alpha calls, from the tree line. He's covered in blood, I freeze and I have a flashback that shakes me to my core. I can see him, standing in the gates of my home. My father's blood on his lips as he squares up to kill my mother. I fight it back, my head spins.

Tonic allows me to slide off as Alpha approaches, lips pulled down, eyes dark with remorse.

"What?" Adriam demands. His eyes are searching, no doubt for Victor.

I can see the big white wolf is rounding up the elves with the others.

"We've had casualties." His voice is distant like he's holding back.

"Well, I figured we would. Who did we lose?"

He glances at Adriam and then to Tonic. "Fleet, Swift, a few of the mid ranks, some lower ranks." Alpha sighs heavily, glaring at the ground as if he was uncertain if he wanted to reveal the loss of the others.

Tonic, sensing the hesitation quickly steps forward. The light blue eyes meet the younger wolf with regret, "Delta." He reveals, preparing himself as Tonic stumbles backward.

"Are you sure?" His voice is small.

Alpha nods slowly. "He went quickly." He tries to sound reassuring. "I'm sorry, Tonic. I know he was your friend."

Unable to comprehend, Tonic lurches past him. "Where is he?" His eyes search frantically, trying to find his body, and Alpha steps in front of him to stop him. "Damn it, show me where he is! You don't know... maybe... maybe Nic could heal him?"

"Tonic, I'm telling you that you don't want to see him. There isn't anything anyone can do, seeing him is not going to bring him back. Tonight, when we send him to Valhalla—"

With a snarl, Tonic shoves back against the bloodied male. "Fuck Valhalla!" Tonic roars, laying his ears back. "That's not what Delta would have wanted! He didn't even believe in this crap! Delta didn't have to die; none of this had to happen!"

"Tonic! Mind the gods!" Adriam hisses.

"Fuck the gods!" Tonic snarls.

Hardened, Alpha narrows his eyes. "You didn't even know his name. Remember your place and remember why you're here." Alpha's tone is sharp and frustrated; he looks away from the smaller gray wolf that shoves past him to find his fallen friend.

Allowing him to go, his attention turns to me. "How's your leg?" He asks me, dismissive of the scene that had caught me so off guard. I'm totally numb, in sensory overload. I cared for Delta too, his loss hits me as hard as the loss for the twins who I had slowly become fond of.

How many more would we lose?

Snapping out of my stupor, I stare at him, almost accusingly. "Don't you think you need to talk to Tonic?" I ask, changing the subject.

His cold tone brings me back to reality, revealing the true intent of the man before me. He was their leader, not their friend. "Tonic needs to figure this out for himself. Nobody can tell you how to grieve." He looks at Adriam. "Have the uninjured gather the dead and take them back to the castle. The injured need to go to town, with you, to get treatment for their injuries." He speaks quickly to Adriam who nods, experienced in the heat of battle. "Victor!"

The white wolf appears suddenly, looking thrilled. "Get everyone home. We need to get out of here before they send another group. We can't afford another hit. Have the uninjured prepare the columns so we can send the dead home tonight. I think after today, everyone could use a drink."

I want to be angry with him, I want to scream at him as Tonic did, but I can only stare. The brutality brings me to the realization that had been building since the start of the run, there was no hiding it from it. He leaves me to join his pack and I wonder if I truly picked the right side.

CHAPTER

Thirty-Two-

Through an Action, a Man becomes a Hero.
Through Death, a Hero becomes Legend.
Through Time, a Legend becomes Myth.
Through hearing a Myth, a Man takes an Action.

I feel numb. I drift in and out of reality from the blood loss, the weight of the situation, and seeing Alpha as the murderer of my family for the first time in a long time. I had thought I was past that but here it hits me, again, with such reality that I'm shaken to my core.

I'm vaguely aware that everyone is moving around me, it looks like a blur but I'm at a standstill. I know the reality of the families of these elves, I know the nightmares, and how they will picture over and over how their loved ones were torn apart.

We have to end this, but at what cost? Could this cold, calculated man truly be the answer?

I realize that I'm trembling and I wrap my arms around myself to absently rub my biceps. The air feels dead and cold as the afternoon begins to turn into evening. I watch the pack gather the dead and I count, one... two... three... seven... ten. My stomach rolls as a large male passes me, Fleet dangles on his back.

I watch his limp paws sway, his tongue hanging from his open muzzle. What I wasn't prepared for is that his eyes are open and it's almost as if he's looking at me. I shut my eyes and look away. Blood. So much blood. When I open them, I realize an elf is on the ground beside me, looking at me with glazed-over eyes. His throat is ripped, his hand outstretched towards his knife.

I admire his porcelain skin.

His long white hair is splayed around him, he looked so much like Haryek it's almost eerie. There are elves all around me, hanging from trees, splayed out on the ground, and now, being led away. So this is what it looks like, this is the destruction that was promised to me.

I remember Sota's words, *'If he is anything, he's absolutely lethal. The Lion spares the lamb, until it's hungry.'* Alpha did this.

One man capable of leading a small force, unarmed, to victory against a larger force. *'If anyone can do this, Alpha can.'* They could pull this off. He could pull this off. I wonder what that will mean to my people if the elves and the humans are forced into submission. Regardless, Loan is right.

In my horror, my resolve solidifies. We need the alliance of the Alpha if we're going to survive this. No matter my thoughts on this, it was time to start making moves. I had to make this work for the sake of my people, no matter what the cost.

"Stop! He doesn't want to go!" Someone is screaming. I squint and almost excuse myself from the dead version of Haryek before I remind myself that, well, he's dead and he's not Haryek. "I'll bury him myself! Just stop!" Sobbing. Hysterical sobbing.

My heart breaks, *Tonic.* I get up and my leg feels better so I risk a jog into the field to see my friend, clinging to the body of his friend. *Oh, Tonic.* I rushed over.

"Just wait for a second please," I ask the male who looks too tired to deal with our crap.

Shoving the body of Delta away, he storms off. "I'm getting Alpha." He says, annoyed.

Delta has been gutted. The chocolate wolf is a sad heap, someone has taken a knife and made his innards his outtards and poor Tonic has him by the neck, holding his head in his lap. His bloodied tongue lolls like a dog in the sun though his eyes are glossed over. He's gone; there is no bringing this one back.

"Tonic..." I breathe. "Honey, he's gone. We can't leave him here." I try to sound patient, I try and think of how I would have felt if someone wanted to drag my mother's corpse through the woods.

The young man shakes his head, here, next to the wolf he looked more like a boy than a man. "He doesn't want this, Nicolas. He told me, ``he doesn't want to go to Valhalla." He shakes his head, burying his cheek against the bloodied forehead. He rocks quietly, Tonic is gone too.

This is a useless husk of emotion, this is grief gone mad. I know it well.

I talk to him as if he's insane, the mentally damaged can't reason. My voice is soft, light, "Maybe we can talk with Alpha. But we have to take him home; we can't leave him out here. We can't leave you out here."

His dark eyes lock on me, "I can't let them burn him." His tone haunts me, he frightens me. I've never seen Tonic like this. Alpha arrives with Victor and they both look disappointed at the emotional display.

"Tonic, it's time to go," Alpha says quietly, he's still a wolf. With the loss of the twins and Delta, he has little help right now save for Victor. Our normal babysitters are dead.

Tonic shakes his head. "No! I'm not going with you. With any of you. You killed Delta." His body tenses, he clings to Delta's frame.

Exhausted, the gray male firms up his resolve just as I did. "I'm not asking you. You're being a child." His response is firm.

"You killed him! You did this!" Tonic is screaming now. "He trusted you! I trusted you! And look at this! Dead! Everyone is dead!" He starts to break down into sobs. Hysterical, heartbreaking sobs.

I get on my knees to hug him and cry with him. I can tell Alpha and Victor are uncomfortable with us but I don't care. Nobody needs to see their friend like this. "Come on Tonic." I coax and slowly I pry his hands away from Delta's neck.

His whole body is sticky, covered in dried blood and hair. My leg is screaming at me from where I was kneeling down. Victor trots over and lowers himself. I help Tonic climb on and I climb on behind him, wrapping my arms around him. I look back towards Alpha and I can see the pain on his face for only a moment.

The entire way back to the castle, the expression haunts me. Was he pained for the disgust of Tonic, the lack of his ability to share in that grief, or for something else entirely? I analyze it as the castle comes into view, anything to take my mind off the stench of death emanating from Tonic.

When we arrive home, I find Adriam and we take Tonic to get him cleaned up in the servants' showers. I pull off my clothes, it doesn't bother me to be naked around either of them. I'm tempted to take Tonic to Stefan's but change my mind. He seems calmer though he's murmuring to himself.

I glance at Adriam. "Do you think he's going to be okay?" I ask, softly.

"Would you be? I wish he hadn't seen—" He stops and sighs. He knew exactly what I had seen, nobody knew better than I did what Tonic was going through. "Nobody needs that."

I can tell he wants to say more but he holds his tongue. We scrub the blood off of him until he's clean and I take the time to rinse myself as well. Adriam washes his hands and arms; the man is covered from the armpits down. His shirt and pants are stained.

"What made you want to be a doctor?" I ask, hoping the conversation will help us all.

"I want to help people. Plus my mother told me it would make good money, little did she know we would be slaves, eh?" He chuckles, the heavy French accent soothing to me, and shrugs. "I was a surgeon. Times have changed a lot. I'd like to go back to school when this is all over."

That makes me smile. When it's all over. What will I do?

I look at Tonic and reach over to brush his wet hair out of his face then I go and grab a towel for us both. "Here, honey." I wrap it around his shoulders and pat him dry. "Maybe we should get you to bed?" I suggest.

He nods, numbly. I excuse us from Adriam, I figure he probably wants to shower and change. I led Tonic to my old bedroom and set him up in there, tucking him into bed where he looks like he could possibly sleep. Or maybe he's just so inside himself he can't fathom that he could be in a position to sleep.

I can only tell him what I had wished to hear, lies, and assurances that everything would be alright. "It's safe here Tonic, you can stay here as long as you need." I lean down and kiss his cheek. It's strange that he doesn't respond but I know he's been through a lot.

I grab some clothes and pull them on. A sweater and some pants. The night air has some bite to it now that I've lost some blood and the activities of the day have died down. I close the door behind me and pull on my clothes, flinching as the pants touch my leg.

Going into the kitchen, I try and find food but I can't eat. I pick up items and put them down, opening cabinets and closing them. I smell a few things, hoping to get a sense to put them in my mouth but the sensation is gone.

I sigh and make my way out of the dining hall and into the main throne room. I realize a door is open and I pad over to see it's one of the balconies and Adriam is outside, sitting in one of the overstuffed chairs that overlook the courtyard. I watch him and clear my throat, he glances at me, smiles, and gestures with his head for me to join him.

Sitting with one leg folded on the other chair, watching through the stone pillars as they light the column of logs, the fire catches his honey eyes. I watch as they load the bodies into the stacks. Ten wolves. Ten dead friends.

"What are they doing?" I ask.

"Sending the spirits to Valhalla, the smoke pillar provides a passageway to the gods and will lead them to the gates." He tells me, his golden eyes reflect the flames beautifully. I watch as he runs his hand through his tangled, thick curly locks. Adriam's feminine features always amaze me, he truly is a beautiful man.

"What is Valhalla?" I don't think Alpha ever answered that before.

Exhaling slowly, he tilts his head back to gaze up at the stars, searching for answers there. "It's where all the warriors go. When you die in battle, you earn a place at Oden's table in Valhalla, the heaven to the warriors. You fight and drink and tell stories all day, remembered forever, remembered for glory. You can listen to the stories of all the greats before us and add your own. It's a pretty important thing to most of us."

Oh. That sounds kind of ridiculous. I see him smirking and I raise a brow. "But not to you?" I prod. I'm not very religious myself either.

"No. Not to me. I'm not really allowed in, well, none of us are. Gods don't like lovers of men I suppose." He sighs and brings his knees up to his chest, curling his arms loosely around them.

I peek at him, curious. "Adriam, almost every man I know here is gay."

He pauses and stares at me for a long moment. "Not quite." He looks surprised. "Victor and I, You and Alpha now, Tonic..." He trails off and shrugs. "Doesn't sound like much to me." I suppose he wouldn't count my friends or Haryek. "I think you just notice the gay ones because they are like you."

I frown. I don't think I'm that closed-minded. Am I? I shrug and lean back into my chair. I can hear a slow drum starting, then it grows and it sounds like a heartbeat. Suddenly, someone starts singing and I realize it's Alpha. The pack joins in, the low hum of the baritones brings the song to life and I'm silenced by the amazing orchestra of voices and drums, low and high in a rhythmic chant to symbolize soldiers marching home to their gods.

The rattling shake of tambourine, the low hum of an aged violin, coupled with the deep voices calling the burning souls home.

"What is this?" I almost whisper.

"They are sending the spirits to Valhalla; it's a song in Nordic about the trip. Wolves are very musical creatures. All wolves can sing." He hums along to it, his light and melodic voice makes me gape at him.

"Nobody ever sings," I complain.

He glances at me from the corner of his eye. "We're trying not to die." Hm. I suppose that makes sense.

I wish I knew the words, the beat is so intense. I find that I like Adriam, I appreciate his honesty and his no-nonsense behavior.

"I'm going to bed. They're all about to start drinking and I'm not one for drunks. I suggest you do the same, these nights get a little rough." He clasps my hand and squeezes it, offering me a kind smile. "You did well today." He reassures me.

I smile back and watch him as he disappears, his petite body makes me wonder how a man of his size could possibly be with someone like Victor. I sigh and watch the ceremony a little while longer before I get up and make my way to bed only to pause when I realize the elf captives are being kept in the throne room.

They are tied up, backs against the wall and in a corner. There are only seven of them. Their battered bodies make me frown. I don't remember some of them being so damaged. I go and get a pitcher of water and offer them all water and some bread. That's all I can do for them for now. They look suspicious of me but they take my offerings.

I end up in my father's room like usual though I suppose it is my true room now. I'm shocked when I see Alpha in there. He's clean, sitting on the window ledge. I stop in the doorway and he glances at me. I can see the emotion in his eyes, he's hurting too. "I figured you went to see your friend." He admits.

"Oh. No. I was just taking care of Tonic. He's pretty torn up." I sigh and close the door behind me. "Why're you in here?" I question.

Alpha looks reluctant to answer. "I always come in here when you're gone, it smells like you." Here he isn't Alpha unless I ask him to be. He's Randy. He's Verando. He's human. It warms me to know he enjoys my smell.

I approach and sit on the sill across from him, looking out the glass. Sampling the air, there is no lingering scent of alcohol as there was last time. "Not drinking?" I ask, curious.

"I don't like losing control like that. It's dangerous. I could have snapped your neck." He tilts his head back against the stone rim of the window. The scars on his neck are shiny compared to the darkened skin. I watch his jugular pulse with his heartbeat directly under those skilled bite marks, envisioning Adriam's story.

He's here before me and I must know if my dream last night was truly a dream. "Were you here last night?" I ask him. "Is your wolf too tired to make an appearance?"

"Yes." He admits after a long moment. "No. He's accepted you. I think you proved your point, you helped to save the pack. That's all he wants."

I swallow, remembering the pact that I made to myself. For my people, I had to make this word, no matter how he gave me pause after seeing him slaughter a company of elves. No matter how I felt about this cold nature to Tonic. "He's a good leader," I say slowly only to see him flinch and I know he doesn't want to hear it.

"*Take the bloody compliment!*" I quote, doing my best to copy his accent. He glares at me but the faintest hint of a smile curls on his lips. I offer a small laugh and he shakes his head at me. Crawling to him, I slip between his legs to wedge myself in his lap. Pressing my ear to his chest, I listen to the pounding beat. "What're we doing?"

With a long, low sigh, he buries his nose into my hair. "Surviving best we can."

"So does that mean you love me?"

CHAPTER

Thirty-Three-

Alpha stares at me, bewildered in my audacity to speak against him so bluntly, to ask such an abrupt question. "Is now really the time for this?"

I can tell he wants to pull away but I'm strategic and I've pinned him here. "It's never the time for it. We could die at any moment." I press closer to him to prevent any hope of escape. If I want this to happen, I have to ensure that this part falls into place. If he could leave me, if he no longer needed me, what would become of my people?

He exhales in frustration at me but I can see my favorite look is coming back. He's irritated but amused at my games. I need Verando right now; I can't deal with Alpha just yet. I wait patiently, like a child waiting for a story. Donning my best look of innocence, I curl into him, nuzzling my face against his neck with an airy inhale.

The effect I have on him is visible, never before have I been able to bend a man to my will in such a way. I was not good at flirting, only offering my services in blunt exchange. This was new territory for me, to seduce and manipulate this man who seemed quite smitten with me in rare moments. "It's possible." He allows it, not looking at me.

I grin against his skin. Anyone else would be upset by the insincerity of it. But it is his way, as it is mine. I find that I'm grateful for the admittance, I don't know if I could handle the full-blown confession right now.

I think of the time with Haryek, with my instructors, and with my one boyfriend. It never clicked, we never matched up. But with him, with Verando, I don't feel so broken. I need to feel dominated but I also need to feel like an equal. I lean back and reach up to touch his face. To brush my knuckles over his stubbled jaw, admiring his full lips and his tanned skin, I swallow back the bravery I had had just moments ago.

Watching his tired eyes; his tangle of gray locks is almost past his jaw bone, I can't fathom what he'd do to me if he found out I was vying for my people's protection just as he was. Perhaps he'd be impressed, it seemed I could never fully predict how he would feel. It distracts me, pulling me away from those deep eyes.

"Are you going to stare at me like this for the rest of the night? I can take it back, you know." He breaks the silence, not much of a romantic. I make a face at him, marveling in our similarities. A dictator and a fallen monk.

Clearing my throat, I straighten. "Way to kill a moment." Standing, I take the time to pull off my clothes and fold them as clean clothes are hard to come by. He observes me, for, of course, he's already naked. I glance over my shoulder. "Do you mind?" I chastise him, yet I stand before him unashamed as he drinks me in.

"Not at all, keep going."

How is it we go from war, to a death ceremony, to this? Maybe it's because we've missed each other and this is an easy distraction. Sex has always been how I cope, how I survive. I slowly roll out of my pants, allowing my hips to follow the sway as I slide them down my legs. I bite my lower lip as I meet his eyes before stepping out of them and gathering them to fold them. "Better?" I ask but he's gone.

I startle as I realize he's in front of me.

"Much." He mutters.

I toss my pants onto a chair and avoid his lips, teasing him, for I need a distraction, too. My intentions were all wrong, I was supposed to be seducing him, not falling back into the comfortable steps of this playful redirect. "So, do you want to go to Valhalla?" I inquire, circling him as my hands find his shoulders and I wind around him. Kneading carefully with my palms, his muscles ripple under my hungry fingers and I wet my lips at the thought of tasting that freshly cleaned flesh.

"Of course." His tone is sarcastic, he's annoyed with me. But I can still hear the hint of amusement; I know I'm safe for now.

"Adriam said you can't get in. Because you like men." I tempt him, I'm either going to get what I need or get what I want. One hand slides up and I trail my fingers across his scalp as I tangle in his hair. I'm rewarded with a growl, it brings a shudder down my spine and I breathe out through my teeth in response.

Alpha's eyes burn, I'm playing with fire as he seeks me out. "Fuck him..." He breathes and turns in my arms but I once more slip away. I take his wrists and put his hands behind his head. He sets his jaw in restraint as he leaves them there.

I brush my lips over his neck, my hands slide down his biceps and it's almost my undoing. I bite him, hard, and he moans as his hands lock on my hips, lifting me up onto his body.

I'm losing this game, losing control of the situation. I'm playing with an expert and for a brief moment, I wonder if we're both playing the same angle. I invade his mouth with my tongue, taking control. My hands are in his hair and I pull his head back, breaking the kiss.

"Haven't I earned an answer?" I ask as I assault his neck once more, grinding my body against his in slow, delicious strokes that threaten to make my eyes roll back into my head. The throat sigh as a growl rolls from his chest urges my fingers to close, raking against his skin.

Swallowing, he composes himself. "It doesn't matter. I've made my peace with it. No, I won't get into Valhalla."

I stop and slide off his body. He pants as he watches me, victorious in his resolve. "What? Why?" This is ridiculous. He's been with women before.

"Do we have to talk about this now?" His lips are on mine before I can blink. My eyes flutter shut and I'm almost lost in him but that nagging feeling remains, I must know. My mission was forgotten, I must know everything I can about this man.

Defiant, I break the kiss, speaking against his lips. "Yes. If you want me to let you finish." I tell him firmly.

He looks at me and almost laughs; it's hard for me to not smile. "Since when are you the Alpha?" He cocks an eyebrow, appreciating my bold behavior, taking me in.

It's my turn to don the Alpha expression, tilting my chin up as regally as I can manage. "Since I rode you. Since I conquered your wolf. Technically, I'm your Alpha." I tease. He blinks a few times and takes a second to process this. "Don't worry, I'll let you keep your job. But right now, I'm your Alpha and I want you to answer my questions."

I don't know why the thought of dominating him thrills me when I'm the one who likes to be choked and spanked. He rolls his eyes at me so hard, it's a wonder he doesn't fall over. In a moment of bravery, I grab his length in my hand. He inhales sharply and almost jerks away but I keep my hold and squeeze him. He pulls air through his teeth and I feel him grow in my hand.

I pull him to me by his shaft and his lips part in surprise. "I've been without you for days while you were trying to get your shit together."

I'm lost in the play, drunk on the intoxicating presence of the warlord before me. It turns me on to see him like this, looking at me like this. "We can talk later. I think I might have other plans for you." I bite my lower lip and he pulls away from me.

"I think you forgot your place." He challenges me. "I think you forget your insolence is the reason we were in this mess, to begin with." I balk. His tone is stern. "You think because you conjure some fog, your insubordination is forgiven? That your behavior is forgiven?" I blink at him and take a step back. He grasps my face, running his thumb over my lower lip. "You are sadly mistaken, I've yet to decide what to do with you. And yet here you are, challenging me." He ponders this for a moment, his body is on fire, his hand slides down to brush over my throat. I can't help but respond to his presence, my body practically bows to him.

I'm hardly in control as I throw myself at him and tackle him onto the bed. Hungrily, I kiss him, commanding control over his lips as I kiss him until I must surface for air. "You would make a poor Alpha." He comments on my impulsive behavior, trading his tongue over my lower lip.

"Good thing I have you to keep me in line," I respond, breathless as he pins my hands over my head.

Alpha looks down at me, a startling boyish grin painted where the scowl usually resides. It dimples his cheek, softening those intense eyes into a look that I had pondered over just a mere night ago. The gentle regard for me, the amusement and the slight hint of something more that I couldn't place. He was looking at me as nobody had ever looked at me before. At that moment, his crimes fade away and my intentions melt with them.

Emotion wells up inside me, this intense feeling is overwhelming. I feel strangled like I'm choking. My cheeks feel wet and I sniffle as I blink away the tears. *What the hell is my problem?*

He looked shocked and unsure as he watched me, sitting up. "What? What happened?" He checks me over, concerned.

"I—" The wave hits me all at once. I thought I had lost him, I'd lost him to the wolf, I'd lost him to the blood lust, I'd lost him to my own vision of what I had seen. "I don't—" I thought he would never come back, that it was over and that if he could ever forgive me, could I ever forgive him for what I'd seen? For a moment, it was over. I don't want it to be over. "I don't want you to go." I manage.

His hand cups my face, forcing me to focus on him as he stares down at me. "I'm not going anywhere. I'm right here. Don't cry, love." He kisses my cheek and I come apart right then and there. I throw my arms around his neck and sob. He stills, conflicted as to what to do with me, and frankly, I don't know how to handle myself either. Maybe it's my 180 in emotion but it took me off guard to feel so strongly for him.

"I thought you were gone. I thought you were never coming back." I manage through the emotion. "I thought... when I saw you out there in battle, when I saw you with Tonic... how could I forgive..." It comes out in sobs, I try desperately to form words as I apologize for ever thinking that I could betray such a creature.

There must be something seriously wrong with me.

Startled, he waits patiently. "I'm here now." He reassures me but it's not the truth. I finally see why I'm so stuck on this Valhalla subject. He wants to die, he had no intention of making it out of this alive. He had to die in battle, if he's going to go to Valhalla. By his own intentions, he would die in battle if he had his say. I completely break down, overcome by the loss of Delta and the twins as well as the realization that I might lose every last person that mattered to me.

I'll have to come back to the fact that these are all the people who murdered my family. "You have to die to go to Valhalla. You have to die in battle, you bastard!" I yell at him, in between breaths. "Damn it!" I push against his chest but he holds me until I stop struggling. "How can you tell me you will be here when you've been planning to die all along?"

"Death is not something that can be decided. I can't plan to die, the gods decide."

Shaking my head, I shove against him once more, angry, hurt, betrayed even if my intentions had been to seduce him into aligning with me not moments before. "But you want to go to Valhalla." I accuse him.

"Nobody wants to die, Nicolas. But Valhalla is the end goal." He watches me with a somber expression.

I can't do this to myself, I can't keep attaching myself to people who don't wish to stick around. "I can't Randy. I can't see you like that, not like Delta. It will kill me." I realize I'm pleading with him because it's becoming more and more apparent to me how painful life would be without him in it.

He just sighs, holding me to his chest. "Everyone dies."

We both go silent and it dawns on me that he's hurting too. I remember seeing glimpses of it, the pained expressions. It is already killing him. The loss of Delta, the loss of the twins, his pack mates, and the loss of Tonic's faith in him. I sit up to look at him, his eyes almost look misty. He offers me a weak smile and I hug him once more.

Alpha, my Alpha, sharing in my grief.

I start to kiss him once more, realizing how much he does for me and my erratic emotions. He plays my games, he sacrifices his own emotions to fulfill my fragile needs, he experiences death and heartbreak and loss and he stands through it because he has a job to do. He doesn't crumble, he doesn't falter. I marvel at him, I'm in awe of him. He understands this is how I deal with loss. That this is how I cope and he's willing to do it for me.

I realize I don't need the fight or the aggression, all I need is him. I kiss him again, melting into him. He's there for me, returning my kiss as I've finally turned into what he needed. Me.

Pulling him on top of me, I curl my arms around his neck as he fills me. My eyes lock with his, pressing my forehead against his as I gasp at the intensity. Alpha's weight pins me beneath him and I'm consumed by the warmth as my fingers clutch his back. The closeness becomes necessary as I cling to him, unwilling to allow a sliver of space to slip between us as the depth threatens to send me over the edge.

He hooks one of my legs in his arm, pinning it up by my side as he braces himself on his knees, staring down at me as I come apart for him. "What're you doing to me?" He asks me again, as he's grown fond of asking me. I could ask him the same question, all my intentions were sullied, I was here serving him once more and unable to fathom doing anything else at this moment. I roll my hips to meet him, hungry for him in response to his question.

The motion brings an airy moan from his lips as he buries his face against my neck. "Gods, Nic." He murmurs against my ear, sinking his teeth into my neck as I groan his name. My free leg locks around his waist, controlling his pace, refusing to allow him to do more than the slow, torturous, grind. I needed every moment of it, savoring it as I climbed.

"Come for me." His voice is hot against my ear as I moan low in my throat, my breathing accelerating as my body begins to tremble. "You are mine."

"Yours," I repeat, breathless as I finish. He groans against my neck as he fills me, I shudder at the sensation, unable to move as I collapse back onto the bed. My head spins and swims, disorientated from such a mind-blowing completion.

He lies on his back and I curl up to his chest. I trace his scars with my fingertips, neither of us can sleep. The day has us wired and emotions run too hot. I want to question him, to pry into him as to how to keep him alive, but he's burnt out on me and I think I've finally learned when enough is enough. "Thank you." I finally break the silence.

"For what?" He yawns.

"I don't know how you're doing it but you're fixing me." I offer a pathetic laugh. It took a murderous warlord for me to realize how broken my life was. He says nothing, he just squeezes me and I sit up. "Hungry?"

"Actually, yes."

I must be grinning because he grins back with a boyish charm that is not typical for him. "Can I actually make some food for my Alpha?" I ask hopefully.

He nods. "You might."

I put on my clothes and encourage him to at least put on some pants which he begrudgingly does. I wrap my arm around him as we walk towards the dining hall. He pauses halfway down the hallway and inhales. "Wow. Does no one shower anymore?" He wrinkles his nose.

"What?" I ask sleepily.

"Blood. I guess a couple of the boys came in and didn't wash up. That elf's blood reeks."

I sniff but I smell nothing.

As we enter the throne room he drops my arm and freezes. Our feet squish in fresh blood. It looks like a massacre. Pieces of elf lie everywhere, blood covers the floor as it pools around freshly killed torsos. A vile trail of fresh red liquid leads to the throne where Tonic sits, with his face buried, hugging his knees to his chest where he is almost too still.

CHAPTER

Thirty-Four-

A better friend would have gone and checked on him, a better friend would not have left him on his own while I romped around with a dictator. My heart sings, plummeting as I see the scene before me. The smell of rust and salt heavy in the air, only this time I'm numb to the gore. All I can see of Tonic, all I can envision is how would he ever recover from this?

"Tonic." My voice is barely above a whisper. I drop Alpha's hand and rush forward, my feet struggling to find purchase on the slippery marble floor, the blood is sticky and slick all at once. The gushing, sucking noises of my feet slipping through the practical silt of remains mixed with the thick life-giving substance. I'm vaguely aware that Alpha has scrambled after me; he throws his arms around my waist and pulls me back.

I fight against him, kicking and shoving at his arms. "He needs me!" I plead. Tonic would not be a victim as I was, alone, and without anyone to understand his pain. He needed me now more than ever and I would go to him. I'd already let him down once before.

"He needs help," Alpha tells me sharply.

I snap my head to look at him, glaring daggers, my eyes burning with resentment that he dare restrain me. "No thanks to you!" I want to go to him. I want to hug him and tell him it's alright. I'm not met with the scowl I was expecting, instead, he holds me firmly, his hands like steel vices on my biceps.

Ever the one in control, the calm and even tone attempting to coax me out of my own hysteria. "We have to get Sota. When this happens... Tonic is very dangerous in this state. We have to wait for backup if we want to help him." He tries to warn me but I shake my head. I don't want to listen to this, hearing him speak of my friend as if he were a murderer.

I had forgiven killers before, in my head I was already attempting to come up with a dozen different ways that would explain him out of this situation. "Tonic would never hurt anyone!" I shove him away from me, freeing myself.

"Look around you! He's proven he will hurt plenty of people, you don't know him, Nicolas! You are not going over there, you are staying here. I'm not giving you an option." His harsh tone cuts through me, echoing off the walls of the chamber, and rattling my confidence. Tonic wasn't the only dangerous one here. "Nicolas!" He commands my response.

I couldn't help Tonic if he banished me from this room. "Yes, Alpha." My voice is low and cold. Tonic needs help but not their help. He needs his friends, he needs to grieve. Despite my efforts, the gore surrounding me, the blood filling my nose, I can't convince myself it's true. It has to have been a setup. To truly be convinced, I must hear it from him and maybe not even though. Dark magic, mystics, shape-shifters, we could be looking at a doppelganger.

"Stay here. Do not move a muscle. Keep an eye on him, I'll be right back." He leaves and my eyes wander the throne room, finally drifting to the motionless young man.

He cut them up.

There are pieces of elf everywhere, parts, and glimpses of what could be a torso strewn across the room in a cyclone of disorder. My eyes pass over the impressions of marble under all that red. I look at the cold faces of those who had fallen victim to whatever this is, the rawest form of expression in a total mental breakdown. The look of shock and terror still remains, their jaws slack, their eyes wide.

War takes more than lives.

The longer I remain here, the longer I stand motionless among the dead, the more I begin to realize that I had been irrational in my justification. With the steady dripping of blood running down the grand stairs, I shudder.

Spotting movement, I see that two elves are still alive; they are battered, bruised, and bloodied. They sit in a far corner, no longer bound but too afraid to move. I steal a glance at Tonic and see that he has not caught sight of anything. His head remained buried in his knees as if he might be sleeping.

I make my way over to the elves. They shrink away from me, one closes his eyes and the other looks relieved that it could finally be over. I cautiously kneel down, attempting to make my face look as gentle as I could manage given the circumstances. "It's okay. I'm not going to hurt you." I reassure them.

"You'll have to forgive us if we don't necessarily believe you." The stronger of the two quips.

"That's what that young one said. Right before he—" The more damaged of the pair shivers as he clutches his companion. My heart breaks for them; the damage to their mental health far outweighs the bodily harm they have endured. Sometimes it's the meek who are unfortunately spared, this young elf would suffer similar trauma to the man who murdered his friends.

The more fragile of the two startles me with a blood-curdling scream.

I wheel around to see Tonic behind me. His eyes are dull; he's covered in gore from head to toe. His face streaked, his hair matted down. I startle, taking a deep breath as I charge my fingertips in preparation to defend myself. The more damaged of the elves screams, incoherent, pleading for his life.

Tonic reminds me of a predator, the way he cocks his head and sets his eyes on his kill. I hold up my hands and glance over my shoulder. "I think you need to quiet your friend down." My voice is soft before I look back towards Tonic. Stepping towards him, his lip curls, warning me not to come any closer. Once more, I exhale down, this is much different than squaring off with Alpha. The feral expression the man held, the crazed look in his eyes, I was not dealing with a sane being. "Tonic, it's okay. Nobody is going to hurt you."

"I know." He responds, dull. "Nobody is ever going to hurt me again. I fixed that problem, I became strong."

I gape at him. *Oh Tonic.* «You've been quite busy.» I allow it.

"It had to be done!" He says loudly and I attempt not to flinch at the barking tone. "They could not be allowed to live, they were dangerous! We should never have brought them to our home, they deserve to die. They are nothing but knife ear scum." His voice darkens as he continues; his eyes are empty and black. They look bottomless, so little of my Tonic is left in this husk of what used to be such a bright and innocent man.

I must reason with him, I must attempt to draw him back out of this before Alpha sees him. Should he attack, there would be nothing I could do to protect him. "You know that's not true, Tonic. They were doing their job, just like you were doing yours. This is war. People die." I find myself quoting Alpha and I'm angry at myself for that. I'm not ready to accept that he might be right.

"NO!" He snarls at me, eyes hard as he glowers down at me. Never before had I realized how tall Tonic was or how intimidating he could be. "None of us should have to die! It's the elves who killed my friend. One of my best friends! My brother! It's your people who enslaved us! Who caused this mess! We don't have to die!" He takes a step towards me. My heart threatens to leap out of my chest, it pounds erratically as I try to stay calm for both of us. "I think it's time someone else died. Someone who deserves it." His rigid arms tremble, every muscle in his body tight, coiled like a spring as he prepares himself for the assault.

Any thought of defending myself vanishes, all I can focus on is the pain he's in and how I desperately want to take it away. "You're right, nobody else should have to die. Nobody. Not the elves, not the lycans and not the magical users." I try to dissuade him, a final attempt to appeal to what part of him I've grown to care for. "You can stop this, right now. Let us help you. You need to grieve Tonic. It wasn't your fault Delta died." I can see I struck a nerve because his jaw sets and his eyes widen.

"Don't say that." His voice is low, hardly audible.

"It's not your fault," I tell him once more, grasping at the light behind his eyes. Some part of him had been reached, some part of him was fighting to come back to the surface. "There is nothing anyone could have done, his fate was already decided." I'm channeling my inner Alpha.

He closes his eyes and for a moment I think he's coming back to me but when he opens them, I know he's lost. "I said shut up!" He bellows and before I can blink I'm being shoved.

The wind leaves my lungs as I hit the wall. My body crumbles as I crash to the ground, my leg throbs almost as bad as the rest of my body. I contort soundlessly on the ground as I try to breathe. I hear my strangled gasps though it sounds like it's coming from someone else. My vision is blurry and shaky as I watch my feet approach me. His hands close around my throat like a vice, elevating me to his full height as he belts me against the wall with an intensity that rattles my bones. I'd groan if I could breathe, my hands wrap around his wrist as I attempt to freeze his hand.

"It's your turn." His voice is empty, hollow of any consideration for my life slipping away in his fingertips. Gasping for air, I struggle to get free but he's so strong. The impact of hitting the stone had sent me spiraling, had I ever been hit that hard in my life?

I'm briefly aware that I'm falling, as I slump to the ground and roll onto my side, my eyes catch the fading form for the cathedral ceiling. The intricate stonework twirls whimsically above my head as my vision swirls in and out of consciousness.

"It's okay. He's alive."

Gagging and sputtering, I'd been in this position before and fought to allow my lungs the vital air they craved. The discomfort of air forcing its way into my chest only meant that I had survived this ordeal but not on my own accord. Someone had come to my aid, I couldn't fool myself that Tonic had spared me.

"I told him to back off!"

This voice is angry. I would laugh if my throat didn't feel as though it had been ripped out of my body. Damaged, I wondered if I'd ever sound the same again from all my interactions with predators and their desire to cut off my airways. This is the second wolf strangling I'd managed to survive.

Slowly, my wits return and I push myself up onto my hip as I reluctantly touch my bruised throat. Even the thought causes me to wince, I dare not press or prod. Scanning for my attacker, I see that Victor has him restrained.

"What the hell were you thinking?" Alpha bends to offer me his hand.

"Well I was using your little speech about death and then I was flying through the air," I tell him sarcastically, my voice is rough and hoarse, reluctant to form the words with the damage. The answering snarl causes me to flinch more than I should, judging by the look on his face Alpha instantly regrets frightening me.

Adriam kneels by my side, his warm fingers gingerly brushing the skin of my neck. "Don't do that. You could have damaged something." I glance at him; he's in Victor's shirt and a pair of short shorts. His tangled curls are bushy from sleep. He looks even younger and smaller without all his accessories. "There is definitely going to be some swelling. I hope you weren't banking on a singing career. There might be damage to your windpipe and vocal cords, he really grabbed you."

"What were you thinking?" Alpha is on repeat, demanding answers.

I have no defense and can only roll my eyes at Alpha's chastising. "I went to check on the living captives, I didn't think he would get up." Disapproving, Adriam monitors my speech with a concerned expression.

"He could have snapped your bloody neck!" He growls and we look at Tonic who is thrashing against Victor's iron grip.

I get up and walk towards him but Alpha grabs my wrist, I swallow back my horror after my ordeal and he instantly releases me. I must have spurred some sort of kindness out of him for he seems to have pity on my current state of shock. "I have to help him, he will help me," I tell him, lowering my voice.

"No."

"Randy." I sigh.

Adriam clears his throat, coming to my aid. "Let him try. They do have a good relationship. I have tranquilizer ready, we have Victor holding him, and we can control him if he gets out of hand." The look of defiance is clear but there is deep respect in that familiarity that makes me envious of the trust between the two. Alpha answers to a few people; Adriam is one of them.

I will have to find out what secret voodoo this man holds to be in such high standing in the community.

Focusing on the task at hand, I begin my cautious approach to the deranged man who had been my best friend not days prior. "Tonic, I'm fine. You didn't hurt me." I try to appeal to what's inside him. Tonic had never wanted to hurt anyone, no matter how they had wronged him.

"I was going to before these traitors stopped me!" He snaps, looking menacing with his crazed expression. Fully exposed, he bares his teeth at me, lurching against Victor's grasp.

"No, that's not true. You would never hurt anyone, I know you Tonic. This is not you. This is not who you are." I am sure of it.

"It's who I have to be!" Savage, he screams at me, wanting free of his restraint with the large Russian.

If I'm going to get through to him, I must be bold. Bold is what it took to reach Alpha, it only made sense that Tonic would need the same. "It's not! We are fighting for another way." *Come back to us, Tonic.*

I near him, putting my hand out to touch his face. Victor's expression warns me, he holds the younger male tightly. As I touch his cheek, I see his expression soften minutely.

"You're right." His voice is barely above a whisper. "I need to make a bigger impact." His body shudders as he begins to change. Victor curses as he tries to keep a hold of him but the wolf fights his way out of the large man's grasp. I slip in the blood coating the floor, his teeth clamp onto my shirt as he pulls me towards him. I feel the canines slip against my skin, the razor-sharp fangs burn as they graze the sensitive flesh.

"Victor, get him!" I hear someone yell. The Russian grips the smaller gray wolf by the neck, squeezing him firmly to cut off his airways. He strikes at us with his paws, refusing to release me. I feel his nails occasionally take purchase; I cross my arms over my face to protect myself from his struggles. He goes limp and Victor drops him as he releases me.

"Is he dead?" I feel tears spring forward from my eyes.

"No. Sleep." Victor tells me and frowns as he takes in my appearance. I'm covered in scratches on my arms and legs.

"We need to lock him up until he has time to come down from this." Adriam commands and Victor nods, lifting the wolf up easily and jogging out of the throne room.

I realize I'm trembling from the shock of the situation. Thankfully none of my cuts are particularly deep, they mostly just sting. My hands tremble as I try not to move. "Am I going to turn into a wolf?" I ask, shakily.

"No. It doesn't work that way with scratches anymore." It's Alpha who answers as he comes to my aid, his touch surprisingly gentle as he examines my arms. His expression is unreadable, not angry, and yet not quite concerned.

In an attempt to gain control of the situation, Adriam instructs Victor to take Tonic to the spare bedroom. "I need to give Tonic some sedation but I'll be back in a moment to treat your deeper cuts." There are no reassurances on what will happen to the young man, nobody tries to reassure me.

I look towards Alpha and he leads me wordlessly out of the throne room, into the servants' quarters where the showers are. He gestures to the showers and I tug numbly at my clothes but I'm too out of it to remove them. He assists me and I try not to make eye contact as he strips me down then turns on the shower. The warm water is excruciating on my cuts, burning into them as if he were pouring hot coals over my skin.

"We've lost him." I murmur, trembling against the chill of the water that only grows colder in my depressed state.

Unreadable, Alpha very gently strokes the dried blood from my skin with a soft cloth. "He's going to be fine, this has happened before. Tonic was not meant for war." He doesn't look at my face, refusing to make eye contact. Thankfully for my shirt, my torso was mostly spared. "We just have to give him time."

I can tell he's quietly seething, fear etches into my mind and I resist the urge to shrink away from him. "Are you going to punish me for disobeying you?" I ask. I don't know if I could handle it right now. For the first time in my life, physical contact is the last thing on my mind for a coping mechanism.

Suddenly enraged, he glowers at me. "Do I look like I'm going to punish you?" He snaps, meeting my gaze with eyes blazing.

Kind of. I don't respond and he rolls his eyes in frustration at my lack of comprehension skills. "There's a time and place, right now is not that time or that place. I think you have learned your lesson. Tonic has punished you enough."

That we can agree on.

CHAPTER

Thirty-Five-

I struggle with the concept that Tonic is mentally damaged. As we crowd around the table in the dining hall, I let my hand rest over my mouth as bucket after bucket of parts are dragged past the cracked door to be thrown on the burn pile that has seen way too much use, in the courtyard.

Alpha and Victor are upset while Adriam exudes concern. I'm lackluster at best, this feels beyond my reach and out of my realm of jurisdiction. My arms and legs bare the marks of his rage. Alpha had the presence of mind to take me back to my father's room to throw some clothes on, soft, loose-fitting clothes that wouldn't bother my deep scratches. In silence, I'm replaying the events over and over in my mind, this is not our Tonic.

He pulled my clothes on me with such care, as I just stared past him. I'm grateful that he's giving me my space, I don't need questions on my actions. Like he had said, I've been punished already. The power of the wolf has never been more real than it is now. My throat aches, it's hard to swallow and even more difficult to speak.

They talk about him like I'm not even here though I suppose I am the servant, I'm not in charge here. It's not my call as to what to do with a young man who, until recently, was my protector. My bodyguard. My friend. I hear words like deranged and damaged go back and forth. A lycan drags an elven torso by his hair and I could almost gag.

How could I forget the massacre when the clean up is almost as graphic?

We have moved the two elves to the guest room after giving them a chance to get cleaned up but they are also dubbed as damaged. The stronger of the two has sucked back, deep inside himself, whilst the weaker one just cries. Alpha believes it's unfair to keep them alive and feels as though we should put them out of their misery, they've seen enough to warrant releasing them from their torment.

I struggle with this but then I think of my own struggles with grief and wonder if I would have wished for the same. What kind of life would they have without a warlord to put them back together? Surely they had witnessed more than I had and I'm still not recovered from the events.

Adriam catches my eyes and sighs, walking over to close the door only to have Sota enter. Everyone goes silent as Ol' One Arm slams the door behind him. He looks at each of us, I feel like I'm in detention only my crime is far beyond anything I could ever have imagined.

I expect him to scold us for allowing Tonic to get to this state, for not doing more to prevent his descent into madness.

"Well. This is a right mess." He says in frustration.

He runs his hand through his long locks which, for once, are down around his waist and loose. It's nothing like the elven perfection I'm used to in long hair. It's thick, dense, and stark white with none of the translucent qualities that elven hair held.

Sota's yellow eyes lock on me and I instantly look away, there is one man I don't push. There is one who brings the Alpha to his knees.

I practically hold my breath and I realize everyone around me is doing the same thing. His tone surprises me.

"Does anyone have a clue as to what the hell is going on?" He's asking us to provide him with answers but honestly, I don't think anyone knows. It's easier when it's someone you're not involved with.

Finally, Adriam speaks. "We think he's mentally deranged. Post-Traumatic psychosis if you will. When he saw Delta, something must have snapped."

I find myself thankful for Adriam's medical training. He sounds so sure, so matter of fact. If we can diagnose it we can treat it, right?

"Isn't that convenient?" Sota practically spits.

I'm appalled. *He's blaming Tonic?*

"So I suppose everyone who hauls off and kills captives gets this excuse? Do we just give a free pass to everyone who cracks under the pressure?" His eyes turn to Alpha and I feel the gray-haired man tighten and grow rigid. He's blaming all of us but it would seem, most of all, Alpha.

"I feel like these are unusual circumstances—"

Sota slams his fist down on the table and everyone jumps but Alpha. It's like a crack of thunder and for a moment, I wonder if he broke the table.

"Bullshit." He thunders. "You have been defending that omega since he was a boy. He costs us valuable support that we could not afford to lose in the ranking ceremonies and now, he has cost us multiple captives that could have been questioned. I've been told you want to euthanize our other two? When does it end, Verando?" He narrows his eyes and leans in on his hand.

He meets the icy gaze of our Alpha and they lock eyes for what seems like an eternity. "This must end. Today. We can no longer afford to sacrifice our lives and our positioning for this omega. We need to execute him or cast him away and you know which I prefer. We cannot allow him to influence our decisions, again, for his weakness."

Before I can think to argue, Alpha narrows his eyes as he squares his shoulder. If there was one thing he was passionate about, it was his people. "He's not ready to be on his own and you know it."

With a heavy grimace, eyes squinted, nose wrinkled, Sota clutches his hand into a fist. "Then I suppose your options are easy. This is what it's like to be a leader, to be in charge. You would do well to remember that friends and lovers are a costly affair. Send me your status report on what we are doing about the attack on Ziduri. It cannot wait any longer, you make the call or I will. The leaves are changing, we don't have any more time for delays."

It's Alpha's turn to slam his hands on the table, outraged that the older man dares to defy him. "We will be going into a slaughter if we march on Ziduri. I have worked it out, we are not prepared for the archery that they possess! I will not sentence our pack to death on the front lawn of their capital!"

Sota snarls back, flashing his teeth as he leans in. "That is not my concern! I'm your advisor, I'm advising you to get your people together. We are moving out, with or without your command. If I must unseat you myself to do it, it will be done!"

It is Adriam who so calmly breaks up their squabble. He clears his throat, smacking the table promptly between the two to gain their attention. "Support for the Alpha runs strong, you would be hard-pressed to unseat him."

Victor nods in agreement. Arms crossed over his chest, he flexes his forearms in frustration.

"I suggest you keep your threats to yourself, lest you forget what cost you your arm in the first place. Now, why don't you go boss the lower rankings around and leave the planning to us. We will march on Ziduri, but not today." Smiling a sickeningly sweet smirk, he waves Sota off, dismissing him with an amount of confidence that I found unsettling.

Sota weighs his options and straightens, pushing his hair back. "Three weeks. With or without you."

As the door slams, everyone exhales and Adriam looks to Alpha. "We need to get this moving. We can assign someone to keep an eye on Tonic. What is it going to take?"

"More?" Alpha sighs, pinching the bridge of his nose. "More weapons, more armor, more training, more men? We just lost Swift, Fleet, and Delta. Beta and John were traitors but they were damn good at training. We can't take another hit like this, we were scrambling around like children out there. At this point we are just throwing bodies at the walls, we cannot defeat the elves if they have their vantage point on top of the castle walls."

It seems like the perfect opportunity. Seamlessly, I shove my anguish back and step into my birthright as a prince in court. With my people at the forefront of my mind, I make my case. "Perhaps it's time we seek outside help? We aren't the only ones who have this problem, the rebellion is wanting to speak with you. There is talk of magical rebellion on the outer cities of Dezna, and Loan says that the elves are trying to come in through the back."

Everyone stares at me.

"How long have you been sitting on this information?" Alpha's sharp voice makes me wish I had said nothing yet I know that there is no time to hide from these facts now. He would have to meet with them sooner or later, it was better to do it now while the wound was fresh and we were in an active need for more. He would have a hard enough time accepting them in the best circumstances, hopefully, our situation would allow for tolerance.

"A few days, we have been busy. Would you speak to them? The rebellion?" I never thought there would be a moment to present this to him, that there would ever be a need for the smaller forces but it seems, thanks to Tonic's mental state, a perfect situation has been offered that might just unite us.

"It would be worth a shot?" Adriam chimes in.

The agreement is tense, I know this is not what Alpha wants. His aversions to the magical community have not come far, he still hates them and blames them for what has happened to his people but there isn't much else for options. If numbers are what he needs, much as he doesn't want to hear it, I offer it in that I can also be of assistance to the cause.

With my ability to conjure up the fog, I've proven my use in combat and as a defense. He brings up that I can't heal myself and it's decided that we can have special armor made for me that is lightweight but can withstand arrow attacks.

I can see in his expression that he feels we are forcing his hand. His jaw is set, he's rigid and mulling things over. I'm too valuable not to use.

"We need all the help we can get," Adriam reassures him.

It's decided that we must speak with the rebellions and gain support, I also suggest that we pay a visit to Stefan for maybe he will have some insight into how to help Tonic. I realize neither of us has gotten much sleep but it's already morning and honestly, I can't sleep with the smell of blood and antiseptic so heavy in the throne room.

I rush to put on real clothes, as does Alpha. I watch as he pulls on his long sleeve and vest. Approaching him, I help him tighten his belt and he turns away from me. I know he's upset but this is how it must be, it can't be done alone. I feel revitalized with the possibilities of alliances between our people, even if they are somewhat forced.

In silence, we make our way to the city and I realize I haven't made this walk with him often, it feels strange to be out here without Tonic or the twins. The sun has just started to peek over the mountains, lighting up the morning frost on the grass.

I'm glad I put on a jacket today, I cuddle up to my captor and when he realizes I'm shivering, he offers me his arm and I relish in his warmth. "Do you ever get cold?" I try and make light conversation. I don't like the icy Alpha, I much prefer the witty Randy.

"Not usually. I'm bred for colder temperatures, my coat doesn't allow for much of a chill." He sounds guarded. "Do I feel cold?" He raises an eyebrow at me and I press my cheek to his bicep, enjoying the warmth radiating off of him.

"No. I suppose not."

We arrive at the armory and he brings me into the back room, it smells of metal and coal here but it's almost welcoming. The coal forges produce a good amount of heat though I still hesitate when I'm asked to remove my jacket, it wasn't often that I found comfort in any dwelling outside of the castle this time of year. My time as a prince had made me soft to the elements, I handled cold quite poorly considering it was my element. "Take off your jacket." He murmurs.

"Is that an order?" I clutch my jacket to my chest in an almost playful fashion.

"Yes." His tone is flat as he sets my jacket aside and takes out a piece of rope. He starts at my neck, gingerly taking the measurement and writing it down before moving on to my chest and my waist.

I watch him with interest considering there are no numbers on the rope and he's coming up with these numbers. "How do you know how long this is?" I ask as he wraps it around my bicep.

"I cut it." He doesn't look up at me as he measures the length of my forearm and the diameter.

"How do you know how to do all this?" Is it so wrong that I just want to know him?

He huffs at me. "We don't need the commentary." He measures my hips snuggly and I can't help but shiver under his touch. As his fingers trail up my inseam and rest just below the seat of my pants, I bite my lower lip. He firmly places the rope and I struggle to remain still.

"I hope you aren't so personal with all your men. I might get jealous. Or maybe I should just have you measure me more often."

"I want this to be exact." He runs his hands down my legs, distracted as he finds where they are in my baggy pants, and takes the measurement of my calf. When he writes down his last measurement, I'm struggling with myself.

I snag his rope and he raises a brow at me. Wrapping it around my hands a couple of times, I give it a few good pulls and I'm satisfied that it doesn't break. "This is some pretty nice rope," I comment, passively.

Regarding me with a warning glance, he shrugs and goes back to writing down further instructions. Watching him, cautiously, I fold up the rope and stuff it in my side pocket. He doesn't seem to be paying me any mind so I leave it at that.

We leave the armory, he seems satisfied with where we left the plans for my gear though I feel as though I got very little input on how the final product will fit and look. I find us heading towards the rebellion and I'm tense all over again about seeing Haryek, after all, we have been through the past few weeks thanks to him but I remind myself that this is what the pack needs and this is the end goal.

We are both shocked when we find Haryek, and a small band, on the path towards us. Both parties freeze. Haryek looks more surprised than we do as we make eye contact before approaching. How can two people who hate each other so much, work together? Maybe this is a mistake.

"Alpha. Nicolas. I was just coming to see you. I've just been told that you have some of my people in your possession? I was hoping I could speak with them." He's got his politician's face on.

I flinch, of course. Oh no. What are we going to tell him?

"Where did you hear that?" Alpha responds, coolly.

"Well. I more so had a scout witness it. We saw the fog, I sent a scout who saw the end of the battle and said you took in seven captives? I'm hoping to get an update on Ziduri." He tries to look as pleasant as he can but I can tell he's uncomfortable being so close to the man who really, truly, would love to see him dead.

"He's mistaken. We have two captives." He doesn't offer any more information and I sigh in relief.

"Oh. Right. Well, can I see them then?"

"Perhaps later. I've actually come to talk to you about what you have been harping on about since you slithered into my path. We need to talk about an alliance. I'm prepared to hear what you have to offer us."

CHAPTER

Thirty-Six-

The look of shock on Haryek's face is almost priceless, giving me almost too much pleasure considering we are supposed to be here professionally, and he takes a second to decide if he should be concerned or not.

I muse over in my head what he must be thinking. Obviously, this is a trap or we wouldn't be coming to him. Casually, he glances around, tipping his body back and forth to see if he can spot the ambush that is surely about to happen. "I never pegged you as a comedian." He comments, dryly.

"You would be correct in your assumption so I suggest you hurry this on, lest you wish for me to change my mind?" There was no claim that Alpha was known for his patience.

I don't much care for Haryek either but surely he can see why one would be suspicious. He had told Haryek, not a week ago, that he would like to have him killed. But I keep my mouth shut. There is a time and a place, I'm learning, and this is not one of them. I offer Haryek a reassuring smile.

With a sense of false bravado, the Elf elevates his chest in an attempt to square up to the lycan male. While they were nearly the same height, Alpha was easily twice the width of the elf. What continued to amaze me was that Alpha was not the largest lycan by any measure of the true mass the beasts could gain.

While he was tall, he ran lean compared to the majority of the muscle-bound masses. Him and Tonic, both, were a more athletic type build when standing next to the sizable Victor. Yet here, next to the Elf, he was a much more impressive specimen.

Clearing his throat, Haryek nods. "Well. Summon Loan. I'm sure he will want to be in on this, if you're going to side with us, I'd like it to be all of us." The elf hedges, looking unsure if he can make such demands in front of such a temperamental guest but Alpha waves him on.

"Be quick, then!" He snaps, crossing his arms over his chest impatiently.

Haryek gestures at one of his men who take off towards the city, I'm sure Loan is with Stefan. Then he turns to us and motions to follow him. I sense Alpha's reluctance but I touch his forearm, giving it a squeeze. This is the right thing, this is what has to happen if we are going to accomplish our goals and if we are going to be able to move forward with this war.

Haryek leads us to the square well outside the range of the rebellion's borders and into the depths of the city walls, much more formal than his humble cottage. It would appear the community was still entertaining giving him any sort of merit here in my realm, for they averted their eyes like scolded boys when they saw us together.

His bum leg gives me a little satisfaction, though it doesn't slow him down as much as I'd hoped.

We arrived in the city hall, much like the dining hall, only the table was round and could comfortably only sit about twelve people. In the center of it, rests a large map of our country. "Sit." He offers and Alpha lowers himself into a chair, leaning back into it and returning his arms over his chest.

Alpha fills the unsuspecting chair almost comically. I would chuckle if we weren't about to discuss the future of our nations. I find myself wishing that Tonic were here, my babysitter always had a way of taking the tension out of all of us. I find myself anxious to see Stefan, my mind wanders to possible cures to his mental state.

The Elf Prince sits across from us, propping his bad leg up on a neighboring chair, as his general sits beside him. "Tea?" He offers his best smile.

The look he receives from my captor silences him and he clears his throat as we wait in awkward silence for Loan. Silence is something a lycan does well, their intensity and heat speak volumes of their opinion. The Solomonari rushes into the room and freezes when he realizes we were waiting on him, he clears his throat and evens out his robes before sitting between us all.

A woman follows behind him, wearing the clothes of a man and a hat, you would guess her a young boy if not for her delicate features. She sits beside him with a smile, the only one in here who looks truly pleased to be here. I suppose everyone else has the same assumption, what good could come from this meeting?

"Did someone die?" She scoffs at the tension, her southern accent heavy.

"Yes. Ten of my men. Good men." Alpha's voice is low and she frowns at him. The casualties were slim compared to the opposing force but to a dictator who hated to lose any man, let alone to elves, it was quite the offense to his tactics.

Perking at the news, Haryek focuses on what he'd been hoping to talk about. "Yes. I had heard there was an attack. How many would you suppose there were?" Haryek attempts, trying not to sound too eager for information. He twirls a pencil between his fingers as a paper is placed in front of him, I'm assuming for notes.

With a heavy scowl, Alpha is not impressed with the elf's attempts to hide his eagerness. "One hundred. They were in the trees, your kind knows better than to attempt an attack on us from the ground." Alpha sits up and rests his folded hands on the table.

"We took care of it but in the process, we took on damage. I just want to make one thing very clear, before we relay privileged information that could put my pack at risk. If any of this is used in a way that could harm my people; I will personally come to your doorstep and ensure your suffering will be long and painful. When you're a slave, you're getting pretty damn good at experiencing the cruelties of Man so I'm sure I could come up with something special. Are we clear?"

Haryek smiles. "Alpha, surely, you can trust us. We have been trying to ally with you for weeks!" It was as if we hadn't spent days trying to help me survive the kind of help Haryek intended to offer. Like a true politician, Haryek's broad grin curls to the softest points in his face in an attempt to make him look more human and less porcelain.

It almost causes me to shudder, looking at him now fills me with disgust. But, this wasn't about me.

Taking on offense, Loan scoffs at the threat. "Maybe you shouldn't threaten the people you need to win this thing?"

The warlord narrows his eyes, there was no need for him to yell, for when he was angry he normally lowered his tone. The menacing set of his jaw sent a clear message. "Oh, it's not a threat. It's a bloody promise."

I shudder at his tone and glare across the table at my schoolmate who gives me a look that says 'you've slept with the enemy'; but, I can't find that I really care.

Finally, he sees it fit to introduce the real reason why we are here. "The pack has lost multiple members of the higher ranks, Lord Darrius was smart to separate those he felt were strong. I know many of these men personally but they are young and lack the experience necessary to form good, tight battle formations that are needed to take on an army of elves, who have bow and arrow on their side. They're mostly footmen, they aren't the free thinkers we need for generals."

Alpha explains that Taryek, the Elf-lord, has made the tactful decision to keep some of the best lycan generals in his own control and it would greatly benefit us to find a way to get to them and retrieve them. This would be difficult because, surely, Taryek knows we would want them alive and might have already killed them.

But, if we could regain even one of two of them; it might be what we need to press on towards the Kingdoms of Man.

Haryek ponders this, he seems to agree that there is a good chance their suspicions are correct. He goes on to explain that, luckily, he brought some of the best elven archers with him from Ziduri and we should all be grateful to his ability to think ahead in case such an event occurred.

He has only thirty elves at his disposal but they are some of the best and have the ability to train others to shoot a bow as well. Physical fitness is at least something they agree on and I zone in and out of their conversation on training, how they could combine some aspects of their skill and combat training.

Surely I get enough exercise.

"Your people would be willing to turn on their own for Lycans?" Alpha doesn't sound convinced.

Haryek's light eyes flick up and his long ears pull down. It is the first time I've seen actual pain cross that stone face. Haryek was a professional, I would give him that, to see him affected by the words softened me in the slightest way. Perhaps there was a soul inside him after all. "It won't be comfortable. But this is war and this is what must happen. Rather be on the side that has the teeth, than the side that receives the bite."

They both turn their attention to Loan who sits up from his reclined position, waiting for any additional requests. He dusts imaginary lint from his coat as he adjusts himself. Unpracticed, unprepared, both my cohorts practically roll their eyes at his ill-kept self and his attempts at a dignified response.

"We are prepared to offer more aid as well, we have magic users and some healers that could keep those alive until I or Nicolas could reach them. Unfortunately, a good deal of our people are refugee women and children. We have been warding off attacks from the elves trying to come in from the neighboring towns but we won't withstand a full-blown attack like the one that went after your group. We will lose much more than ten. What we truly need, in exchange for our magic users, is aid."

Alpha sighs only to slump back into his chair, it audibly groans, as if it'd like to crack but it was too frightened to fail. He mulls this over, tapping his fingers on the table. I can tell by his expression that he's disappointed, he had hoped for numbers or perhaps some hidden threat that could have made the alliance worth his while.

I begin to dread the outcome, too much had been revealed to a man whom I knew to be merciless. With all their cards on the table, they were at risk of total exposure to the wolf who sat just outside the sheep pen. Suddenly, the urge to protect these men curls into my stomach, to protect my people from what could be a very dangerous man should he decide to act on our current weaknesses.

"Don't discount what magic can do, remember who the cursed one here is." Loan adds, wryly.

His female counterpart is surprisingly silent, I figure she must be here for backup in case the feral Lycans turn on him.

I narrow my eyes at my Solomonari counterpart. "Not helping, Loan." I snap and look towards my captor. "Maybe we can send the younger wolves to aid Loan's people? They could get experience there?" I offer, expecting a harsh response but he glances at me sideways. I realize everyone is looking at me because I'm a part of this meeting as well.

Am I not here as a servant?

Though I suppose nobody knows about my position except for me. I swallow and stand up to take a look at the map.

"I have offered to lay down cover fog as our foot soldiers move in. It helped greatly considering most of the wolves are forest colors and blend right in with the fog." I gesture on the map towards the open fields that separate us from the neighboring towns. "I don't know how much use it would be here, it works best around water and as you can see there is little to be found if we meet in the open."

The cool eyes observe my trailing finger, he brings up his hand to quietly comb his stubble and consider my proposition. "On foot, the pack is too strong. I'm not concerned with the head to head, it's the elves on the walls of the capital that will stop us in our tracks. They, no doubt, will have oil to dump down on anyone who can get close enough. Taryek, surely, has amped up his defenses. He knows we are coming for him."

"No doubt." Haryek sighs.

Clearing his throat, Loan sketches out a quick diagram on a sheet of paper. "Our magic users can put up small shields on a force that could run in and break down the gates?" He suggests. We look at him, collectively. Alpha pulls his lips down into a frown, it was clear whom he trusted and Loan was not one of them.

"It would take a monster to knock down those gates." Haryek scoffs.

"I have a Russian." Alpha sits up to rest his elbows on the table in quiet observation. He asks Loan to show him where the rebellion lies and Loan, hesitantly, shows him with his finger. Only a dozen or so odd miles from our borders. Right on the edge of Dezna.

I can tell he's weighing his options, he doesn't want to split his pack but the offerings of the rebellion and magical aid are difficult to turn down considering we are at a surplus of muscle and lack of those to control it. "Do you trust him?"

In the dead quiet of the room, I realize that he's talking to me. Not looking at me, he waits in complete patience for my answer, as if I had to mull it over. My eyes dart to Loan then back to Haryek, in truth the answer was no. As my lips part, I quickly consider where my alliances would land me. He would surely blame me if this went wrong but admitting a suspicion could cause the whole plan to crumble.

Swallowing, I straighten in my seat. "I trust them to align with us as long as it benefits them. Our cause benefits them."

"How many do you need?" He asks.

Loan blinks and looks like he really hadn't planned to get this far. "Um. I don't know. How many do you have?"

Alpha rolls his eyes and I can tell his patience is growing thin. They settle on sixty. That leaves us with a remainder of two hundred, it will also help with the hunting on land that is about to reach winter when prey will be much more scarce. "We have three weeks to make this happen." He concludes and I can see both of our new allies pale.

They weren't expecting such a close date.

Collecting his papers as if he wished to run before the warlord could change his mind, Loan stammers through his demands. "I'll need time to get my men here and get your men there, we will need yours first before we can send ours, we can't afford to be vulnerable right now. Our leader will want to meet with you, he has plans to form a sort of council where we can all communicate openly. We have others that will need to be brought in once the elf kingdom is conquered. Dams have been built that block major rivers for many of the magical community—"

Alpha raises his hand to cut him off.

"Let's get one thing clear. The lycan force is not staying here. Once we conquer Ziduri, we are pushing forward towards the kingdoms of Man. Any, and all, complaints go directly to your new leader of Dezna, Nicolas. He will be left in charge once I'm gone."

Thirty-Seven-

He had intended to give my kingdom back to me? This hits me with an amount of surprise that floors me. I can't allow my face to crack, not here, not in front of these people who wish to end us if it saw them fit.

Me?

It was never supposed to be me. My father must be rolling in his grave at the thought that I would replace them as the King of Dezna, the standing king of one of the most powerful communities in all of Romania.

My throat goes dry, I blink away the shock and offer a polite smile and nod. While I sit here, overwhelmed by the proposal, all I can think is that my time is slowly running out. Not my life, not my moments to freedom, but my moments with this strange, irritating, infuriating, incredible man.

I feel myself sag.

Three weeks.

In three weeks he will be gone, out of my life. There was a time I would have rejoiced and say it couldn't come soon enough but now I'm at a crossroads. Nobody had ever believed me capable of much of anything.

In my training with my siblings, I had never stood out as exemplary in any one task. Fencing, art, music, any of the gifts my siblings were blessed with had fallen short of my skill set. I sang much like a wild animal in a trap, I played instruments on par with the hearing impaired street beggars.

When it came to the arts and politics, I tended to fall quite short in creative nature and influential pieces. I was apathetic, coasting through this life as if I had known all along that it wasn't meant for me. A part of me had even been understanding when they sent me away to a school I could never return from. Their mediocre son who couldn't even be married off would no longer be their problem.

Yet, here, I had begun to thrive.

I had sprouted into something more than I'd ever thought capable. I was beginning to grow and develop, I had friends even if they were few and far between. I was finally becoming someone who didn't look like a stranger when I looked in the mirror. In this moment, thinking of the end, all I could think of was how desperate I was to never give this up.

The euphoria of the damned living among the sinners. The captive clinging to the captor. I was intoxicated with the thought of living this life.

"Alpha." Haryek starts, using a patient voice. "You will all be killed if you take on the kingdoms of Man." He emphasizes the multiple kingdoms, as if Alpha might not understand this. Part of me wondered about his intent for the warning, I could only assume it was to prevent his protection from offing itself. There would be no returning from that battle, so few could not stand against so many.

"There is no glory to be won there. You could go on in peace here." He gestures with his hand to our nation, trying to show him the ample space he would have. "Live out your days in your home land, humans are not a bother to us, humans are not going to come after us." The collective laugh between him and Loan makes me pause.

I didn't believe that for a moment and I could see that Alpha didn't, either.

There is no great look of malicious intent. There is only certainty, he had picked his path and he would not deviate from it. "Not whilst the biggest portion of my people remain slaves in their kingdoms. Their wolves are locked away, there is no one to show them how to free it and control it.

"Until the curse is broken, every untrained Lycan is a ticking time bomb and it won't be long before they are calling for our heads more than ever. Man is weak but they are smart, they will come for us if we don't come for them. You're all fools if you believe they aren't waiting to see if we all kill each other before they make their move."

His hand drifts to the expansive kingdoms. Weathered and worn, the scarred knuckles draw my eyes almost more than the various rings on his fingers. "This is nothing compared to what will come once word gets out that Lord Darrius is dead. This land will be up for grabs and we are a prime target. Men are frightened of what they don't understand, we are a nation of oddities and at odds with each other. Look around and ask yourselves if you wouldn't take advantage if you saw fit."

Of course, Loan did not agree but he came from simple means. I knew, for myself, that my father would never have hesitated to take over more lands when it came to men. But, their numbers were so vast, fights with them never panned out without large losses of life. As magic users, we couldn't stand to fight in expansive wars for there weren't enough of us. We would wipe ourselves out long before denting the forces of humans.

Haryek lightly taps his lower lip with his index finger, raising a perfect brow. "And what say you for your brethren when this is all over? Hmm?" He tilts his head, translucent locks tipping and swaying as he observes us. "Would you dare say that you would then be the next big threat? What happens to all your lycans when this is over?"

"Haryek!" Loan spits, bewildered by the elf's boldness. This does not surprise Alpha as his arms flex and his jaw settles into a firm clench of resilience. He was fully aware of the fear he would leave behind in his wake.

"What?" Haryek mewls, pursing his pouty lips with the smallest of grins. "I'm only suggesting that we could be showing all of our cards to our next adversary." His eyes flick up and down the tall male in a linger of curiosity as his teeth drag over his lower lip. "We should ask these questions now before we all get in line to suck that infamous cock."

Disgusted, I want to get up to leave but Alpha holds his hand out to stop me. "My kind will be searching for a cure. Then we will be gone, a bad memory. If a cure is not found... well... perhaps you should be quite focused on finding it? There will be nothing to hold back my rage if I am to find out that I am stuck this way for the rest of my days. Immortality and what have you, I suppose I'll be paying each of you a visit." His dark voice doesn't faze me, I'm used to it now.

Haryek's right hand elf panics, gripping his sword. "What gives you the right to threaten us?"

Alpha smirks, a small flicker of amusement on his face. "Not one of you dare stand against me, so there's that. It's not a threat, it's a promise. Cure me, we won't have any issues."

I want to blurt out that there would be nothing left to cure when this was all over, that marching on man would spell the end of the lycan race. I want to reassure them that this was a non-issue, a final threat of a man with a death wish. He must know? He must know that there was no way to cure him.

They exchange worried glances for they do not know him, they had not seen beyond this exterior that was meant to protect his people. He wanted them worried of his return, for it would mean that they would do whatever they could to keep their borders safe which would ensure the safety of their people. Which, in turn, would keep man busy while his own disappeared. He would subconsciously arm us with fortresses meant to keep him out and it would save our lives.

Clearing his throat, Loan sits up in his seat. "Well, now that that's out of the way. Our leader will be here within the week, I'm sure he'd love to hear your speech. We need defense, we need an alliance. We can't afford to be caught off guard again, even if it's just training until your people move on. If you're going to go on another war path, we'd take any training you can give until you go."

Loan was like me, he had gone to school, seen the atrocities. A warlord could not deter him from his goal, he could step right into it just as I could for that was how we were trained.

Haryek nods in agreement, they might not like Alpha but he is single handedly running an army that took down one of the most powerful beings in the world. His young warriors went from common slaves to a machine that runs and functions in mere months. Time is not on our side, we don't have long to make the same leaps with our own people.

Alpha had done, multiple times, what many had deemed impossible. With Haryek's silence, I assume he was thinking the same thing that I was. If we didn't befriend him now, we might be facing him again in the future on much different terms. The words from before could be just that, a threat and nothing more. Haryek was testing the waters, biding his time, trying every angle and pushing every button.

I couldn't help but wonder if we were passing or failing, Haryek could not be trusted. He showed his hand too often to feel that any of his words could be the truth.

Yet, in that same strain, the ache curled in my chest once more, bringing me out of my focus.

Was I ready to let him go? Could I possibly relinquish the only thing that had pulled me from my own emotional solitude?

Tired of the discussion, Alpha waves him off dismissively. "I'll bring you your sixty tonight. Go to your people, bring back one lycan with you to confirm the conditions, bring your leaders and men. The quicker we do this, the more time we have to train these people. You're lucky that I am kind."

Sixty. Sixty was all it would take to defend an entire city. In the crystal eyes of the elf prince, I see fear. They were both getting a grand look at this dictator and seeing exactly what I saw. There would no longer be any question as to why I sided with him, if I had had a choice or not. My father had succeeded in creating the perfect killing machine, Haryek had been right in that none of us were willing to receive the punishment of that intent.

Any thought that I had in my mind that I was the one controlling him had begun to falter, there would be no room left for such falsehoods. I was not manipulating him to do anything he didn't want to do, so then what was it that drew him to aid us?

Nodding with a slow exhale, Haryek stands as it seems he's had enough of us as we had of him. "I'll have my own men ready in the morning to begin training, we will need to acclimate to each other. I will have to find a way to distinguish our elves from those of my father."

Alpha stands as well and I follow him. "We can discuss this more tomorrow. For now, I have business to attend to."

It's finally beginning, the alliance we were all hoping for.

Thirty-Eight-

We walk through the city in silence. I walk close to him instinctively, his warmth drawing my chilled body. Afternoon will quickly be upon us and we will be forced to part with the youth that everyone seems to always complain about, I didn't even know them and yet I already feared for them, almost missing them as odd as it seemed.

I think back to how many conversations they had to have had about the younger wolves of the pack. Even during our first days together, I recall the need for training and management. Youth makes for unpredictable lycans, I suppose.

It's hard for me to think of the person I was before, to experience the fear that used to torment me. I know it's still there, like a scar on my physique, I get glimpses of it when he shifts and when he wears his warlord expression as he is now.

I find myself staring at him with a puzzled expression and he glances at me and makes a face of disapproval. Nobody stares at the Alpha but I'm feeling confident and not in the mood for rules. Besides, I got what I wanted and that was the opportunity to draw information out of him.

"I thought you hated magic users?" I can't help but pry. While his introduction hadn't been the warmest, he had still agreed to help us despite Haryek's questions.

Alpha sighs, keeping his gaze fixated ahead. "Hate is a strong word." He grumbles, not amused by my apparent need to know his reasonings behind such uncharacteristic behavior. I know I should just be happy that he's cooperating but I find that it's never been good enough just to accept good deeds from this man.

He's so calculated. *What's the catch?*

"And you're okay with sending sixty of your pack members away to bunk with a bunch of dirty mages? For gods know how long?" I don't think I've ever seen him change his mind on something but as that thought crosses my mind, I take it back. Me. He had changed his mind on me, hadn't he?

Slowing his stride, he considers my reasoning as his jaw tilts in my direction though his gaze remains in the distance. He never stopped surveying, never let his guard down. "If it's what must be done." His response is too cool, too collected.

I furrow my brow. "Okay, now you're just playing hard to get." I accuse, knowing that I'm had in my quest for his intentions.

The hint of a smile curls onto the corner of his mouth. "A leader does what he has to to ensure the safety of his people. Even if it means being uncomfortable. I have seen these men grow up, I know their families, it won't be easy to send them away. But it's the best way to keep them safe and get them the training they need. If we get ambushed from behind by an elven army, we have little chance of surviving that kind of assault."

The city opens before us in a bustling commotion as people dodge around us and resume their lives as if we weren't even there. The low hum is barely a whisper with my engagement in the conversation, all I can see is him. I assume he figures I should start feeling the same way of my own people though I have to admit, I'm lackluster when it comes to my future as King of Dezna.

"You're showing your age." I complain with a sigh. I didn't sign up for a father figure, I didn't need a lecture on how I should behave and carry myself.

Alpha doesn't take my joke lightly. "I am almost twice your age."

I don't need to be reminded of my apparent daddy issues. In an act of defiance, I hop up on a small stone ledge, walking carefully along its edge. I find it symbolic to our current situation as we are constantly on the edge of losing everything. I watch my feet as I cautiously place one in front of the other, when I glance up it's my turn to be stoic as I see he's watching me.

We were stark opposites, he and I. He had a strong sense of order and discipline, I insisted on acting like a child when situations became too real. Reality was terrifying and the prospect of facing it alone did not sit too well with him. I wanted to be angry with him, accuse him of lying to me, I was supposed to be dead. Things weren't supposed to work out, not like this.

"You are going to have to step up and rule this place you know." Alpha speaks slowly, a more patient voice.

I roll my eyes and march forward as I shake my head. The heel of my boot scuffs the cobbles much to my satisfaction, the cuffs of my long sleeve billow dramatically under the sleeves of my jacket as I storm forward. This wasn't what I was asking for, this wasn't what I was looking for. He wasn't supposed to care about me, he wasn't supposed to interview me.

His hand catches my wrist and I jerk out of his grasp. "A kingdom wasn't exactly something I prepared myself for." There's no one else to rule but me. I'm the last of my line, the last of the royal family. When do I get what I want? Where is my prize for surviving? Most would assume a castle would be enough.

"That's why you're right for the job." He offers his hand and I glare at him but take it and hop off the ledge. Always pulling me off the edge, always the ground when I'm lost in the abyss. I must be spending too much time with Stefan because I've become too dramatic even for my own tastes. I turned away from him, not wanting to look at him now that he'd seen me. Now that he'd glimpsed the real me.

"Do you need me? I'd like to go see Stefan about Tonic and see if he knows of some treatment. That's the task right? To cure you? To cure all of you?"

Do I need to ask permission after today? What am I now? A servant? A slave? A king? An ally?

My tone is cold, cutting.

"Ask if Tonic can stay with him for a bit, would you?" His question surprises me but I nod, sneaking a glance over my shoulder at him. He's giving nothing away. Warlord. *He knows his role at least.* He would not play my game, he would not pursue me. He had his own mental health to protect. Even a dictator knew that I was toxic.

The world turns on as if flipping the switch to light the oil in a lamp. I'm so used to being alone with him. People flood around us, passing us by as if we were two normal beings. The sounds of the busy village crash into me as if I had just come out of water. When I'm around this man, the world closes off and it centers around us. I clear my throat and run a hand through my hair.

"See you later." It's a plea, I don't want him to go, I don't want him to turn away from me as I had him.

"Of course." He leaves me to my flustered emotions and I quickly retreat towards Stefan's house. I don't knock, I just enter and make myself some tea as I wait for him to sense my presence. The Strigoi appears mere minutes later, yawning and rubbing his eyes.

"To what do I owe the pleasure? Glad to see you're alive. Nobody has been to visit me since all the mess with your elf occurred." His feelings are hurt though I can't say that I blame him. My eyes sting as I meet his gaze and he rushes to me to wrap his arms around me. I don't know what I want, everything and nothing all at the same time. I've never felt this way before, I've never been so conflicted.

I take a deep breath and fill him in on all the gory details about the conversation I had with Adriam, spilling my guts about how I felt knowing I might lose Alpha. My leg twinges, reminding me that I had been shot. I do my best to reanimate our epic battle with the elves and how my fog saved the day, what it was like to be among a horde of lycans.

I find myself lost for words as I explain it, how it was to lose our own and see the elves fight a hopeless battle. He stops me when I gesture to my leg and he gets up to gather some herbs out of his cabinet with the help of his house spirit.

"You'll die of infection, idiot." He so easily pulls me to my feet and yanks the side of my pants down to look at my leg but I've taken the wind out of his sails because I have been taking care of it. He examines the stitching and runs a cool finger over it carefully.

"You're growing up." His expression softens. "I never pegged you for the war type." He mumbles and watches me with those deep red eyes. His long black hair is pulled back into a loose bun, strands falling to frame his frozen face.

How much do I reveal? To Stefan, I bear all. "This is different." I came back quickly.

He watches me so knowingly. "Because of him?"

I bristle. "No." I snap, because lashing out suits me right now. "Because of my people. Because I think it's the right thing to do. I want to help the resistance. We are marching on Ziduri in three weeks." I can't speak of it, not right now, not when I can't trust myself.

"Not a lot of time." Disapproval replaces curiosity as Stefan packs my injury.

"Well I didn't get to the real reason I'm here. Tonic had a mental breakdown." I run through the scenario and I watch the careful facade start to crumble as I explain the situation. His hand covers his mouth, as if an icy breath could escape his corpse lungs. I bring up my own hand to trace over the fading bruises on my neck.

My voice still isn't the same though I try not to let it devastate me. Maybe it will make people think I'm older? "He needs you right now, Stefan." I conclude. *He needs all of us.*

"Of course he does. He's a sweet innocent boy! He should never have been in that fight!" The concern on my friend's face brings a flutter of hope in my heart. He's fallen head over heels, himself, it seems. Stefan catches a glimpse of my misty eyed expression and swats at me.

"Don't you start! These damned dogs are really doing a number on us." Exhaling shakily, he nods. "Bring him here. I can work on him, he would be the safest here plus maybe he can help me hunt. With so much activity, I'm reluctant to go out much."

I nod, feeling good about this decision. "I'll see if I can coax him down here tonight. One more thing, do consider joining the rebellion, Stefan. You have plenty to offer the cause. You're the only unbiased one."

It's wishful thinking, Stefan was never one for politics. We make idle conversation until I feel as though I need to get back to see the inexperienced lycans off.

It's strange to think of them that way, considering most of them are older than me but nonetheless, they are the ones deemed unfit for organized battle. I make my exit and it's not hard to decide which direction to head in.

The large group moves through the city, five wolves wide. Each carries a pack of his personal belongings. My eyes wander over all the different coat colors though I find I don't recognize anyone, save for Alpha leading at the front of the battalion. I jog up to walk beside him and the wolf regards me quietly.

It's eerily quiet, like a funeral, as we march towards the rebellion. Loan is waiting for us, looking surprised that we showed up. I can't help but look smug though I admit I had my doubts. "Wow." I watch him mouth.

I glance at our large group, the height of the wolves never ceases to amaze me and I imagine Loan hasn't really gotten to look too closely at them since he arrived here. Haryek nods in agreement as he limps over.

"Can you imagine what it would be to control them?" He marvels. "Hypothetically of course!" He holds his hands up apologetically and I instinctively place my hand on Alpha's shoulder.

The wolf struggles to speak, rough in his tone. "These are your sixty. They're young but they're good soldiers and they are ready to defend your rebellion. You don't need to feed them, don't heal them, don't save them. Let the gods' will be done." His voice is firm and I can see Loan hedging.

"What? You want me to let them die?" He stammers.

"Yes. It is the way of our ancestors, to die in battle is to receive glory and to deny them that is high treason. Take it or leave it." I watch his lip curl, his ears erect and his body rigid.

"Fine." Loan practically spits. Alpha gestures with his muzzle, and a white wolf with black tips appears.

"Tejo will be leading them, you go to him with requests. Frost will be the one you send back. Keep them out of your liquor, probably smart to keep them out of everything in general. Put them to work." He says the last part to Frost, mostly. I remember this wolf, he babysat me once before.

I remember his black rooted hair.

"I expect frequent reports. You'll send him back as soon as you arrive to confirm the conditions and to bring back your people. Are we clear?" His commanding voice makes the small pack avert their eyes and some even lower themselves.

"Sure." Loan crosses his arms over his chest and sighs. "Let's get going. I want to be there before night falls." Frost trots over and lowers himself, Loan looks exasperated but hesitantly climbs on as well as his female companion. The group moves off soundlessly and I feel the tension as Alpha watches them leave. I can't help but feel uneasy.

His attention turns to Haryek. "Have your people ready by morning, we go on a run and I expect your men to be there."

Haryek scoffs. "Surely my people can't keep up with wolves."

"Didn't say you would be runnin' with wolves. We're going on foot." Slowly he approaches Haryek and I watch the elf grow rigid and cross his arms over his chest. "I hope you prove your worth, you've given me very little reason to keep you around. So maybe show some initiative tomorrow, yeah?"

"Just try to keep up." Haryek counters.

Alpha smirks and we depart, once out of sight, he surprises me when he lowers himself to allow me to climb on. I'm relieved because my leg is starting to ache. "Thanks for not killing him." I stroke the scruff of his neck.

"Yet." He grumbles as we walk through the town.

"Are you alright?" I ask him quietly.

"No. But I have to be for now." I notice we are heading towards Stefan's and pull him to a stop.

The heavy shoulders shrug casually. I marvel at the variety of coat colors beneath my fingertips with various shades of pale silvers and deep grays. "Where are we going?"

"We are doing what Lycans do in times of stress. Drink and eat. Your friend has graciously agreed to host. When we leave, Delta will bring Tonic and leave him with Stefan. He's been banished from the pack, he's free to do what he wants now." I flinch and straighten.

"What?! I was just there?!" My mind reels.

"It's really the best thing that could have happened to Tonic in this situation, Tonic cannot remain after what he's done and it's not safe for him to be among the men. Banished, it will be against our laws for anyone to harm him. It is for the best this way. And, as you said before, everyone likes Adriam, so arranging this gathering was quite simple." He gestures with his muzzle and I see Adriam waving at us in the distance.

Thirty-Nine-

I'm bewildered that a party is something any of these people would want to partake in right now. But I allow myself to be led to my friend's home and I hop off my wolf companion, guarding my leg.

He shifts and I can almost hear the bones grind as he becomes himself once more. His naked frame before me makes me sigh and I almost wish we were going home. My libido has skyrocketed since my 'almost' reveal of a more emotional side of myself. Despite my hesitation, he pushes me into the house and I'm surprised when I see that it's rather alive inside.

The torches are lit, the home is warm and welcoming. There's the smell of food, actual food, being cooked and I ponder what it is. I almost fear it's Victor who's making it but then I notice he's just willingly sampling whatever it is.

Adriam is putting together a meal from his home country, a bowl of onion soup with some chicken and vegetables for the main course. I'm amazed he managed to find a chicken in these parts, the vegetables catching my eye more than the bird carcass the rest would be partaking in. I steal a glance at Alpha, who I notice is gone. Probably off to find clothes.

Our small group had finally come together.

"I figured it was time to get away from the castle and have a night out," Adriam says lightly though he sounds mildly disappointed. "Your city is really behind the times, you know. No nightlife at all. How can anyone have a good time here? Thankfully, Stefan is cultured." Adriam offers my Strigoi friend a small smile.

I check the Strigoi over, hoping he's okay with this but he's beaming. His house has been empty for so long. Our small group's tremendous heat even brings a little life back to his ashy skin.

I allow myself to relax in just the slightest amount. "When I'm in charge, the first thing I'll do is remedy that." I tease as I sit at the kitchen island, I didn't know how to do this. How was I supposed to interact socially and yet remain casual? Everything until this point had been so structured, I find myself painfully aware of my own awkwardness.

"I don't think your town is ready for his kind of entertainment." Alpha chimes in, I turn and see he's clothed and I'm almost disappointed at the simple pants and shirt, yet the V of his neckline saves it for me. I never get to see him as a civilian, I'm not used to a 'tame' Alpha.

Seeing him brings me comfort, I could speak to him much more easily than the likes of Adriam. "Why? Does he tear the place down?" I chuckle, surely it can't be that bad.

Raising an eyebrow, his cheek dimples with amusement.

It's Victor who answers. "*She* can be a real party girl." Victor snorts, dipping a slice of bread into the pot of soup and wrinkling his nose as he's swatted with a wooden spoon.

"She?" I murmur, confused.

Adriam cocks a hip and points his spoon at me. "Not everything is as it appears, honey. I don't normally look like this." He shrugs and stirs the pot. "Can't really have a lady running around during an active war though can we? Heels in these conditions just wouldn't do." He takes a taste and I stare at him.

This isn't really a known subject for me, I'd never seen a man pretend to be a woman. Stefan appears between us, gazing at the pale wolf.

"You're a crossdresser?" He muses, intrigued as his eyes rake over the shorter, feminine man.

Put on the spot, Adriam considers his answer. "Something like that. It's just what makes me happy." He waves him away and Stefan reappears, seated next to me and Alpha.

I look at my wolf overlord and see that this is no surprise to him. How is it that a savage society is more accepting than those who are supposed to be the civilized ones? In my time among the population, I'd always been shuffled and hidden to prevent revealing my dreaded secret. Here, it was widely accepted by most.

Alpha stands to get us both a bowl and spoon, settling back in his seat beside me as he sets the bowl down.

Victor gets his own and dunks his bread into it, taking a rather dramatic bite of the loaf and groaning in appreciation. Adriam rolls his eyes as he chews a piece of bread. "Dig in, it's not often I get to cook anymore."

I'm almost offended when I see Alpha eating with actual enthusiasm. "Okay, what gives?" I've been trying to feed the bastard for months. "Now you eat? This? I'm appalled. It's good, don't get me wrong, but I've tried everything to get you to eat."

The rumbling laughter warms my cheeks, "I raised him." Adriam chuckles. "Sort of, anyway. He knows better than to turn my food down, let's say that." Alpha shrugs apologetically. "Besides, if you feed him too well he might get fat. He's gotten lazy since you've been around."

With a snicker, Victor walks over to clap Alpha on the back with his massive hand. "Too busy chasing the tail," Victor adds between bites, waggling his hips in a lude fashion.

"I'm plenty busy," Alpha responds shortly. The back and forth warms my heart. It's almost like a family. I try and envision Delta, Tonic's blush, and the ever-vigilant brothers trying not to gag. I attempt to be excited that we are here, together. It's not over yet but for now, we are not all lost.

I savor the taste of the food and the warmth. I can't help but enjoy the back and forth between the three, it isn't often I get to see Alpha relaxed or even hear much from Victor. I periodically glance at Stefan and I'm pleased to see he's enthralled with these creatures.

Their existence among humans must give him hope. Adriam dives into a tale about Alpha when he was a child and it warms my heart to hear him call him Randy. About how he would play horrible pranks on his sister, Temptrest.

"Where is Temptrest?" I ask casually.

The mood shifts and Alpha frowns, glancing down at the empty bowl in front of him. "Who knows. I haven't seen very many women of our kind." Alpha responds, almost too quickly. I instantly regret my prying, for all I knew she could be dead.

Taking a deep breath, Adriam clears his throat. "Tempy is tough, she's alright," Adriam reassures him.

Clapping his hands, Stefan distracts us all, I jump at the suddenness. "On that lovely note, what's this I hear that wolves can sing? I've heard Tonic sing a little and he says all wolves can sing?" He swirls his glass, of what I now smell is wine, his eyes scanning the three lycans.

Adriam grins, flashing all of his perfect white teeth in a beaming smile. "Some are more gifted than others. That one," He tilts his chin towards Alpha, "Actually sings fairly well."

Dismissive, Alpha is in little mood to participate. "Not much anymore," Alpha grumbles and gets up to grab the bottle of wine, pouring himself a glass.

Unashamed, Stefan pleads openly. The dim lighting in the home reflects off his pale skin, causing his eyes to glitter dreamily as he focuses on the gray-haired male. I can say that I can't blame him, there were times when the man could be quite charming. There was allure in the brooding lycan.

"Oh come on! I'm a music connoisseur! I play almost every instrument known to man, the least you can do is sing for me if you're going to drink all my wine!" Stefan complains, his voice light and hopeful.

Filling the man's glass, Adriam bumps him with his hip. "Come on Randy." Adriam encourages, leaning on the counter beside him, and grabbing the bottle out of his hand. He takes a long swig and rests his head on the larger man's shoulder. "We are going to drink all his wine." He reaffirms.

Sighing, Alpha settles on his face, downing a large swallow of his glass.

"Of all the money,
that e'er I had,
I spent it in good company,
And all the harm I have ever done,
'Alas it was to none but me."

He starts slow, in a low tone. Adriam straightens and smiles. He joins casually in the words, obviously a familiar song to him. Victor looks amused and carries the baritone.

"And all I've done for want of wit,

To memory now I can't recall,

So fill to me the parting glass,

Goodnight and joy be with you all."

Stefan disappears only to reappear with a violin. "I love Irish songs." He gives them a melody as Adrian and Victor join in with a melodic humming. Alpha carries the song, I never pegged him as a singer, and of course, he would choose such a song.

"So fill to me the parting glass,

And drink a health whate'er befalls,

Then gently rise and softly call,

Goodnight and joy be to you all."

"Of all the comrades that e'er I had,

They're sorry for my going away,

And all the sweethearts that e'er I had,

They'd wish me one more day to stay."

I begin to realize the song is about death but their tune is so joyful. Stefan follows their lovely melody perfectly and I find it hard to think of it as a sad song. It dawns on me that this is the divide between us and them, and now, it seems, Stefan is one of *them*.

I did find it odd that he accepted them so quickly but it must be because they do come from similar terms. Forced into a life that they didn't ask for. The Lycans don't view death as the end, it's the beginning of their eternity. It was only me who was stuck with the inconvenience of mortality and all its shortcomings.

"But since it fell into my lot,

That I should rise and you should not,

I'll gently rise and softly call,

Goodnight and joy be to you all."

"Fill to me the parting glass,

And drink a health whate'er befalls,

Then gently rise and softly call,

Goodnight and joy be to you all."

Alpha pulls me out of my stupor, he takes my hands and brings me to him, surprising me as he whirls me around the room in a small dance. He looks so joyous and I can't help but laugh.

I was never a good dancer but I don't feel shy here, I allow him to guide me and marvel at his happiness. Adriam joins him in the melody, leaving Victor to harmonize as Stefan begins to lower the tone. The song begins to come to an end.

"Fill to me the parting glass,

And drink a health whate'er befalls,

Then gently rise and softly call,

Goodnight and joy be to you all."

They all join together for the end verse and I briefly realize I'm probably the only person here who can't carry a note. Stefan sets his violin down and claps. "Well worth the wine, boys! Well worth it!" He calls, excitedly.

I blink, breathless, and brush my hair out of my face as I focus on the stunning, smiling man before me. I throw my arms around his neck and kiss him, catching him off guard. The catcalls make me flush and I break the kiss as I capture his eyes with my own. Panting, our mouths rest mere inches apart and I so desperately want to kiss him again just he seems intoxicated by my very presence.

Swallowing, I catch my breath as I step away from him with a nervous laugh. "I didn't know wolves could sing, I never heard anyone sing." I manage, picking at the vegetables left on my plate.

"We sing at all the ceremonies," Adriam responds. I suppose they do, it was just different than the electric joy filling the room. Stefan rallies us to continue and I find that most of the night is overflowing with songs and stories, coupled with genuine happiness.

We run through folk songs though I don't offer up my horrid voice, I am good for clapping along to the beat. I'm just as happy being a guest at this concert as I would be as being a part of it.

Though it's bittersweet, for eventually those who have passed work their way into our minds and I find the night ends the way it began. With the 'Parting Glass' only in a much more somber tone in remembrance of our lost ones. I miss Tonic and I think I'm ready to go home, the others seem to read my mind.

Stefan yawns, he hasn't had this much company in a century.

"I'll have the guard bring Tonic by," Alpha reassures him and Stefan nods.

"I'll be here." He says cheerfully. "It was truly a lovely evening."

Adriam and Stefan exchange cheek kisses. I laugh as Victor and Alpha quickly depart to avoid the formality. I kiss Stefan's cheek and hug him. "Thanks." I breathe against his shoulder.

The walk home is quiet, everyone is tired and a little buzzed. It's a fun walk home as Victor has to practically carry Adriam. The small French man is rolling in his arms, belting out old-time Broadway-style themes and getting the occasional shush which only seems to egg him on. "I've picked the wrong job. I should have been a star!" He purrs and clings to Victor's neck.

"Biggest one we know." Victor chuckles. We part with the Russian as he totes our ringleader off to bed and I'm pleased to find Alpha follows me to my bedroom.

I turn to him and tug him out of his clothes, he catches my lips and I press against him as I kiss him. I'm surprised to find that I'm perfectly content. My libido poises like a jungle cat, ready to strike, but I call it off with a well-timed yawn. Today has been long and I'm exhausted. I'm pleased to find, he follows my train of thought as I guide him to the bed and he curls around me under the down blankets.

"Good night and joy be to you all." I attempt with a chuckle.

I feel his grin and it spreads to my own face. This miraculous man was slowly fixing me, perhaps I was fixing him, too. "Don't quit your day job." He responds sleepily.

CHAPTER

Forty-

It's slow going the next few days. I feel as though the days creep by but the week is catching up on us faster and faster. Nobody has time to fill me in on much, I catch up on what I can but I hardly see anyone I know.

It's odd really, I look for familiar faces in the crowds and remember the people I'm looking for are dead. I find myself missing my twin bodyguards, their quiet demeanor which I used to find fairly creepy is now something I feel lost without. My new guard, Frost, isn't much company.

Unfortunately, he's very good at his job and he's appreciating the promotion from babysitting young wolves and his younger brother, Havoc. What is interesting about the two is they are almost exact opposites.

Frost has his startling white hair that is black at the roots, his icy eyes are nearly clear as if all color has been leached out of them. His pale skin reflects that thought and I find that maybe his personality has gone with it. He's bored by me and finds my attempts to be a part of society frustrating instead of amusing.

Havoc, on the other hand, is someone I'm fond of and is a good replacement for Tonic who is currently out of commission. Havoc is fun and cavalier.

My head reels as I try and come to grips with Tonic's removal from the vicinity. The way Alpha decided to help him is to cut him off. Banished from pack life, he was sent to live with Stefan. I didn't pretend to understand it nor do I really care to. It doesn't seem right to mess with someone's head then ban them when they become an inconvenience though I do suppose at this point, he was a liability.

I did visit him once and he seems better though he doesn't talk much or let on to what was going through his head. I suppose I'm just not that good of a friend, but I trust that Stefan is taking good care of him and I know that strange wolves make my Strigoi friend very uncomfortable. Especially when they look as 'by the book' as Frost does.

But with attention to detail comes commitment, I have finally found someone willing to train me in some form of combat so every morning, earlier than I would like, I cram down breakfast and get my ass handed to me for about two hours. Frost is kind though, he has no intention of hurting me even though at times he forgets I'm about half his size.

He's teaching me a basic hand to hand, something that Havoc reminds me is taught to children but considering I've had very little combat training I'll take whatever I can get. I would much rather get this beating from Frost than from Alpha or one of his minions.

Though I would welcome even seeing Alpha, since that night with Stefan, he's vanished and is so wrapped up in preparations it's a wonder how anything gets done.

Frost plays on my wandering eyes, I find myself scanning our surroundings which have become so different in these mere days. Elves are among us, magic users and humans. At the castle, in the city, in the courtyard. The refugee magic users from the outer rebellion look half-starved and battered.

They gorge themselves on our bountiful food and I think it embarrasses our wolf overseers. Tensions are high but this is a must if we
are to march on the elf kingdom in only a week's time. I cry out in
surprise as Frost knocks me and brings his elbow up to just mere
inches from my face. "Focus." He commands.

"Sorry." I breathe. I'm not much of a fighter, my time in the school
had deadened me to hand to hand, I responded much better to a
dragon trying to eat me than a lycan attempting to cut my throat.

Frost is a good teacher, ever patient. "Again." He tries to be en-
couraging. It makes his job easier if I can keep myself alive if I were
to get stuck somewhere.

I try to defend myself, when I can pay attention I find that I'm
really not half bad. But I don't think elves will go easy on me. Frost
lands me on my butt and I cringe, exhaling in frustration. He senses
my annoyance and helps me up.

"We'll do more later. You are distracted."

I want to argue with him but I know I'm looking for someone
in particular and I won't be satisfied until I find him. "Can I go into
town with Havoc?"

He knows that means I want to investigate. Knowing that he's
against everything that stands for, he shrugs and gestures to his
haphazard brother who trots over excitedly. My prisoner status had
been lifted, I was free to do whatever I pleased as long as I stayed out
of the way, there was no denying me.

"Done with the zero?" He quips.

We collectively roll our eyes at him but I follow him to town and
try to catch my breath from my training with Frost. Thankfully, Havoc
is not much of a talker and I'm left to my own devices as I scan every
face that passes me.

It's odd to rule a kingdom and know very little about those who live in it. I wonder about their tasks and jobs as we walk, examining their clothes and various states of disrepair. My town was mostly farmers nowadays, some specialists but they were simpler people. Just as I'm ready to give up, I spy the jogging group of half-naked men and my eyes fall on my prize.

Alpha leading them in a death march.

My heart quickens though I silence it for I remember that I'm upset with him for disappearing on me. I wonder if he will even stop and, for a moment, I will tell them not to but I realize Havoc is waving them down and I pinch the bridge of my nose.

They come to a slow halt and their panting makes me feel less terrible for stopping though Alpha and the few lycans towards the front don't look nearly as winded as the elves and magic users gasping for air behind them.

"Breaking in the new meat, eh?" Havoc grins like a schoolboy, amused by the suffering of others.

"Something like that. Don't you have a job to do?" Alpha responds shortly, frustrated at the interruption.

Havoc elbows me with a goofy grin. "We had a question for ya." Havoc's street kid accent seems to hit our leader's ears like nails on a chalkboard. I realize everyone is looking at me and I flush while I clear my throat. I hadn't intended on asking any of my questions, I forget Havoc is not Tonic and he has no means of nosing around until we find out intended answers.

"I'm wanting to know what's going on, as far as the planning. I know Loan is supposed to bring their leaders back shortly?" I take a wild guess, they haven't come yet, and surely we were running out of time. He looks like he doesn't have time for my questions but I cross my arms over my chest. "I'm part of this too," I tell him firmly.

Rolling his eyes as dramatically as he can, Alpha glares at the lycan beside me. "Havoc, take over this run for me." Alpha steps out of line and I hear a sigh of relief that makes me laugh a little. I'm delivered a deadly look and I bite my lip but I'm amused nonetheless.

Havoc yanks off his shirt and runs a hand through his locks. "Come on ya sorry bunch!" He practically skips as he leads the deflated group away.

Alpha shakes his head and looks towards me. I drink him in, his body glistens and steams in the light peeking through the trees as I take in his naked form. He's only wearing a pair of sheer shorts that leave little to the imagination, my mouth practically waters. "Well?"

Blinking, I stammer my way back into the world of the living. "Well, what? I'm happy to see you, it's been almost a week since we've done anything but a glance at each other. I hope that means progress." I find myself feeling awkward around him, shy almost.

"Loan is bringing a man named Bogdan around some time to-morrow. He is supposedly the true leader of the outer rebellion."

I blink a few times. "Bogdan? The Bogdan?" I'm appalled they could get him to choose sides. I'm appalled that Alpha would meet with him. Unless he doesn't know?

"I suppose. Strange enough of a name." He grumbles in response.

"Stranger than Verando?" I tease. He glares and I roll my eyes. Why did I miss this man? "I'm just surprised. He is not a man, by the way, he's a dragon who takes the form of a half-man. I'm not surprised Loan left that out, it's not something many people know. He is a great power, his kind is some of the dragons who teach at the schools for the Solomonari. They are very powerful, no wonder their city is still intact, no elf would stand against such a magic user." I give him a moment to take this in and he seems to be mulling this over.

"Great." He responds with little emotion and I'm unimpressed.

"It is. He's a great ally if he agrees to our terms. If he stands with our alliance, a lot of users will follow him. If he doesn't, we will never get the support we need." The pressure makes me flinch a little, this is pretty serious. Was he not going to tell me? While I respect the wolves and what they are doing, they aren't exactly known for their polite company.

"I'll add it to the list." Alpha starts walking back towards the castle and I hesitate but I follow him.

"What's wrong with you?" I ask, bluntly. Single-handedly, he had ripped me out of the daydream that I somehow had longed for his company. Why had I missed him at all?

Alpha crosses his arms roughly over his chest at the command, "I didn't ask to rule your people and my own. It's a lot without you making requests." The dark rings around his eyes bring me to pause, he was exhausted and cranky, probably hungry. Yet, that was no excuse to take it out on me.

The answer seemed simple. "Then stop, let me rule my people," I tell him, simply.

But the scoff I get in return says not many believe I'm capable of that. I suppose I haven't much proven myself as a leader with my dramatics and ability to get in trouble, the last time we'd spoken of it I had told him as much. "Then teach me." I sound much more firm this time, determined to cut through any preconceived notion.

Shaking his head, he begins to walk away. "I don't think it's something that can be taught." His response is tired and I shrug.

I follow after him, scrambling to walk up beside him. "I'm the best you've got. Unless you've got another of my siblings in there that I'm not aware of."

We finish the walk in utter silence and when we get inside, we are informed that Haryck has called a meeting towards the outer boundaries of the city. It doesn't surprise either of us that he would want to be far away and truthfully, it's a very Haryek thing to do. Difficult and mysterious.

With some prodding, I convince Alpha to at least let me clean him up considering we are both sweaty and sticky and it will be far too cold by the time we return to run around in our current outfits.

Washing him brings a familiar calm to me, I trace over his muscles with my cloth, washing away the smell of man and the woods that the heat of his body emits. I'm reminded of that first time, the way it felt to wash him and I hate this quiet that has grown between us. I'm about to burst, my voice climbs up my throat like a caged animal as I wish to call him out on his dismissal.

My lips part, then he speaks. "This is nice." He says, exhaling. I glance up at him like he's lost his mind, raising a brow. "The quiet." His voice is low only to look amused at my obvious discomfort.

I sponge his chest with a huff. "I forget how old you are sometimes," I tell him as I spin him to scrub his back. I earn a chuckle and shake my head though some of the tension is gone. Sitting in silence is not something I'm accustomed to but if he likes it then so be it. It defines us; he's secure in the silence while I feel it taunts me, only providing mystery and unknown.

I wrap my arms around him from behind, soaking my thin shirt. "All clean." I can't help but feel as though our time together was too fleeting to allow something so ridiculous to prevent me from enjoying it.

385

"I'm looking forward to showers in Ziduri. If you want me to visit, you'll have to get proper plumbing in this place." His comments make me pause and I press my cheek into his warm back, smiling against his skin.

He meets me halfway, a gentle encouragement that this was difficult for him, too. "Who says I want you to visit?" I tease.

Alpha turns in my arms and his lips find mine, I deepen the kiss and curl my arms around his neck. Alpha lifts me to his height and I wrap my legs around his waist, clinging to him. When I come up for air, he looks amused. "You're stronger."

I try not to be offended, I am much stronger. Stronger than I've ever been in many ways. "Frost is a good teacher." I bite my lower lip, setting the trap. "Not bad looking either." I practically giggle and get a growl in return. His teeth are on my neck and I arch my back and find his hair with my fingers. "Got to love a man with presence."

I gasp as my back hits the cool wall and pull myself impossibly closer to his warmth. Sliding off of him, as my feet touch the ground I push into him to flip our positions. He pulls air through his teeth as he feels the cool stone, I grin as I stretch on my toes to kiss him firmly.

"Awfully bold." His voice is rough with restraint, his eyes bearing down on me.

Bold is an understatement. I take a step back from him. "How come you don't train with me?" I ask as I take a few steps away, allowing my hips to lazily sway.

It was as if he believed that was obvious, grumbling to himself at my ignorance. "I don't want to hurt you." He tells me sternly, taking one stride to close the gap but I curl away from him and near the tub. I had not been expecting him to reveal a weakness like that.

He wanted to protect me, he didn't want any harm to come to me, especially by his own hand.

"I bet I could take you on." I twiddle my fingers at him and he rolls his eyes so dramatically it's a wonder he can stand upright. I can't stand for the room to fill with unnecessary confessions when I'm so close to getting what I want.

Amused, he scoffs. "Not without magic." He takes no prisoners. The bath turns to a thin sheet of ice as I quickly push off and land on the other side of the tub.

"And what're you without your wolf?" I comment. He flexes and it's my turn to roll my eyes. "Hmm," I mumble and he almost catches me but I quickly skirt away to find myself in the bedroom. He appears in the doorway and I swallow. Nowhere to hide now. "Fight me. If you win, I'll follow your rules in combat. If I win, I'm on the front lines with you." I wager.

Alpha thinks of this, he already has his own terms he seems to think I will follow but I know he's smart. He knows, as well as anyone, I'm not famous for following orders. "Deal." He growls.

I wonder if I've made a mistake.

Alpha circles me slowly, a hunter stalking his prey. I quiver with anticipation but I refuse to let my nerves get to me. Frost has trained me well not to allow tactics like this to get under my skin. I exhale and he makes a few moves that I easily dodge though he comes closer than I would like to allow.

He's fast and he goes every which direction. I would think his shoulder would slow him down but blocking his advances is like being hit with a hammer. I'm proud of myself, I'm keeping up and doing well. He looks impressed as he takes a step away from me to reassess. "Not bad." He allows.

I bow sarcastically. "Well, I am half your age." I tease, baiting him.

This brings on an onslaught I was not prepared for. It's all I can do to dodge and block, I'm on the offensive and there's no wearing him down. I see my chance and I take it, I aim for his sternum with my elbow and direct all my energy there.

That's when I fly through the air as he sweeps my legs out from underneath me and everything spins as I realize I'm off the ground. He grabs my hand and I'm mere inches away from kissing the stone floor. With a strong yank, he pulls me to my feet and his elbow pauses before my cheek.

"I win." He breathes. The restraint was clear in his voice. I'm panting, exhilarated at his strength and speed. I should be afraid but I'm trembling with so much more than fear.

I throw myself at him and practically knock him to the ground, kissing him. I take him by surprise as I yank my shirt off and scramble out of my pants. I want him, here and now. I pull him by whatever I can grab and shove him onto the bed, taking his length in my mouth I suck hard and he groans in response.

He writhes as I attack him relentlessly. There are things that I beat him in and he should be more appreciative that this is one of them. I torture him, teasing him, watching him come apart as I wait until I feel like he can't stand it and I climb up his body to kiss him deeply.

His tongue invades my mouth and I lower myself onto him, moaning against his lips. He thrusts into me and I clutch at his chest, cursing under my breath. He flips us, shoving my legs up towards my chest. I grip the sheets as he takes me, incoherent as I call his name. I don't know whether to fight back or surrender and I'm not left guessing long. We chase our release together and I'm left panting as I finish.

Alpha flops down beside me as we catch our breath, this is a good quiet. I can deal with the silence that follows this. A small smile curls onto my lips. "I win."

CHAPTER

Forty-One-

We scramble to get dressed, our antics making us later than my captor ever cares to be. I can't help but grin every time I'm directed an annoyed look. "Worth it." I mouth to him as we make our way out of the castle and down the path towards the city, as we reach the tree line and I'm sure there's not a chance we might turn around, I decide to ask my question. "So, why are we meeting Haryek by ourselves?"

To this, Alpha does not seem amused. "Gathering a small force to take with us would take even more time and we are already late as it is. I won't give that elf another damned thing to look so smug about."

At times, it's hard to remember that beyond his inhuman mentality, he was still a man. "Really? We're going out on our own because we're running late?"

Glowering at me, his expression speaks for itself and I swallow back my sarcasm. "It's Haryek, I'm sure he's found something or wants to make some sort of threat. I very much doubt that he has anything that could surprise me. It'd be a waste to gather any sort of party for something so simple and then what? If he attempts to ambush us, the pack would never forgive him. Then we would truly have to execute him and you seem unwilling to do that."

I take in his tight long sleeve and sigh as I force myself to focus on the task at hand. Haryek will certainly be displeased with our tardiness. As we leave the city limits, he starts to slow. "I haven't seen Sota in a while, have you?" He mentions and I give him a look that suggests Sota is the last person I want to see.

"If I had, you would be the first I'd come to find. The man practically wants me dead." I can't help but be bitter at the fact that Sota would do anything to keep us apart. "So you're saying it's my fault that Haryek is alive?"

With a devious grin, he shrugs one shoulder. "If the shoe fits. I'd much rather see him dead. It continues to amaze me the things I do to appease you."

Crossing my arms over my chest, I laugh at him in a dry tone of disapproval. I decided to ask a different question that might satisfy me a bit more. "Was banishing Tonic really what was best for him?" We have a long walk ahead of us, and might as well fish.

Alpha tracks the tree line as he speaks, cautious in his steps and yet confident in his path. "Yes. He's free of the bounds of an omega. He can do whatever he wants now. Besides, anyone who kills him is breaking the law now and nobody wants that with this power struggle going on." I realize that I'm not up to date at all with what is going on.

We exchange back and forth as I try to fill in the gaps of my knowledge about pack politics. Frost really has been promoted to Delta position. Havoc is trying to gain the general position but there is stiff competition. When Ziduri is taken, they will have a real ranking ceremony and redetermine ranks but for now, this is the way it has to be.

Older wolves aren't happy with the lack of dedication to tradition and I find that I think it's a good thing the traditions are dying off. Society would have such an easier time accepting them if they weren't a war based culture. The fact that they take after Vikings and believe in war-torn heaven is a little off-putting.

"Are we ready to move on to Ziduri?" In the short answer, no. In the long answer, who knows? Alpha explains to me that the magic users are trying but the elves are struggling to teach the lycans how to shoot Elven bows.

The bows are too small and not a heavy enough weight for lycan strength but Alpha is currently working with a rebel from the outer magic camps who has seen a longbow that could be used from the breast. With Bogdan due tomorrow, the lycans are struggling to find many positives and morale is low.

With a heavy sigh, I see his shoulders begin to relax as he speaks to me. "Nobody wants to die. Even if you believe as we do that glory is to be won in battle. War is ugly, I think it's settling in that we are moving out and there's nothing anyone can do about it. It's hard to look at your brothers and wonder which ones you will never see again, which ones you'll carry home and if you will come back yourself."

A small chink in the armor. They don't want to die, we can all find common ground in that.

"We can do this. We have a lot of different angles to hit the elves from. They won't know what's coming." It's the truth. They won't be expecting elves and magic users to side with the lycans. In reality, I don't think anyone was. Together, we stood a real chance. Together, this wouldn't be so impossible. Ultimately, it was the fact that I wouldn't, yet, have to say goodbye that brought me the most peace.

We take the time to discuss battle tactics. He pulls a knife out of its sheath and slowly runs it across a sharpening stone while he walks. This is where he's the most at ease, casually walking and talking about how he plans to slaughter a whole nation. *My* warlord. It's not just the battle, it's the woods and the freedom. He's outside, in his element.

I watch as he scans while he talks, Frost tells me all the time that I'm not vigilant enough, and watching 'The Alpha' in his natural environment I can agree with him. Nothing passes him, he watches the flutter of the leaves, he tracks soundlessly over the ground as if he knows where the bare spots are. I feel like a child clamoring next to him and making a conscious effort to walk more quietly.

It is unrealistic to expect to keep him locked away in a castle when this is all over, you can't domesticate something that's wild. I wrap my arm around his and lean my cheek on his shoulder as we walk, the chill air nips at me through my robes and I find myself wishing I had worn warmer clothes. I listen to him talk, the most he's ever really talked about, about books he's read and how the armadillo shell he intends to build with shields could protect them from any skyward attacks.

There is also the option of tunneling under the walls but we lack the manpower and the time to perfect that. Besides the fact, a tunnel failure would be catastrophic.

Listening to him talk about this makes it feel too real and I shudder, squeezing him closer. "I could give a fog cover? You can't hit what you can't see. Let them waste their arrows." I expect retaliation but for the first time, he nods.

"If we could keep you out of sight, that might actually work to our advantage. Especially if we can get them to come out of the walls, which I doubt. If we could get the fog high enough, we could potentially even scale the walls." The constant talk I hear about having hot oil at the castle's disposal makes me reluctant to entertain the idea of climbing any walls.

I tune in and out of his excited babble about the possibilities and the different ways that could lead them to victory or failure. It seems like there's a very small window of opportunity to make this work. We pass a small stream and in the distance, I can hear the roar of what could be rapids but it's too distant to tell. I'll have to remember to make a trip there on our way back, it's always good to map out potential water sources on these treks.

Suddenly, he slows. I feel his tension and see him inhale. "What?" I try to avoid asking him too much like a dog. His lips part as he savors the scent, settling on an identity for whatever had paused him.

My notice seemed to have almost embarrassed him as if it were involuntary. It causes me to smirk just the slightest, it wasn't often I got to see him caught off guard. When he was with me, it was the closest he ever seemed to near relaxation. "Nothing. I just smell elves. Still getting used to it I guess." He mumbles, wrinkling his nose a little.

"I'm sure it's just Haryek," I mumble, trying to be reassuring. "We are meeting him you know." I don't want to talk about Haryek, I want to go back to where we had been in our conversation. I press my lips to his bicep as he stiffens at the affectionate gesture. "Is this not okay?"

Clearing his throat, he purses his lips to get a hold of himself. "I... no, it's fine. Sorry, I am just a bit overwhelmed, the elf scent is really strong. It just smells different, but honestly, the man wears so much cologne it's a wonder we can tell him apart from the garden."

I chuckle at this because it's true. I'm reminded of my time with the elf, how everything smelt so fragrant. "Well, maybe I can distract you?" I offer, trailing my fingers along the inside of his arm.

With a heavy exhale, he slips his arm out of mine for some distance. "Oh, believe me, you distract me plenty."

"I prefer the woods," I tell him with a click of my tongue.

An arrow whizzes by us and he instinctively pushes me to the closest tree.

"Hey! You called us here, asshole! Watch what you're shooting!" Alpha snaps angrily. He looks at me, "It didn't get you did it?" He checks me over and I shake my head, panic rising to my eyes as I remember the last time we were under arrow fire. "Hey..." he murmurs, capturing my face with his hand. "It's fine. Keep it together."

"No, I'm not—" I'm cut off as an arrow pierces his chest. The sickening thunk stops my heart and I'm sure he will drop dead but it seems to have pierced his lung because he remains standing.

I clutch his shirt and prepare for the next arrows but all I hear is a congratulation on a good shot. Out of the woodwork comes a small party of shiny elves, all dressed up in sterling silver armor that reflects the leaves like glass. One of the elves removes his helmet and he bears a startling resemblance to Haryek.

"Taryek." Alpha spits.

How could I have been so foolish? So naive?

Elves. So many elves. This was it. They had found us.

Forty-Two-

How did he find us? My heart drops into my stomach and I swallow back the nerves that threaten to overwhelm me. I can't break now, we have to look united. I scan the elves for Haryek but I don't see him, though it's possible I can't recognize him in the armor. We didn't know it was Taryek because he was distracted, we were too relaxed in each other's presence to think that this was a possibility.

"Dog." Taryek addresses Alpha which brings forward a raspy growl, he flinches and grasps the arrow. I plead with myself that he doesn't just yank it out.

"You have caused an awful lot of trouble, you know. Stirring things up... eliminating a good resource for us. I wouldn't have thought your kind was smart enough to fabricate a plan so elaborate. Cutting off our trade routes, keeping us far away from the city so we wouldn't know what you were doing down here. In fact, we really wouldn't have the slightest idea of how elaborate this whole thing was if we didn't have a little help." A grin pulls over his face and I watch his porcelain skin, wondering if it'll crack.

His lips are too solid, his cheeks without an imperfection. It reminds me of polished stone. How many centuries has this elf been alive?

"Don't flatter yourself, I knew your kind wasn't smart enough to figure it out. So tell me, who's helping you?" Alpha retorts through gritted teeth.

Taryek slowly approaches though he knows better than to get too close, Alpha might be wounded but he's still plenty dangerous. He gestures towards me and all archers raise their bows. He raises his hand, fingers poised to snap. I charge my fingertips, feeling for the water source from earlier but it's far from my reach.

In my training with Frost, I had been neglecting my magic. I was weak, too weak to pull water from so far away.

"There is an order here, mutt. A line, which you have so thoroughly crossed. There's a rumor, I want to see how true it is. I'm going to kill this one, the boy." Taryek sounds so amused, I blink and take a step back.

Surely I'm more valuable to him alive? Though I suppose it's possible my reputation has come with the message and I'm not worth much to him with my disobedience. I swallow hard and glance at Alpha out of the corner of my eye.

"You'd be doing me a favor." My warlord's muttered words burn me and I glance away. I convince myself it must be a ploy though a part of me reminds myself that our relationship was doomed from the start.

I try to steady my breathing as I watch Taryek's fingers snap. My eyes snap shut with it and I hear the arrow leave the bow, I must look like a pincushion. I wait for the pain, for the cold, but I feel nothing.

When I open them, I see Alpha is in front of me and a laugh leaves the elf lord's lips. Another arrow, he's taken another arrow for me. The upper left pectoral muscle, at least there's no joint involvement. I can see his strained jaw, his stoic expression can't hide the pain from me.

For me, he would stand. For me, he would defend. Why did it take me until now to realize that this was all for me?

"Remarkable. I didn't believe it honestly. I'm glad it's true because I would have been very disappointed to lose the only son that remains but truly remarkable." Though disgust crosses his face. "Laying with a man. A true disgrace to your people. The best they can send and it's a bloody queer."

Alpha rolls his eyes, blood seeping from his lips as he holds firmly onto the arrow. "Take a seat, the ranting might be a while." He grumbles and flinches when Taryek's hand grips the arrow in his shoulder to twist it. He growls through clenched teeth and I'm startled that he doesn't leap into an attack.

But he can't attack, because I'm here and if he makes a move, they will surely kill me. I will myself to do something, I pull at the snow, the ice, anything to give me strength.

"Stop!" I demand. "Take me, take me instead!" All I have to offer is my life. I suppose I would only have to kill Taryek but I scan over his armor again, it's without a flaw. Pulling magic to my hands, I call upon the wind and step to slice down upon the small band. I was attempting to move against Taryek but the direction in my desperation had been miscalculated.

Taryek yanks his sword, pressing the blade to my neck. I move to attack but Alpha stops me, gripping my surging arm. "Stop. Stop." He begs, his voice strained as he coughs. "He's just a kid."

"In due time." Taryek spits and twists the arrow again, forcing Alpha to his knees. Blood seeps from between his lips, the arrow in his chest taking effect. Taryek snatches his jaw, meeting his eyes. "This is where a slave belongs." He hisses and glares towards me.

I remain in my defense position, the cool steel of the impeccable sword pressed to my throat. "This is a lesson. To you. Your people. You think you can rise above the ash because a group of slaves storms in and throws their weight around? This is what war is like. This is what happens when you mess with the balance of things." Directing his attention back to the lycan, he tests his theory.

He shoves Alpha's face away and delivers a kick to his stomach with his shin. I don't think he expects the resistance he's faced with because he almost looks like he regrets it as Alpha glares at him with his steely eyes. "You were always a tough one." Taryek seems unimpressed with the Lycan's lack of groveling and writhing.

I could not admire my warlord more, he says it all in complete silence. Tears well up in my eyes, "Alpha, let me waste this asshole!" I manage through my teeth.

"Be quiet." Alpha snaps back at me. Taryek slices my shoulder, my arm drops limply to my side and I cry out, stepping back quickly.

Amused, he brings the sword to his lips to lick the blood curiously. "Hmm... that was a nerve, nothing permanent, just can't have you trying that again. I have big plans for you."

Alpha snarls, baring his teeth but I gain Taryek's attention as I belt out a challenge. "You don't have to kill him, if you're so confident in your victory then defeat us at your home gates!" I defy the elf lord who laughs like I've told a good joke.

"That's the thing, I don't have to. I can end this, right here, right now. And I intend to. I told you, this is a lesson. A learning opportunity. We are everywhere and everything your childish rebellion thinks it's hiding from us, we already know. The most important rule you must learn is never to leave a job unfinished." With that, he grabs the arrow from Alpha's chest and yanks it out.

Alpha gasps and clutches the hole the arrow leaves as blood coats his hands. I scream, attempting to rush to him, he had been trying to defend me and now he would pay a price that I gladly would have paid.

I rush to him but Taryek stops me, pointing the arrow at me like a sword. The motion spatters me with blood and I flinch.

"Another step and I stab him in the neck." He snaps and I will myself to conjure up anything but I have nothing. With one arm, I'm defenseless. Why had I let him stop me? Why hadn't I used the wind to slice him in half? Around this man I couldn't think, I had been lulled into obedience and in that hesitation, I lost my only opportunity.

I watch my warlord start to pale, his hand red, his ragged breaths. My element had failed me, he had failed me. Why didn't he see this coming? I want to scream at him, I want to shake him and tell him to fix this. "Do you find me a fool? I know you would heal him. You will do no such thing. Instead, I want you to watch this. Watch and remember this feeling. That you can do absolutely nothing."

"It's...okay." Alpha manages, looking at me through his tangle of gray locks. Reassuring me because seeing me suffer caused him much more anguish than his own wounds. I watch his blood-stained teeth, and hear him struggle to breathe.

"Don't tell me it's okay, asshole." I plead, my voice shaking, not caring who's around to hear. He rewards me with my favorite look only to flinch and cough. It's not okay, I'm not ready to watch him die. I want to be beside him, telling him that it's okay instead of needing the comfort myself. He was always the strong one.

Taryek motions for two elves to come over, both have ropes in their hands. Taryek kicks the lycan over, his chest heaving from having to be on his back. I jerk for him but I find that I'm being restrained. I thrash against the two elves with everything that I have, getting to him just long enough to push him onto his side so that he can clear his throat.

I'm yanked away, kicking and screaming at this point as I fight to use my numb arm. I feel the fist hit my jaw and I feel my world spin for just a moment. I try to recall if I've ever been punched before. When my eyes focus, my hands are bound behind my back. They are tying the other rope to Alpha's ankles.

They are taking him.

I see red, my vision blurs as magic surges to my limbs and I fight against my restraints. They freeze solid, threatening to shatter. "He's dying anyways!" I call them, fighting to get upright, willing some entity to come for us.

"Never leave loose ends. No unfinished business." Taryek 'tsks' me, walking over and delivering a kick to my abdomen. It effectively knocks the wind out of me and he looks much more satisfied with this kick. "I'll drop him off somewhere when I'm sure he's dead. Lycans take forever to die, we could be here all day and I grow bored of this. You have a message to deliver. Surrender and hand over the slaves or we will come and take them and level your city to the rubble it started as. This is a whole new era, Nicolas." He watches me thoughtfully and smirks.

"Don't worry, I'm sure my whore of a son will keep you entertained. Don't disappoint me, there is still something we could do with this hell hole." He motions to his men and they begin the process of dragging Alpha away. "Follow us and I force the change and skin him alive—" He tilts his head as he watches the limp form.

"Hmm... scratch that. Follow us and I'll skin you and ship you back to your people in a box. Pity, I thought it would take much longer than that. I was looking forward to the walk home." He shrugs and pats my cheek before following after his group.

My chest heaves in panic, I plead with my magic, attempting to force any spark to come from my body. But there is nothing, nothing can fix this, nothing can replace this real pain that trumps any fear or anguish I might have felt before. I'm incapacitated by the grief of loss.

I stare after the shiny forms until they're all gone. I don't have a single tear, this is something beyond what I'm capable of feeling. I watch the spattering of blood slowly disappear as the leaves roll around on the floor.

The drag tracks are faint as the wind rolls through the forest and it carries on with its day, turning the page on the events that just occurred. I numbly untie myself and scramble over to the spot, pushing the leaves away and finding the blood-stained earth. I want to scream but all I hear is silence.

I dig my fingers into the earth, pulling the bloodied soil up and holding it in my hands. Cold and thick and sticky, my hands tremble at the thought and I leap away like I've been shocked. Gasping for air, I manage to get to my feet and run back towards the castle. His pain is my pain as I struggle to breathe, fighting for air with him as I try and push the thought out of my head.

Alpha was immortal, he had told me himself. There was a chance, there had to be a chance, that what I had seen had not been a reality. I had to get back, to warn the others, to gather a party and go after them.

It's almost dark by the time I reach the castle and I'm exhausted. I throw open the doors to the dining hall. "They took him! Taryek! Taryek took him!" Like a mad man I sob, wheezing and choking on my own exhaustion as Adriam grasps my wrists.

"What has gotten into you?" He commands, horrified by my appearance. I'm coated in blood from my shoulder and grit from the blood-soaked earth.

"Randy." My voice is a hushed whisper. "Please, please, we have to save him. Please."

Sota appears in the hall, staring past Adriam to lock eyes with mine, I was the last person he was expecting to see by the look of it. "You turned him over to Taryek!" He barks, pointing a finger at me. His skin pales as if he's seen a ghost.

I can't speak, my eyes lock on the leaf litter on his boots, the snow, and the grit. "Sota—" Something hard connects with the back of my head and the lights go dark as I collapse onto the tiles.

Forty-Three-

I'm alone now.

I awake in my room and I suppose I shouldn't be surprised that I've ended up here. I recall the events of the day prior. He's dead, that's all I can think of that they would lock me up. There's no reason to keep me around anymore, no Alpha to protect me, no one to claim my worth. I must have thought wrong, it was foolish to think any man could survive an arrow to the chest.

I'm just an inconvenience, and it's finally time to rid the world of me. I feel right about this, that I should go shortly after he does. Though I do find it strange that I'm so attached to someone who I never really knew but then, he knows me better than most. I suppose that I would never get the answers to my questions, how I wished I had asked better ones in the time I had had.

I'm cast on my floor, the cold stone is soothing to my aching jaw. I can't lay here forever, I slowly climb to my feet and stare down at my hands. They are still covered with blood and dirt, it's caked under my fingernails and up to my wrists in the rich soil that could only come from the forest.

I go into the bathroom and I'm thankful that I usually keep a bucket in here for quick cleaning. I'm numb as I slowly scrub my hands, trying to wash the muck, grime, and blood off. But it won't go, it's stuck and stained; I scrub harder.

I take the fingernails of my other hand and rake them against my skin I scrub violently until my skin reddens and threatens to bleed. I cry out in anger and shove the bucket away, spilling water all over the floor and I fall to my knees and lean back against the wall.

I look at my hands, stained with blood. The cracks of my hands bear the blackened dirt. A reminder, a reminder that he's gone and that if I had just done what I had been trained to do he might still be alive.

But, I can't shoulder all this blame. It was something we did together, something we both consented to. Lost in time, we had allowed our guard to slip as we drifted closer together. Our greatest weakness had become the other, he played his own role and I was furious with him.

I will myself to cry, I can feel the sob wanting to roll through me but it doesn't come. I feel empty, lost. I stand and go to the window, looking out. Nobody stirs, not a soul is outside the castle and it's well into the morning. The eeriness overwhelms me.

I remember this moment, looking out into the courtyard and willing one of these beasts to appear so I could see who murdered my family. Once more I do the same only, now, they are my family.

I hold my breath, willing him to come in the door. I can only envision the silent open and close. I don't wheel around, I wait but I don't feel the familiar presence. His overwhelming heat, the way the scent of the woods followed him, and now follows me. It clings to me, burned into my hands mixed with the smell of rust and iron.

When I focus my eyes, my reflection startles me and I could break the glass as the intruder stares back only to realize it's me. I'm haunting, my face splattered in blood. My hair is a tangled mess, my bruised jaw, and my slightly swollen face.

My clothes are peppered with spatter marks. I can only imagine what I looked like with my blood-soaked hands. I blink a few, slow times. I could almost laugh, Alpha would be pleased. I look like a regular killer. The realization hits me like a ton of bricks and my eyes lower to my clothes.

I grasp my shirt between my fingers and extend it away from my body. The blood spatter almost makes me flinch. I rip it off as fast as I can, needing to get away. Rushing back into the washroom, I scavenge what little water remains in my tossed bucket and scrub my face, ignoring my tender cheek that screams every time I run my cloth over it.

But the damage is done and there's not much I can do to erase the mental image I've burned into the eyes of every lycan in the dining hall last night. That I, Nicolas, killed the Alpha.

Alpha had warned me to stop, to get back, possibly even to run. Had he foreseen what they would see? Did he realize that it was too late for him but not for me? Taryek had made sure to spray me with blood, the rest I'd done on my own, yet it surely wouldn't have looked that way.

Something so unreasonable and yet so possible in the eyes of a society terrified and untrusting of magic. I want to burn my clothes, they remind me too much of him but I struggle with ridding myself of the only evidence I have. So I toss them aside and find new ones, my civilian clothes.

Maybe they will make a public announcement before they kill me and there's a chance that I can be rescued by Loan or Stefan but somehow I find that I don't want that at all. What I really want is to be with Alpha.

"Damn you." I curse him, gritting my teeth as I throw myself against the wall and fight against my own mental exhaustion. Running my hand through my hair, I grip it at the roots as I pound my fist against the stone. I couldn't hate him, much as I tried, for I did, truly, care for him.

That's why we were in the mess, wasn't it?

Regardless, I pace and plan as I wait for my captors to come and find me. Maybe I'll be briefed on my fate. I won't ask for a pardon, I won't even ask for my life. All I want them to know is the truth, that Taryek is coming and they must protect Dezna. I'm not waiting long before Adriam comes into the room.

He's tense, he doesn't look at me. His eyes are red and puffy, he closes the door and leans against it. I don't speak, I just hold my breath. I'd rather Victor than Adriam, somehow the Russian who hardly speaks English is more reasonable at times. "Adriam, it's not what it looks like—"

"Did he suffer?" He breathes.

I flashback, I hear him gasping, I see his bloodied mouth. I watch his blood pool and his heaving chest, I watch my hands as I roll him so he can get the much-needed air. I swallow. "Not for long," I respond in a whisper. "Adriam, he might not be... he's immortal?" I want confirmation, I want him to say it with his own words.

Adriam gasps and clasps a hand over his mouth. I can see the tears spilling over his face and yet I have none to join him. I'm totally numb, unable to feel the true weight of my loss. "Why?" He murmurs.

"Would you believe me if I told you I didn't do it?" My voice is weak. I don't sound like I even believe myself. "I'm not even sure if he's dead."

"Bullshit!" He screams. I flinch, I've never seen Adriam lose control. "You were covered in his blood! You look like shit! It was you! It was obviously you!" He sobs a heart-wrenching sob. He slams his fists on the door in frustration, shaking his head. "Sota said he saw you take him out of the courtyard this evening completely alone. He said that you told the guards to not follow. Why on earth would Alpha meet Haryek by himself?"

I was asking myself those same questions. "Adriam. It wasn't me. I would never—I could never—" How could I explain that killing that man was the last thing I would be capable of doing? That I fought to save him, that I wanted to save him so badly? "I didn't do it." I finish firmly. "Taryek did this and right now, Alpha could be in their grasp, very much alive."

"He is more skilled than most of us combined and Taryek managed to kill him? I find it hard to believe." His tone is accusing. It sounds unlikely but I believe that was the intent. Taryek had said this was a lesson, a message.

I blink. *I'm the message.*

It wasn't about what Taryek could do just to the city but the internal workings. Without Alpha and I, what was there for the alliance? From the inside, he would corrupt until there was nothing left to do but march in and take over.

"Taryek," I tell him slowly. "Taryek set me up."

"A sick joke. How would he know where we are?"

It all makes sense to me now. "For this exact reason. To frame me. To destroy us. Because he's scared; because he knows we will win." I feel stronger as I speak like I'm starting to believe it.

Sniffling, he rubs his eyes with his palms. "You can see how I find this hard to believe." He shakes his head weakly like he's dealing with a child. "Sota is my family, one of my good friends, and he has you dead to rights leaving with Alpha. All of a sudden, you show up bloody and blame Taryek, who, no one has seen?"

"Adriam, please. You know I cared for him. He was—" I pause and don't know what to say.

The Frenchman shakes his head. "Exactly. He was." He breathes and presses his back against the door. "I'll be meeting with Haryek and Bogan tomorrow. The alliance still stands, for now, we will decide your fate. You're being accused of murder and treason." He looks like he might cry again and I hold out my hand.

"Adriam, I love him."

At that moment we both pause.

"Don't. You don't get to do that. You killed my family, my son, my brother, my friend... our only hope at getting out of this. Your only hope. You can't bring him back, Nicolas." He retreats from me, wanting to get away, wanting to escape from my truths.

I move towards him, quicker this time as he bares his teeth at me. "I love the way he looks when he sleeps, the way he dimples his cheek when he laughs or when he looks at me as if he might wish me ill but couldn't bear the thought. Adriam, I did not kill Alpha and if we don't do something, there is not going to be anything any of us can do. He truly will be dead if he's not already."

The French man takes in slow shaky breaths as he considers this. "He would want me to give you a fair trial and I will do just that. I'll see you in court." With that, he leaves.

I feel the tears want to come but I have nothing, I want the heat, the comfort of my warlord. I think of the smell of the woods, his brooding gaze. How he watched everything, the way his eyes would scan and calculate. I take a deep breath and sit upright to curse myself. It took me this long to realize just how much I cared about him.

Looking at my hands, I slowly close them. *It's okay.* I hear his words all too clearly. It is going to be okay, I tell myself. Those words meant more than my mental state. He was not the only strong one, I've become strong. I've become more than I ever thought possible. "It's okay," I say out loud to myself.

I'm strong enough for both of us like he had to be time and time again. I can do this. I can be the leader my people need me to be, I can lead the rebellion.

Slowly, I rise to my feet. Come tomorrow, I will make my case before the alliance. Whatever decision they make, I must convince them—No. I will convince them that I'm innocent of this act and that Taryek is coming from us. He did this because he was scared. He knew we would win. He thought he could break us but I will prove that he only brought us closer together. Bonding us over one common goal.

Freedom.

I'm alone again and for the first time, I don't feel alone.